THE JEWEL OF FATE

"I have come for your ruby," Ker said in a trembling voice. All his bravery had vanished.

In reply, Derethigon stood. He seemed to expand until he towered over Ker like a giant over an ant. Then his scalp parted like a ripe melon—the rip continued over his face and into his chest. Brilliant light burst from inside his body, brighter than the sun. And Derethigon reached inside himself and drew out a dazzling red object. It spun from a silver chain, pulsing like a beating heart. A sun glared from its core, like a single, bloody eye.

Ker managed to tear his eyes away, to throw himself to the ground, prostrate, hiding his face. If he looked longer, he feared he might go mad.

Worlds of Fantasy from Avon Books

THE CRYSTAL SWORD
by Adrienne Martine-Barnes

FIRESHAPER'S DOOM
by Tom Deitz

THE PIG, THE PRINCE & THE UNICORN
by Karen A. Brush

TALKING MAN
by Terry Bisson

VALE OF THE VOLE
by Piers Anthony

WINDMASTER'S BANE
by Tom Deitz

Coming Soon

THE DRAGON WAITING
by John M. Ford

NIGHTREAVER
by Michael D. Weaver

THE SHADOW OF HIS WINGS
by Bruce Fergusson

THE BLIND ARCHER

John Gregory Betancourt

AVON
PUBLISHERS OF BARD, CAMELOT, DISCUS AND FLARE BOOKS

THE BLIND ARCHER is an original publication of Avon Books. This work has never before appeared in book form. This work is a novel. Any similarity to actual persons or events is purely coincidental.

AVON BOOKS
A division of
The Hearst Corporation
105 Madison Avenue
New York, New York 10016

Front cover illustration by Romas
Published by arrangement with the author
Library of Congress Catalog Card Number: 87-91631
ISBN: 0-380-75146-1

First Avon Books Printing: February 1988

Printed in the U.S.A.

K-R 10 9 8 7 6 5 4 3 2 1

For the writers
who most shaped my view of fantasy:
Hannes Bok, Robert E. Howard,
and Clark Ashton Smith.

1

Castle Orrum

> Sight is an innate talent. A parallel can be drawn to magic, which is also an innate talent. Those who can use magic are like the sighted in a world of blind men. But the blind men, never having known sight, do not miss it, and continue to live in blessed ignorance. How I pity them.
>
> —Neraff Tev
>
> *Meditations on Magic,* Volume LXIV

The roses were closing in around him.

Thorns bristled like the hackles of a dog; blood-red flowers opened and closed like so many toothless mouths. Thousands of skeletons of birds and other small animals hung, skewered, on their stems.

Ker Orrum took a step back, but the rosebushes had circled around behind him. A quick flash of fear made him shiver in excitement. The danger heightened his senses. He drew his only weapon—a short wooden training sword—and held it just as Nowandin had always taught him. He'd learned well.

A long stem with a large red bud at its tip rose from the mass of tangled, thorny stalk. It turned toward him. Several of the flower's petals quivered, then spread open in a sudden burst of movement: it *lunged.*

Ker flung his arm up and deflected the blow, but several of the thorns tore through his sleeve and punctured his arm like the fangs of a snake. He felt a pulse of fiery pain along his forearm for a second, then the poison began to work and he lost all feeling from his elbow to his fingertips.

Cursing softly, he slashed with the wooden sword, severing the stem that had wounded him. The rose flopped on the ground for a second, then lay still. The other roses swayed and made a soft whispering sound, as if mourning their lost companion. Then they turned toward him and began to move again.

Their stems wove back and forth, back and forth, and he had the impression of eyes watching him, evaluating him. He tensed and prepared himself for another attack.

It came in a second, and from two different sides. Rosebuds opened and slapped forward almost faster than he could follow. Their stems lashed at his arms and face like small, thorny whips. Ker parried, slashed, parried again, dancing back, then forward, until at last he began to tire. Still the rosebushes pressed their attack, never slowing, never hesitating. Ker moved to block every thrust—*parry; slash; slash*—until the inevitable happened and he misjudged his swing. Thorns caught in the back of his right hand and scratched deep, tracing three parallel lines in blood.

Crying out in pain, Ker dropped the wooden sword. The roses reared up before him like an angry dragon prepared for the kill.

He spoke the magic word of binding that Lerrens had made him learn before he could walk. It was the one true defense against the roses.

As Ker said it, they pulled back to clear away from the path. He knelt and rubbed his hand, massaging numb fingers, kneading the palm. In a moment, he felt the pins-and-needles of returning circulation.

He stood and cursed softly to himself. He'd been so sure he'd win today—but again the rosebushes had gotten the better of him. He retrieved his sword and tucked it back in his belt; he'd need it again soon enough, he knew. Whistling softly, he picked up one of the severed roses, twirled it once, then cast it aside so it could take root once more.

He continued down the wide gravel path, past the roses, and into a more mundane section of the garden. Here flowering bushes grew in huge white clumps, and ancient beds of iris and ximenia threw out bright red and yellow and pink blooms. The rich, heavy scent of pollen filled the air.

His disappointment with the rosebushes faded. There would always be tomorrow . . . and the next day, and the next. Ker knew he'd never be leaving Castle Vichir and its lands. It was a trap, a cage. He would've given anything for a day of freedom just now.

He wondered if he could steal a horse from the stables before the grooms noticed. He'd never been able to do it before, but today—with the first flush of summer in the air—*today* they might be sleeping . . .

Deep in thought, Ker walked the garden paths of his father's castle. He was twelve years old and had more on his mind than the musty old books waiting for him in the castle's library. Summer was here! Perhaps he could ride through the castle gate before the grooms caught him and brought him back to face his teacher's wrath . . . Ah, to charge across the pastures, driving enemies before his sword like sheep to the slaughter! Only they *would* be sheep, he realized, and his sword would be made of wood. But perhaps he could do something else . . .

A distant shout interrupted his musings: "Ker! Where are you? *Ker!*"

He recognized the voice at once. It belonged to Lerrens, his father's counselor, to whom his education was, seemingly, the most important matter in the barony—in the world. What did summer plantings mean to Lerrens when he could keep Ker locked indoors, reading volumes of bad poetry—or, even worse, having to write it. Dactylic hexameter sounded like some demon to battle.

And yet Ker knew, deep inside, that he ought to be studying. As the second son of Baron Orrum of Vichir, he would never be baron—his older brother was destined for that—but he could still be something important, a learned man, a scholar. His duties would be solemn and dull, just like his life.

How he longed for excitement, for adventures in the woods to the west where magical creatures were said to walk, or in the lands to the east where countries fought great battles and kingdoms rose and fell. He thought for the thousandth time of the tales the storytellers wove at night . . . the glory of following a noble lord into battle, the thrill of victory, the romance and adventure: these were the things he wanted.

And they were things he would never have. The gods had decreed it, as Lerrens never let him forget. He winced at the thought. His father had gone to the Oracle the night he was born, and the Oracle had burned with the bright spirit of Shon Atasha the Creator, speaking with His voice:

"Ker Orrum will lead many in years to come, and his words and wisdom will always be remembered."

That was it; no more. The wisest men in the barony had interpreted the prophecy, saying Ker was destined to be a great scholar. Since the Oracle's words always came to pass, Ker knew his future was set. He would never fight, never lead men into battle, never have a single adventure.

He knew Lerrens would soon come down the path between the hedges of rosebushes, for his teacher had spotted him as he slipped out the side door and into the garden, and Ker had ignored his call to come at once for the morning's lessons.

Running through a gap in the hedge to his right, Ker followed a thin trail to an ancient grove of oaks. Once a gray marble bench had rested between two trees, but passing centuries had crumbled it to almost nothing. Gathering a handful of small stones from its base, he tied them in the corner of his shirt. Then he ran to the nearest oak, grabbed its lowest branch, and pulled himself up. He climbed until he was about thirty feet above the ground, perched in the V formed by two large branches, and grinned. Since he wore riding breeches, boots, and a loosely woven linen shirt rather than the tunic or robes Lerrens would have preferred him to wear, he had no trouble keeping his position.

He steadied himself with one hand while he took out the stones, setting them in a row along a relatively level branch to his right, within easy reach.

The counselor called again, sounding nearer. Ker guessed he was on the hedge path and smiled in anticipation. *Now* he'd get even for hours of learning past!

The day was warm, the sky unclouded. Small winged lizards hummed like a thousand bees in the trees around him, flitting from branch to branch in blurs of green and gold. Through a large gap in the oaks' leaves he could see the castle's outer wall, and just beyond it Vichir proper, with its narrow, winding streets and sprawling buildings. But beyond *that*—still misty with the morning's fog—lay lush fields and rolling hills, and even farther, the dark smudge of a distant forest. An ancient road paved with giant blocks of some jet black stone cut straight through the fields, heading due east and west.

I ought to be riding there, he thought. *Maybe—*

Hearing light footsteps, Ker looked down. Lerrens stood directly below, glancing around in exasperation.

The counselor's shoulder-length brown hair fluttered lightly in the breeze. He'd gathered his long yellow robes up around his knees, as he always did in the garden, to keep them from getting soiled. Ker noticed too that Lerren's narrow jaw was set and his cheeks flushed from more than the morning's heat.

"Ker Orrum!" he shouted. "Come here at once or your father will hear of this!"

Since Baron Orrum wasn't home at the castle, the threat didn't worry Ker. He knew nobody really blamed him for anything he did in play, not even Lerrens, since there weren't any other young nobles in Vichir. Even Minnan, his older brother by eight years, had never played with him—Minnan had been sent to the castle of Baron Lastyn of Nochal eight years earlier (to learn how to be a good ruler, Ker guessed)—so Ker had been truly alone most of his life. His only companions had been adults and servants. He'd seen his brother once in the past five years, and then only briefly. Minnan had no time for children.

Ker turned his attention to the counselor once again. He struggled to keep from giggling and giving his position away. Picking up one of his stones, he threw it in a high arc so it landed somewhere in the bushes to his right, with a crashing sound and a dull thump.

Lerrens whirled about with a low cry of triumph and stalked out of sight. "Come out of there!" Ker heard him shout.

Ker threw two more stones in quick succession, both to Lerrens's left. They crashed into the rosebushes, sounding like someone moving, and Ker glimpsed the counselor stalking along the length of the hedge.

"Come out, I said!"

Ker couldn't suppress his laughter this time, and he started to fall out of the tree. Rough bark raked his fingers as he grabbed at the branch in front of him—and missed.

The garden spun dizzily, leaves whipped by his head, the ground rushed toward him . . .

2

Threnodrel

Who knows the way wizards think? They are like the wind, unmoved by any human hand, or like the seas, without channels to guide them.

—Avden Prish
The Aeglian Chronicles

Eyes squeezed shut, Ker felt himself begin to scream, but somehow couldn't make a sound—

He didn't hit anything. For a second he thought he'd died and gone to meet the Dark God.

Slowly he opened his eyes. He hung suspended three feet above the ground. The world was strangely quiet; nothing stirred. Time seemed to expand. He felt his heart pounding in his chest; a ringing filled his ears. He gaped at the trees above him, where winged lizards hung suspended in midflight between branches, looking like statues set into the sky—

And then he fell the rest of the way, abruptly, and the breath *whoosh*ed out of his lungs. Slowly sitting up, dazed, he stared uncomprehendingly around him. What had happened? What had stopped his fall?

Perhaps it was a god, he thought, awed. But why would a god save him? What could he matter to one of them?

Lerrens had spotted him by then. The counselor hurried forward, robes still gathered up around his knees. He seemed about to yell, but managed to control himself. He shut his mouth, and Ker could see the lines of tension around his eyes and lips.

"There you are," he said briskly. "I'm tired of your stupid games. Thank the gods I won't have to watch you now!"

Ker looked at him. "You won't have to watch me?"

The counselor carefully held his face expressionless. "Go to the main hall," he said.

"But I never study there!"

"Did I say you were going to study? Your father has sent someone else to be your teacher, and good luck to him."

"Who?" Ker asked eagerly, putting the fall from his mind. It didn't seem that important, all of a sudden. He must've been lower in the tree than he first thought, and anyway, Lerrens would only have yelled at him for climbing in the first place.

"You'll have to ask him yourself, I imagine. Go on—he's waiting." He allowed himself a tight-lipped smile. "Maybe you'll even like him as much as you like me."

Ker ran past him, down the winding trail and through the gap in the hedge, turned right, and kept on going. He passed the magical rosebushes before they could notice him. His thoughts raced ahead. A new teacher, someone from a different country. What would he be like?

I hope he's not like Lerrens.

Maybe he would be a knight from one of the Great Lands to the east, someone who could teach him about battles and fighting. Maybe he'd fought in some great war. *Maybe—*

He stopped. *Maybe he's here because of the Oracle.* Ker would be thirteen in a month, required by law and custom to go to the Oracle to hear for himself, if he wished, the prophecy that would determine his future. Not that he had to go to know he'd be a scholar, whatever his desires. Perhaps his father had sent the new teacher to prepare him for his visit?

Reaching the side door, he fumbled with its catch, then eagerly flung it open and hurried down the wide stone corridor. He passed small meeting rooms, antechambers, storerooms. At last he got to the huge oak door to the main hall, pushed it open, and entered.

It took a minute for his eyes to get used to the dim light. When he could see, he barely glanced at the ancient tapestries covering the walls. He knew each picture by heart: the scenes of Vichir's history and the history of the world. All the gods were there—the eleven in their palace in the sky, and the one who ruled in Hell—along with the Oracle, and Shon Atasha the Creator, who had made the Earth from His flesh in centuries long past.

Ker could make out a dark figure seated at the far end of the room, where tables and chairs had been set up in front of a huge stone fireplace, and he walked forward, boots clicking on the cold stone floor. The man didn't stir, though he had to have heard Ker's approach, and the boy felt a sudden flush of anger tinged with nervousness. Who was this stranger to ignore *him,* a son of the Baron of Vichir?

When he stopped ten feet away, he realized his new teacher couldn't possibly be a lord, or even a common soldier. The man slouched in his chair, thin and frail and old-looking. It must've been a labor for him to stand—let alone fight. All Ker's hopes crashed down.

Slowly the man shook his thin, silver hair and brushed wrinkles from his plain gray robe. He sat up straighter. Something glimmering and white lay on the chair beside him; it was long and thin like a willow branch, only perfectly straight and smooth, as though it had been carefully carved by a master craftsman.

Without a glance in any direction, the old man reached over and picked up the white stick. Slowly he straightened his shoulders and sat bolt upright, humming softly to himself.

"Well?" Ker said, after a minute had passed.

The humming continued.

"Say something!" Ker said.

"You are an ill-mannered lout with stones for brains." And the odd little tune went on, scarcely missing a note.

The boy didn't respond. He stood silently for a minute, trembling with anger, his fists clenching and unclenching. Nobody ever treated him like that. He felt the rage building inside. Who was this stranger to talk to him as if he were a commoner? Turning, he stalked back the way he'd come.

I'll show him! he thought. *I'll get Nowandin and we'll go off to the meadows to practice archery now, instead of this afternoon. Father will have this—this—*teacher*—thrashed and thrown out when he returns and finds he hasn't been able to teach me anything!* He swore he wouldn't cooperate with the stranger no matter how hard he tried to teach.

He wished he were an adult so he could order the man thrown out *now.* He would've done it in an instant, if he thought the guards would obey. When he'd told them to do things before, they'd only laughed and done it if they felt like it, saying they didn't obey children, not even the son of their baron. And of course his father had never done anything about it, never told his men they should obey Ker too. The baron never did *anything* but watch in silence, neither smiling nor frowning, looking only the slightest bit wistful, as though his thoughts were someplace far away.

But if I *were baron—*

"Wait," the stranger said, in a voice so low Ker almost didn't hear it. Ker stopped and considered for a heartbeat, then slowly turned. He decided he might as well hear what his new teacher had to say—it would have to be an apology.

He mistook me for one of the servants, Ker thought, *and now he wants to say he's sorry.* He smiled a bit, triumphantly.

The man was on his feet, watching Ker. Strangely, he didn't look so frail or old now. He seemed taller, and his deeply tanned face, lined by years of exposure to the weather rather than age or infirmity, was strong and sure. He held his glimmering stick toward Ker.

"I have something for you," he said. "Take it. If you can."

"What do you mean, if I can?" Ker snapped, his patience gone. The old man didn't seem to be apologizing. "And who are you to call me names? My father—"

"Your father isn't here to baby you now."

"But—"

"Surely you're not so incompetent you can't do anything for yourself. Do you need to call servants to take a little stick?"

Ker frowned. Hands balled into fists, face hot and flushed, eyes narrowed to slits, he longed to hit the man, and barely managed to restrain himself. One time he'd hit Lerrens, and the counselor had come back with a stick and hit *him*—many times, and so hard and in such places that he hadn't been able to sit down for a week without being reminded of his beating. There was a difference between playing tricks and hitting someone larger and stronger than he was: he'd learned that lesson well. So he said nothing and glared at the stranger with all the hatred he could muster.

After a moment his would-be teacher said, "If you're anything more than a little boy who runs crying to his father, you'll have to prove it to me. You can do that by taking my wand. *If* you have the strength."

Ker stalked forward and snatched the stick with his right hand. It burned his fingers. He dropped it with a cry of pain. Clattering on the floor, it rolled over and stopped at the man's feet.

"I knew it," the old man said. "You're no better than—"

Ker ran forward and snatched up the stick again. It burned him like a white-hot ember. His right hand was on fire—he'd never be able to use it again, he knew it! But still he refused to let go. He grasped the wand tightly, waving it in front of him like a sword.

"Do you feel it burning?" the man said, voice low. "Do you feel the fire spreading down your arm like water, so you must let it go or watch the flames char your hand away before your eyes?"

Ker stared at the wand, his fingers wrapped tightly around it.

Liquid fire seemed to spread down his wrist, to his elbow, to his shoulder. Every muscle screamed in agony, his skin on fire, his bones charring . . .

Gritting his teeth, he held tighter, determined not to drop the wand, as his teacher obviously expected. Tears filled his eyes—he bit his tongue and tasted salt, *he had to let go—*

"No!" he shouted. "I don't feel anything!"

Then the pain was gone, vanished to a dull ache in his arm, where his muscles still bunched. His breath was ragged, uneven, and he found himself soaked with sweat. He sagged forward, but caught himself and forced himself rigidly upright, shoulders square, head back.

"There," the man said. "That wasn't so hard, was it?"

Ker snapped the wand in two and threw it down at the man's feet. *Hah!* he thought. *That's your wand now!*

His teacher blinked once, almost in surprise, and stared at the two pieces of pale wood lying on the floor. Slowly he bent and picked them up, fitting them together. He hummed as he worked, tracing the grain of the wood with his fingertips, and in a moment the wand was whole again. Ker looked closely but couldn't see where he'd broken it. He gaped.

"You have my sincere apologies, Ker," the man said, bowing low. "You are indeed more than I originally thought you were. That will be all for today. You may amuse yourself for the rest of the morning, and then spend the afternoon with that soldier, Nawdul."

"His name's Nowandin, and he's captain of the guard."

"That's what I said. Now that I've met you, I have some unpacking to do. Your lessons will start promptly at sunrise tomorrow morning, whether you're there or not. Since I'd hate to leave you behind, I suggest you show up—but the matter is totally up to you."

Ker stared at him in surprise. "Up to me?"

"Certainly. It's to your benefit to be there, not mine. I get paid regardless. Teaching you or the walls of the library—it's all basically the same. Good day. And try not to fall out of any more trees; you might injure yourself." He nodded once, then walked past the tables and between two pillars. Darkness seemed to swallow him.

Ker turned away, thoroughly confused. *What kind of teacher is he? Why did he make that stick burn my hand?*

And how did he know I climbed a tree to hide from Lerrens?

Who is *he?*

"Wait!" he shouted. "What's your name?"

Faintly he heard, "Threnodrel."

Ker murmured it to himself. "Threnodrel . . ." It was an odd, foreign-sounding name, unlike any he'd heard before. He wandered out to the garden again, heading for the oak trees, and found Lerrens still on the path. The counselor had been staring absent-mindedly at the roses. They twitched faintly.

Lerrens cleared his throat when he noticed Ker. "Well? Did you find him?"

"Yes. He said his name was Threnodrel—what kind of name is that?"

"It's a wizard's name. He let you go already?"

Ker shrugged. A wizard! That explained the man's strange behavior—everyone knew they didn't think like normal people. This was the first time he'd ever heard of one coming to Vichir, though. Wizards were in legends—Ker never dreamed he'd have one for a teacher. The wand and the pain it had caused him no longer mattered; he didn't care how the man had berated him.

A wizard! Like in all the ancient epics.

What had Threnodrel said after he'd apologized? That Ker was more than he'd originally thought? What did *that* mean? Did *he* have the talent to use magic, too? Or was it something else?

The counselor was shaking his head in bewilderment. "I don't see how he can possibly teach you anything, letting you run off like that." Lerrens turned back to the roses and sniffed, more in disgust than anything else.

"I think Threnodrel's wonderful!" Ker said, seeing it annoyed the counselor.

He didn't wait for Lerrens to ask another question. He darted through the gap in the hedge, only this time he didn't head for the oak grove. Instead, he decided to go see Nowandin, to tell him about the wizard and ask about a trip to the meadows beyond the peasants' fields. If they left now, they'd be there by noon, and if they were lucky they'd flush quail or other game in the tall grass.

Of all the weapons Nowandin had taught him to use, Ker liked the longbow best, and he practiced with it every day. Already he was as good as most of the men in the guard. He knew he'd have no trouble bringing down whatever birds they flushed from cover.

Through an open door at the far side of the garden Ker saw two grizzled old guards, Dero and Rammur, lounging against the wall of a small, well-lit hallway. They had been in the baron's service as long as he could remember. For some reason both were wearing finely wrought leather breastplates, dark leather pants and red capes—dress uniforms. Why would they wear them on guard duty?

Ker frowned. Everything seemed strange today, he thought, so why should his father's men be any different? Perhaps they knew where Nowandin was. He hurried over.

Rammur straightened a bit and gave him a half-serious salute. "How're you today, Master Orrum?" he asked.

"Fine," Ker said. "Where's Nowandin?"

"Went to see some peasants. Some sort of disagreement over a newborn calf. Nothing you need to worry about." He ran his hand through his short gray hair and grinned. "He'll be back by noon, though. Wouldn't want to miss the baron's arrival, after all."

Ker started. "My father's coming?"

"Didn't you know?"

"No. Lerrens didn't tell me." He thought angrily of what he'd do to the counselor once his father was gone. Maybe burrs in the robes Lerrens prized so much.

The guards exchanged a quick glance.

"Master Orrum," Dero said slowly, "did you want something?"

"No. Nothing." Ker turned and headed back toward the center of the garden, kicking at the grass in front of him. So his father was coming home, probably to check on him and his new teacher as much as the barony. And nobody'd bothered to tell him. Somehow, he wasn't surprised: Lerrens had been rather secretive of late.

The baron had only been gone six months this time; usually he took as much as a year between trips home. Maybe this time he meant to stay for the summer? Ker hoped so—things were always more exciting when his father was home. Often ambassadors came, or other minor lords, or traders. Once even a large troupe of performers from the city of Zelloque had come, and they'd kept the castle in an uproar for days with their jokes and bawdy songs, dancing, juggling, music, and short plays. It had been six years since they'd been there, and Ker longed to see them again. He'd heard all the local storytellers' tales a dozen times.

Glancing up at the morning sun, he guessed he still had a few hours left to get ready, if the baron came at noon as he usually did. He turned and ran for his room.

It was twelve, and almost too hot to do more than stand quietly as they waited for the baron. The initial flurry of activity had lessened somewhat; the cooks in the kitchens labored over the night's meal, but elsewhere everyone had finished preparations.

Most of the guard stood on the battlements, watching for the baron and his troops to ride into view on the old, jet black stone highway. Already peasants and townsmen were gathering in front of buildings along the dirt road to the castle drawbridge. Extra guards had been posted by the gate, watching people passing in and out, holding steel-headed pikes proudly upright. Like the other guards, they wore dress uniforms of polished leather and red capes. Plumed helmets shaded their eyes from the high, bright sun.

Ker stood on the walls beside Nowandin and Lerrens, looking out to the east across red-tiled rooftops for the first sign of his father's approach.

A cry went up among the guards on the battlements to their left: *"The baron! The baron!"*

A proud line of men on horseback came into sight through the trees in the distance, soldiers sitting straight in their saddles, holding swords high over their heads. The sun gleamed so brightly on their sword blades and steel breastplates that the whole procession seemed to glow. Ker's father rode at the head of his men, brandishing his sword with a war cry, urging his horse to a gallop. His men quickly followed suit.

The guards on the castle walls let out a wild cheer.

Heading up the final stretch of road between long lines of peasants, the baron allowed his horse to slow to a canter. He and his men rode over the drawbridge and through the gate.

Nowandin, Lerrens, and Ker hurried down the stone steps at the end of the battlements to the main courtyard. Already the baron and his men had dismounted; stableboys and grooms led their foam-flecked horses off toward the stables.

Baron Orrum coughed, brushed dust from his eyes and sweat from his brow, and turned to his men. "Go and relax and have some wine from the cellars. Tell the steward I said to give you nothing but the best—you certainly need it after that journey!" He almost smiled.

The soldiers murmured their thanks and slowly headed off toward the kitchens, looking tired and worn and glad to be home.

"My Lord," Lerrens and Nowandin said as one, bowing.

"Hello, Father," Ker said.

"Greetings," the baron said wearily. He gestured toward the nearest door to the castle. "I'll speak to you while we walk, Lerrens, and you, Nowandin, after I've had a bath and a shave."

He rubbed the week's growth of beard on his chin and cheeks absently as he turned away.

Ker stood silently beside Nowandin, feeling alone, forgotten—betrayed. He swallowed and found a lump in his throat. The air seemed to take on an unnatural clearness as he struggled to keep from showing how bad he felt.

His father and Lerrens headed toward the nearest door, talking earnestly about crops and the next harvest's expected yield, oblivious to all else. They'd hardly noticed him—they didn't care—

"You'll have plenty of time to see your father tonight, at dinner," Nowandin said, putting his arm around Ker's shoulders. "Until the baron calls for me, I'm at your command. What would you like to do first?"

Ker watched the door shut behind his father, then turned to look at the captain of the guard. He swallowed several times before speaking. Even that didn't quite hide the strain in his voice. "You said you'd teach me tracking."

"That's going to have to wait until we have a whole afternoon to ourselves. How about swords and daggers? You need practice on that. You fight like an old lady with one bad eye."

"I do not!"

"So prove it!"

And Ker ran to get the wooden swords and daggers.

Late that evening, in the banquet hall, Baron Sernal Orrum sat down to eat with Ker, Nowandin, Lerrens, and Threnodrel. None of the other minor officials of the barony were present, just the people the baron had told to come, and Ker.

Torches flickered from their niches around the room, providing a warm, yellow light. Great tapestries decorated the walls with scenes of famous battles: of Ilyundis, where Ker's grandfather had stood and died, of Zelloque and Peldath and Kiy-len, where the gods themselves once fought. Ker had always enjoyed eating here, where he could look at the pictures and dream of the great battles his ancestors had taken part in—all his ancestors except his father.

The baron had never joined any of the other lords to the east in their (often century-long) squabbles. And partly as a result, his lands had never been invaded, his castle never lain under siege during his lifetime. He traveled to the other baronies and visited other barons instead, arranging trade agreements, signing treaties. Lerrens called Sernal a diplomat and had made Ker learn the word and all it meant. From the books the counselor made him read, Ker guessed he was supposed to be a diplomat, too, and follow after his father's scholarly ways.

Servants carried in a roast pig smothered in baked apples and set the platter on the table, along with numerous bowls of fresh vegetables and plates of sweetmeats. The baron took the best of each plate and set it aside as tribute to the gods, then nodded and the dinner began. Quickly, serving girls dressed in white robes fetched pitchers of wine and stood close at hand, ready to fill any empty goblet.

"Ah, Threnodrel," the baron said softly. "Tell me, what do you think of my lands?"

"They are indeed splendid, baron—rivaling any I've seen. If we were in the East, your barony would be one of the most powerful in the world."

"That's not the life I want."

"Yes, yes." Threnodrel sighed, glancing around at the tapestries on the wall as if noting them for the first time. "Your father and grandfather thought differently, though, I see. Still, what's done can be undone by sword or by magic."

"Do you question the baron's actions?" Nowandin demanded, half rising.

Baron Orrum quieted him with a wave of his hand. "What are you getting at, Wizard? I know your kind—you never say or do anything without purpose, so speak now. I haven't the patience for court intrigue and innuendo tonight."

"Are you sure you want me to speak about your son now, with the others present?" Threnodrel pressed his hands together, then pulled them apart and his wand was suddenly there, one tip pinched between each thumb and index finger. He stroked the wand gently with his fingertips.

Ker stared at him.

"A common enough trick," Lerrens said. "Surely you can do better."

"Enough, Lerrens." The baron gestured to the servants and they quickly filed out. In a minute, the five of them were alone. Ker could feel the tension as he watched—more was happening here, he realized, than he saw. Both Lerrens and Nowandin were trying to steer the conversation away from magic and the governing of Vichir. Why?

Threnodrel smiled a bit. "I would rather speak to you privately," the wizard said. "I don't mean to insult your counselor or captain of the guard, but the matter is . . . *delicate.* And Ker must certainly not hear this from any of us, for it concerns him in such a way that it might . . . endanger him."

"I'm almost a man!" Ker said. "My thirteenth birthday is barely a month away. I'm old enough to hear anything you say about me."

His father thought for a minute, then nodded curtly. "Very well, Wizard. Ker, leave us now—a servant will call you when we're done. Lerrens and Nowandin will stay. I have no secrets from them. How could they serve me well if I did?" Nodding, he ran his fingers through his hair and cocked his head to the left.

Ker relaxed immediately, recognizing the signal: he was to listen from the other room.

When Threnodrel turned and looked at Ker, the boy slowly stood and walked to the door. He slipped out and closed it. Turning left, he jogged down the corridor to a smaller hallway, then turned left again, pushed open a tiny wooden door, and entered a storeroom adjoining the banquet hall. He'd listened here before.

Light from the hall revealed stone shelves loaded with dried spices, crates of fruit, and bags of grain for the kitchens. At the back wall he slid aside bundles of gray-green *baata* roots, one of Vichir's few native delicacies, to reveal a row of fist-sized stones that formed part of the banquet hall's fireplace. One stone was loose in its mortar. He slipped it out without a sound, revealing a clay pipe that had been built into the wall when the castle was new.

Lerrens had shown Ker the listening tube years before, when the counselor had instructed him in the secret ways of Castle Vichir. At that time Ker had also learned the system of hand signals that the baron used when strangers were around.

Glad his father trusted him enough to let him overhear the conversation, he swelled his chest proudly. He was, after all, almost a man.

He pressed his ear to the tube.

THRENODREL: . . . have no idea how important it is! The boy took my wand *and broke it!*

LERRENS: But surely—

THRENODREL: Listen! The boy is young enough. Let me take him with me. After I've finished teaching him, he can be apprenticed to another wizard and trained to master whatever power is in him. And I know it's more than I have. I was barely able to take my master's wand, and even then I managed to hold it for only a few seconds. Ker took my wand *and broke it without a second's thought!*

Ker opened his mouth in surprise. So the wizard *had* been startled when he broke the wand—it had meant something after all, some sort of test to see if he could use sorcery. And Threnodrel said he could!

He almost missed his father's low answer.

BARON ORRUM: My son is not to leave Vichir. I did not hire you because you're a wizard, but because you're the greatest scholar I could find. I gather you did not understand that fact. I have plans for my son here. You will not interfere with them, by the gods!

THRENODREL: I believe the Oracle will determine the boy's future, not you—his thirteenth birthday is almost here.

BARON ORRUM: I know his future.

THRENODREL: You may be endangering his life. I know you will refuse—but consider this: if he discovered he could work magic and didn't have the proper training, he might open up a Gateway.

BARON ORRUM: He will not know magic.

THRENODREL: He already does, and there is nothing you can do to prevent him from learning more.

LERRENS: What do you mean? How can he know magic?

THRENODREL: This morning, when I first got here, he sat in a tree playing a trick on you. When he laughed, he lost his balance and by all rights should have fallen from the tree—but floated down as lightly as a feather. He didn't know he'd done anything magical, I could tell—he just did it, like you or I might raise a hand to protect ourselves from a falling roof-tile. That was when I decided to test him.

BARON ORRUM: You had no right to do that.

NOWANDIN: Masferigon's Fingers! Do you think he could be—

BARON ORRUM: Quiet, Nowandin! There will be no more such talk in my castle. Ker will not leave Vichir. And tomorrow, Threnodrel, you will return to your homeland—or anywhere else you please, except Vichir. I will *not* have you interfering with my son.

THRENODREL: I see that magic has hurt you sometime in your past. Very well, Baron, I will take my leave of your lands in the morning. I knew you would not listen. Until then, though—

Ker didn't wait to hear more. He carefully returned the small stone to its place and shifted the *baata* roots so the wall behind them didn't show, then went back to the corridor and waited for his father's shout.

He could use magic! He *had* used magic—that's how he'd managed to save himself from falling! But it hadn't *felt* like magic—it hadn't felt like anything at all. He found the memory more than a little disappointing.

Maybe magic is like that, he thought. *Maybe you just think about something, and it happens. I wish Threnodrel were staying. If only the Oracle tells me to become a wizard . . .*

He shook his head, knowing that would never happen. Just as he could never be baron, he would never learn magic. His father's decisions were final.

"Servants!" The baron's shout carried through the door.

The man leaning against the wall sprang to life, snapping his fingers for the others to follow, but Ker beat him to the door and threw it open. He took his place at the table again, noting how his father, Lerrens, and Nowandin now stared at him. He shifted uneasily. Threnodrel looked off at the tapestries on the wall, his distaste obvious.

"What's wrong?" Ker asked. "Father? Nowandin?"

"Nothing," the baron said emotionlessly. "Threnodrel will not be staying with us after all. Lerrens will resume his duties as your teacher. For the moment."

"What?" Ker cried, pretending shock. *"Why?"*

"That is my decision. Threnodrel is not the proper teacher for you, and Lerrens will suffice until I find another. In a month the Oracle will confirm your destiny: you will be a scholar. Nothing else. You must study to help meet your fate or the gods will not be happy."

"But I'm too old for teachers now. I'm almost a man!"

"Ker," Threnodrel said gently, "one learns all one's life, and only stops at death. I'm still learning. There's much about human nature that still gives me reason to ponder." He glanced pointedly at the baron. After a moment, the wizard sighed and rose, nodding to them all. He seemed tired and old all of a sudden, as though the argument had drained the last of his strength. "Good evening, then. I must pack, if I'm to leave at sunrise."

"No!" Ker said. "Father—please don't make him go!"

Baron Orrum shook his head, and Ker knew better than to argue further.

After Threnodrel left, the meal continued on a grim note, with nobody saying anything more than what courtesy required.

Threnodrel had said that magic once hurt his father? Ker had never heard that before. Perhaps magic was the reason the baron stayed away from Vichir so much, why he never spoke of his wife, Ker's mother, who had died long, long ago.

Ker didn't know. From his father's bitter expression he guessed Threnodrel would never be spoken of again.

Ker was the only one at the gate to see the wizard off the next day. Threnodrel seemed surprised to find him there, but smiled as he lifted a light pack to his shoulder and pulled a long gray cape tighter around his shoulders. The drawbridge was down and the day looked to be fair enough. The bright morning sun was just beginning to burn away the night's fog. Peasants moved in the fields, dark phantom-shapes, and far off a cow lowed loudly.

"Well," Threnodrel said, smiling a bit, "it was a pleasure meeting you, Ker. I only wish we'd had more time together."

"So do I," Ker said. "Why do you have to leave?"

"You already know why."

"I—"

"There's no need to lie. I know you listened last night—and no, I didn't tell your father you disobeyed. I'm glad you heard for one reason—I won't have to come back to warn you. Listen well: do not try to use magic without training. It has ruined hundreds of others like you. Heed my warning!"

"I don't understand," Ker said. "How could I use magic? I don't have a wand or anything!"

"You don't need a wand. It is merely a tool, a channel for whatever power lies within you. Just as an artist uses a brush instead of his fingers to paint, so do wizards use wands. Ah, I feel your father's eyes upon us now. I will say no more. Good-bye, Ker Orrum. We will meet again." He smiled and waved, starting forward.

"Good-bye," Ker called after him. He stood there and watched until the fog closed around the wizard, shrouding him from sight. "Good-bye," he whispered.

Despite Threnodrel's words, he knew they'd never see each other again—banishment meant death for the wizard if he returned to Vichir. Ker had a feeling he would've liked Threnodrel, if he'd gotten to know him. That only left the Oracle as a chance to see real magic . . . and the thought of that meeting made him shiver.

Many tales were told of the Oracle and how the gods could change and twist people to suit their needs, if they chose.

Ker jumped, startled, as a heavy hand dropped on his shoulder. Lerrens stood behind him.

"It's time for your lesson," the counselor said.

Sullenly, Ker followed him back toward the library.

3

The Oracle

Jasel Urithgard was the first person to travel completely around the world. He started in Zelloque and headed north until he found the Edge—a fearsome place of toothy black rocks and giant winged monsters. There, after gazing into the dark emptiness upon which the Earth floats like a ship in the sea, he went mad. He became obsessed with the idea that the world was sinking and set out to find and stop the leak. He turned to the right, with his retinue of fifty loyal men (Jasel was very rich), and started walking. Forty-seven years later he returned to Zelloque, having walked in a complete circle, for the world is round as well as flat. All the years Urithgard had spent in the shadow of the edge, though, had made him more insane than ever. He later became a famous Oracle, for in madness lies the truth of the gods.

—Anonymous
A Child's History

The following weeks passed with painful slowness for Ker. He kept away from Lerrens and his lessons as much as he could, and since Nowandin and the baron were gone most days, visiting the remotest corners of Vichir and making new estimates for the harvest, Ker found time weighing heavily on his hands. One of the other guards had been assigned to him as instructor while Nowandin was away, but Ker, thinking the man fat and clumsy, avoided him. He took to retreating to the little-used rooms of the castle, and there he reread ancient epics, the tales of heroes and gods and those they fought—writings that Lerrens never approved of.

The tales of the twelve gods fascinated him the most. Their names made a roll call of adventure, and he'd whisper them softly to himself, always careful lest one should overhear: "Faramigon and Hevtherigon, Masferigon, Derethigon, Tanagon and Ladarigon,

Solmarigon, Vermithigon, Ghelmerigon and Pathanigon and Berigon." And the Dark God, the God of Death, whose name nobody would speak for fear of capturing his attention.

And yet, even the ancient epics were not enough to occupy him, and he often wandered the castle, bored and frustrated. He took his anger out on the servants and Lerrens. Soon, he noticed, he never came upon unoccupied servants in the corridors or garden. Lerrens grew more dour, and the lessons in the library grew more complex and demanding—the memorization of long poems and essays, essays, and still more essays.

One day as he walked in the garden, he passed an open window. His father and Lerrens stood inside, and he couldn't help hearing their words.

Lerrens spoke quickly: "His manners are terrible, and he's becoming rather vicious toward both me and the servants."

"Ah." The baron considered for a moment. "Children are insane and can't be blamed for their actions, as you know."

Ker flushed with anger. A child! His birthday was tomorrow, and then he'd be a man!

"Yes," Lerrens said, "but he has such potential! He could be an excellent scholar, if only he'd set his mind to it."

"That will come with time and patience, nothing else. Wait, my friend, wait."

"But the servants—"

"I will take care of the matter. That will be all."

"Yes, Baron."

Ker turned and moved away, scuffing at the ground with the toes of his boots. *What did he mean when he said he'd take care of it?* he wondered. *I'll show him I'm not a child tomorrow, when I go to the Oracle!*

Ker woke early the next morning. At first he didn't know what had disturbed him, but a moment later he saw one of the shadows against the far wall move. He tensed. The shadow drifted past the far window, became the silhouette of a man. It was hard for Ker to see in the silvery, predawn light, but he was certain he glimpsed a sword in the stranger's hand.

Ker caught his breath and held it. *An assassin?* he wondered. His fingers slid under his pillow, groping for the knife he kept there.

The man shifted; for an instant light caught the blade of the sword he carried and made it shine like sun on water. He moved toward Ker's bed, nearer, nearer.

Ker sat up, holding his knife ready. Still the stranger approached. Again the man passed an open window—and this time light shone full upon his face. Ker recognized his father and sank back with a nervous laugh.

Baron Orrum looked at the sword. Then he tossed it on the foot of the bed. His face remained expressionless, cold, aloof—as it had always been.

"A present," he said, "along with new mail and the finest stallion in my stables. You can't go to the Oracle looking like a commoner. Get dressed." He turned and went into the hall, his footsteps fading away.

New mail and a horse! Ker could hardly believe his good fortune. Shivering, he slipped from the covers and padded barefoot across the cold stone floor. On a chair against the wall sat a supple shirt of chain mail. He ran his fingers over the tiny links and wondered at the construction, as fine and light as human hands could make. It had to have come from one of the great Eastern lands, he knew—no smith in Vichir could have duplicated it. He put it on over a padded undergarment, along with riding breeches and boots, and hung the sword at his belt. He wondered for a second if he'd need it at the Oracle.

Then he went to the banquet hall, where his father waited. The baron sat alone at the long table. In the uncertain light of the torches, the silver in his hair gleamed, and odd shadows moved over his face. The remains of breakfast lay before him—cold meat, bread, ale.

"You may neither eat nor drink," he said, "until you return. That is one of the Oracle's laws."

"Yes, Father." Ker glanced around the room. No servants stood in attendance, and the counselor was nowhere to be seen. "Where is Lerrens?"

"I have decided you no longer need his lessons. You must spend time with *me* now, if you're to learn all I know."

Ker swallowed, then sat down and waited. The silence grew thick and heavy. By custom he wouldn't leave until nearly dawn. He felt hungry and thirsty already, and shifted uneasily.

The tapestries around them seemed to stir as the torches flickered. Again he looked at the famous battles they displayed, at Ilyundis and Zelloque, at Pethis and Kiy-len. He felt rising within him the familiar longing to take part in the adventures they showed.

If only the prophecy would let him be a warrior! Just one adventure could've made him happy.

The baron made no effort at conversation, staring off into space.

"Father?" Ker asked.

"Yes."

"What did the Oracle say to you when you were young?"

"When my father went at my birth, it was foretold that I would be a good baron. When I went on my thirteenth birthday, I chose not to have my future cast. I did not need to know more."

"And . . . do I need to know more?"

"No man can tell you what to do now, Ker. The choice is between you and the gods. I will say this: you know you're destined to be a scholar. Such is Shon Atasha's will. Should you risk the Oracle's magic by asking more?"

"I don't know," Ker whispered.

"The Oracle said you will be a scholar. *I* say you should be a scholar. Let your brother fight battles and negotiate treaties. He will be baron after me—not you. You must make your own mark on the world, and there is no other way than through learnedness. I wish one of my sons to be a scholar: you."

"Yes, Father." And the silence fell again.

When the cocks began to crow, they went to the front courtyard. Night's last breath chilled the air. A soft breeze from the east ruffled Ker's hair. *When I see the sun,* he reminded himself, feeling the strangeness of the day, *I will be a man.*

The drawbridge was down and the main gate stood open. Through it Ker saw several buildings belonging to the sprawling town that surrounded the castle, and beyond the buildings he saw fields dimly lit by the false dawn. Sheep clustered in some; others were newly plowed. Among them stood the shacks of peasants.

A servant held his horse ready. The stallion pranced impatiently, then quieted when he climbed into the saddle. He spurred his mount with a cry of joy, laughing in his exuberance. Then he and his horse almost flew over the drawbridge and down to the ancient road, turning west, passing among the houses and fields and patches of wood.

It would take all day to get to the valley where the Oracle lived. Ker's stomach abruptly growled. Looking at the vegetables growing in the peasants' gardens, he knew it would be a long, uncomfortable trip. He kept his eyes on the road until he left Castle Orrum behind.

* * *

In the afternoon, when the sun slanted down through the tops of the trees, casting long, dark shadows, he came to a high wall built of rough-hewn fieldstones. Behind it lived the Oracle. At the wall's small gate a boy wearing long yellow robes met Ker and took his horse's reins.

"Go in," the boy said in a voice oddly hollow, as if his body were merely a shell and empty inside. "The seer waits."

"I know!" Ker stalked forward, glaring at everything around him, trying to hide his growing fear.

The path to the temple curved to the left and wound out of sight among the trees. He hurried down it until he came to worn stone steps. Statues of many gods stood on them, looking down imposingly. Ker recognized Faramigon and Masferigon from the old tales; Hevtherigon too. They seemed to watch him as he passed. At the top of the steps sat a small marble building—the temple. He ducked through the low archway into the darkness.

Inside, sweet-scented herbs smoldered in a small brazier. Smoke writhed above it like dancing figures, making his eyes sting and his head spin. Glowing embers cast weird shadows on the walls. After a moment, Ker's eyes adjusted and he could see the Oracle. The old man sat bathed in darkness.

"Ker Orrum," he said, voice wavering with age. "Your father has already made a gift to the gods in your name."

"My father!"

"Yes. That is the price of the prophecy. You may ask me to cast your future now. Or you may tell me to stay my hand."

Ker hesitated, torn between the choices. All the stories he'd heard of the Oracle's powers frightened him. They said that whenever you asked an Oracle to look into your future, he took a bit of your soul as payment, that you could never be the same again. And whatever the seer said about you came true—it had to!

What if my father bribed the Oracle? he suddenly thought.

But no, that couldn't happen—the gods couldn't be bought.

Then Ker thought of the ancient epics, of the heroes and their adventures. He knew what life he wanted: oh, for the glory of battle!

And if he couldn't have any adventures in the baronies to the east, at least he'd have one in Vichir . . . if only for a moment. He had to take the chance and ask for a prophecy.

"Cast it!" he whispered.

"Very well." Reaching to his side, the seer drew away a black cloth. Beneath it sat a golden wheel. Gems sparkled on its surface, diamonds and emeralds, sapphires and rubies. The wheel shimmered even in the dim light.

The seer turned it once. It spun slowly, around and around for what seemed an eternity. At last it stopped. The old man leaned forward, mumbling to himself.

"Well?" Ker demanded.

"I see a journey. I see the gods. I see a gem: a ruby as big as a boar's heart. You must win it." He looked up. "It is the great ruby of Derethigon, the blind archer."

"*What?*" Ker cried, shocked.

"Your fate is cast. Your task has been set."

"But Derethigon—he's a *god!*"

"That is all. Your prophecy is over." The seer watched him with dark, shadow-filled eyes.

Ker stared back in bewilderment. He wanted to believe the prophecy, wanted to believe it more than anything in the world— But, like the promise of all his secret dreams fulfilled, it seemed too much to ever expect in life.

"What else did you see?" Ker asked, afraid for the first time. "Tell me!"

"You may go now," the seer said, and he rose and went off into the shadows.

Completely bewildered, Ker stumbled back to the gate where his horse was tethered. He climbed into the saddle and rode toward his father's castle at a gallop. A quest! The gods! How could he be a scholar and a warrior at once? Why hadn't his prophecy made sense? But the gods couldn't be wrong—it was unthinkable!

Night came and still he hurried on. At last he reached the castle. Sleepy guards nodded to him as he entered the courtyard.

"Well?" Ker demanded when everyone just stared at him. He was tired and frustrated and had no patience. "Take my horse—*you!*" His gaze fell on one of the retainers.

The old man hurried forward. "Yes, Master Orrum." He bowed his head and took the reins.

Now he was a man and they had to obey his orders at once!

Glancing up at the night sky, Ker guessed midnight had already come and gone. To the left, lights gleamed in the main hall's windows. He knew his father waited there, and he hurried through the side door and down the hallway.

Baron Orrum was seated on his low throne. Ker stood before him, waiting for permission to speak.

"Tell me what happened," the baron said.

Ker told him of the statues of the gods and the seer in the temple, of the golden wheel and the prophecy he'd asked for. His father listened intently as Ker told of his quest to seek the great ruby of Derethigon, and the Oracle's strange behavior.

"What did he mean when he said I was to win Derethigon's ruby?" he asked. "He didn't say anything about me being a scholar!"

"The Oracle is wrong," his father said. "The only task the gods have for you is writing about the great philosophies. There is nothing further to discuss."

"But it's my prophecy!"

"So? I forbid you to go. You're far too inexperienced in the world; there are many things you've yet to learn, if you're to be a scholar. I didn't have my future told, and *my* life's been good enough. Ignore what the Oracle said—and that's an order."

"Father, I'm a man now, and as a man I'm old enough to make my own decisions. I'm going on this quest. I'll find Derethigon and win his ruby. I swear by my honor!"

"What do you know of honor?" the baron demanded. "What do you know of quests? What do you know of gods? *Nothing.*" He spat. "Few men defeat the gods, and you are little more than a boy. I forbid you to leave."

"But the Oracle said—"

"The gods know when mortals seek them," his father said. "If you search, Derethigon may find *you.*"

Ker swallowed. A god searching for him—the thought was terrifying. The old tales warned of what happened when the gods took a special interest in a man. He could be turned into a monster or rewarded with wealth and power beyond compare. But if he really *was* destined to win the ruby, surely nothing could happen to him? Ker didn't know what to think.

"I'll do what's best," he promised. Still, he couldn't help but feel excitement at the prospect of leaving the castle and journeying beyond Vichir to seek a god's treasure.

"Good." That seemed to settle the matter, for the baron rose with a curt nod and headed for his private chamber.

Ker too went to his room, let a servant help him remove his armor, then lay down. But sleep didn't come. He considered his father's gifts: a good sword, a mail shirt, and a fast horse.

The Oracle had given him a quest. And the Oracle's prophecies always came true. At least, that's what the storytellers said. And if he *was* destined to win Derethigon's ruby, what right did his father have to stop him?

Silently Ker rose and dressed, then went to the main courtyard. All the torches but two had been extinguished, and these sputtered feebly, almost out. A boy lay on a bench beneath them. He woke when Ker's boots clattered on the flagstones.

"Yes, Master Orrum?" he asked, looking at the ground.

Ker glanced at the drawbridge and saw it was down. Since nobody had reason to threaten Vichir, security at the castle was lax at best. Now it would serve him.

"Fetch my horse," he said. "Put trail provisions in the saddlebags, and make sure there's plenty of water."

The boy hurried to obey. Ker sat on the bench and waited, impatiently stroking the steel of his sword, preparing for his battle with the god.

He rode past the nodding sentries at a gallop, and the sharp sounds of steel-shod hooves on the paving stones brought the men to their feet with shouts for him to stop and identify himself. Laughing, he looked back over his shoulder and crouched lower, urging his horse to greater speed.

Finding the ancient stone road, he turned west, heading away from the great lands and toward the almost-unknown wilderness. True, men did live there, but they were wild and arrogant, ungoverned by any lord. Since Ker could recall no recent accounts of gods walking among the men in the Eastern lands, he figured they'd have to be in the other direction. After all, that was the way the road went—and no men could have built it. Perhaps the gods made it to bring travelers to their door.

And so he traveled for many days. At last the paved road became a dirt track that meandered through dark forests and empty meadows. The few villages he came to were clusters of rude huts, and the men had strange, coarse accents that were difficult to understand. Always he asked about the god Derethigon. Always they shook their heads.

As he traveled farther and farther from lands he knew, the plants and animals became more and more bizarre. Flocks of hairy birds flew overhead, their singing voices as sweet to the air as any woman's. Six-legged deer loped through the forest. Rabbits as large as dogs leaped from the path as he approached.

Once he found the spoor of a giant serpent larger around than his horse, but turned away from its trail. It would have taken a small army to kill such a creature, and he didn't like the thought of facing it alone. Quickly he rode on.

One evening he chanced upon a tall, long-legged, two-headed bird nesting beside the road. One head was feathered as black as coal; the other as white as new-fallen snow. Its speckled gray body must have weighed as much his horse. Wings folded back, it sat upon a huge pyramid of pebbles, making soft crooning sounds as it watched him.

Ker dismounted and drew his sword to kill it at once, with little thought except to eat, but as he advanced toward the bird, it regarded him solemnly with its four dark eyes. He hesitated, wondering if it was intelligent. The dark head dipped forward; the beak opened and a long black tongue, forked like a serpent's, flickered out for a second. Then the other beak opened and from that mouth the creature spoke with a woman's voice:

"You have come to the Toolam. One serves Time; one serves Fate."

The black head rasped, "One will prevent your journey."

The white said, "One will help you on your way."

Together they said, "You must decide which of us to trust and which to kill. You are bound here until you do, or until we grow tired of our sport."

"How would you prevent my journey?" Ker asked.

They said nothing.

He turned to run, but found his horse had vanished. A grove of trees appeared before him, the trunks so close together that he never could have squeezed through. His heart pounded like a drum in his ears.

Magic!

Fear was a tinny taste in his mouth. He bit his lip, tasted blood. His legs felt like thick wooden stumps, his muscles so weak he could scarcely move. Shivering, he turned back to the bird.

"W-what do you want?" he managed to whisper.

"You to ask us one question," the white head said, "to help you decide."

"Consider it well," said the black. "One of us may lie to you."

"Consider it well," said the white, "for you will die a thousand times if your decision is wrong."

4

The Toolam

When Shon Atasha left our world, the gods grew wild and full of mischief. They made the rivers run uphill and the seas burn like oil; they made forests walk and mountains laugh; they made all creatures into toys and all toys into creatures. It is a miracle mankind survived. Fortunately the gods have grown old and tired and uninvolved in the latest age. Still, the remains of their jokes and amusements can be found in the odd corners of the world. Let the traveler beware.

—Pere Denberel
Atlas of the Known Lands, Revised

"I thought heroes and adventurers got three questions," Ker whispered.

"You are neither," said the black head. It regarded him silently for a moment, then snorted and looked away. "Hurry up, manling."

"How long do I have?"

The black head reared back. Strange sounds—like a man choking—came from its beak. After a moment, Ker realized it was laughing at him. Then he realized why. He'd asked a question.

"That doesn't count!" he said.

"It does! It does!" And it continued its mad laughter. At last it stopped: "*Your time is up, your question answered.* Choose, that your fate be decided."

Ker hesitated. Which head? The black one hated him. The white one wanted to help. They'd said Fate would help and Time delay him . . . so that meant the black one had to serve Time. Or did it?

"Decide!" the black head screeched. "*Decide! Decide!*"

It was the Fate of Oracles and Shon Atasha that the old tales said men had to thwart—man's predestined Fate always formed an obstacle! Wouldn't a servant of Fate be the same? And wouldn't the outcome of his decision already be known, already be part of his personal fate?

He shook his head. It was all too confusing.

Making his choice, he raised his sword and stepped forward. The black head shrieked with laughter while the white one looked on with cool detachment. He struck, felt the sword bite through flesh and bone—

Then the white head flopped limply at his feet. No blood spurted from the severed neck, and when he bent to pick up his trophy, it seemed to melt away in his fingers, becoming ghostlike in substance. Standing, he found the bird whole, both heads in place, as if he'd never struck it.

"You have chosen correctly," the black head said, cackling. "You have gained your freedom from us. Listen, then, and harken well:

"The quest runs long and hard.
To tarry is to stay the wheels of Fate.
Bow not to the East, nor North, nor South."

With that, the creature spread its wings and flew away in a great rush of wind.

The grove of trees behind Ker had vanished, melted away like a revealed mirage. His horse stood cropping grass where he'd left it. Only the Toolam's nest remained, reminding him that the two-headed bird had actually been there.

Cautiously, he approached the pyramid of pebbles and looked over the edge. Oddly twisted human faces lined the inside. They had been carved of some pale stone, he thought at first, but then one, then another, then another opened its eyes and stared back at him.

With a cry of fear, Ker turned and ran to his horse, leaped into the saddle, and spurred the stallion on down the path. He rode in silence for some time, thinking about the faces, about the staring white eyes—and shuddering. They had to belong to men who'd lost the Toolam's contest.

The weeks wore on and still Ker searched the wilderness. Fortunately the weather remained warm and fair, for the most part, and game was plentiful. He slept out under the stars and looked to the heavens for inspiration. Even so, he found no sign of Derethigon—

or any of the twelve gods. If not for the omen of the two-headed bird, he would have turned around and gone home to Vichir in disgrace, failed at the task the Oracle had set for him.

As the weeks became months his hair grew long and wild, his armor tarnished, his boots scuffed and dirty. Still he asked about Derethigon whenever he found a small village; always the towns-people shook their heads.

One evening Ker came upon an old man standing motionless in the center of the road. He wore a tattered blue cloak and a hood that kept his face hidden in shadows. Only his eyes showed, gleaming white like pearls.

"Move aside," Ker said impatiently. As a horseman, he had the right of way, and he intended to use it.

"I know whom you seek," the old man said. "I am Biur. I serve Derethigon. You will meet him soon."

Ker regarded him suspiciously. "How do you know who I'm looking for?" He looked around, nervous: all his life he'd heard tales of the bands of outlaws who lived in the wilderness, far from his father's soldiers and Vichir's laws.

"I serve Derethigon. You seek my master."

"Why are you telling me this?"

"Be at peace," Biur said. "I will do you no harm."

"Then what do you want?"

"Merely to answer your questions. You are young and do not know the ways of gods. Ask and I will answer, child."

"I'm not a child, and I don't need your help!" Ker spurred his horse, and the old man had to leap aside to avoid being trampled.

Angry and frustrated at being called a child, Ker rode for several minutes in brooding silence. He'd find the god himself—surely it wouldn't be that much farther, if he was already finding the god's servants.

Then he noticed a figure standing motionless in the middle of the road ahead, wearing a tattered blue cloak and hood. Quickly he looked over his shoulder. The man behind him had vanished.

He forced his horse to a gallop, and again the old man had to jump from his path. Ker smiled and slowed, glancing over his shoulder. Strange—he was gone again!

He looked ahead: the old man stood motionless in the center of the road, watching him. He reined in his horse.

"What do you want?" Ker asked, eyes wide. His hand trembled as he patted the stallion's neck.

"It takes more than years to make a man," Biur said. His voice grew stronger, more commanding. "I serve Derethigon. Ask me your questions."

"Then," Ker said, bolder now that he was sure of the old man's station, "how may I win Derethigon's ruby?"

"You must best Derethigon, the blind god, at archery. Any man may win. Many have tried; all have failed—so far. They thought it would be an easy victory against a blind opponent, but Derethigon is a god and sees without sight. Surely *you* are not such a fool as they."

Ker's face grew flushed. "Where is he now?" he demanded.

"To your left, in a clearing a hundred yards into the woods. He listens to the music of a water nymph."

"I'll win if I challenge him, won't I?"

Biur shrugged. "I see the present, not the future. It has been prophesied he will lose one day. Perhaps you are the one who will win. Now I must go; a thousand duties call." He stepped to the side and continued down the road as though nothing unusual had happened.

Ker stared after him for a long minute, then dismounted and led his horse to the edge of the woods. He strained to hear sounds from ahead, and thought he heard splashing and the delicate music of reed pipes.

After tying his horse to a tree, he took his hunting bow and a quiver of arrows from their straps on his saddle, then pushed into the underbrush. Branches he couldn't see in the long evening shadows scratched his face and tore at his clothes. At last he broke through a bramble bush and stood, blinking, at the edge of a grassy glade. Many flowers grew alongside the small stream that pooled to his right.

On a log beside the water sat a tall, dark-haired, dark-skinned man wearing sweeping red robes. His eyes were closed and he remained expressionless, slowly rocking back and forth as if to the sounds of some musical instrument Ker couldn't hear.

Ker stood there for a moment, watching, waiting. Where was the god? Nobody waited here but an old man! His face grew hot; he almost turned back, angry at having been made a fool.

Then he recalled how Derethigon was said to have wandered the Earth in centuries long past, disguised as a blind beggar to reward those few men who were good and generous. He stopped and looked more closely.

The man's skin seemed to glow with an inner light, and how graceful his simplest movements were! Ker knew then that this had to be the god he'd searched for, and suddenly his throat went dry and his nerves jangled.

Somehow, he found the strength to approach the pool.

"I have come for your ruby," Ker said in a trembling voice. All his bravery had vanished.

The god made no reply; his eyes remained closed. Slowly, wind ruffled the hem of his robe. He seemed oblivious to the world.

"I want your ruby," Ker repeated, louder.

In reply, Derethigon stood. He seemed to expand, swelling to fill the glade. He towered over Ker like a giant over an ant.

A mask of electricity shimmered over his face. Raising both hands to his head, tangling his fingers in his dark, curly hair, he pulled.

His scalp parted like a ripe melon. The rip continued down his face and into his chest. Brilliant light burst from inside his body, brighter than the sun, brighter than anything Ker had ever seen before. Stark shadows cut through the clearing. Light seared into Ker's eyes, burning, driving all thoughts from his mind until all he could do was scream and scream and not look away—

And then Derethigon reached inside himself and he drew out a dazzling red object. It spun from a silver chain, pulsing like a beating heart. A sun glared from its core like a single, bloody eye.

Ker managed to tear his eyes away, to throw himself to the ground, prostrate, hiding his face. If he looked longer, he feared he might go mad.

He's going to destroy the clearing, Ker thought. *He's going to kill me.* He could think of nothing else. It ran through his mind over and over like an endless chant.

At last the god spoke. His deep voice held the roar of the oceans and the songs of the birds. It seemed to pick Ker up and carry him along for miles. "We must wager on the contest," he said.

Ker uncovered his eyes and looked up, shaking all over, still awed by what he'd seen. Derethigon looked human again—yet the memory of the god looming high above, half split in two, light roaring from his insides, tied his tongue in knots. He tried to speak but could only stammer helplessly.

The god set the gem on a log by the water. It looked like any other ruby now, only larger, more perfect.

"What do you wager?" he asked.

Ker could think of nothing. He wished he'd never come, that he'd listened to his father and ignored the Oracle, given up his quest. How could he win against a god?

"It does not matter," Derethigon said. "I will take what I want when the match is over."

Ker pressed his face to the ground again. The smell of damp humus was smothering.

"G-great Derethigon," he managed to stutter. "I apologize for bothering you. I have no spells to guide my arrows; I know no sorcery. Surely you know that. Have mercy!"

The god stood in silence. Ker felt cold all over, as though winter had come and chilled him to the bone. He knew Derethigon was angry. He climbed to his feet and took a hesitant step toward the trees. The god shifted slightly, eyes still closed. He seemed to see everything.

"You are cautious," he said at last. "How mortal of you. I am a master archer. I have practiced more centuries than you've seen years. I use no magic when I shoot."

"I'm sorry—"

Derethigon cut him off with a wave of his hand. A tree at the far side of the clearing writhed, then folded in upon itself. It changed to a silver pedestal. On its top stood a slender needle, and on the tip of the needle balanced a tiny emerald. It glinted green in the dim light.

"Strike the gem and the ruby is yours," Derethigon said.

Ker didn't know what to do. A bit of his old confidence returned. *Maybe I can win,* he thought suddenly. *He's destined to lose someday. He said he won't use magic. I'm a good archer! I can hit his target—it's not so hard! Maybe I am the one who'll take his ruby. Why else would the Oracle have sent me?*

And then he thought of Threnodrel. The wizard said he'd used magic when he saved himself from falling. Maybe he'd be able to use it now. He *had* to be the one destined to win Derethigon's prize. It had been prophesied!

He steeled himself and picked up his bow. "Who shoots first?"

"You do," Derethigon said.

Ker put his quiver on the ground and selected his best arrow. It was long and dark, carved from the heart of a giant oak tree. He set it against the bow's string, pulled back, aimed for a long moment, then let fly.

He knew he'd missed the instant he shot, felt it deep inside. A numbness swept through him as he watched, a sense of doom about to descend.

The arrow missed by half a hand.

Derethigon produced a bow and arrow from nowhere, it seemed, and turned toward the target. His eyes remained closed. Without aiming, he shot. His arrow hit the emerald with a tiny *ping* and glided off into the darkness.

"I have won," he said slowly.

Ker backed away, terrified. What had the god said? He'd take what he wanted? *My soul?*

"You cheated!" he cried. He drew his sword and brandished it wildly. "Nobody could've hit that target without eyes!" Ker turned and fled into the woods the way he'd come, heading for his horse.

Five minutes later, he emerged at the dirt road, gasping for breath. Derethigon stood there waiting for him.

"I have won," the god repeated. "For my prize I claim your face."

He loomed higher, blue electricity shimmering over his skin. His eyes opened. An intense whiteness burned in them, a thousand times brighter than the sun. The god was blind, and yet he seemed to see! One hand stretched toward Ker, growing longer, stretching to infinity.

Then the god's hand touched his skin. It felt cool and smooth as ivory as it circled his jaw, then traced its way across his forehead. Ker wanted to scream, to cry, to run away, but he couldn't move. The god's hand covered his eyes for a second. He had a sense of vertigo, of flying, though his feet never left the ground.

Derethigon shifted his fingers. Looking between them, Ker saw his body standing five feet below. The front of his head was solid now, covered with fresh, pink skin, without place for eyes, nose, or mouth: his face had become a mask and Derethigon lifted it away.

Then he found himself back in his own body again, yet he remained without sight or smell. A fire burned in his lungs. He was smothering!

"Fear not," Derethigon said softly. "I free you from your need for air and food. Rejoice that I have spared your life. Think on your mistakes, and do not let false pride bring you to me again."

And then he was gone.

Ker sat and cried without tears for a long time, too stunned to really think about anything, then he crawled to the pool's edge and splashed warm water on the skin where his face had been. He still heard the noises of the night, the insects, the birds, the babble of the stream—but they did little to comfort him. His face was gone, he couldn't talk or see or eat or smell, and there was nothing he could do about it. Despairing, he lay down and waited for death.

After many hours, a light hand touched his shoulder. He jerked away, startled and frightened.

"Be still, child. It is only Biur, servant of Derethigon," a kind voice said.

Ker turned until the other could see his facelessness.

"I know what my master has done, and I grieve for you. Always before he took only eyes. You must have angered him."

Ker nodded.

"But do not be without hope," Biur said. "It is still possible to get your face back. Derethigon wears it now, but soon he will grow tired of it and discard it, for the interest of a god is fleeting. If you swear to serve me for five years, I will get it back for you when the time comes. Do you agree?"

A little of Ker's spirit returned. Become the servant of a servant? The son of Baron Orrum—serve another? *Never!* He shook his head vigorously, then struggled to his feet. Strong arms helped him rise. He shrugged them off.

"As you wish," Biur said. "I will come again. Perhaps you will change your mind."

Ker shook his head more strongly than ever, but Biur was gone.

Later, he crawled along the road, finding his horse by touch. He untied the reins, climbed into the saddle and gave the stallion his head, riding blindly on, away from the Oracle, away from the lands of Vichir. He could never return home, he knew, so great was his shame. He hadn't listened to his father, and now he'd lost his face to a god.

How long he rode, he didn't know. The air grew cool and he no longer felt the fiery warmth of the sun on his skin. Night birds sang. Dismounting, he led his horse, one hand outstretched, to the side of the trail until he found a sapling. He tied the reins to its trunk, then fumbled around in his pack until he located a light blanket. He made camp there for the night.

His sleep was haunted by dreams of evil spirits and shape-shifting gods who stole his face. And over it all he heard Biur's disgraceful offer: "Serve me, boy, and I will get your face back . . . your face back . . . your face . . ."

Suddenly awake, he was shaking with fear, and his hands flew to his head. It wasn't a dream—his face was gone!

He sat up, almost drowning in waves of self-pity. He wanted to kill himself. He'd fall on his sword, like the ancient heroes did when all hope was lost—that was the answer.

His hand fumbled at his scabbard and found it empty. Remembering he'd left the sword where he dropped it, he cursed his own stupidity. Why did he have to forget it? He'd never find it now. He couldn't even do a good job at killing himself.

He lay down again. His body shook with unspent sobs.

Morning came, and he hadn't managed to sleep any more. He heard the doves begin to sing. When he stood, the breeze was warm on his head, friendly, inviting.

Sitting with his back to a tree, he thought. He had nothing else to do, no future to look forward to, no home or hope for one. How could a faceless man be a scholar? How could a faceless man be *anything* but a hopeless cripple? Who would ever want him around? Certainly not his father!

He heard horses' hooves on the road, a dull vibration spreading through the ground. Before long he heard the shouts of men as they saw him, and the rasp of swords being drawn.

They reined in, calling to each other. Then they stood over him, blocking out the sun.

My father sent them, he thought.

"He's got no face!" one of them said.

"A god must've taken it—he's cursed!" said another.

They'll drag me back so he can see how I've disgraced him.

"Shut up," growled a third. "Take his horse, Urm. We'll get his mail."

Or maybe they're outlaws.

Ker tried to hit the man who began unfastening his armor.

"Got a little spirit left, have you?" He pinned Ker's arms to the ground. The others stripped him of his mail and scabbard, leaving only the underpadding.

"Want to kill him?"

"No. Who's he going to tell?"

Ker wanted to beg them to kill him. He tried to speak, but could make no noise. He couldn't do anything, couldn't even beg to die. A lump in his throat choked him. Swallowing wouldn't make it go away. He tried to stand and the men pushed him down.

They laughed. Ker blushed with shame at his helplessness, his ears burning.

The bandits rode away.

* * *

After walking and crawling down the road as best he could, Ker's hands and knees grew bloody from tripping and falling on sharp rocks. He crawled to the shade of a tree and rested there for a long time, thinking.

There had to be some way he could get his face back, he decided. All he had to do was find it. Of course, there was always Biur—but he promised himself he'd never be the servant of another, no matter what happened. All he had left was his pride.

There must be another way! he thought.

How had the god taken his face? He'd just reached out, traced a circle, and removed it magically.

But Threnodrel said he'd used magic, too. Could he somehow get his face back the same way he'd saved himself from falling out of the tree? He didn't know—but he decided he had to try. What did he have to lose?

Leaning back, he tried to remember everything he'd ever read about wizards and their craft. Thank the gods Lerrens had made him read so many books, and memorize passages he'd thought important in them! *The Chant of Creation* came to him first:

> . . . And Shon Atasha the Creator carved the world from the dust of the void, but it was without form, and dark. From his body he took his bones, and laid them out as a foundation for all the lands of Earth, and the mountains were there, and the valleys, and the hills and the plains. His tears were the oceans, the rivers, the streams, the springs, but still his creation was empty. He gathered more dust from the void, breathing on it, forming it into Man, Animal, and Plant. From his own flesh he formed the Gods and Magical Animals, giving up his body that they could roam across his world . . .

It was interesting, but did little to help him. Hadn't there been an epic about the wizard Karkashon and his battle with demons he accidentally let into the world?

As much as he tried, Ker couldn't remember it. Sighing to himself, his thoughts turned again to Threnodrel, and he remembered the wand the wizard always had with him. *Do wizards need wands to use their power? No—it can't be that. I didn't have one when I used magic.* Still, it couldn't hurt.

He knelt and ran his fingers over the ground around him, soon finding an old, dead stick about the size of Threnodrel's wand. Peeling away its bark, he held it in front of him and tried to stroke the grain of the wood, make it smoother, more perfect. He concentrated on it, picturing the stick in his mind as it was now, and again how he wanted it.

His palms tingled with the same fire he'd felt when he held the wizard's wand, and he moved his fingers faster, smoothing the grain of the wood, *willing* the magic to be done.

When he stopped he found his dry, slightly twisted branch had become as smooth and cool as carved ivory, exactly as he'd wanted it, and he gave a mental cry of triumph, hardly able to contain his excitement.

And now to make a new face! he thought.

It would be easy—already he could picture it in his mind, the blue of the eyes, the nose, the curve of his lips.

The wand moved in his hand, and he imagined himself drawing a picture in the air, sketching his own face with lines made of blue fire. First the head—the chin and cheekbones, the rough outline . . .

He felt the power in his hands, the fire coursing through his body. For an instant he grew disoriented. The world seemed to be spinning around and around, a blinding vortex of blue within blue within blue. He tried to open his eyes and for a moment saw himself, as through a pool of deep, still water.

He gazed up at his crouched body, looking straight at his head. The place where his face had been was flat and featureless skin, without place for eyes or nose or mouth. His hair was shoulder-length and filthy, full of twigs and dead leaves. In his right hand he held a glowing blue rod of light—the wand!

His hands moved of their own will, it seemed. The wand grew larger in his field of vision, and then he felt it stroking his face like a painter's brush, the touches soft and feathery on his cheeks and chin and forehead. He felt at once removed from his body and part of it—as though he were two people simultaneously, one giving pleasure, the other receiving, both him. The sensation was unnerving. Then he realized he was looking up from the picture he had sketched . . . that the face had truly been shaped and he was gazing out from it—feeling what it felt!

His eyes grew heavy and cold. He felt his eyelids forced down, down, down by some pressure other than his will. He seemed to be drifting away from himself, away from his new face.

Then he was back in his own body. In his mind he saw the face he had shaped. It was perfect, smooth, beautiful as an ivory mask. The eyelids opened, and instead of eyes Ker saw darkness—as though the eyeholes were windows into another, darker, world . . . where something moved.

It was a shadow. Snakelike, it wisped through the eyeholes and twined upward, spreading out, taking form—

And reached toward him. Ker felt a coldness touch his heart; the chill spread through him, numbing his fingertips, deadening his legs. His hands twitched, dropped the wand, seized it again—without his willing it.

Then his hands began to draw.

Something was wrong. Fear tightened in his throat. He couldn't stop himself: around the face he drew a neck, then shoulders, arms, legs, a chest and stomach—the body changed and blurred, still like his own in shape, but twisted out of proportion, grossly distorted.

For an instant a brilliant white light flared around the drawing. The body vanished, replaced by what seemed a hole in the fabric of the universe. A cold, cold wind blew through it, and through it Ker saw blackness. Strange stars—tiny pinpoints of light—slowly winked into existence. They were arranged in constellations unlike any on Earth, distorted, disturbing. Too late he recalled Threnodrel's warning.

The wizard had said never to use magic without training—that he might open a Gateway. But what *was* a Gateway, and where would such a Gateway lead—and what might come through it?

He tried to break away, to stop his hand from finishing the picture, but he couldn't. His arm refused to obey his thoughts.

In his mind he saw spheres of shifting yellow light coming through the eyes of the face he'd drawn. Each carried a tiny bit of darkness within. They floated all around him, bursting softly like soap bubbles, releasing the shadows. And with each bursting bubble the cold within him increased. At last it burned like a flame in his chest, and the pain grew and grew, swelling inside him like a thing alive. His chest felt as though it would burst. Far off, in another world, he heard himself screaming.

The shadows from the yellow spheres slowly drifted around him, a dark cloud hovering. He felt their cold, malignant presence as much as he saw it. They seemed to be feeding on his pain, growing stronger and stronger.

The wand in his hand blazed with light, a beacon in the shifting, shadow-filled darkness. He tried to focus his attention on it, and as it became larger and larger before him, drawing closer, he felt its heat soothing the pain. He could feel his fingers again. Life seemed to be flooding back into his body, the ability to move, to think—

He tried to drive the wand into his body, and it passed through his flesh like a knife through water, through his stomach and up into his heart. There it lodged against something cold and hard. He felt its heat spreading out through his body like ripples in a lake. The warmth shone through him like the sun breaking through clouds, driving back the shadows, driving back the darkness.

Now his whole body burned in the fire of his creation.

But the figure he'd drawn began to move without his will, stretching its arms and legs, twisting its head to see. It seemed *alive*, somehow. The tiny bits of shadow flowed into it, entering through the mouth, nose, and ears.

And then it laughed. It was a cold, sharp, evil sound that made the hair on the back of his neck stand on end.

It stepped forward, and darkness rose like a tidal wave to drown him.

5

The Eye of the Demon

When Shon Atasha created the world, the world cast shadows throughout all eternity. The shadow-worlds mirror our world in myriad ways. One way of special note is in life: twisted creatures, dark parodies of man and his kind, live in the shadow-worlds, breeding and practicing magics there. These creatures, or *demons,* have not been fully studied. The few that manage to enter our world have all been tyrants, more interested in power than science, and they murdered all scholars who tried to get close enough to study them. See also TYRANTS, and DEMONOLOGY.

—Rel Tayobi
A Treatise on the Facts and Fictions of Life in the Shadow-Worlds

Ker woke trying to scream.

Every part of his body hurt, from his head to his feet. After a minute, he realized he was lying on sharp rocks, and managed to lift himself up enough to roll over onto softer earth. Groping around, trying to find out where he was and what had happened, he finally realized he lay beneath two trees. From the needles on the ground, he knew they were pines.

The wand, the figure—had they been real, or a nightmare from some black corner of his mind? His fingers searched among the pine needles, but couldn't find anything to tell him. If the wand existed, it wasn't there now.

It must've been a dream, he thought with relief. Yet he couldn't help but wonder . . . he remembered it as though it had actually happened. The scene was set in his mind forever.

At last he roused himself and stretched the aches from his body. As he crawled back to the road, he found a stick the size of a cane. It helped him walk more than he'd believed possible.

He thought again of trying to use magic, but somehow he didn't have the strength to even try. Why torture himself? He had no hope of getting his face back. He knew it now; the thought burned in his mind.

He didn't know where he was going. He had no plans—only to get as far from his father's lands as possible. He didn't want to disgrace the name of Vichir, the home that would have been his. It was the only thing that mattered, the last thread of sanity he clung to.

After many days of wandering, he came to a small village. He heard the people moving about their tasks while he was still far away—his hearing seemed to have grown much keener—and he hurried a little. Perhaps they would comfort him. Perhaps they would let him sit by their fires at night and listen to their conversations. Surely they would be kind to a faceless man.

Children were the first to find him. They danced in a circle around him, laughing and taunting, grabbing his arms and spinning him around until he didn't know where he was.

At last he collapsed to the ground and they swarmed over him, shouting, poking him with his stick. Ker hid his head in his arms, mentally screaming for them to go away, to leave him alone. And yet he couldn't seem to hate them, for they were only children, and had no real knowledge of the world.

Finally they grew tired of their sport and drifted away. Ker didn't move. Later, the children returned, and this time their touches were gentle, amid soft whispers and giggles.

He felt a light, feathery touch where his face had been. When he raised his hand to brush whatever it was away, the children pinned his arms, their giggles growing louder.

"Hey there!" a woman shouted. "Stop that! What are you doing?"

The children scattered. Ker heard the woman's footsteps as she ran to him, calling, "Mister, are you all . . ." Her voice trailed off. Then she screamed.

"Demon! Demon!"

The children took up the cry. *"Demon! Demon! Demon!"*

A rock hit him in the arm. Then another. And another. He struggled to his feet, stumbling back down the road the way he'd come. Still more stones pelted him. Cries of *"Demon!"* echoed all around.

A last rock struck him in the center of the back, and he stumbled forward, his body twisted in pain.

"If ever we see you or your eye again," a man shouted, "we'll do more than stone you! Remember that, demon! And tell your brothers in Hell!"

Ker brought his hand to the spot where his face had been, touching what felt like grease. He wiped it off.

The children must have painted a giant eye in the center of his forehead, he thought. No wonder they thought him a demon.

He crawled from the road into the bushes, huddling there and waiting—for what, he didn't know. Perhaps it was death. He would have welcomed release from his torment.

In that instant, he felt closer to his father than he'd ever been before. He should never have left home. He didn't have to ask the Oracle or the gods to know his father had never been angered by him, or tried to punish him by making him stay in Vichir and study. Lessons could only have made him a better scholar! And then he realized he'd only been a child in his father's eyes, and not responsible for his actions. Just as he couldn't blame the children in the village for marking him a demon, neither could Baron Orrum blame *him* for being rash and quick to anger, or for playing tricks on Lerrens and the other servants.

The two of them shared a common pain—that of loss. The baron had lost his wife, all that he loved in the world. Ker had lost his face and his life in Vichir, all he'd ever known. Deep inside him was an ache he thought would never go away.

He felt truly like a man for the first time, and would have smiled if he'd had a mouth, had a face.

"I make my offer a second time," a voice said. Was it another hallucination? He'd heard his father and his long-dead mother speaking to him, and all the friends he'd thought he had. They'd laughed and tormented him, telling him to hurry and die.

Ker sat up.

"I am Biur," the voice continued. "Surely you remember me? If you swear to serve me for five years, I will get your face back. Do you agree?"

This time, Ker nodded. What did he have to lose? If this was but another waking nightmare, it could do him no more harm than all the others.

But now strong arms helped him rise, then guided him through the night of the world. He heard many strange sounds on their journey—the cries of nameless animals, the howl of the wind as it passed over some great chasm, the clanking of chains as a gate was raised. The air grew cold with a wind that tore through his clothes and lodged itself deep in his bones. Still they went on.

Then the air was pleasantly warm. Ker heard the sharp crackling of a fire.

"We are in Theshemna," Biur said.

Ker knew of it. Many legends told of Theshemna, the palace of the gods. It moved through the heavens at night, they said, and the lanterns in its windows mixed among the stars. It was said to be the most wondrous sight on Earth.

He couldn't find it in himself to feel elation, though, at being in a place few mortals ever saw. A dismal apathy had settled in.

At last his new master sat him down on a thin pallet. There were sounds all around them, the babble of voices, meat hissing as it broiled, the clanging of pots and pans, the sharp rattle of plates and cups as they were cleaned and stacked: the noises of the palace kitchens.

"Wait here," Biur said, and then he left.

For how long he sat, Ker didn't know. Hours, days, weeks—it mattered little. He remained slumped on his straw mat, unmoving, listening to those around him go about their duties.

They told stories of the gods to one another as they worked. He grew to know every voice like an old friend. The rich, heavy tone of the master cook; the sharper voices of the scullery maids; the voices of the other cooks and serving people—he knew them all.

And the tales they wove in their few free hours! Tales of the grand old days when the gods had walked the world with men, tales of great battles where the gods had drawn up sides and divided the world between them, tales of noble deeds and fearsome monsters to be slain.

He listened to the tale of Masferigon, who created a tribe of men who knew nothing of evil. One day a young man had gone out from the tribe to see the rest of the world. When he returned, he'd been changed, warped. He slew his neighbors and made himself their king. He made the tribe learn war, and fighting, and evil.

Then Masferigon had returned to see his tribe, had destroyed it in his rage. The wrath of a god is a fearsome thing: he turned the Earth in upon itself, burying the city, save for two children who knew nothing of evil. These two he changed—one into a monster to guard the ruins, one into a storyteller to wander the world and make men heed the warnings of the gods.

That tale Ker heard—and others. Tales of the strangest corners of the Earth, where the seas cascaded into darkness and the land fell away in cliffs no man would ever climb. Tales of monsters who had once been men. Tales of everything imaginable.

Several times a woman came to see him. She bathed his head in warm water, trimmed his hair, spoke soothingly. "You must rest," she would say, very softly. "Soon Biur will return with your face."

Other times he retreated into fantasy, imagining himself back home with Lerrens and Nowandin and his father. Sometimes Threnodrel was there, too, and life went on peacefully.

Someone touched his arm. He raised his head, the dreams slow to leave.

"I have your face," he distantly heard. "Here—give me your hands, take it."

It was wrapped in soft cloths. Ker brought it out, hands trembling, and ran his fingers over the smooth skin. Then he turned it over and brought it to his head, fitting it in place.

It stuck. And then the pain began.

He felt a thousand tiny needles piercing the skin beneath his face, like circulation returning to a bloodless limb. A brilliant light blazed through his head. The world shrilled at him. His eyes burned. His lips ached. Then white-hot brands seemed to bore into his face, searing his flesh, pushing deeper and deeper, piercing into his brain. He tried to scream. A choked gurgle slipped from his lips.

His hands were at his face, clawing madly, trying to tear it away, trying to free himself from the agony—

He heard a soft voice singing. The words rose around him, making him sleepy, easing the pain he felt. At last the world receded and he drifted on a soft, silent ocean.

6

The Halls of the Gods

> The twelve gods do not use magic, they *are* magic. They are shaped from the flesh of Shon Atasha the Creator, and they serve His dark purposes. Yet also do they serve the Earth, watching it, guarding it from harm. Could it be that they are bound to our world as flesh is bound to bone in man?
>
> —Tellerion
> *Speculations*

After what seemed hours, he heard a voice—as if from a great distance—calling to him: "Ker! Wake—*Ker!*"

It seemed to be getting closer, louder, rising all around him like the walls of a trap. The world grew dark and he felt someone shaking him.

"Ker!"

He opened his eyes and saw. Biur crouched over him, still dressed in a tattered blue cloak and hood, face still hidden.

He opened his mouth and cried out.

He breathed deeply, smelling the roasting meat, the stale wine, the boiling vegetables around him, the sweat of the cooks as they labored over open fires—all with equal ecstasy.

And he wept with happiness, thanking Biur again and again. He didn't even care if he *was* the servant of a servant, so great was his joy.

He collapsed suddenly, shaking all over, legs no longer able to support him, a coldness like that of deepest night running through his veins.

Biur caught him and carefully lowered him back down to the mat.

"Sleep now," he said. "Your body must get used to having senses again."

Ker pulled the blanket tighter around his shoulders and lay back.

Soon he slept, dreaming black dreams of the empty world of a faceless man.

It seemed he'd slept for only a minute before Biur woke him again.

"Come with me," his new master said. "You're a mess, and it's time you were cleaned up."

Ker looked down at his clothes and saw it was true—his boots were scuffed and muddy, his riding breeches torn at the knees and caked with dirt and dried blood from where he'd fallen, the under-padding for his armor ripped and as filthy as a beggar's rags. Self-conscious, he nodded.

Biur led him through countless empty hallways until at last they arrived at a small door. It opened easily at his touch, and he gestured for Ker to enter.

The room seemed more a cave than a chamber of the palace—long, transparent crystals, some as large around as a man's fist, hung down from the ceiling and grew from the floor, forming walls. They radiated a soft, soothing light. Dry white sand covered the floor, sloping down to a bubbling, steaming pool of water. Two marble benches lined a sand path to the pool's edge.

"Do not leave here," Biur said behind him.

Ker turned and found his master—and the door he'd entered—had vanished, replaced by a solid wall of crystals. He inspected it carefully, but couldn't find a way out. That the new crystals joined into the others in the wall puzzled him until he realized they must be magic—that everything around him had to be magic, for the gods themselves lived here!

The thought of Derethigon sent a shiver of excitement and apprehension through him. What would the god do when he discovered Biur had returned his face? Would he take it again? Or had he given it to Biur willingly?

He wandered around the room. Idly tapping one of the crystals with his finger, he sprang back in alarm when it rang like a bell with a loud, clear, high-pitched note. It echoed around and around the room, growing louder instead of softer, a shrill scream that bored through his skull. He covered his ears and backed away.

Then the sound ended.

With a grating noise, the wall to Ker's right slid back, revealing a dark, narrow passageway that curved out of sight. The stone walls glistened with water. Cautiously, he moved toward it. Light from the crystals spilled around him, providing enough illumination to see ten feet down the corridor.

He paused and listened. Wind moaned softly from the blackness, sounding like a low, rough, human voice.

Where does it lead? he wondered. *Back to Earth?* The doors of the palace of the gods might lead anywhere. He felt a familiar urge to explore, to see what lay just out of sight.

I might return to Vichir!

He rejected the thought before it tempted him further. *No. I gave my word—I have to serve Biur for five years, and there's nothing I can do about it.*

He heard the moan again, and this time it didn't sound like wind.

Maybe somebody's hurt, he thought. *I ought to get Biur!* Looking back at the crystal wall, he didn't see a door, or any other possible way to summon help. The sound came again, louder, definitely *not* the wind this time.

Maybe someone's dying!

Ker bit his lip. He couldn't just listen to the moaning. His master hadn't known there'd be someone in need of help! Cautiously he started down the passage.

The darkness seemed almost tangible; it hung over him like a shroud. When he'd taken five steps, the door behind him swung shut with a harsh grating sound, leaving the passage pitch black. He jumped, startled, then cursed. Why did everything have to go wrong at once? How would he get back to the crystal room? And what would Biur do to him when he found out?

Feeling his way back to the dead-end stone wall where the door had been, he pounded on it as hard as he could. His fists made faint slapping sounds, and hurt—but that was it. He gave up and felt for a hidden catch. The stones were slick and smooth, firmly set in mortar. None moved.

Shivering, he turned around, tasted bile and swallowed hastily—he was blind again, fumbling his way along the road.

Stop that! he told himself. *You can see! It's only a dark tunnel—there's nothing to fear now!*

Then he grimaced at his own nervousness. A wail echoed through the passage, half-human, a raw, animal cry that quickened his pulse and made him tense with excitement. Wary, he started forward, one hand on the stones to his left, the other outstretched, feeling the way. The passage seemed endless.

After an eternity, he saw light ahead. It was dim, but definite.

When he raised one hand, it was silhouetted against the corridor ahead.

He grinned in relief. At least he wasn't trapped in an endless dark maze, as he'd begun to suspect! Now curiosity edged concern, and he walked faster.

Rounding a turn, he came to a rough-hewn wood door set in the wall to his left. Stark white light leaked into the passage around its edges. He stopped in front of it and watched. The light flickered like a candle's flame, only infinitely brighter, as bright as sun on water. He wondered what fires would cast such a light. The sun itself? Did the door lead—to Earth?

As he watched, his body grew cold and numb. His thoughts drifted. He felt himself drawn forward, as if in a dream. The world hazed, strangely textured, and there was a blankness in his thoughts, a fumbling for words—

WHO?

He felt his hand rise to push the door open. He walked into whiteness. The world was white, pulsing like a beating heart. Again came the fumbling in his mind, the question formed:

WHO?

It was a roar that drowned out all else. He couldn't think. He couldn't see. Ice and fire, burning—

WHO?

There was nothing in the world but white. It swept over him. He drowned in it . . .

Then:

The world pulled itself together. All the whiteness spun into a whirlwind, rose, coalesced into a ball of white flame that hovered a yard above the stone floor. He saw, briefly, that he stood in a bare stone chamber; then his eyes fogged over and he couldn't see. He tried to rub them. His hands wouldn't move. He shook.

The sphere of light grew brighter, burning in his mind. Tendrils of fire reached toward him, touching his face in a caress like a rush of cool water.

THOU SHALT SERVE ME WELL . . . GO WITH THY MASTER, HUMAN.

And Biur was at his side, taking his arm, leading him back into the dark passage. Ker couldn't see. Bright spots glowed before his eyes. A ringing filled his ears. He began to cough and couldn't stop.

"Forgive the disturbance, Great One," he heard Biur say.

No answer came. Then the door creaked shut and Biur led him back to the crystal room. His master said nothing until they reached the pool. Slowly Ker's sight returned. The crystals on the walls, the two benches, the path to the pool of water—the room hadn't changed.

"Clean yourself up. You could have been killed." Biur shook his head. "I told you not to leave here. Next time, listen."

"What—" Ker began. He blinked and his master was gone.

Theshemna was full of surprises, it seemed. Next time, he'd listen to what Biur told him, no matter what happened! What could possibly be next—dragons in the sleeping chambers? unicorns in the banquet halls?

Shrugging, he stripped and left his clothes on one of the benches, then waded into the water. It was pleasantly warm. Bubbles rose around him, tickling where they touched, seeming to scour away the accumulated layers of grime and leave only tingling pink skin. When the water was up to his chin, he grabbed a quick breath and ducked his head under, and again the bubbles worked their magic. At last he rose to the surface, gasping for air, and felt truly clean for the first time in weeks, *renewed* somehow, as if his body had just now come to life.

He climbed out onto the sand and found his old clothes had vanished. That didn't upset him—they'd hardly been wearable. Hadn't Biur said he looked a mess? It wouldn't do to wander around the palace of the gods like that.

A soft woolen towel, a silvery gray tunic and a pair of soft-soled sandals now sat on the bench. He dried himself and dressed, then turned to look at the crystals once more. The door had returned.

Ker opened it and ventured out into the featureless passageway. Biur stood outside. His master still wore a tattered blue cloak and hood.

"Ah, much better," Biur said, nodding slightly. "Now you are fit for anything."

"What next?" Ker asked hesitantly. "Food?"

He'd noticed a growing hunger as he bathed, and he realized his appetite was back—and making up for all the time it'd missed when he hadn't had a face.

"That will do for a start. We'll return to the kitchens and get something for you there. I should have realized you would require a meal—magic is very draining."

Magic again! Ker thought. What magic had there been this time? He'd put his face back on—but it seemed to have stuck and become a part of him all by itself when he set it in place. Perhaps Biur meant the magic Derethigon used to let him live without eating or breathing? Or was it something else?

And what did Biur know about magic? Ker had been too busy with everything else to wonder about his master. Biur had known of his search for the god, and been able to disappear and appear when Ker tried to run him down—did that make him a wizard?

The more Ker thought, the more questions he had. It didn't look like he'd be getting any answers in the immediate future, though. Biur remained silent as they walked—he seemed more interested in the corridors than his new servant—and since Ker wasn't certain what was expected of him, he didn't ask. He knew he'd be told soon enough.

The palace kitchens were large and hot. Huge stone hearths along three of the walls held fires, and over the fires hung skinned and skewered oxen, sheep, goats, and other animals, as well as iron kettles filled with bubbling soups and various other liquids he couldn't identify. Old women and fat men—the cooks—rushed from one dish to another, basting the meats, stirring the sauces, adding seasoning or more vegetables. The smells made Ker's mouth water, and again hunger gnawed at him.

Biur sat him down at a small table and went to get his meal, soon returning with a plate heaped with roasted meats, stewed vegetables, and small yellow fruits with a sweet, slightly spicy taste unlike anything Ker had ever eaten before. When he bit into one, juice spurted out and dribbled down his chin. He stopped and stared at it in surprise, then finished it in one bite. Biur watched in brooding silence.

After he'd eaten, Biur led him through the winding, featureless corridors again. Ker quickly became lost. As soon as he thought they were going in one direction, they'd double back and go in circles . . . or so it seemed. Shaking his head in bewilderment, he followed blindly. As usual, Biur offered no explanation.

At last his master stopped before a small wooden door, took an iron key from his belt and fitted it into the lock, then opened it. The door swung back. Biur moved aside, so Ker could enter first.

The room was a library, large and crammed with shelves full of books—more than Ker had ever seen in one place before; more, in fact, than he'd thought existed in the whole world. It would have taken centuries to read them all! A cluttered desk stood in one corner, covered with stacks of papers and scrolls. Two low, padded couches covered in soft fur the color of snow sat in the center of the floor facing each other; a high, empty wooden table stood between them.

When Ker seated himself, Biur paced before him, seemingly lost in thought.

"I don't really need a servant," he said at last. "What am I to do with you?"

Ker stared at him in surprise. "Then why did you bother to get my face back?" he asked. "I thought—"

"Derethigon told me to."

"Derethigon?"

Biur shrugged. "The gods are mysteries, even to those who serve them. Perhaps he wanted to humble you for greater things to come. Perhaps he merely took your face to amuse himself. I doubt if we will ever know. I suspect he doesn't care whether you can see or not, and telling me to make you my servant was something to pass the time. There is little else to do in all eternity."

"But if he took my face . . . then, why wouldn't he want to keep it?"

"You don't understand the gods," Biur said. Then he chuckled. "It's the sport that matters, not the prize. Since Derethigon can have almost anything he wants just by wishing it, material things are meaningless to him. But to win something with the strength of his arms and the sharpness of his sight—Ah! That's something else."

"But he's *blind!*"

"He has other senses that serve him as well. Gods are different from men, you know—that's what makes them gods!"

Ker stared at him, mystified. It was Derethigon who had decided to give him his face back, not Biur—his master didn't care whether he served or not. It didn't make sense! What could he possibly do that the god could have foreseen? *Nothing*. Only the Oracles could foretell the future because the spirit of Shon Atasha the Creator burned in them—an Oracle would have to have told Derethigon to save him. But come to think of it, an Oracle *had* sent him on his quest for the god's ruby! Was *that* a coincidence, or part of the plot? *Was* there a plot?

He shook his head. No—he had to be mistaken! His pride had made him seek Derethigon's ruby, not the Spirit of Shon Atasha. Shuddering slightly, he put the idea that he'd been manipulated by the gods and the Oracles from his mind, concentrating on what his master said.

"But still the problem remains. What to do with you?"

"Let me serve Derethigon too," Ker said without hesitation. He was surprised at the vehemence of his outburst, then swallowed and continued. "Teach me to use magic—I know I can! A wizard told me I had the ability, and he even wanted to take me to one of the Eastern cities to apprentice me to another wizard!"

"You're rather old to begin lessons."

"I can still learn!"

"Then answer one question for me: what magic have I used with you since you got your face back?"

Ker hesitated, wondering if this were some sort of trick question such as Lerrens sometimes used. The pool of water sounded like the best answer—what else had Biur done? Then he remembered the way the corridors turned and seemed to double back, going in circles, and how strange they were to be empty.

"The corridors?" he asked slowly.

"Very good. There may be hope for you yet; recognizing magic is equally as important as using it, especially in a place like Theshemna, where everything must be regarded as magical until proven otherwise. You'll soon be injured here, if not killed, if you don't keep alert."

"Tell me," Ker said eagerly, "how do the corridors work? What was that pool? Will I see the gods—"

Biur held up his hands. "One question at a time, Ker. If you are to be my apprentice, you must be patient. All will be explained to you. There is more in the world than I could possibly know, and there is more in Theshemna than I can possibly explain to you when you don't know of magic. How does one explain light to the blind? Magic is like that. Perceiving it is the hardest part; once you can sense magic, *feel* it around you, you will be able to manipulate it to your own designs."

"How long will that take?"

The wizard shrugged. "Days. Weeks. Months. Maybe years. Who can say?"

"When did *you* learn?"

"Two months into my apprenticeship. It was quite a surprise when it happened." He sounded almost wistful. "Magic can be a curse, at times. I have never been as happy or as free since I came into my powers."

"The gods," Ker said to change the subject. "Will you tell me about the gods?"

Biur sighed, then seated himself on the couch opposite his

apprentice. "I suppose I must," he said. "That information is important to life in Theshemna."

Leaning back, he began.

There have always been gods in the world (Biur said), since Shon Atasha the Creator started time. Some have faded away, or simply vanished, never to appear again. No one can say for certain what became of them: they are simply gone. Now eleven gods live in Theshemna, some of whom walk the world from time to time, some of whom merely watch, some of whom try to dream away eternity, locked in chambers no man will ever see.

Derethigon has always walked the world, searching for something; he knows not what. There is a great melancholy upon him, a great desire to leave Earth and venture among the stars, to join with the spirit of Shon Atasha the Creator, for that is the one thing denied him—and all the gods. When Shon Atasha created them from his flesh, and breathed life into them, he bound their names into the very essence of the world and now they cannot leave it.

Truly the world is in a dark age now: Few gods walk the lands of men, and magic is slowly being forgotten. Humans multiply and spread over the Earth from one end to the other, and with each generation they remember less and less of Shon Atasha. Perhaps the day will come when the gods are but a wistful fever-dream. Who can say for sure? The gods do not speak of the future, and the Oracles burn with the bright spirit of Shon Atasha, and will reveal no more than hints of times to come.

These things all wizards know, and they bide by them, working to postpone the loss of magic and keep the memory of the gods alive for as long as possible. That is why I serve Derethigon, and why wizards must always serve the gods.

Biur stopped talking and seemed to listen. "Derethigon calls me now," he said, standing quickly and starting for the door. "Come."

Ker followed him from the room, feeling euphoric. He was in Theshemna, the palace of the gods, he had his face back, and now he was to learn magic from a wizard who served a god! He knew his father never would have approved, but then—if he hadn't agreed to serve Biur, he'd still be waiting to die as he lay in the bushes beside the road. What else could he have done?

When Threnodrel said he had the ability to use magic, he'd

longed to learn how. And now he *would* learn! He could think of nothing in all the world that he wanted more.

As they walked through the winding corridors, his master began to speak, and Ker listened carefully to every word.

"Theshemna is more than merely a place," Biur said. "She is alive with magic, always changing, never the same for more than a few seconds. She can feel your very thoughts. When humans walk through her, they must keep their destination firmly in mind, and she will change the passageways ahead of them to guide them wherever they want to go. Remember that."

"Yes, Biur," Ker said. Then he grew silent, letting his master concentrate on the corridors ahead.

Biur opened a small door and stepped through. Ker followed, surprised to suddenly find himself on a low, rolling hill overlooking miles and miles of forests and fields, meadows and hillsides. Had they somehow returned to Earth? He looked back through the door into Theshemna's featureless corridors and knew they hadn't.

It took a minute before he realized they stood in an enormous room, a room with a ceiling so high clouds rolled across it, a room with walls so far apart he could barely see its far side, a room built of thousand-foot-high blocks of granite. Since the door opened onto a hill, he had a good view of everything below. Giant trees with trunks fifty feet in circumference stood like toys amid lush, green-grassed meadows, and men and women moved among them like ants.

It was a miniature world, this room inside the palace of the gods—to the right, misty in the distance, sat a magnificent castle surrounded by farmed lands, and to the left the gigantic trees grew thicker, becoming a forest whose like no huntsman on Earth had ever seen. Ker could scarcely imagine what sort of animals would live there.

"Come," Biur said, starting down the road paved with jet black stones. It led from the door to the distant castle. Ker could see it cutting across lush, green fields in the distance, exactly like the road past his father's castle in Vichir.

"Where are we?" he asked, trying to see everything at once.

"The throne room of the gods. Derethigon is in the castle now, and he commands me to hurry. Listen! Can you hear him calling?"

Ker strained to hear beyond the rush of the wind and the dry rustle of insects' wings in the grass. A low, throaty roar like the blast of wind through some great chasm filled his mind, but it vanished when he shook his head. The smooth, frightening voice he remembered Derethigon using did not come to him. "No," he said at last.

"Then you must learn—that will be one of the first things I teach you. One must always obey the gods when they call."

They reached the bottom of the hill. There a woman dressed in a deep green robe waited for them, the reins of two coal black horses in her right hand. Her hair gleamed like new-minted gold, her face ice-pale save for the faintest flush of rose in her cheeks.

The stallions behind her shifted, uneasy in the presence of strangers, but she rubbed their noses, speaking soothingly, and they didn't pull away again. The horses wore bridles, but no bits, Ker noticed—their riders would be unable to control them. But they were sleek, their muscles rippling like water beneath their coats, their eyes glittering and wide, and he knew they were wild things, tamed only by their love for the woman. To ride them like normal horses would kill them.

"Derethigon wants you," the woman said.

"I hear him," Biur answered. "These are for us?"

"Yes. Keep them well."

"Thank you, Lady."

She smiled suddenly, and it was like a golden burst of sun through cloudy skies. Her face was unbearably beautiful, like that of some nymph, full of simple innocence and wisdom beyond her years. She turned to look at Ker, and he smiled shyly, glancing away. Never had he seen a woman like her! Her beauty rivaled that of Queen Rathelsia from the ancient Zelloquan epic *The Perisomidon*—a thousand nobles had died in a great dueling competition to see who would win that queen's hand, or so the poem said. He'd never believed it before, but seeing this woman put the ring of truth in its lines. There *was* such a thing as love at a single glance.

He wished he could tell her how beautiful she was, but found himself at a loss for words, struck dumb for the first time in his life. Lerrens had never taught him what to say to women beyond the empty phrases court etiquette required, and those would ring false when put to this woman.

Biur had simply called her "Lady." It was a title that fit her quiet charm and dignity.

"And how are you, Ker?" she asked, as though they were old friends.

Surprised, he asked, "You know me?"

She only smiled. Then he remembered the soft voice and the hands that had bathed his face when he first came to Theshemna. He stammered his thanks, blushing at his awkwardness.

"Ker," Biur said, "I present the Wind Senessa d'Alshia nar Mian Ellysiaf."

Ker smiled and bowed, his training taking over. "I am pleased and honored by your acquaintance, Lady." He longed to ask Biur what he meant—a Wind?—but knew better than to do so in the woman's presence.

She laughed, a light patter like a breeze through chimes. "Please, Ker, call me Liana. 'Lords' and 'Ladies' are best left to castles and courts, not meetings of new-discovered friends."

"Thank you, Liana," he said. "I am honored by your friendship."

Again she laughed, a purely joyful sound. "And I am honored, Ker, to know you." She turned to Biur. "My friends will let you ride them to the castle. I hadn't known there would be two of you, or I'd have asked another horse to come. I will get a ride and catch up with you soon."

She asked the horses to come? Ker wondered.

"Thank you, Liana," Biur said. He swung into the saddle of the horse to her right, motioning for his apprentice to follow suit. Ker needed no urging. He climbed into the saddle and sat quietly, feeling the stallion shift beneath him, all power and speed. This would be a ride unlike any other.

Her friends?

He'd known there was some special bond between her and the horses when he'd first seen them together. The stallions had grown calm beneath her hands, restraining themselves for her, eager to serve her wishes. And Ker would have served her just as willingly, if she'd asked.

Could she be a wizard? he wondered. He'd heard of female wizards in the Eastern lands, and read about women who'd used magic in a few of the old epics, but it had somehow never occurred to him that they would be beautiful. *And what did Biur mean by calling her "a Wind"?*

Liana turned to her horses. "Go now, my friends," she said softly. They pricked up their ears and listened, snorting impatiently, then wheeled about and started down the road, slowly at first, then faster and faster, at a gallop, then more than a gallop. Wind drove tears from Ker's eyes. He tucked his head down and clung to the reins, letting his horse run in its wildness. It knew the way and needed no help from him.

On the softer ground at the side of the road, the sharp clatter of hooves became muted. The world blurred by faster than anything Ker had ever seen before. Men pushing barrows on the road were gone in a flash, fields whipped by; wind roared like a demon in his ears. The speed exhilarated him. He hoped the ride would never end.

The horse's supernatural speed dropped abruptly, and he looked up to see the castle looming before him. Like the walls of the giant room in which they rode, it was built of stone—seemingly carved from a single block of granite. As much as he looked, Ker could find no breaks in its walls to tell it had been assembled.

They rode over the drawbridge and through a thirty-foot-high stone arch into the main courtyard. A line of men, all wearing blue and gold breeches, shiny steel breastplates inlaid with silver, and large, deep blue capes, stood at attention as they rode past. Long, slightly curved swords, unlike any Ker had ever seen before except in the oldest tapestries of the banquet hall in his father's castle, hung at their sides. He wondered for a second if these were the same men who fought side by side with the gods at Kiy-len and Peldath—but that had been hundreds of years ago.

"Yes," Biur called softly, as if sensing his thoughts, "this is the gods' honor guard. They will serve here for eternity, rather than face the Great Abyss and the Dark God."

"Forever . . ." Ker whispered.

They passed the lines of men and came to the central building. It was hundreds of feet tall, built of granite like the outside walls, with many high turrets and spires. Banners flapped overhead, bearing various emblems—and one of them was a single blue arrow on a field of white. Ker guessed it was Derethigon's standard—the blind archer's symbol of power.

They dismounted. At once the horses turned and trotted back the way they'd come, hooves clip-clopping on the pavement.

Biur watched until they'd vanished from sight. Then he dropped one hand on Ker's shoulder, and his voice became hard and humorless. "Derethigon will be waiting inside. Say nothing to him except what he asks of you."

"Yes, Biur," Ker said.

"Good." Slowly, he drew back his blue hood and shrugged off his cloak. His slightly stooped back straightened and he seemed to grow four inches. A light breeze blew his short brown hair into disarray. His skin—smooth and firm, unlined by age—almost glowed with health, with youth. He couldn't have been more than thirty years old.

Ker stared at him in shock. "You're—" he began, then stopped himself, biting his lip and wishing he'd kept quiet.

"Not ancient and decaying?"

Ker nodded.

"Do all wizards have to look like they're on the Dark God's doorstep?" he asked with a short laugh. "I *am* older than I look—I feel as though I have seen all there is to see, done all there is to do. The press of time is heavy on my soul. Like all the gods' servants, I do not age when I am in Theshemna. It will be centuries before I am old and wrinkled, and millennia before I die."

"But why do you wear that hood and cloak?"

"Sometimes there are benefits to looking old. Would you have listened to me in the lands of men if you saw me as I truly am?"

Slowly, Ker shook his head. "No."

"Most humans are like you. They base their judgments on what they see with their eyes. Appearances are irrelevant; it is the mind—the *thoughts*—that count." Clearing his throat, he folded his cloak and hood and draped them over his left arm, then led the way through a large door that had been left open to the breeze.

"Follow me," Biur said, "and remember what I told you. Say nothing to Derethigon; his whims are sudden and dangerous."

Apprehensive, Ker nodded. They passed through the door.

The great hall inside was cool, and their footsteps echoed with unnatural loudness in its confines. As Ker's eyes adjusted to the near-darkness, he stared openmouthed at the wonders around him.

The room stretched back a hundred times longer than the main hall of his father's castle, a dozen times higher. Pale globes of colored lights—reds, yellows, greens, and blues—slowly circled overhead in a stately dance, providing dim illumination for the spectacle below. A thick blue and gold carpet sprawled across the entire floor. Intricate designs woven into its fabric shifted as he watched, constantly changing, constantly different. Along the walls to the left and right stood hundreds more of the gods' honor guard, all dressed in the same type of uniform as the men outside. Eight of them approached and formed a cordon around Ker and his master, escorting them forward.

At the other end of the hall stood eleven enormous thrones carved of gray marble, each designed to hold a figure more than three times as large as any human. All were empty save the one in the exact center.

Derethigon sat there.

The god was huge and splendid in sweeping red robes, majestic and somehow more frightening than ever before. The air tingled with energy, surrounded him with an almost tangible barrier. The hair on the back of Ker's neck bristled and stood on end, his skin pricked as though a thousand ants crawled over him. Every sense in his body jangled preternaturally sharp. The dark, crushing walls seemed to close in; he felt lost and insignificant before the god. Quickly he averted his eyes. Then he forced himself to look up, to see all that went on, for he knew it would concern him greatly if his master was right and Derethigon *had* made him come to Theshemna for a purpose—for some great deed yet to come.

Shadows cast by the shifting spheres played across the god's skin, forming a kaleidoscoping pattern. Yet despite the shadows, his whole body glowed faintly, as a bright light might seep through a heavy curtain, or filter down through the depths of the sea. Again Ker had the impression that the god's skin was paper, and fires blazed beneath. Ker knew, then, that this was not the god's true form—that Derethigon was something beyond all comprehension, that no man could look on him as he truly was and not go mad. The god took on this guise to deal with humans as a man might don a cloak to go out into the rain.

Finally Derethigon spoke. His voice was low, full, melodious—more so than Ker remembered—rich and terrible with its power.

"Biur," the god said slowly, "we have sensed a disturbance in the world, a great unrest. Since a man—some wizard—must be responsible for its cause, you are to find him, and bring him back to me."

"Yes, Derethigon," Biur said.

"You must go to Ni Treshel. That is where the disturbance starts."

"As you will, Derethigon."

"That is all. Leave me."

Biur bowed and slowly backed away, motioning for Ker to do the same.

The honor guard escorted them outside.

As they stood on the pavement, Ker found himself overflowing with questions. Where was Ni Treshel? What did a great disturbance—an unrest in the world—mean? And why did Derethigon send Biur rather than go himself?

But Biur waved him to silence before he could speak, putting on his tattered blue cloak and hood again, assuming the appearance of an old man. "There will be plenty of time for that later. Now we must prepare for the trip." His shoulders bent forward and his words took on a different texture, a certain slurring and tremor as if someone truly old were speaking.

Ker didn't know what to think about his master. Biur seemed to know magic well, but hardly ever stopped to explain anything! How was he supposed to learn if he couldn't ask questions? And then there was his master's disguise . . .

His thoughts turned to the god. *He didn't say anything about me—I guess that means he had Biur return my face just for sport, like Biur said.*

He guessed he wasn't destined for greatness after all—and immediately felt like a load had been lifted from his shoulders. There would be no burdens of responsibility laid on him—at least, not yet. When his service to Biur ended, he'd be able to do whatever he wanted—and he'd be a wizard! He could go to the Eastern lands and visit the great cities at will, or travel through the wilderness, protected by his magic. Or just return home to Vichir and surprise his father and Nowandin.

And then he remembered what Derethigon had said.

"I'm going to Ni Treshel, too?"

"Of course," Biur said. "Where I go, my apprentice goes. That custom is as old as the world. How could you possibly learn anything if I kept you locked in a room all your life?"

Ker didn't know what to say. Biur thought Lerrens and his father had been wrong in making him stay in the castle library to read old books! A sense of euphoria filled him, a sense of completeness and happiness. He knew, then, that this was the life he'd always longed for.

They headed for the gate. Liana waited outside for them, only this time she rode a sleek gray mare. Two more horses cropped grass five feet away—another black stallion like the ones they'd ridden earlier, and a brown and white mare. All the horses bore large packs—he guessed they held blankets and provisions for their journey.

"Well?" she asked Biur. "What did he say?"

"Some wizard is creating a disturbance in Ni Treshel, so I'm to go and put a stop to it."

"Ni Treshel! But the bones—"

"Even a madman would not touch *those.*"

Ker couldn't contain his curiosity any longer. "*What* bones?" he asked.

"The bones of Shon Atasha the Creator," Biur said. "Surely even your people have heard of them."

"The Chant of Creation says they're under the world."

He sighed. "So your people do not know of the Rashendi and their divine task? So much has been forgotten on Earth! It is indeed a dark age."

"Who are the Rashendi?"

"They worship the spirit of Shon Atasha the Creator. As the elements expose splinters of his bones in the distant corners of the Earth, they gather them up and bring them to a shrine in Ni Treshel. It is one of the most holy places in the world, and almost every Oracle comes from their people. The spirit of Shon Atasha favors them."

"And they are very important to the gods," said Liana.

Biur shrugged. "We are wasting time."

Ker still hesitated. "We're going to ride there?"

"Yes, of course. Ni Treshel is too far away to walk."

"But how—"

"I will open a Gateway. You know nothing about Gateways, either?"

Feeling foolish and ignorant, Ker shook his head. He remembered Threnodrel mentioning them, but the wizard hadn't said what they were, just given a vague warning and hinted of terrible things that might happen if he opened one by accident. But surely there wouldn't be any danger with Biur, would there?

His master sighed. "I see we will have to start at the very beginning. Do you know *anything* about magic or the gods?"

"Only what you've taught me."

"There will be time for that later," Liana said. "We must go."

"I had not realized you were coming with us," said Biur.

"I am."

"Very well." He turned to Ker. "You will ride the other mare. Mount up!"

"Yes, Biur," he said. He climbed into the saddle and watched to see what his master would do.

Biur stretched his right arm in front of him. Ker was surprised to see a glimmering white wand in it—the wizard had never before used it in his presence. Wind billowed Biur's cloak out behind him, and he moved slowly, cautiously, with restrained power.

He raised the wand higher, tracing a pattern in the air. The world around him grew darker, and blue fire flickered over his body, giving the land an odd, surreal look. Grass in fields to the left and right stood out in stark relief, blades sharp as razors; the road's jet black paving stones took on an oily sheen; the very air grew misted and thick.

Biur pointed the wand at the ground in front of him. Dazzling light leaped from his arm in a low arc, then roared up, a blazing wall of liquid-blue flames that slowly faded away.

A matte black rectangle perhaps fifteen feet high and five wide now stood where the flames had been. Its surface shimmered, rippling like water in a lake, but they could not see through it. A bone-chilling cold oozed from its depths. Gazing at it, Ker felt a sense of vertigo, infinite darkness, infinite void. Terror clawed at him—he was falling into it—*falling*—

He tore his eyes away.

Liana didn't hesitate. Her horse cantered forward, then leaped into the rectangle, disappearing from sight. Biur turned and ran to his horse, swung up into the saddle, then spurred the stallion forward with a touch of his heels. They too leaped into the darkness.

Ker felt the dappled mare gather herself beneath him, then she followed a split second behind the others. The speed of it all took his breath away. A leap, and they plunged into a sharp, knife-edged cold worse than the coldest winter Ker could remember. He coughed, gasping for air as the chill settled into his lungs, stealing his body's heat. And still his horse ran on, muscles rippling smoothly, effortlessly.

He clung to the saddle as before, trusting the mare to find her way. He knew he wouldn't have been able to follow Biur and Liana on his own if his life depended on it.

7

The Weird of the Rashendi

On darkest eves the twilight wind
Brings sounds of fiends' delight;
Cavorting demons kill and maim
Throughout the thick of night.
Beware until first light!
Beware until first light!

—Traditional

A wave of searing heat blasted over him, and he almost screamed in agony. It took a minute for him to realize his horse had stopped. Prying his eyes open, he found himself in the middle of a vast plain. Thick green grass stood as high as his horse's chest in all directions; clumps of stunted trees dotted the horizon to his left—and that was all.

He shivered, the chill slow to leave. After another minute he realized the day was no warmer than any other; the sun on his face only seemed unnaturally hot after the icy cold of the Gateway. And that reminded him—

Twisting around in his saddle, he found Biur and Liana already dismounted and talking quietly. They'd found a wide game trail and were standing in the middle of it. He hopped to the ground and pushed through the grass to join them. His horse followed more slowly, browsing as it went.

". . . should be no trouble," Biur was saying. He nodded to Ker. "I see you have recovered somewhat. Do not be concerned—it will take time for you to become accustomed to traveling through the shadowlands."

"Where are we?" he asked. "I've never seen grass like this before!"

"You're at the edge of the world," Liana said, "where the sun goes to die at night. We're not far from the valley of the Rashendi." She shaded her eyes and looked west. Already the sun hung low in the sky, a fading crescent. "It is perhaps an hour's ride from here, and another three hours' ride to Ni Treshel."

"Then we must start at once," Biur said. "I have no great desire to sleep in the open tonight."

"Why don't we go through another Gateway?" Ker asked.

"No," Biur said. "I have not the strength now."

Liana called to the horses. They pricked up their ears and trotted to her, snorting impatiently, trampling the grass. "The road lies to the left," she said, climbing into the saddle.

"I remember it."

Ker watched as his master slowly mounted his horse. Biur seemed oddly tired, as if opening the Gateway had drained him of all his strength. And, wearing his cloak and hood, he looked more like an old man than ever before. He slumped in the saddle and let his stallion trail Liana's horse.

Ker climbed onto his mare. It seemed Derethigon's task was more important than anything else to the others—they made no effort to wait for him, nor did they even look back to see if he'd followed.

The horses plunged through a barrier of high, thick grass, and they found themselves on the road. It sat a hundred yards from where they'd arrived, cutting a straight line through the plain. Paved with enormous blocks of black stone, just like the road that went through Vichir, it stretched as far west as he could see.

Liana whispered something and laughed, then the horses trotted. Ker expected them to break into a mile-eating gallop, as they'd done in the throne room of the gods, but they didn't. Relaxing at last, he urged his horse to catch up with Biur's.

Head still covered, his master glanced over at him. Wind billowed his cloak and whipped at his hood, but didn't push it back far enough to show much of his face.

"Will you tell me more about Ni Treshel?" Ker asked.

"What do you want to know?"

"What are the Rashendi like? Are they human?"

Biur said nothing for a minute, and Ker began to wonder if his master had heard him. At last he said, "Usually. The spirit of Shon Atasha burns brightly in them—they are the only people who can see the future, when the Creator wills it."

"Do you mean they're all Oracles?"

"Yes."

"Oh." He rode in silence for a time. "Have you visited them before?"

"Yes."

"You don't say very much!"

His master turned and looked at him again. "One learns most by listening and watching."

"But—"

Biur shook his head. "Listen. Watch. Learn." There was a note of impatience in his voice, so Ker grew silent and did his best to examine everything around them. The grass stretched in all directions like an endless yellow ocean, broken only by the road and scattered islands of trees; and the sky overhead remained a cloudless azure. Bored, Ker decided there was nothing to learn there after all. He tucked his head down and rode in silence.

Liana reined in her gray mare. They caught up with her.

"What is it?" Ker asked quickly.

"We're coming to the valley where the Rashendi live."

"How can you tell?"

"I've been here many times." She gestured down the road. "There is a strangeness in the air, a heady whisper of power—and more than power. Can you feel it?"

Ker thought he could feel it then, too. It hung just on the edge of perception: a sense of unease, an odd disturbance in the air.

They continued more slowly. Ker saw they were approaching a drop-off of some kind, where the black stone road ended abruptly and the land fell away in steep cliffs that stretched straight down for what looked like miles. Far below, misty and fair, spread an enormous valley. Patches of lush green fields, neatly planted orchards, and scattered groves of trees made a pleasant checkered pattern. White buildings dotted the landscape, and a small town sat far to the east, full of glittering gold spires and brilliantly white domed roofs.

"That is Ni Treshel," Biur said unnecessarily, pointing. Ker felt the ancientness of the place and knew its holiness. "The bones of Shon Atasha the Creator are kept there."

Ker heard the reverence in his master's voice. He too felt a sense of growing awe mixed with apprehension. The bones of Shon Atasha the Creator were here, the bones of the god who had made the Earth, made the gods, made everything he'd ever known.

And yet . . . something indefinably alien seemed to hang over the city like a shroud. Deep inside him, a sense of foreboding grew, as though the city's facade of placid beauty hid some inner disturbance. Suddenly he didn't want to enter Ni Treshel. He had the impression that both the city and its people would be hostile—full of solemn men and women bound to ritual and grim religion, full of vague threatening portents and mysticism . . . and the ancient magic of Shon Atasha.

Then he noticed that the road didn't quite stop. A narrow dirt track, scarcely wide enough for a wagon, wound down the side of the cliff. It was steep and full of switchbacks.

Biur moved forward quickly, his eagerness apparent. If he sensed the dismal atmosphere hanging over the city, he made no sign of it. Turning, he glanced back at Ker for a second, as if urging him to hurry, then prodded his horse to the edge of the dirt track. They all paused there for a time, Ker secretly dreading the descent.

"There's someone on the road ahead," Liana said.

It took Ker a minute to spot the small, gray shape slowly making its way up the road. He guessed it would take an hour for the man to get to the top—if not longer.

"Biur?" he said.

"What?"

"He'll know what's happened in the city! If we wait . . ." He didn't quite voice his reluctance to enter Ni Treshel.

The wizard sat in silence for a long minute, then nodded and dismounted. "I will get him," he said. "Perhaps he will save us a trip into the city."

A wand appeared in his hand. It crackled with blue fire that leaped away from him and traced a tall rectangle in the air. When the shimmering black Gateway appeared, Biur ducked through. In a second he stepped back out, followed by another man. The Gateway collapsed in upon itself, disappearing with a sudden gust of cold wind. The road ahead of them stretched empty for miles.

Ker looked at the strangely dressed newcomer with amusement. He wore a shirt of some silvery material that shimmered where light touched it. His pale gray pants, cut of some silken material, puffed out balloonlike from waist to ankle. Equally gaudy—and equally improbable—silver sandals covered his feet.

In Vichir, Ker thought, only a traveling entertainer would have dressed in so outlandish a costume, and everyone would have laughed at the joke. This man, though, looked grim—not at all like part of a troupe of players. A light pack had been slung over one shoulder. And yet, for all his strangeness, he had a pleasant, half-familiar face—quick gray eyes, firm chin, thin nose. His long, black hair had been tied loosely behind his head. It took Ker a minute to realize he looked like the Oracle in Vichir—not exactly the same, but close enough that they must have come from the same people, if not the same family.

The man set down the pack he'd been carrying.

"Greetings, pilgrims," he said wearily. "Thank you for saving me a long climb. I thought I couldn't take another step!"

Biur said, "You are of the Rashendi, I see."

"No more," the man sighed. "I have been cast out. And I advise you to turn away. Go back to your homes, for there is much anger and distress in Ni Treshel, and strangers would not be welcomed now."

"I have been sent by my master, the god Derethigon," Biur said. "All the gods have felt a disturbance in the world that comes from Ni Treshel. A wizard is at fault, it seems, and I will bring him back to Theshemna."

"What?" he cried. "How can this be true? What wizard would dare to steal from the Rashendi?"

"I said nothing of stealing," Biur said. "What happened here? Tell me!"

The man stared at him, then closed his eyes and slowly swayed back and forth, making a soft crooning sound that set Ker's teeth on edge. Ker thought back to the sound Threnodrel made when he fixed his broken wand—but it wasn't the same. Threnodrel's humming had been melodic; this stranger's was discord on discord. *More magic?* Somehow, he knew it was.

The man opened his eyes. They were liquid blue, without pupils or whites, and small flecks of azure fire seemed to hang in their depths like birds in the sky. "You are a wizard," he said to Biur. Turning, he gazed at Liana. "And you are not human . . . a Wind." He glanced at Ker. "And you are . . . a boy?"

"My apprentice, Ker," Biur said. "I am Biur. And this is Liana. You have seen who and what we are; now, by the gods, I command you—tell me what happened in Ni Treshel."

He called Liana a Wind, too! Ker thought. *What does that mean?* He longed to ask, but knew it wasn't the right time. Perhaps tonight, after they'd set up camp.

"I am Zeren Kentas," the Rashendi said. He blinked and his eyes returned to normal. "Once of the Servants of Shon Atasha the Creator." He sighed heavily again. "No more, no more. I have been exiled for my carelessness and stupidity."

"What happened?" Ker asked.

"Several of the bones of Shon Atasha were stolen while I stood on duty in their shrine, keeping lamps burning for latecomers. I saw no one, I swear!"

"The bones!" Biur said, stiffening. "Why—"

"You say a wizard has done this thing. I do not know. The bones are gone nonetheless." He sank to his knees. Anger and pain twisted his face as he stared at the road. "I have been sent to find and retrieve the lost bones, or never to return. I will die in foreign lands, under foreign lords for the rest of my life. How can I go on with my disgrace?"

"You will come with us," Biur said. His voice and manner had softened.

"A wizard is responsible! We have never trusted your kind. How do I know you haven't been sent to lead me from my mission?"

"I have sworn to serve my god until I die. I can give you no assurances beyond the simple truth—which is enough for any mere man. Since our tasks appear to be the same, I ask you again to come with us. This evening you will spin your wheel and show me what happened."

Zeren shook his head slowly from side to side. "The high priests tried, but the spirit of Shon Atasha the Creator would not come. They saw nothing!"

Biur shifted impatiently. "I am Derethigon's servant, and with his power I will help you search. The bones of Shon Atasha are sacred to all the world, not just the Rashendi. Together we might be able to accomplish what neither can do alone—retrieve the bones!"

"It was Shon Atasha whose spirit led me to take the path here," Zeren said, nodding slightly. "Perhaps it's his will that I accept, even though you *are* a wizard. Very well—I will accompany you." He picked up his cloth bag and looked at them expectantly.

The suddenness of the Rashendi's decision startled Ker.

Biur said. "You will ride my apprentice's horse; he will sit behind me. Will that be satisfactory, Liana?"

She nodded and laughed, softly stroking her mare's nose.

"But I warn you, wizard," Zeren said. "If you try to steal the bones, or keep me from my task, I will not hesitate in doing whatever I must to stop you. This I have sworn before Shon Atasha!"

Biur made no reply.

* * *

They rode east throughout the afternoon.

There seemed no need to hurry as yet; though he protested its uselessness, Zeren promised to cast his wheel that night, when the stars were out and Shon Atasha's spirit moved most freely in the world.

They traveled the only road from Ni Treshel. Biur had mentioned that it divided into five other roads not far ahead. Until they had a direction for their search, little could be done—a hard day's ride might take them many miles from the bones and their thief. They had to have a destination before they picked one path—it would take years to travel through the entire world, and a mistake could cost many months.

Toward late afternoon, they came to forested lands, and lands sparsely settled by farmers. Patches of wood had been cleared for wheat and corn; sheep and cattle grazed in small, fenced meadows. The road continued straight ahead as far as they could see.

Bone-weary, Ker was glad when Biur at last led the way down a narrow dirt track toward a farm. They rode to the main house and there dismounted, unloading and unsaddling the horses. Zeren groaned and stretched, rubbing his back, but made no complaint. Ker smiled to himself, guessing the Oracle hadn't ridden in years—if ever.

Liana whispered something in her horse's ear; with a snort, the mare led the other two off into a meadow to browse.

The farm itself was small, consisting of several carefully plowed fields with green just beginning to show between furrows, a house built of logs, fieldstones and thatch, and a small barn facing the front of the house. Stables and a scattering of other buildings lay behind. Trying to see everything at once, Ker turned in a slow circle. He noticed a face at one of the house's windows. With a flutter of dark curtains, it disappeared.

"Biur," he whispered, "someone's watching us!"

"I saw him."

"Why hasn't he come out to meet us?"

"It *is* strange."

Zeren nodded gravely. "He should have recognized me as an Oracle. Send your apprentice to talk to him. I want him brought out here, where I can make certain that this isn't a trap of yours."

Biur almost bristled with anger. "I put up with your insults on the road, but I will no longer stand for them. If you wish to remain with us, you will act like a civilized man, not some pampered child! You have no right to command anyone but yourself, and I have given you no cause for fear or suspicion. If anything, I want the bones found sooner than you do so I can be rid of your company! If you want to talk to the farmer, do so yourself."

Zeren paled, hands clenched. At last he bowed slightly. "I am sorry if I offended you, Biur," he said tersely. "It is often difficult to put aside one's feelings. I ask your forgiveness, and tolerance."

"Then we will forget the past," Biur said, almost reluctantly. "We must concentrate on finding the bones."

Nobody said anything for a long minute.

"Biur?" Ker asked. "I'll talk to the man."

"Go, then," he said.

Drawing a deep breath, Ker started forward. Before he'd taken five steps he heard the sound of a door slamming somewhere behind the house. He decided it wasn't important at the moment—there'd be plenty of time to investigate the back later, if necessary.

Reaching the door, he knocked and waited. Nobody answered. He knocked again, louder, then tried the handle. The door seemed barred from the inside—it wouldn't budge an inch. Stepping over to a window, he cupped his hands over his eyes and tried to peer through the cloudy green panes of glass, but it was too dark inside to see anything. All the bones of Shon Atasha could have been five feet away and he wouldn't have seen them.

He glanced back at Biur, hoping for instructions, but his master wasn't paying attention. The others had formed a small circle and were talking with quiet voices. Zeren and his master seemed to have forgotten their argument. He strained to hear, but their words blended together into a single note. Shrugging, he started for the back door he'd heard slam—perhaps the farmer would be there.

With a clatter of galloping hooves, a horse and rider rounded the corner of the house and tried to run him down. They'd managed to sneak up without making a sound. Caught by surprise, Ker didn't have a chance to leap aside.

"Biur!" he screamed.

The man's left foot swung out and grazed the side of his head. He felt a burst of pain—*the world reeled up at him*—

"Liana!" he heard Biur shout. "Send the horses to bring him back!"

More hooves clattered down the road.

—then everything went dark.

The next thing he knew, Biur and Liana were leaning over him, pressing wet cloths to the side of his head. He groaned and raised a hand toward the wound. Liana took it instead. Her skin, he found to his surprise, was cool, like stone or water from a spring. *Or like the wind.*

"Rest a moment longer," she said.

"The man—"

"The horses will bring him back. Do not worry."

Biur stood. "Nothing seems to be broken. You have a scalp wound, with lots of blood and no real damage."

Ker felt a sudden flare of anger. He started to say there *was* damage and he could feel it, but then stopped and thought better. *Biur knows what he's doing,* he thought. *If he says it's a minor wound, then it must be so.*

Liana pressed another cloth to the cut. He winced. The pain helped to clear his mind.

By then he had his balance back and could see straight. He was lying on a pile of hay beside the barn, a pack from one of the horses under his head. Sitting up, he watched the world tilt uncertainly, then settle back. His head throbbed. He rubbed his eyes and looked out across newly plowed fields. On the black stone road, fast vanishing in the distance, were the man and horse that had tried to run him down—and Liana's horses were catching up.

"Are you feeling better?" Liana asked, still not smiling.

Numbly, he nodded. "I didn't see him."

"It was the will of Shon Atasha," Zeren said. He walked closer. "Thus do you learn caution." Smiling, he turned to watch the end of the chase.

Biur too looked out at the horses. "They have caught him," he said. "We will soon have answers."

Liana's horses had formed a cordon around the other horse and were leading it back at a slow canter. They gave the rider no chance to dismount. One of the mares nipped the farmer's horse in the flank when it slowed, and it scampered ahead and didn't try to stop again.

Liana carefully removed the cloth from Ker's head. He noticed it was red with blood. She studied his wound for a minute.

"Just a scratch," she said.

Ker struggled to his feet.

"Something frightened the man," Liana said. "I saw it in his eyes."

"Yes. But what?" Biur turned back to Ker. "Go around to the back and come through the house. I want the front door unbarred."

Ker hesitated. "What if others are waiting back there?"

"Ah, caution!" Zeren whispered, just loud enough for him to hear.

"There is no one else. I feel it."

"Yes, Biur." Ker didn't want to miss the stranger's return, so he hurried around the side of the house—but more cautiously than before.

The building had been made of wooden beams and mud bricks. The thatch roof, yellow-brown in the fading sunlight, jutted out over the walls, shadowing them. In the back, two curtained windows looked out toward the stables and a couple of smaller tool sheds. A small back door, slightly ajar, had been set between windows. Ker pushed it open and went in.

The kitchen looked as though it had been turned inside out—and upside down. Broken glass and furniture covered the ceiling, along with twisted steel farm implements and iron pots and pans—held up by forces he could only begin to imagine. The floor was bare earth.

Magic! he thought suddenly, awed. *What sort of wizard would want to do* this *to a room? And why?*

The place disturbed him. He shivered, his apprehension growing.

He went on, more slowly now, past a door that had been torn off its hinges. Deep marks—from claws?—had been gouged into the wood. The next chamber was a bedroom. As in the kitchen, everything breakable had been broken, and the debris littered the ceiling. Straw mattresses looked as though they'd been glued in place, along with jagged bits of colored glass and more shattered furniture. Ker poked his head into two other rooms and confirmed that they too lay in a similar state.

Then he entered the front room and found the corpses.

A middle-aged woman and two children of perhaps eight or nine had been bound in ropes and tortured. Their bodies floated three feet off the floor, held up by magic. The overpowering, sickly sweet stench of death and decay hung over them. The woman slowly spun, around and around like the axle of a wagon. She faced him in a moment. When he gazed upon her full face, blood poured from her mouth and nose, streaming up to the ceiling like water from some macabre fountain.

Retching, Ker tore his gaze away and ran to the front door. Unbarring it, he flung it open and hurried out into the clean sunlight. He closed his eyes and leaned back against the house, suddenly dizzy, wishing he hadn't been the one to find the bodies.

His head pounded and he couldn't see anything for a minute. He swallowed again and again, thinking he'd throw up.

He finally forced himself upright, thinking of the great epics he'd read, of all the dangers the ancient heroes had faced. This hadn't been so bad—only a few dead people, nothing that could hurt him now!

The horses had returned with their captive. The farmer now stood before Biur, shaking a little, face swollen and pasty. A web of bright red cuts covered his cheeks and hands. Shoulders bent, long black hair wild, clothes disheveled and caked with blood, he looked half-conscious at best, a distortion of humanity. A grimace seemed frozen on his face. Though Biur was questioning him, he remained silent, a lost, far-off look haunting his eyes.

Liana turned slightly, noticed Ker. "What's wrong?" she asked quickly.

Trying to keep his voice from shaking, he said, "The wizard who stole the bones was here, and he killed three people and did strange things to everything inside." He stopped and swallowed. "The dead bodies are floating, and there's blood—*blood* . . ." He choked and grew silent.

"What do you mean?" Biur demanded. "Floating bodies? What blood?"

Numbly, Ker pointed to the door. "They're inside."

Biur stared at the house and seemed to hesitate. At last he raised his right hand; the air shimmered for a second, then the silver wand appeared there. He muttered a single word, too low and fast for Ker to catch, and the tip of the wand flared with a cold, blue light. Biur touched it to the farmer's forehead.

The man gasped and tensed, but didn't cry out or try to escape. His muscles strained as if against invisible bonds. Then he sagged forward, unconscious. The lines of stress faded from his face. Biur tucked the wand away and caught the man before he fell.

"Liana, Ker—take him to the barn," he said. "Zeren and I will see to the house."

Ker hurried forward and draped one of the farmer's arms over his shoulder, Liana doing the same to his other side. Between them they managed to half carry, half drag him to the pile of hay by the barn. They set him down, making him as comfortable as possible.

Ker turned to watch the house. Zeren and Biur had gone inside, shutting the front door behind them.

"I do not understand. What did you see?" Liana asked.

He told her about the broken furniture on the ceilings, and how the woman and two children had been tortured to death, and how the bodies floated in air.

"They will burn the house, then," she said. Softly, she added, "Those who came before us must have made the farmer watch while they tortured his family. No wonder he wanted to escape us—we were strangers to him, and strangers meant death and pain."

"Why would anyone make him do that?"

"You must ask Biur. I don't know."

A minute later, Biur and Zeren appeared from behind the house, both silent now. The Oracle's face was pale as starlight. He stared at the ground. The two of them joined Ker and Liana by the barn.

"What happened there?" Ker asked. "Biur? What will you do?"

His master took him by the arm and drew him aside, away from the others. "Now is the time for your first real lesson," he said. "Remember all you saw within the house. It is a perversion of magic, a sign of wizardry gone awry. Magic can turn on you in an instant if you are weak. It can open the door for other . . . *things* to take control of your mind. The ancient scrolls describe it thus: 'Like a jaw closing upon a limb, so did that darkness close on me; while I was under the Dark One's spell, I moved as if in a dream, and spake not but what He willed, and did things most base and unwholesome to further his dark designs.' The wizard Lij' Ahranoteb wrote that passage four hundred years ago. He was only spared from his possession by accident, when the Dark One tried to bring his own body to our world and loosened his hold on Ahranoteb for an instant—long enough for the wizard to fight back and close the Gateway, trapping the Dark One in the netherworlds—or shadowlands, as they are also called. This sort of possession may be what happened to the wizard we now seek."

"The same one who stole the bones came here," Ker said. "I can feel it!"

Slowly, Biur nodded. "There can be little doubt."

"Liana said we must burn the house."

"Yes. It is tainted and will be a place of death and misfortune until it is purged. Fire is the best way."

"Not magic?"

"Fire is a prime facet of magic; so in a way, yes, it will be magic. But come, we must do it at once, before anything further happens. I saw torches in the barn. Get them."

Ker hurried to obey. Just inside the barn door he found a stack of long sticks, each with oil-soaked rags or straw tied in a tight bundle around one end. He brought an armload out to Biur.

"Give me one," Zeren said. "I'll light it." He seemed to be trying to help as much as possible, so Ker dumped the torches on the ground, picked one out, and offered it.

The Rashendi took it with a slight nod. "Thank you." Crossing the yard to where he'd set his pack, he rummaged through it, then took out flint and steel. Sitting with his back to the breeze, he struck sparks over the torch, bending to blow them to life. On his second try it caught fire.

Biur took two more torches and hurried forward, touching them to Zeren's. Ker did the same, then stood back to see what the others did.

The Rashendi approached the house and threw his torch through one of the windows in the front. Glass shattered; the dark curtains became a sheet of flames.

Biur hurled both of his high onto the roof, setting the dry thatch ablaze.

Ker hesitated a second, then threw the torches he held through windows, as Zeren had done.

The house burned quick and hot, and soon the three of them had to move back to watch. With a low roar, the house's roof fell in. Sparks streamed into the heavens like fireworks. A thick, gray column of smoke rose, but twilight had fallen and it was almost indistinguishable from the night sky. No anxious neighbors would see it and run to help.

At last Biur turned away and entered the barn. Ker followed hesitantly.

"What is it?" his master asked.

"I just remembered . . . inside the house was a door with claw marks on it."

"I saw it."

"Do you know what made them?"

He shrugged. "Some monster from the netherworlds—that is why I suspect magic turned on the wizard who stole the bones. The first thing a demon would do is bring the creatures he rules into this world, making him more powerful here. Or so I would guess. Ultimately he will try to bring himself to Earth—and that must be prevented at all costs!"

"Why?" Ker asked.

"There is no telling what ruin he would do! Demons do not bind themselves to the rules and customs of our world, and if history is proof of the future, any demon in our world will thirst for slaves and power—*human* slaves, and the power that comes from conquering armies."

"But why would he bring himself to Earth? Why not conquer the lands he comes from?"

Biur shook his head. "The netherworlds are cold, and harsh. They are pale images cast by the Earth's shadow moving through eternity, insubstantial and vague. I have told you that. Why conquer a shadow when you can conquer that which *casts* the shadow?"

Ker frowned. "I understand, I think. This wizard—or the demon that controls him—must be stopped!"

"Indeed."

"Maybe he's going to use the bones to bring himself to Earth!"

Biur stood stone still, as if shocked. "No," he whispered. "Surely not even a demon would use the bones of Shon Atasha for such a purpose. It might destroy the world!"

Ker shivered, suddenly cold. Destroy the world! How could anything destroy the Earth? Then he remembered the colossal forces that had shaped Theshemna, the radiant power of the god he'd found in its chamber. There was more power in a god than he could imagine—how much power must there be in the being that had *created* the gods?

"It was just a guess," he said softly. "There's no way to know!"

"We will not discuss this further when the others are around. Do you understand?"

"Yes, master," Ker said.

Biur turned and looked out at Liana, then drew back his hood. The burning house reflected in his eyes. Ker thought he saw new lines etched in the wizard's face. "There is no reason yet to frighten them. We will recover the bones and end the problem—there is no choice."

"Yes, Biur."

He watched the fire for a time. It seemed to be dying down. "Watch Zeren closely tonight, when he spins his wheel. I can tell there is much power in him, and it will be the purest sorcery, not the tricks of some would-be Oracle. He should have much interesting to reveal . . . if Shon Atasha is willing."

"Are all the Rashendi like him?"

"No. He has a sour disposition . . . perhaps because the other Rashendi blamed him for the loss of their bones. Here he comes. Stand back and do not touch his wheel, for that would ruin its magic."

Zeren entered the barn carrying a golden wheel at arm's length in front of him. He'd taken it from his bag while they talked, and it sparkled with gold and silver inlay, with rubies and amethysts, emeralds and sapphires. He carried a square of night blue cloth draped over one arm. Liana followed him.

Carefully, as they watched, Zeren spread the cloth out on the earth floor. It was smaller than Ker had thought—scarcely seven feet to a side. The Rashendi sat in one corner, placing the wheel in front of him, and motioned for everyone else to sit as well. Ker found himself in the corner facing Zeren, with Liana to his left and Biur to his right.

The Oracle spun his wheel gently, touching it now and again with long, thin fingers, and began to hum a soft, haunting, discordant tune. It swept Ker up, carrying him away from the *here* and *now*—back to Vichir, back to his father. He saw a dusty banquet hall with a tired old man sitting there for a second, then time seemed to roll back. He saw his grandfather, whom he knew only from tapestries in the banquet hall, and Castle Orrum as they once had been, tall and splendid. Banners taken from conquered lords hung in the banquet hall, and people moved like streams of ants through Vichir. Entertainers, noble lords and ladies, ambassadors . . . the barony was alive as Ker had never known it.

Then the power of his vision carried him on, away from Vichir, up away from the Earth and into the dark spaces between stars. And in the darkness he saw himself.

He sat, with Liana and Zeren and Biur—and a golden wheel spun between them. He gasped and opened his eyes. It took a minute to focus them.

It took him another minute to realize Zeren was speaking, and longer still to comprehend the words: "*. . . Shon Atasha, Maker of All Gods and Men, Giver of Life . . .*" The universe seemed strangely blurred, dreamlike. Zeren slowly swayed back and forth, eyes closed, and his wheel now moved by itself, faster and faster until it made a whirring sound as it turned. The singsong voice Zeren used was a drug on Ker's senses, rhythmic, melodic, imploring. Again Ker floated free of his body, up into the heavens.

He found himself above a white marble building, the rest of the world dark. He drifted down, down, through rock and into a chamber lit by thousands of smoky white candles. He saw Zeren there, dressed in robes of gold and red, moving among immense blocks of white stone.

Slowly realization came: the white blocks were the bones of Shon

Atasha the Creator, those few that the Rashendi had gathered from the corners of the Earth.

He felt a thrill of elation that lasted for hours.

And then darkness swept across the temple like a shadow passing. It vanished in a second, but left an aching cold in his bones. He tried to call a warning, but his body seemed frozen: he could only watch with horror as Zeren collapsed to the floor, unconscious, barely breathing.

Dark creatures stole through the night. They were like men—only not men; they dressed in solid black, with hoods draped over their heads, and walked in a stooped-over shuffle—on hands and knuckles as much as feet.

They moved quickly, though, and dozens of them filed into the temple where Zeren lay unconscious. They went to the nearest of Shon Atasha's bones, lifted it, bore it off into the night.

The whole world seemed to sleep: not a single person appeared to challenge the theft, not a priest stirred. The night grew heavy. Dark clouds rolled across the heavens and filled the sky, obscuring much of the creatures' activity. They took more bones—three, four, five . . .

Ker floated behind them.

A great engine waited not far away, its tall masts, full of tattered sails that could never hold an Earthly wind, looming high above the houses and temples of Ni Treshel. It was like a giant ebon sailing ship—only it had twenty-foot-high wooden wheels and its hull had been breached with huge portals in several places. The dark ones carried the immense bones of Shon Atasha up ramps and into the hold one by one, set them down in piles of straw that they would not be damaged. *Seven, eight, nine . . .*

A single figure stood on the engine's deck. It seemed to be a man—he stood upright, a strong breeze billowing his black robes—but somehow, Ker wasn't certain. The man seemed familiar, but he wore a black hood over his face. The wind tugged it back for a split second and Ker glimpsed a gold mask leering out into the night.

The figure on deck called orders to the dark ones below, directing their movements, but Ker could not hear the words. Abruptly, the last of a dozen-odd bones was stowed away inside the great machine. The dark creatures poured through gaping portals and into the hull, swung shut immense wooden doors.

Slowly, ponderously, the engine moved forward. Ker could imagine the gnashing and clanking its gears made, the creaking of its wooden frame, the whistling of wind through its ruined rigging. It glided forward and through the streets of Ni Treshel. The buildings remained dark. Still not a single Rashendi came out to stop them; the whole of the city seemed frozen in a moment of time.

Abruptly Ker felt himself drawn back, away from the city and the remaining bones of Shon Atasha the Creator. The stars flowed like water around him. The Earth appeared, an enormous disk of brown and blue, green and gold, floating unguided through the heavens. Its edges were jagged, unfinished, full of broken rocks and twisted trees. He fell toward it, faster and faster, the lands rushing up at him—

He opened his eyes and sat in the barn again, darkness thick around him. He looked at the others. No one spoke for a long time. Then Zeren reached out and stopped the spinning wheel.

"Demons," he said.

"And the wizard we seek," Biur said.

Ker asked, "Why didn't anybody stop them?"

"Sorcery," Zeren said. "The whole of Ni Treshel slept while they moved through the temples, stealing—" His voice broke, and he said no more. At last he stood and picked up his wheel, carrying it out toward his pack. Tears glistened on his cheeks.

"Perhaps the farmer will be able to talk now," Biur said. He too stood.

Ker and Liana followed him out to the pile of hay. The man sprawled out, snoring gently. He seemed at ease, quiet and relaxed.

Biur touched the man's forehead. The farmer opened his eyes. Surprise and fear showed in them. With a cry of alarm, he scrambled away, then climbed to his feet.

"Who are you?" he demanded. He turned and gaped at the smoking ruins of his farmhouse, moaned softly. His muscles stiffened. His hands made fists.

"I am Biur. I serve the god Derethigon, and am here by his will. Sit back—we will do you no harm."

"I don't . . . understand. A god did this?"

"Others came here. Do you remember them?"

"Others? What others? What do you want here? And where are my wife and children?" Then he caught sight of Zeren and hurried forward, dropping to his knees in front of the Rashendi. "Master! I didn't see you! What do you want of me?"

Biur sighed. Zeren glared at him, then looked down at the farmer.

"What is your name, friend?"

"Loq Tarrin." He looked around, bewildered. "Master, where are my wife and children?"

Zeren said nothing for a long moment.

"Master?" A tremor broke his voice, as if he sensed something wrong.

"The Dark God has taken them."

"No!" He leaped to his feet. *"No!"*

He ran to the ruins of the farmhouse, tried to open the door—but the fire had blocked it from inside and it wouldn't budge. Finally the heat drove him back, sobbing, to the barn. They followed him more slowly.

"You can help us find the ones who killed them," Biur said.

Loq didn't answer. He stared at the burning ruins, tears running down his cheeks. His lips moved, but he said nothing.

"Loq!" Zeren shouted.

The farmer turned to look at him. "What do you wish of me, Master?"

"Answer Biur's questions quickly and truthfully."

"Do you remember the others?" Biur asked.

He shook his head.

"What is the last thing you recall?"

"I . . . Feeding the animals. I was in the barn while Nia cooked breakfast for me—" He wept again.

"He remembers nothing," Biur said.

"Such is Shon Atasha's wisdom," Zeren said. He turned to Loq. "Go to the barn and sleep. There is nothing further you can do."

Slowly, the farmer turned and wandered away. He hardly seemed aware of his surroundings. Perhaps that was best, Ker thought. He wouldn't dwell on his family's death until later, when his wounds were healed and he'd recovered as much as he ever would. Perhaps he would sell his farm, move away—find a new wife and start over again.

"Come," Biur said to them all. "It is time we ate; we will need our strength in the coming days."

Ker stifled a yawn, but his master noticed.

"Then we sleep," he continued. "We will leave at dawn."

Taking blankets from their packs, they made beds in the hay in the barn. Ker lay down and found himself suddenly wide awake and unable to sleep. He couldn't get the picture of the dead woman out of his mind—*her blood*—

He shuddered. His thoughts slowly turned to other things, to all that had happened to him since he'd left Vichir—was it only a month before? Two? He had no way of knowing, short of asking Biur, and his master was asleep. It seemed an eternity: life in Vichir was as remote as the stars in the sky.

He thought of meeting Derethigon and losing his face—how had he ever been that foolish?—and of Biur's offer to get it back. Why had he refused the first time?

I was a fool, he thought. *I was the worst kind of fool—one whose pride won't let him admit he can make a mistake.*

He promised himself it would never happen again.

After a time, he slept.

And then the nightmares began . . .

8

Demons in the Dark

The Rashendi are alternately loved and hated. They are Shon Atasha's chosen people—and arrogant in their position. They foretell the future, but twine it in riddles and shroud it in half-truths. They are powerful, but come to the aid of none but their own kind . . . unless it suits their purposes. They are the great schemers of the world. They would welcome a chance to rule the Earth and all its people.

—Pere Denberel
Atlas of the Known Lands, Revised

Ker dreamed of falling through darkness. He dreamed of cold, wet things that clung to his back and wouldn't let go. He dreamed of death and life and blindness, of running, forever running—

He fled down endless corridors like those in Theshemna. Behind him came the scuttle of claws on stone, the shuffle of padded feet. He heard a rough wolflike panting and smelled the fetid breath of monsters at his heels.

Something howled close behind, a shrill scream of a sound.

The passageway twisted before him, bringing him farther and farther from his pursuers. His chest ached until he thought he'd never be able to draw another breath. At last he rounded one final corner—and knew he walked alone. A strange, brooding silence filled his ears. His footsteps echoed sharp and loud, unnaturally loud, on the flagstones.

After he'd walked for hours, he heard a soft voice whisper his name.

"Ker Orrum . . . you are mine . . . come to me."

He stopped, recognition slow. Then he turned.

He stood in the banquet hall of his father's castle. Baron Orrum sat alone at the head of a great oak table, wearing his finest ceremonial robes; a goblet of sacramental wine and a plate of sweetmeats had been set before him. Covering his face was a gleaming silver mask with his features carved into it.

"Father," Ker heard himself say, "where am I?"

"Home. Safe. All your friends are safe." A pause, then: *"Come, sit with me."*

Numb, Ker moved forward and sat at his father's side. The tapestries on the wall shimmered, colors unnaturally bright. Their pictures were familiar, reassuring. He was home. Safe. The ceiling curved high above, as it always had, as it always would. Nothing could get him here. *Safe.*

The room grew chill, suddenly, and he shivered. His breath misted the air.

The man behind the mask sat in silence, looking at Ker. Ker looked back. The baron's eyes glimmered blood-red through the slits in his mask, hot and bestial. Still Ker said nothing. The cold slowly settled into his bones, pervading his thoughts. His breathing grew more and more shallow. Then the air seemed to grow warm around him, like a thick, smothering cocoon.

He became aware of how sleepy he'd become. His father leaned forward, eyes crimson, expectant.

"Sleep," he whispered. *"Sleep."*

Then Ker noticed his father's breath didn't show in the cold air. The thought grew in his mind. It was as if the baron weren't breathing—as if the cold radiated from his body, driving away all that was warm and alive. Ker sat up straighter. A thin layer of ice had formed over his clothes and now it broke away and fell to the floor in slow motion, tinkling like a thousand crystal chimes.

He reached forward, managed to hook his frozen fingers under the edge of the baron's silver mask, jerked back and up. The mask came away, revealing smooth, ice-pale flesh that held no place for eyes, nose, mouth.

The baron had no face.

Ker screamed soundlessly.

The baron reared back, knocking his chair over. It made no noise as it struck the bare stone floor. But Ker was on his feet and running by then, back the way he'd come, out into the endless castle halls.

Behind him, animals bayed. Something hissed like a serpent from the depths of the sea. He turned to look back, tripped over an uneven stone, plunged headfirst into darkness—

Again he walked the roads to the west of Vichir, searching for his face, only this time he could, somehow, see. The world was a desert, sand bleak against the gray slab sky.

He walked forever. At last he came to a great dark house. Noises drifted out from within: laughter, low voices singing, shrill cries of joy. He fumbled his way up hard stone steps, reeled drunkenly into the great front hall. It was empty, desolate. Dust covered the floor like a carpet, mushrooming around his feet as he moved forward.

Happy sounds called him. He followed through barren room after barren room and seemed to go in circles, the voices and sounds mocking him wherever he turned.

He moved into shadows as thick as the space between stars, dank and cloying. Something ice-cold and sharp reached out and sliced his cheek like a knife. A burning pain shot through his face. He staggered back, felt hot blood streaming down the line of his jaw, dripping from his chin. Tense, fear arching through his body, he strained to hear.

Rough breathing. Near. To the left—no, right—no, behind—

He felt another quick, bright burst of agony as something struck his other cheek. He leaped forward, swinging his arms wildly. Someone grabbed his shoulders. Hands like bones forced him to the floor, pinning him there. A thousand voices whispered, "*We have your face . . . your face . . . your face . . .*"

He could almost see the speaker—tall and dark, face shrouded by a glittering gold mask, skeletal hands reaching out, ripping the clothes from his body, tearing into his flesh.

He had to scream—

Gasping, Ker woke. He didn't know where he was and barely fought down panic. He reached for his face—found mouth, nose, eyes. Then realization came and he could relax. *It was only a dream.* His blanket had wrapped itself around his throat during the night, half choking him. He straightened it out and lay back down again, listening to Biur's soft breathing beside him. All the others still slept.

The fire in the doorway had burned down to ruddy orange embers. Now deep shadows filled the loft overhead and the storage bins in the back; the thick oak beams supporting the roof became dark, solemn giants, the piles of straw beneath them full of watching eyes.

Sitting up, he shook his head, the last remaining wisps of nightmare slow to leave. Through the open barn doors he glimpsed night sky. The stars had faded to vague pinpricks of light; dawn would soon come. Already he heard animals stirring outside, soft cackles of chickens, a horse's neigh from the stables.

He didn't think he'd sleep more that night. Standing, he wrapped the blanket around his shoulders, then went out into the yard. The farmhouse still smoked a bit, hazing the sky, but the fires had died down and soon would go out. To his surprise, he found Loq sitting against the barn's wall, gazing up into the night. He seemed to be searching among the stars for Shon Atasha and the reason for his misfortune.

Ker didn't know what to say. He knew he wouldn't have slept, either, if his father and brother had been killed like the people in the house. What would he have done? Nothing but watch the stars and curse the gods.

Sitting beside the farmer, Ker silently waited for dawn.

A cock crowed and Ker started. He'd dozed off, much to his surprise. Blinking at the orange crescent of sun hanging low in the east, he turned and found that Loq had vanished.

He struggled to his feet.

Zeren sat alone by the crackling fire in the barn's doorway, slowly stirring something in a pot on a flat stone. He glanced up and nodded, then went back to his cooking. Ker sniffed and smelled eggs and some kind of meat.

"Where are Biur and Liana?" he asked.

"They went ahead half an hour ago, to try and find a trace left by the wizard's engine. I sent Loq to stay with his neighbors—they'll take care of him."

"Biur and Liana left without us?" Ker cried, shocked.

"We will join them soon enough. You didn't sleep well last night, and there was no need for more than two to go out to search . . . one to watch each side of the road." He shrugged. "Thus is Shon Atasha's will served."

"But the horses—"

"They left us one." He nodded toward the far field, where one of the mares cropped grass. "Enough. Eat." Picking up a plate beside him, he ladled a large portion of scrambled eggs mixed with some sort of shredded meat onto it, then handed it to Ker along with a fork.

"Thanks," Ker said. He sat and ate, surprised at his hunger, while Zeren cleaned up and extinguished the small fire. Finishing his work, the Rashendi settled back on his heels and watched Ker polish off the last of his food.

"You want to be a wizard," Zeren said.

Ker nodded, leaning back. "Yes," he said cautiously. "If Biur will ever teach me!"

"Ah. You must have patience if you're to learn from him. Wizards pick their own times and places for lessons. It may take you many years to master even the simplest magics."

"I know," Ker said.

"I'll let you in on a secret: much of the mystery of magic is just for show—the way a juggler will toss knives with much foot stomping and great flourishes. It's more impressive that way."

"That doesn't make sense!"

"Doesn't it? How would a man react if he realized he was a cripple in comparison to a wizard—and that the wizard had done nothing to earn his magic skills except be born with them? He'd say, 'It isn't fair that a wizard should be so much more powerful than me,' and he'd get his neighbors and together they'd try to kill all the wizards they could. Apprenticeships are mostly wasted time; a wizard's powers come to him naturally. He just has to be able to say he *earned* those powers through years of hard work."

"Biur said there were dangers—"

"Nothing common sense can't handle! Would you stick your hand into an open flame? Of course not. The same applies to magic."

"I'll wait and see," Ker said slowly. He didn't like the way the conversation was going.

Zeren was smiling. "And yet there are more ways to learn than from Biur . . . Did you know that?"

"What ways?"

"You could serve Shon Atasha the Creator in Ni Treshel. I perceive the power in you—I know you would serve Shon Atasha well. It's not too late. Seldom do we let outlanders join the people of our city—but you would be admitted. And perhaps, if I were to take you back with me, they might let us both remain, to serve in the temples."

"But what about the bones of Shon Atasha?" Ker cried.

"They are bones. What can be done with them? There are many more in the world; the missing ones can be replaced in time. It is *men* whom the Rashendi need—men able to use magic. Men like you."

"What would Biur do if he found out what you wanted?"

Zeren shrugged. "He won't find out—unless you tell him. And I know you won't."

"How?" he demanded.

"I was like you once, young and in love with the idea of magic. Not all of my people are touched by the spirit of Shon Atasha, but I was among the lucky ones. Once I began my service as an initiate in the shrine, the powerful old Oracle of Peldath came to me, asking me to be his apprentice in that city. But I refused, preferring to stay closer to the bones, closer to the heart of all magic. It was a decision I never regretted—and one I have never spoken of, until now."

"I don't understand," Ker said. "Why didn't you tell other people?"

"Because it didn't matter. Because I knew, deep inside, that the decision I made was correct. I had been destined to serve Shon Atasha in this way and no other. Anything I might've said could only have made things more complicated—and that wasn't necessary. Think of the possibilities of serving Shon Atasha. Biur is just a wizard—what loyalty do you owe him?"

"I swore to serve Biur for five years, and I will!"

The vehemence of his words surprised him. For the first time Ker realized he intended to keep his word and serve his master no matter what happened. Loyalty was as much a part of being an apprentice as learning magic. Even if Biur *did* give him permission to leave with Zeren, he knew he wouldn't go. He intended to see their task to its end—they'd find the stolen bones and bring them back to Ni Treshel, and nothing would stop them!

Zeren shrugged, but still smiled a bit. "As Shon Atasha wills. Perhaps you were not meant to be other than what you are. Still—think of all I have said. Think of the power you could command as one of the Rashendi. We would teach you all you want to know of sorcery." Stiffly, he climbed to his feet. "Get the horse, boy. I'll wait for you here."

Ker stared at him for a second, then started for the meadow. Halfway there he realized Zeren had called him a boy—and somehow it didn't matter as much as it once had. He knew he'd made the right decision.

I will always stay with Biur, he thought.

The mare trotted down the black stone highway. Ker sat behind Zeren and watched the passing land. The woods gave way to another plain filled with tall, golden grass; the road stretched far ahead of them.

Ker thought again and again of what Zeren had offered him: a chance to serve Shon Atasha the Creator in Ni Treshel. He thought of that city, with its glittering domes and spires, of the bones, of the magic an Oracle commanded. Once, he knew, he would've given almost anything for the chance. But to be apprenticed to Zeren . . .

He thought of what would happen if he told his master what Zeren had offered him. What would Biur do? He shivered a bit, his imagination running wild. He imagined Zeren vanishing forever into a cold, dark Gateway, or suddenly floating up into the sky and out of sight, never to be seen again.

I won't tell Biur, he decided at last. *I've told Zeren my answer. Nothing he can say or do will change it. There's no need for more trouble.*

By noon they could see, far in the distance, the place where the road divided and continued in five different directions. A horse and rider stood at the crossroads, and as Ker watched, he suddenly realized the man was Biur. He dug in his heels and the mare obligingly quickened her step. Zeren clung awkwardly to the reins, shifting his weight to keep his balance as best he could, but made no complaint.

At last they reached Biur. The wizard still wore his dark blue cloak and hood, concealing his face, but he called a cheerful greeting.

"Did you find the road?" Zeren called back.

Ker dismounted and ran to Biur's stallion. His master took his hand and swung Ker up into the saddle behind him.

"Yes." Biur pointed to the second road from the left. "That one. The wizard's engine ran off the edge of the pavement, crushing the grass, about a mile farther down."

"That branch passes through several large towns, then ends at Zelloque," Zeren said.

"I have friends there who will help us," Biur said, "should the need arise."

"Where's Liana?" Ker asked.

"We each tried different roads. She will return soon, when she finds the one she chose was not correct. Ah—here she comes now."

Ker twisted in the saddle and looked. Down the middle road, far in the distance, he saw a horse and rider galloping toward them. It was Liana, her long, golden hair streaming out behind her like a banner. She drew close in minutes, pulling up before them. Her mare snorted, barely winded, and again Ker wondered what sort of horses these were—they moved unnaturally fast, acted almost as smart as men at times, and never grew tired. *Magic!* But where had they come from, and what else could they do?

"Did you find it?" she asked Biur.

Nodding, he told her about the crushed grass and wheel marks he'd found.

"Good," she said. "Let's go—we have a day's travel to make up, and we're wasting time here."

They started down the second road from the left at a mile-eating trot.

"Why don't you open a Gateway?" Ker asked. "We could catch up with the wizard in Zelloque!"

Biur sighed. "No, Ker, that would not work. Think about it. We do not know that the wizard went all the way to Zelloque—he could have stopped anywhere along the way. And, too, wizards can sense magic around them. If a Gateway were to be opened in Zelloque, the wizard would know and be warned of our coming."

"But how would he know?" Ker persisted. "He wouldn't see us!"

"If I threw a stone into a pond, you would see the rings, even if you missed the stone hitting the water. Magic is the same way. Everything you do that involves magic will spread like rings in a pond—the greater the magic, the larger the rings."

"Oh," Ker said.

They rode in silence for several minutes before he spoke again. "How do you know whether something is magical or not?"

"You must look at it the right way."

Look at it the right way? Ker wondered. *What does that mean?* It didn't make sense! But little of what he'd seen or heard the last few days made sense. He thought about it for a long moment.

"How?" he asked at last.

"You will have to find the way for yourself." And his master would say no more about it.

Remembering Biur's promise that he'd learn everything in time, Ker sighed and slouched a bit in the saddle. In time! He wanted to learn *now.* Then he recalled Biur's saying he'd learn best by watching and listening. But how could he listen if Biur never said anything, and how could he watch if Biur and Liana rode off and left him sleeping? It was all so frustrating. He promised himself he'd stay close to them from now on.

He supposed his master meant for him to discover everything gradually, learning as he went along. Perhaps magic couldn't be learned like literature or any of the other things Lerrens had taught him in Vichir. Perhaps magic would just come to him naturally, if he let it. And Biur would be there to help him whenever necessary, to give him advice and steer him in the right direction.

But what did he mean, I have to look at it the right way?

He stared at the grasslands to his right. They stretched as far in all directions as he could see, broken only by scattered clumps of ancient, gnarled trees. Nothing magical showed as far as he could tell.

Turning a bit, he looked to the left, at Liana. She rode several paces ahead, keeping her eyes on the road. He knew she—and her horse—were magical. Perhaps he'd perceive it, if he concentrated . . .

He stared at her until his eyes hurt, but still saw nothing but the clothes she wore, nothing but her almost unnatural beauty. Studying her horse, he noticed nothing save the smoothness of its gait, the sleekness of its coat. It was a horse to all appearances, just as Liana was a woman. But Biur and Zeren were able to see her as she truly was—a *Wind*, whatever that meant.

His eyes ached. He squeezed them shut, rubbing them. And then he saw a lingering blue afterimage—the outline of Liana on her mare. And the outline seemed traced in blue fire, just like the Gateway Biur had created.

Ker's eyes flew open and he grinned, scarcely containing his excitement. He searched for the glow in daylight. There, he found it—a subtle halo that surrounded Liana. Blue sparks clung to her hair. Bands of indigo crisscrossed her skin, clung to the folds of her robe, traced her profile. It became clearer and clearer each second:

Her skin was a translucent bubble with swirling blue waters trapped inside. No, not waters—it was as if a wild wind raged within the shell of her body.

He turned slowly. In front of him, blue static ghosted over Biur's cloak and hood. The horse beneath them shimmered, its coat a gleaming cyan.

Twisting in the saddle, Ker gazed back at Zeren—and found the Rashendi also ablaze in blue fire. Intricate blue patterns wove across Zeren's skin.

Light radiated from them all—from everything! The whole world leaped vibrantly to life. Blue static crackled across the golden heads of grass to his left and right; the air swam with sparkling drops of turquoise; the black stones beneath the horses' hooves washed in shimmering, electric blue.

Looking down at his own hands, he saw brilliant azure replace tanned skin. He willed it to stop—and found it wouldn't. He couldn't control his sight; everywhere he looked, the world gleamed blue on blue on blue. He squeezed his eyes shut, tried to force the images from his mind. They refused to fade. The world grew distant, unreal, his thoughts twisting toward dream and nightmare. Azure, turquoise, indigo, sapphire . . .

"Biur," he whispered.

"What is it?"

"My eyes . . ."

The horse swayed beneath him. Everything felt blue, fuzzy blue, out-of-focus blue.

"Ker!" he heard a voice shout, very far away.

He heard nothing more as he slowly sank into an ocean of blue.

9

The Feast of Masferigon

> The world is not limited to what the eyes reveal. When you look beyond what you normally perceive, who can say what lies there? Perhaps reality is like a paper mask, to be peeled off at the end of the festival known as life.
>
> —Tellerion
> *Speculations*

The blue pulsed through Ker's mind like waves pounding the shore of some wind-tossed sea.

He seemed to walk alone, hardly aware of himself. The world was blue, so blue—that's all he saw in every direction. Blue pounded through his skull until he wished he'd never seen the color. Blue filled him utterly.

Slowly he began to notice traces of dark and light. Jags of almost green, dashes of almost yellow floated at the horizon. Above, glistened pinpricks of purple and white.

He sat in nothingness and watched them drift.

It was as though a giant picture were slowly settling in place around him. The yellows drew together; the greens and reds and pinks; the dashes and dots of black and white; the oranges and purples and all the shades between. The universe around him swirled with rainbows.

And suddenly the colors dropped in place and he could imagine everything around him again. It was as if a dam had burst and the world flooded over him, drowning his senses with a million sparkling bits of information. Eyes closed, he slowly built a picture in his mind: the shimmering cloak of the sky overhead; the long, straight, black stretch of road before them; the clack of steel-shod hooves on stone, striking sparks now and then; the gold of Liana's hair, the pastel blue of Biur's cloak and hood, the brown and gray of the horses—

And then he stepped into the picture.

* * *

He woke slowly, dry eyes grinding in their sockets. Every muscle in his body ached and his neck hurt when he twisted it. Light screamed into his head when he opened his eyes. The world swayed dizzily.

Abruptly he sneezed, smelling the thick, musty smell of horse. Then his eyes began to water and his vision cleared and he could see.

He found himself strapped, head and feet dangling, across the back of Biur's horse. Biur and Liana rode together on one of the mares, twenty feet ahead. Zeren rode next to Ker, smiling at him.

Ker struggled to undo the straps and sit up.

"Don't be alarmed," the Rashendi said, yawning slightly, as though bored. "You've stepped into a larger world. Your mind couldn't accept everything you showed it at once; it happens to all who follow the ways of magic, when they look beyond the edge of perception for the first time."

Ker groaned softly, feeling his wrists chafe against the leather.

All the horses drew up together. Biur slipped to the ground, then walked back and unstrapped Ker, slowly helping him to stand on the highway.

The world wobbled. Gritting his teeth, Ker forced himself to stand still, ignoring his pain and dizziness. He massaged his wrists, his arms and legs tingling with returning circulation.

The sun hung low in the west, he noticed at once, and the grasslands had given way to heavy forests full of oaks and beeches. Only the road broke through the tangle of trunks and branches. He thought at once of the woods where he'd met Derethigon—where he'd lost his face—and the forest around him now seemed to grow darker and more ominous. Far off, a bird chittered, its cry raucous and out of place. The silence that followed was worse.

Although the trees hung back twenty feet from the highway's stones, as if some magic held them at bay, Ker could imagine them slowly creeping forward at night, to be driven back with the rising sun. Shivering, he marked the lateness of the hour again. He hoped they wouldn't have to spend the night in the forest's gloom.

As his strength returned, he began to feel better. How much time had passed? At least half a day or more. Had he really been unconscious all that time?

"What happened?" he asked Biur.

"You have come into the world of magic. You forced your senses to recognize that which mere men can never know—the forms and patterns of power bound into everything by Shon Atasha when he created the world. I know now that you were right: you can be a wizard, in time, with patience and practice."

"Then the hardest part is past?"

"Is all one's life not a struggle?"

"That means 'Yes,' " Zeren said.

Biur frowned. "The rest is like learning to walk. First you crawl, then you stumble, but finally you *do* walk, and walking, think it so easy you should always have been able to do it. And, as with all skills, you must learn the responsibility that comes with magic."

Ker felt a sudden tightness in his chest, a sense of building excitement until he thought he'd burst with pride. He'd used magic—actually *done* something this time instead of just watching Biur and Zeren.

The breeze had gotten stronger, and a good deal colder. He shivered, suddenly empty—as though all the magic had been burned out of him.

"How do you feel?" Liana asked him.

He looked up at her radiant face. "Tired."

"You will feel better tonight," Biur said. "You need to rest—and to eat. Magic drains your body's strength." He rummaged through one of the saddlebags and removed a white cloth with something tied inside. Unwrapping a stack of round, moist oat cakes, he offered one to Ker.

"Thank you," Ker said, taking it. The cake was warm and sticky with honey. It smelled sweet and delicious. He took a bite, chewing slowly to savor the taste.

Biur mounted his stallion, then offered Ker his hand. Ker took it and the wizard swung him up into the saddle as if he weighed nothing. His master's grip was strong and sure. Stuffing the rest of the cake into his mouth, Ker wrapped his arms around his master's waist.

"Follow!" Biur called to the others. Then he lightly touched his heels to the stallion's sides and they were off.

The horses moved in the same breathtaking gallop they'd used in the throne room of the gods in Theshemna. It was as if Biur wanted to make up, in one quick surge, for all the time lost while Ker had been unconscious—as if he wanted to catch up with the demons and wrestle the bones from their gold-masked leader. Zeren grumbled a bit, but managed to keep up.

The forest blurred past on either side, trees formless streaks of brown and gray, leaves dark green. Ker laughed in joy, raising his face to the wind, reveling in their speed. His muscles eased and his pains faded, quickly forgotten. The horses raced the sun across the sky.

They slowed when they came to places inhabited by men. The grim forest had given way to lush grasslands. Brilliant green hills, dotted with grazing sheep, rose around them. Small thatched cottages stood like lonely sentinels, thin gray plumes of smoke rising from their chimneys.

But the sheep appeared untended, the houses abandoned; not a single shepherd came forward to call a greeting. Studying the lands around them, listening to the desolate whisper of wind, Ker grew uncomfortable—as though he were being watched.

"There's something wrong," he whispered. "Where are all the people?"

"Look carefully," Biur said. "What magic do you see?"

At first Ker hesitated, thinking of falling into blueness, of how he'd become lost in the magic the last time he'd looked. Half a day had passed before he'd awakened. Rubbing his neck, he thought of the pain.

But he let his fears slip away and concentrated on the road in front of him. Now that he knew how to look, the sight came easily—the air took on a crystalline quality; the magic glowed strongly around him. Biur, Liana, and Zeren, the horses, the road—all shimmered blue. He looked around, scanning the horizon. Sparks danced lightly among the grass and sheep, played among the trees. He gazed at the nearest cottage.

It seemed alight with blue—not a brilliant, fiery blue, but a dull, faded glow, as if something magical had been inside and the force of its presence had only now begun to vanish. Turning, he examined all the other buildings in sight and found the same soft glow in each.

He knew, then, that the other wizard had been here, and he felt a sudden pang of apprehension. Had the demons killed everyone, as they'd killed Loq's family? Or merely driven them away?

"Did Loq's house look like that?" he asked quietly.

"Yes," Biur said.

He let his sight slip back to normal, then slumped a bit in the saddle, strangely tired by the effort. "Will we look inside the cottages?"

"No. There must be a town ahead; we will find out what happened there."

The sun settled lower and lower into the west, slowly disappearing into a crease between hills. Still they pressed on. Soon the houses grew larger and closer together, and huge plowed fields came into view. The rows of new furrows, with their dark green shoots of corn and oats just beginning to peek through rich black earth, reminded Ker of Vichir.

He suddenly wondered what his father was thinking about. The harvest, perhaps, or some war between Vichir's neighbors? Or was he thinking about his children . . . ? *About me?*

What would he think if he knew I was tracking down the bones of Shon Atasha the Creator with an Oracle, a wizard, and a Wind? What would Lerrens think? He almost found the idea funny. The counselor would have sniffed and looked away in disapproval. His father would have made him go study.

But those days were gone, and he knew things would never be the same. His time had come to go into the world—and he didn't know if he could ever go back, even if he wanted to.

As they topped a final rise, a town came into view. It sprawled out before them, a rambling collage of wood and stone buildings—far larger than Vichir, far larger than Ni Treshel or any other town Ker had ever seen before. Hundreds of shops and houses clustered along narrow, twisting streets. Many buildings stood four or five stories tall, some even topped with domes that shone with gold, or tall, slender spires that rose far into the darkening sky.

With twilight, lanterns had been hung from poles along the streets. A soft, warm glow washed over everything. And yet there were no signs of the people who'd set the lanterns in place. Ker allowed his eyes to look for the soft blue glow again; it spread over the town.

"Where are we?" he whispered.

Zeren answered: "I believe this is Rhimalga, but I've not been here before. It seems a fair enough place." And then he too grew silent.

The night seemed to swallow speech, making everyone uncomfortable and reluctant to talk. Ker could feel the tension among them. Even the horses seemed aware of it; their hooves clicked more quietly on the paving stones and their breaths grew softer.

They entered the town, passing among the tall buildings, staring at all the dark, curtained windows around them. Thick glass panes reflected the lanterns' light in weird patterns.

Ker strained to hear any sound above the clip of hooves, the soft rustle of clothes, the creaking leather of the saddles and tack. There—was that a sound ahead?

It came again, louder than before, a high-pitched whistling that moved up and down the scale in a wild, half-animal howl. He shivered, fear rising within him. What would make a noise like that? Some monster, or—

Then he heard other noises: what sounded like the whistle of a flute, the low jingle of a tambourine, the *pam . . . pam . . . pam* of a drum. He relaxed with a nervous laugh. The townspeople must be ahead somewhere—

A man suddenly stepped from a shadowy doorway in front of them, blocking their way with a steel-headed pike. He wore only black—matte black pants and shirt, with black leather gloves covering his hands. A silky black cape, lined with dark fur, had been drawn across his shoulders, and a tight-fitting black hood stretched across his head and tied under his chin. Only his smooth-shaved face showed. His skin was very pale. The effect was striking in the darkness; his face seemed to float loose in the air.

The horses shied back. They steadied only when Liana whispered to them.

Ker shivered, remembering his own facelessness. *Why would he dress that way?* he wondered. It seemed a part of his nightmares—a fragment of some half-remembered dream that disturbed him in ways he couldn't name.

"Who are you?" the man with the pike demanded.

Zeren pushed past them. "I am Zeren Kentas. Don't you recognize one of the Rashendi?" He gestured vaguely. "Stand aside and let me pass."

The man raised his pike until its point almost touched Zeren's chest. "Get back with the others."

"Bring me to your superior! I demand—"

"Do as you're told!"

Zeren shut his mouth with a snap and let his horse edge back a bit.

"I am Biur," Biur said, "and the others are traveling with me. Let us pass; we serve the god Derethigon."

The man lowered his pike. "Why have you come here?"

"We are traveling to Zelloque. This is the right road?"

"It is."

"Then we will seek lodging for the night."

"Very well," he said. "Follow me."

He turned and seemed to flow into the darkness. Ker heard the man's footsteps ringing somewhere ahead of them, then glimpsed his silhouette against the lanterns ahead. The horses walked down the center of the street just behind him, past more dark houses, past closed shops. Their hooves clicked loudly in the empty streets.

"Ignorant fool," Ker heard the Rashendi muttering.

Slowly the savage music grew louder. It was shrill and strange, gyrating wildly, unlike anything Ker had ever heard before. It reminded him of wolves howling at the stars, of the ancient tales of screaming monsters at the edge of the world. Then the buildings fell back and they entered a wide square with a bubbling fountain in its middle.

Several taverns were open, and music and light spilled from their open doors and windows. More light came from giant orange lanterns strung between tall poles set in the corners of the square. Ker gaped at the crowds of men and women wrapped in night black clothes; only their pale faces showed. High tables had been set up all around the square's edge, and people clustered around them, eating and talking and drinking wine and ale. Off to the side, more men and women whirled in intricate dances, their black-gloved hands linked as they circled around and around.

All noise ceased as the four of them rode into the light. The dancers stopped. The drinkers turned to stare.

"Please, sir, come with me," the man with the pike said to Biur. "Your friends may wait here with your horses until arrangements are made."

"I won't—" Zeren began, but Biur cut him off:

"Watch the horses, please, Zeren. I need someone I can trust here."

"I know what you're doing. I'm not some child you can manipulate, like Ker! I'll do what I choose." He glanced at the circle of townspeople now staring at him, then swallowed. "I'll stay here."

The music started again, and the people danced once more—but not so wildly as earlier. Talk slowly resumed.

Ker hopped to the ground first, then Biur dismounted, stretching tiredly. Only Liana said nothing, watching those around them carefully. Ker realized, then, that she was aware of everything around them, her eyes missing nothing. If she saw any danger, she gave no sign of it.

"What's going on?" Ker asked the man. "The music and all."

"Today is the Feast of Masferigon, when we celebrate our

town's patron god. We had not expected visitors. Come this way, Biur."

"My apprentice will accompany me," Biur said.

Ker looked up in surprise, then grinned.

"Of course." The man nodded. Turning, he went up the wide wooden steps and into one of the taverns, and the two of them followed.

Inside, Ker looked around in surprise. The tavern's somber atmosphere made a sharp contrast to the festival outside. Tallow candles flickered, dripping wax, from nooks in the stone walls. Ancient, scarred oak tables sat against the walls. Some had been screened off with black curtains; high, straight-backed chairs surrounded others. Old men sat at the tables and slowly spun crystal spheres of various sizes. It seemed to be a game of some sort; copper coins changed hands every few seconds.

The man who'd led them inside leaned his pike in one corner, then turned and said, "Wait." Going to one of the screened-off booths, he spoke quietly through the curtain, then turned and gestured for Ker and Biur to join him.

"The Lord of Rhimalga will speak to you," he said.

"Thank you," Biur said.

He stepped around the edge of the curtain. Ker followed him into the booth, wondering if the lord would be like all the other nobles he'd met.

A small lantern burned clear and bright on the table before them. Ker stared at the old, wrinkled man who sat there. Like everyone else in the town, he was dressed in black with only his face showing. His beard was gray, his eyes dark and rheumy.

He looks like he's ruled for years, Ker thought. He bowed low, as he'd been trained by Lerrens. Biur only nodded slightly.

"I am called Nessoq, Lord of Rhimalga," the old man said. His low voice quavered with age, but still held a sharp note of authority.

"I am Biur. This is my apprentice, Ker."

"Is it true that you serve the gods?"

"I serve Derethigon."

"Then you must tell me what evil"—he coughed for a minute—"what evil passed through Rhimalga."

"What do you mean?" Biur said. "Tell me what happened here, I bid you."

"Last night they came, in a ship as dark as night. Its sails were shrouds that flapped in the breeze, and it rolled on wheels twice as tall as any man. I thought it was a portent of our god's return at first. But it creaked to a stop in the great square, the doors in its side swung back, and I saw deep shadows gather in the opening. They had eyes, these shadows, that burned and seemed to watch us. And yet they touched no one, nor made any move to leave their ship. As I watched them, the clouds grew lower, the sky darker. The night seemed about to break in storm. Then the doors swung shut, the ship's great wheels slowly turned, and they sailed down the highway toward Zelloque. So did it happen! Tell me, you who serve the gods: what does this mean?"

"Evil times are upon us," Biur said. "I can say no more than this: we are following that engine you saw, and we will see its creatures dead or banished from this Earth."

"Evil times," the old man whispered. "Evil, evil times." He looked from Biur to Ker and then back again. "What must we do?"

"You can do little to help, Lord Nessoq—this we must do ourselves. Will you give us shelter for the night, and food?"

"Of course, sir." He rose a bit uncertainly, holding the edge of the table for balance. Then sweeping aside the black curtain, he called, "Tiyar!"

Tiyar—the man with the pike—hurried over. "Yes, Lord?" he asked.

"Biur and his companions will stay this night in my house. Escort them there and see to their needs. I will summon servants to wait on them."

"Thank you, Lord Nessoq," Biur said, bowing slightly. "Your generosity will surely not go unrewarded."

"It is my pleasure to serve you." Then he settled back in his seat and drew the black curtain between them.

"This way," Tiyar said softly. He led them outside, back to Liana and Zeren and the horses.

He escorted them through the wide, dim streets of Rhimalga to the edge of the town—to a tall, splendid house topped with tapering silver spires. There they dismounted. Zeren groaned and stretched, rubbing his back again. Ker grinned when he thought the Oracle wasn't looking. Then he and Biur unstrapped the saddlebags from the horses and slung them over their shoulders.

"You may leave your horses here," Tiyar said. "Stableboys will be around in a moment. The animals shall be well taken care of."

"Thank you," Liana said.

"This way." He led them up broad marble steps to the wide oak doors. Taking a large brass key from his pocket, he slipped it into the lock, twisted it once, then swung the doors open.

They went into a huge entry hall. The floor was a checkerboard of gray and white marble squares; pillars stood in even rows to the left and right. A small fountain gurgled happily in the center of the chamber, and small fishes slowly circled in its wide, shallow pool. In various recesses in the walls stood magnificent statues of the gods. The golden figure of Masferigon stood taller than the rest, grim eyes staring down at them as they entered—as if warning them not to intrude on their host.

Ker swallowed. He'd only seen statues like these on the steps of the Oracle in Vichir. They seemed out of place in a home.

Servants, also dressed like Tiyar so only their pale faces showed, glided out from dark corners. They took the saddlebags at a curt gesture from the pikeman and carried them away silently.

"I assume you wish to wash, then eat," he said.

"Yes," Zeren said. "It's the least you can do, after treating us as you did."

Tiyar ignored him. "The servants will set a table in your sleeping chambers. You may wash in the fountain room at the top of those stairs." He nodded to the left. "Your rooms are also on that floor. I trust you will find them agreeable. Now I must go. Have a pleasant evening."

"Thank you," Biur said. "Your kindness is appreciated."

Zeren snorted derisively.

Bowing, Tiyar turned and left, shutting the front doors behind him. Ker glanced around, but saw no trace of the servants.

Zeren started up the stairs. More slowly, the others followed.

After they had washed the road's dust from their hands and faces in the intricately carved marble fountains, they wandered into the second-floor hallway again. Ker ran ahead, opening doors and glancing inside. The first few contained nothing but beds, the next few had no furnishings at all. He hurried on.

At the end of the passage he found two rooms with open doors. Inside the first sat a pair of beds already made up with sheets and light blankets; the saddlebags had been draped across a padded bench in one corner. In the second room stood another pair of beds, as well as a large table spread with food. His mouth watered as he looked at the fresh fruit, dried strips of salted fish, sliced vegetables, and cold pastries. There were pitchers of water, some sort of sour-smelling ale, and large loaves of a peppery brown bread spiced with ground *baata* root. Four hard-backed chairs had been neatly arranged around the table.

Not a single person stood in attendance to serve the meal, which Ker considered odd. It would have been considered bad manners for guests to serve themselves in Vichir, but Ker reminded himself that customs differed across the world, and he was too hungry to care, anyway. With a shrug, he sat and waited for the others to catch up. Taking a cold meat pastry from the platter in front of him, he nibbled one end.

"Ah!" Zeren appeared in the doorway and sniffed, savoring the smells, then entered and flopped into the chair opposite Ker. He looked the food over eagerly. "At last, a civilized meal!"

Biur and Liana followed him in, sitting to either side of Ker, and after they'd set aside a libation for the gods, they began to eat.

When they'd all had their fill, Zeren leaned back in his chair, rubbing his stomach contentedly. "Excellent, excellent," he murmured. "Far better than I expected, in this barbaric place."

"What happened to the servants?" Ker asked. He noticed, for the first time, that the house seemed very quiet—as if they were the only people within.

"They probably went back to the celebration," Biur said. "They will return in the morning. I plan to sleep now, and recommend you do the same."

"I think something's wrong," Ker said. "The servants should've remained to wait on us."

"It does not matter," Biur said. "They set out the food. It was enough."

"But there are other things wrong, too," he said, recognizing for the first time everything that bothered him about Rhimalga. "What about the sheep outside the village? No shepherd would abandon his flock, even for a festival!"

Zeren shrugged. "The sheep will be safe here. Not all the world is filled with monsters."

"And," Ker continued, "why is the city glowing blue? And the outlying cottages? Biur said the demons visited them, just as they visited Loq's farm! That means they *must've* done something other than watch from their engine!"

"But why would Lord Nessoq lie to us?" Biur asked.

Zeren nodded. "Why?"

"But—" Ker started. He broke off. Why *would* Lord Nessoq lie to them? He had no reason to, unless he wanted to help the thieves. But if he were trying to aid the wizard, then why would he let them stay in his house? Nothing made sense. "Perhaps you're right," he admitted slowly.

"Of course I'm right," Zeren said.

"You are tired, as we all are," Biur said. "Lie down—rest. The world will seem different when you wake."

"Yes, Biur," he said. He glanced at the two beds in the room. "Where do you want me to sleep?"

"You and Zeren will spend the night here. Liana and I will sleep in the next chamber." He rose and nodded slightly. "Good night."

Liana rose as well, saying, "Sleep in peace."

"You too," he said.

Despite Biur and Zeren's assurances, Ker couldn't help but feel uneasy. He lay in his bed and stared at the low flame in the oil lamp. He was restless, and his stomach felt cold and full of lead. A sheen of cold sweat covered him.

Listening to Zeren's light snores, he waited, counting seconds, then minutes. Time dragged on. Nervous energy filled him. His palms itched and he couldn't sleep.

At last, unable to stand it any longer, he threw back the covers and rose. He stole softly to the door. Pausing for a second, fingers on the handle, he pondered his actions. What if the Rashendi woke and found him gone? What would Biur do if they discovered he'd sneaked out? He wasn't disobeying, exactly—his master hadn't told him not to go out and look around the house. He'd just take a quick look around.

He opened the door a crack and peered out. A small lamp sputtered feebly from a nook in the wall, providing little light. It would soon be out of oil. Deep shadows swept up and down the hall. Still the house seemed deserted.

Cautiously easing through the door, he held his breath as Zeren mumbled something in his sleep and rolled over. Then he stood, trembling, in the hall, and shut the door quietly behind him. Tiptoeing past Biur and Liana's room, he came to the half-open window at the far end of the hall. It looked out on a small, dark alley. He leaned forward and stared down at the twenty-foot drop in disappointment. The building's smooth stones provided no handholds for him to climb down, and it was too far to jump.

Turning, he padded past the doors to the other end of the hall, then down the broad stone steps to the entry hall. His breath grew short; he tried to quiet the thunder of his heartbeat.

Not a single person stood in attendance.

Ker knew, then, that something was wrong. What if Biur or Liana wanted something during the night? What if more travelers came? Who would greet them here if Lord Nessoq offered them the hospitality of his house? Such a breach of courtesy would never be tolerated in Vichir! More disturbed than ever, he searched the rooms one by one.

The first floor's windows were mere slashes in the stone walls—too narrow for him to squeeze through. Pale starlight glimmered through them. He wandered through the front hall, the banquet hall, the kitchens. No servants worked in them. He explored the recesses of the entry hall, where velvety shadows crouched and seemed to watch his every move. Then he found his way into a small, dark storage room with a bolted door at its very back. From the door's position, he guessed it opened onto the alley he'd seen from the second-floor window. Perhaps deliveries were made here, or garbage taken away.

He slipped the bolts and swung the door open. It creaked slightly. Easing into the alley, he glanced up and down its length, then nodded in satisfaction. It was deserted. He shut the door behind him and started toward the street.

Hearing a sound ahead, he tensed. It was a light shuffle, like that of padded feet. He crouched and ran forward, darting between pools of shadow. Reaching the alley's mouth, he risked a quick glance around the corner.

A mass of townspeople moved through the street in front of Lord Nessoq's house in a grim, silent procession. Their faces seemed to float against the darkness of the night. The lanterns lining the street had grown dim, providing little illumination, but Ker saw the telltale glint of drawn swords. He ducked back before they saw him.

Why would they bring weapons? The lord had seemed friendly in the tavern. Why would he want to kill them now?

He stole a second look.

The people had stopped in front of the lord's front door. There they began to disrobe, removing first their gloves, then their cloaks. The night made their bodies indistinct, vague, dreamlike. Then they drew back their tight-drawn hoods for the first time.

And they seemed to peel their faces away.

It was as if their faces were masks, bound in place by their hoods. Ker stared in growing horror. He wanted to hide from the sight, but he forced himself to stay and watch, to learn what they were doing. The world had drifted into nightmare and he couldn't look away. His stomach lurched and he thought he'd be sick. He shook all over.

All those faces . . .

Unbidden, his fingers rose and followed the line of his jaw. He could still see, still breathe, still taste. He proved it to himself over and over again. He *had* to prove it to himself.

The townspeople cast their faces into the air. The world was moving very slowly. Spinning end over end, the paper-thin masks floated down the street like a line of fallen stars, glowing faintly white. Their eyes were shut. Their mouths gaped open.

Still Ker stared in shock. The faces had been masks. *Masks!* He was suddenly reliving his own facelessness again, his blundering through the dark of the world. Every mask had been his face. Shuddering, he knew the faces had come from the townspeople.

Where were their bodies?

He knew what had happened to the shepherds and the farmers, to the Lord of Rhimalga, to all the people. The wizard had been here. He'd sent his creatures roaming through the town, stealing faces. And his demons had worn them as masks.

He opened his mouth and screamed silently with all the pain that had built inside him; he knelt in the street and pounded the stones with his fists till his hands ached and bled. Then, through a haze of tears and with a heavy pain in his chest, he dared to look at the demons again.

They stood like statues. Swords gleamed in the dim light. They had come to kill.

Something hardened inside him. Ker sat up. He would not cry again.

These were the same sort of creatures who'd helped to steal the bones of Shon Atasha, the same sort of creatures who'd loaded the bones into the Dark One's engine. They stretched, limbs twisting in unnatural directions, and he caught a sour, bestial stench in the air. Then they drifted up the steps toward the front doors. More swords rasped from scabbards.

The noise woke him from his trance. Scrambling back down the alley, he made no attempt to cover the noise he made. His feet slapped loudly on the pavement. He reached the pantry door just as a low, bleating cry sounded at the mouth of the alley behind him. A spear *whoosh*ed through the air—inches from his head. Then he was safe inside. He slammed the door shut and rammed the bolts home.

His breath came in ragged pants. His heart pounded wildly.

Already he could hear the front door being torn asunder.

10

The Streets of Rhimalga

What many do not realize is that the Earth has two sides. The eleven gods in Theshemna rule the top, and with their benevolent help the world has grown tame and fruitful. The other side of the Earth, the side where the sun pales to but a feeble remnant of its glory by day, is ruled by the Mad God, the God of Death, whose sport is madness and whose toys are the souls of the dead. It is strange that such an equilibrium between light and dark, life and death, can exist so peacefully here.

—Pere Denberel
Far Lands and Shores

Ker glanced around in panic. He had to warn the others. He ran through the storage room and into the kitchens. A back staircase for servants stood in the corner. He bounded up its steps three at a time.

In the second floor's hallway, he stopped and listened. Hearing light breaths and lighter footsteps, he guessed the demons had gotten into the entry hall below. Soon they'd be creeping up the stairs . . .

Running silently down the corridor, he found himself reliving his nightmares. *Faceless creatures chasing him down endless halls in Theshemna—*

He reached Biur's door and threw it open. His master woke at the noise and sat up in bed. Liana had been standing by the window, gazing up at the stars. She too turned, startled by the noise, and stared at him.

"They've come to kill us!" Ker whispered loudly.

"Who?" Biur demanded.

"Demons from the wizard's engine. Hurry! They're on the stairs!"

"Wake Zeren," Biur said without hesitation. He rose and dressed quickly, throwing on his cloak and hood. Liana packed the saddlebags.

Ker stuck his head through the doorway. The demons hadn't yet reached the hall. He imagined them slipping up the steps silently, their eyes burning red in the darkness. Darting down the hall and into the room where Zeren slept, he crossed to the bed and shook the Rashendi awake.

Zeren rolled over, blinked, and cursed. "What is it?"

"Demons—they're coming up the stairs!"

"Go back to sleep—it was just a nightmare—"

"Listen!"

Ker could hear them now, a soft padding not far away. Zeren tensed, swallowing quickly. He leaped to his feet and began pulling on his robes.

"Where are Liana and Biur?" he demanded.

Footsteps pounded outside. From somewhere farther away came shrill cries and animallike grunts. Ker peeked around the corner of the door. Liana was running down the hall toward him with one of the saddlebags while Biur followed with the other two. The demons stood in the shadows at the head of the stairs, a writhing mass of dark bodies. They surged forward, throwing clubs and spears wildly.

Liana shot through the door, gasping for breath, with Biur two steps behind.

Then a spear hit the wizard just as he reached the doorway. Its point ran through his right shoulder and the haft snapped off with a dry, brittle sound. Dropping the saddlebags, Biur slipped, and Ker thought he'd fall for an instant. But somehow he stayed on his feet and staggered into the room.

Ker slammed the door and bolted it closed, then he and Liana slid the beds and the table and chairs from dinner in front of the door, blocking it as best they could.

Already the demons stood outside; the door shook as heavy fists pounded on it. Metal rang on wood as they hacked at it with swords.

Ker glanced wildly around the room for something—*anything*—to add to the barricade. Nothing remained but the carpets on the floor, and Zeren had pulled them up and piled them in the corner for Biur to lie on.

The Rashendi had removed the spear point, a ragged, clawed bit of steel, from Biur's right shoulder, and now the wound bled freely. He used Biur's blue cloak to sponge off the blood; then, tearing sheets from the bed into strips, he bound the wound tightly. Biur tensed, then groaned as the Rashendi tied the final knot. His face twisted in agony.

"Help me up," he whispered. His voice rasped harshly.

"You must lie still until the bleeding stops," Zeren said.

"If I do, we will *all* die." Biur placed his palms flat on the floor, then slowly raised himself. Ker ran forward and took his master's good arm, helping him to his feet.

Biur pushed Ker away and stood by himself. The wizard no longer seemed aware of his wound. Raising both hands over his head, he whispered something softly, then began to sing in a quiet, lilting voice. Ker couldn't understand the words, though at times the meaning seemed almost within reach, just at the edge of his mind.

The room grew very still. The demons' sounds seemed muted, as if they came from a great distance away. The air swam with dewy drops of azure.

Sheets of electricity crackled over Biur's skin. His face was a glowing mask. He raised his right hand higher; his wand suddenly filled it, glowing white-hot like the sun. A tense silence filled the room. Biur's face was wrapped in blue flames; he smiled faintly, as though he looked beyond the world, beyond the demons in the hall outside. He laughed with power.

Raising his wand, the wizard shaped the air before him. Ker watched in awe as the fabric of the world twisted, darkened, tore apart. Patterns formed and vanished in the blue fire. A hole appeared, slowly expanding until it stood almost as high as their ceiling. Its edges showed, ragged and half-formed.

The Gateway.

An icy wind struck Ker in the face.

"Get through!" Biur shouted, his voice strange.

Zeren hurried into the Gateway, then Liana. Ker hesitated, staring up at his master's brilliant face.

"*Go!*" Biur shouted.

Ker turned and dove into the darkness. Cold bit into him. The room around him disappeared, replaced by—nothingness. The world glowed white and empty in all directions. Raising his hand, he stared at its silhouette against the brilliance.

The Gateway world, he imagined, must be bleak and desolate, filled with ice and snow. He watched as the air misted from his breath. Ice crystals formed, spinning into patterns like snowflakes.

He seemed to be standing in a cavern that stretched to infinity, beautiful and pure, waiting for him.

He moved as if in a dream, the cold forgotten. He grew warm; his thoughts drifted like leaves in the wind.

Then he saw the other end of the Gateway a few feet ahead, glowing like a beacon, calling him forward. He meandered drunkenly toward it and stepped through.

He stood shivering in the middle of a narrow, cobbled street. The air seemed stiflingly hot. Ice covered his clothes. Fingers numb and blue from cold, eyebrows and eyelashes frosted white, he shivered and stamped his feet to get warm.

"What took you so long?" he heard Zeren whisper. "And where's Biur?"

"I d-don't know!" he stammered.

Liana and Zeren stood before him. Shivering, he looked around. They were still in Rhimalga. Buildings loomed, tall and dark, to his left and right. Lanterns jutted out over the street on thin poles. Their wicks had been turned low to save oil; the light was dim.

"Where are we?" he asked.

"Shh!" Zeren whispered. He pulled Ker into the shadows.

Far off, they heard the raucous voices of demons and the slapping of splayed feet against the streets' cobblestones. At first they seemed to be getting nearer, but slowly the voices grew more distant. He guessed the creatures had passed on the next street over and sighed with relief. What would they do if demons discovered them *here?*

He turned and watched the shimmering Gateway. Its surface rippled and chopped like a lake in a storm. Then Biur appeared and the magic collapsed in upon itself, disappearing with a soft sigh of wind.

Zeren ran forward. Biur collapsed into his arms.

"Help me!" the Rashendi hissed.

Ker ran forward and draped Biur's left arm over his shoulder, bearing as much of his master's weight as he could. Biur's flesh was cold and damp with sweat. Fresh blood showed on the bandages.

"We must"—Biur gasped—"get to the . . . stables. The horses—"

"Where are they?" Zeren asked.

"Find them—"

"Yes."

Ker helped him half carry, half drag Biur into the shadows. They laid the wizard down in a doorway where the shadows were so thick nothing could be seen. Then Liana bent over Biur for a second, stroking his face softly.

"He will be all right," she said. "He must rest."

The Rashendi turned to Ker. He moved quickly now, like a cat, all efficiency. His decisions were quick and his bearing crackled with authority and power. Ker stared at him for a second, trying to figure out what had happened. His opinion of Zeren did an abrupt turnabout. The Rashendi had taken over from Biur with no hesitation—suddenly gone from an obnoxious fool to a leader, as if everything he'd said and done before had been a lie and he some player in its game.

"Wait here with Biur," he ordered.

"But—"

"No." He shook his head. "I'm counting on you to guard Biur, to make sure he doesn't try to get up and help. Liana and I will find the stables. Now that we know what happened here, we will be prepared for what must be done. I know I can depend on you. Your showed your loyalty to Biur at Loq's farm. Now, *do it!*"

Ker nodded gravely. "Yes, Zeren."

"Good." He turned. "Come, Liana."

They melted into the night, silent as two ghosts.

Ker crouched in the shadows next to Biur, listening to his master's rough breathing. Everything had gone wrong! The demons wearing human faces, the loss of the horses, Biur's wounds . . . If only Zeren and Liana could find the stables so they could escape before anything else happened.

"*Hurry,*" he whispered. "*Hurry!*"

It seemed as though years had passed since Zeren and Liana left. Ker began to fear they'd been caught. He even considered going to look for them, but thought better of it. No alarm had been raised; he'd heard no sounds of fighting. Therefore he had to assume they were still safe—just lost, or still looking. Staring down at Biur's dark, shapeless form, he wished they would hurry. He couldn't tell whether his master still lived.

A slight noise came from the right. Ker tensed. Dark forms moved in the shadows, and he heard hooves striking stone, a horse's low neigh. He climbed to his feet, taking a hesitant step forward.

"Zeren?" he whispered.

A meaty hand clamped over his mouth from behind. "Quiet!" the Rashendi whispered. "We found the stables."

Ker relaxed and Zeren released him. As the Rashendi bent to examine Biur once more, Liana led up four tall, proud stallions. She was crying softly, tears glistening on her cheeks like drops of silver.

"What happened?" Ker demanded. He had a sudden hot, angry feeling inside. He knew something had gone wrong. "Are you hurt?"

Liana didn't answer. Ker turned to the Rashendi. "What is it?"

"The horses have been . . . murdered. Butchered for food." Zeren sounded strangely withdrawn. "There was no reason. I do not understand—" He broke off and looked away. Ker could see him struggling to get his emotions under control.

Ker's legs suddenly went weak and he sat down next to Biur. He found it hard to accept. A lump in his throat made it hard to breathe. *Dead.* He tried to swallow and couldn't.

Staring down at his hands, he could just make out the crusted blood from where he'd cut them in the alley. *Dead.* Everything he loved was slowly being ruined. He wished for a sword, suddenly. He wanted to go out and kill the demons for all they'd done. More than that, he wanted to kill their master, the wizard who commanded them. He *would* kill their leader! He swore it over and over to himself until the words became meaningless sounds. And yet thoughts of revenge gave no comfort; he felt nothing but helpless rage and betrayal.

"We must go," Zeren said. "The longer we stay, the more chance they have of finding us. Take Biur's arm. We've got to get him on a horse."

Together they got Biur to his feet. In the dim light Ker could see deep lines of pain etched into his master's face. The wizard seemed to grow aware of them, for his eyes opened and he looked up.

"Do not worry," he said weakly. "I will not die. My time has not yet come to face the Dark God."

"Biur," Ker whispered.

The wizard closed his eyes. "Help Zeren."

Ker released him and went to get one of the stallions. As he took the reins, he noticed Liana's face had darkened. "Are you all right?" he asked. Hesitantly, he took a step toward her.

Liana moved forward, opened one of the saddlebags, took out a knife. She ran to Biur and knelt before him. "Set me free!" she begged, pressing the knife's hilt into his hand. "Flesh has become a curse! Never did I care for such creatures until Hevtherigon forced me into your form. I claim all that you owe me, Biur! I beg you, free me from this guise. They must not die unavenged."

And then she wept. Her long hair tangled across her face.

Slowly Biur pulled her to her feet and put his arms around her. He held her for a long minute, his face creased with pain from more than his shoulder. Then he pushed her away.

"No," he whispered. "Now is not the time. If you would have revenge, save it for the one responsible, not his minions. Your human life would be wasted if you spent it to destroy just a handful of demons. Is that how little you value your friends?" He sank back and closed his eyes.

"No," Liana whispered. "I value them far more than that."

Ker led the stallion forward, then Zeren and he each took one of Biur's arms. They helped him over to his horse. The wizard walked as best he could, but he was so weak from loss of blood that he could scarcely stand. Getting his foot into the stirrup, they swung him up into the saddle.

"There's rope in one of the saddlebags," Zeren said. "Get it."

Ker rummaged through them until he found a coiled length of cord. He held it up. "Will this do?"

Zeren took it and snapped it taut several times. "It should." Picking up the knife Liana had dropped, he cut the line in half and handed part to Ker. "Tie his foot to the stirrup so he can't slip."

"Yes, sir," Ker said. He bent to the task, looping the cord around his master's foot and tying it securely.

"Can you take the reins?" Zeren asked Biur.

The wizard nodded. "Yes."

Zeren and Ker climbed onto their horses; Liana followed more slowly. The Rashendi led the way down the street, spurring his mount, followed by Biur, then Liana. Ker brought up the rear.

Before they'd gone fifty yards, Ker heard angry cries behind them. Crouching, he risked a glance over his shoulder. Demons swarmed from the side streets behind them.

He looked ahead. Seven demons appeared from an alley twenty feet ahead. They raised their weapons, but Zeren whipped his horse on and charged straight through their midst. The creatures broke and ran to the side, casting spears uselessly after him. Then Biur and Liana were past, and Ker dug his heels into his own mount's sides. He felt his stallion straining beneath him. Foam already flecked its coat, and its eyes rolled in terror.

He galloped past the demons, too, following after the others. Their horses ran out of control now, nostrils flared, sweat streaming, their wild whinnies of fear ringing in the dark.

They met no more resistance. Within minutes they were outside the bounds of Rhimalga, and the city's gold domes and silver spires grew more and more distant. At last they passed the outlying buildings and farms, following the straight black road as it cut across the fields. Ker realized, then, that they'd come out through the wrong side of the town. Ni Treshel lay ahead, not Zelloque!

"Where are we going?" he shouted to Zeren.

The Rashendi looked back and called an answer, but the wind snatched his words and Ker heard nothing.

They rode for another five minutes. Zeren let his horse slow to a trot, then a walk. Ker caught up and the four of them rode side by side for a time.

"Where are we going?" he asked again as he began to catch his breath.

"To the forest we passed on the way into the city," Zeren said.

"That is not a safe place," Liana said. "We must not go there!"

Biur straightened in his saddle. "No," he said. His voice was stronger than before, more commanding. He turned his horse from the road and spurred him up the small, grassy hill to the left. "We must stop here first."

Ker followed him at once, wondering what he meant to do.

Zeren sighed but wheeled his horse around as well.

From the top of the hill, Ker looked back across the grasslands to the city. The central square blazed with light. He could just make out dark masses of demons assembled there. Even over the distance he heard the rousing cry of a horn.

The demons were being summoned together. In minutes they'd be an army—and then they'd march from Rhimalga in pursuit.

He could already see scouts streaming from the city gates.

The demons were heading toward Biur's hill.

11

The Forest of Gar Galimu

It is said Shon Atasha loved the creatures he created more than anything else, and that to each He gave a great gift. That is why some creatures speak with the sweet voices of women, why others walk like men, or fly, or swim like fish through the ground underfoot. These are the beasts we know. How many marvels must there be in the parts of the world where man has never trod?

—Tellerion
Speculations

"Untie my feet," Biur said.

Ker slipped to the ground and ran to his master's horse, fumbling at the knots until Zeren dismounted and handed him the knife. Then he slit the cords and they fell to the ground.

Biur dismounted without help and walked to where he could see Rhimalga clearly. The stars shone bright and sharp, ghosting the landscape in whites and grays. He faced the city across the fields and low hills for a long time. Then he raised both hands as if in greeting to the demons below.

Zeren ran forward and pulled Biur's arms down. "No!" he shouted. "You'll kill yourself, and there's no point in that! We can be in the forest before they reach us, and they'll never find us there!"

Biur faced him. "This city cannot remain. You know that."

"I need your help to find the bones, and you can't help me if you're dead!"

"What noble sentiment," Biur said angrily. "I know my own limitations, Oracle, and this will not kill me." He turned back to the city.

"What are they talking about?" Ker asked Liana. She still sat on her horse, staring off into space. Her face was a pale teardrop in the darkness.

"It matters little," she said. "All is the same in the end."

Ker turned and watched Zeren and Biur again. The Rashendi seemed to give in, for he nodded and backed away. "As you will, Wizard. You know your abilities better than I."

Biur raised his hands a second time and began to whisper softly to himself. Ker could feel the magic in the air, an electric pulse that made his skin prick. The atmosphere was close, oppressive, like a storm about to break. He shivered suddenly.

"You are a fool, Biur," he heard Zeren whisper to himself.

Ker turned. "What do you mean?" he demanded.

"Look!" The Rashendi pointed toward Rhimalga. "He will destroy the city, and himself with it! He is too weak to survive any great magic. He had enough trouble opening a simple Gateway. And even if he *were* strong enough, it would surely injure him, perhaps forever. All magic takes its wage. I fear he will die this night."

"No!" Ker cried. He lunged toward Biur, but Zeren grabbed his arm and forced him back despite his struggles.

"You must do nothing. The magic is started, and no one may interrupt. Watch, boy, and learn, if you can!"

Ker stared. Sparks whirled around Biur in a fantastic dance, faster and faster, brighter and brighter. The top of the hill burned with their fire. Still Biur shouted to the elements. Still he called upon the power of the gods. Overhead, dark clouds rolled like waves across the sky. Blue lightning flickered like the tongues of serpents. A hot, dry wind howled across the hills and fields, flattening the grass, uprooting the trees, destroying everything in its path.

Ker raised his arm to protect his face from stinging grains of sand. His hair blew wildly and he was almost forced off the hill. Zeren stood firmly beside him, a rock in the wind.

"I can't see!" Ker shouted. "What's Biur doing?" But the Rashendi could never have heard him over the roar of the storm.

Ker shielded his eyes with one hand and turned once more toward Rhimalga. The lights of the city went out one by one, street by street, as if waves of darkness crashed across the buildings. Here and there glowing tornadoes coursed through the streets. Houses and shops shuddered and collapsed. The towering spires snapped like twigs. Even the golden domes that had shone like the sun grew dented and dull. Clouds of dust rose like banks of fog, first shrouding, then revealing, then shrouding all that went on.

The roiling clouds overhead grew lower, darker. Lightning lanced the sky again and again, striking the city. Stone blocks chipped and cracked like ice. Wood beams blasted apart in splinters. Thunder roared like all the monsters of the underworld.

The few standing buildings seemed to shimmer like a heat mirage as pillars of fire leaped hundreds of feet into the air.

Rhimalga folded in upon itself. The ground chopped like the Insel Sea. A grinding, ripping noise followed, as though the Earth itself were being torn asunder, and still more clouds of dust and smoke rose to cloak the city.

Lightning flickered in great sheets against the black-velvet sky. The ground beneath Ker's feet trembled like a thing alive. Far off, he heard the hysterical neighs of horses.

Then the lightning stopped; the winds blew themselves out. The world paused, dark as pitch, silent.

Abruptly the clouds broke and rolled back, flowing toward the horizon like spilled wine, vanishing from sight. A desert of fine white sand now lay beneath the stars where Rhimalga had stood. Each grain of sand glistened faintly, as though wet. A light breeze stirred, building dunes, rippling them, sculpting them into fleeting shapes of men and monsters.

Finally even the breeze died. For an instant not a sound could be heard. The stars glittered overhead as though nothing had happened.

Not a sign remained of the city or its demon inhabitants.

Ker blinked and it was as if a bubble had burst. He could move again. Biur lay facedown on the ground ahead of them. He ran to his master's side, knelt beside him, gently rolled him over onto his back. Fear and concern made his hands tremble.

Biur's face looked dry and brittle, covered with a web of fine wrinkles that hadn't been there before, as though he had aged fifty years in the last five minutes. Even his hair had thinned and silvered.

And yet Biur's deep-sunken eyes were open. They gleamed feverishly, reflecting the stars overhead. "Is it done?" he asked slowly.

"Yes," Ker whispered.

Zeren stood over them. "We will make camp here," he said, "until you recover."

"My wound . . ."

"It will heal enough for you to travel in a week."

"No!" Biur said. "The spear was poisoned. I feel its coldness now, moving through my veins like ice. You must find a healer."

"But that will take weeks! Liana's horses are gone!"

"Find . . . Gar . . . Galimu." Biur closed his eyes.

"What happened to him?" Ker demanded, shocked. He couldn't look away from Biur's face, now grown so old.

"You have witnessed what few humans ever see. Magic takes its toll on those who use it. Biur used more magic in a breath span than most wizards use in a lifetime, and it has sucked his body dry. He is like an empty husk."

"Will he be able to use magic again?"

"If he lives. But always carefully, and never as before."

"Who is Gar Galimu?" Ker asked.

Zeren shrugged. "I have never heard the name. Perhaps Liana knows."

Turning to look for her, they found the hilltop empty. Liana and the horses had vanished.

"She won't have gone far," Zeren said. "She must have taken the animals to where they wouldn't be frightened, else they might have bolted. Find her while I tend to Biur."

Ker scanned the nearby hills, looking for any trace of them, but saw nothing. The wind had flattened the grass, obliterating any trail the horses had made. Starlight silvered the world.

All he could think about was Biur's face. He'd become so *old!* Ker couldn't help but wonder if the same thing would happen to him, if he became a wizard. *Is it like losing your face,* he wondered, *when you wake up and find your body old and weak?*

No, he decided, nothing could be like losing your face, not even *that.* It wasn't the same as being totally shut off from the world, only able to hear. At least Biur could still see and breathe.

"Liana!" he called.

He paused, listening to the echoes of his voice, and thought he heard a distant reply from somewhere over the next rise. Jogging down the slope, then up to the next hilltop, he finally spotted Liana and the horses in a low fold between hills. Liana seemed to be talking to the stallions as she rubbed them down with handfuls of dry grass.

Ker joined her, saying, "Biur turned the city into a desert."

"What did the magic do to him?" she asked.

"He's old now. But that's not the problem. He says the spear that hit him was poisoned. He wants us to find a healer for him, someone called Gar Galimu."

Liana stiffened at the name.

"Do you know who he is?" Ker asked.

"Yes. He rules in the forest we passed through yesterday. He makes toys of people for his mad games. Is he truly the one Biur asked for?"

"Yes, only him. Where will we find him?"

"One need but ride in the forest to find Gar Galimu."

Ker thought back to the dark, oppressive forest they'd passed through before coming to Rhimalga. That had to be the place Liana meant, where they'd find Galimu, whoever he was. Ker didn't look forward to the meeting.

"Let's go back to the others," he said.

Liana passed him the reins of two horses. He started up the hill, leading them, then turned and waited for her. She caught up and they walked together for a time.

"Liana?" he asked at last.

"Yes."

"I wondered . . . about the other horses. Who made them so different?" He hesitated. "If you don't want to talk about them, it doesn't matter."

She sighed. "No; what was done is over. Nothing can change it. I will tell you about the horses. Perhaps you will learn from the tale, as Biur says he learned from it.

"Once, many years ago, the gods fought among themselves. This you know. It was then, at the end of the battles, when peace was made and all the lands made into splinters for men to rule, that the Mad God took flight and carved out his own kingdom in the underworld. When he was gone and all the fighting ended, the gods returned in triumph to Theshemna. They rewarded those who had served them well, whether man or beast, as they saw fit. It was then that soldiers came to serve the gods in Theshemna, and with them came their horses.

"The soldiers set their steeds free to run wild in the forests and plains of the throne room, and there the herds thrived and grew. Whether the presence of such great magic worked upon them or whether one of the gods reshaped them in his idleness, I know not—but nevertheless the horses changed. They grew faster, more intelligent, beautiful and arrogant in their wildness. The gods watched them and laughed for a time. But that was many centuries ago, before the gods grew bored and drifted away from man.

"I came to know the horses, for I was a Wind and newly formed in mortal guise. I longed for freedom and speed at times, and when the horses would let me ride, we would circle the throne room, or race through the endless halls of Theshemna. It was their pleasure to serve me, and mine to serve them. I would brush their coats and comb their manes and tails, and we were happy.

"Thus it was our pleasure to follow Biur to Earth, to run free on true land for the first time in ages."

They had reached the place where Biur lay. Liana hurried forward and sat beside the wizard, softly stroking his forehead, murmuring something in his ear.

At last she looked up at Zeren. "How is he?"

Zeren shrugged a bit. "I dressed and cleaned his wound, then worked some of Shon Atasha's magic over him. He is still weak from loss of blood, and the poison is still within him."

"Will he live?"

"For a day or two, perhaps a bit more—but certainly no more than that, without a healer. He mentioned someone named Gar Galimu."

"Ker and I will get Galimu and return as quickly as possible. Stay with Biur until then?"

"Of course."

"Come, Ker," Liana said, rising smoothly. She took a set of reins from Ker's hand and swung up into the saddle, spurring the stallion toward the black road.

Ker scrambled to keep up.

It was still dark when they reached the edge of the forest. Ker sat up straighter, massaging the tired, knotted muscles in his hands.

He didn't like the look of the place. Trees hung back a little from the road, their branches dark tangles, their trunks ebon pillars. He had the impression of a thousand eyes watching their every move, for shadows gathered beneath the trees ahead. Some seemed to writhe with movement while others remained still. Somewhere far away, night birds sang strange melodies. Insects chirped and small animals scurried. The forest breathed with life.

The stars, almost finished in their nightly orbit around the Earth, had begun to fade; dawn would soon come. Yawning, Ker stretched. His horse plodded wearily onward.

Only Liana seemed unaffected by the night's travel. She rode in the exact center of the highway, as if daring the watchers to show themselves.

Ker spurred his horse and caught up with her. "Where will we find Gar Galimu?" he whispered.

"He will find us," she said in a normal voice. "Look for a path. I know we passed several yesterday."

"Is he human?"

She laughed. "Sometimes. He is a dream, a creature older than man. He will take whatever form he chooses. Often, it is said, he roams the forest as a giant boar."

"Oh." They continued in silence for a few minutes, then Ker said, "Will he cure Biur?"

"Yes."

"How do you know?"

"It is part of his nature to care for all living things. He is as an uncle to the Winds, and will not refuse my request once we get beyond his games. Amusing him for a moment will be the price of his aid. If ever we find the path to his home!"

As though in answer to her request, a small, winding game trail appeared on the left. Low-hanging branches made it impossible for them to ride, so he and Liana dismounted.

The thick, damp smell of humus and growing things filled the air. Without hesitation, Liana dismounted and started down the path, tugging her horse's reins. Reluctantly, it seemed, the stallion followed.

Ker hesitated an instant before ducking after her.

"Stay close behind me," Liana said. "If you get lost, we may never find each other again—unless Gar Galimu wills it."

The trees seemed to close around them; the trail grew narrower. With a thick mat of leaves overhead blocking out the starlight, it was impossible to see more than a few feet ahead. Ker couldn't see Liana at all, and her horse—scarcely three feet ahead—seemed more shadow than substance.

The trees swayed in the wind. Their branches rubbed together, whispering, squeaking. Ker found the noise unnerving and quickened his step.

"I think the trees are moving!" he called ahead.

"They are. I can see them drawing back to make the path for us. It's Gar Galimu's doing—he knows we're here. Ignore his tricks and we will meet him soon enough."

Gnarled roots stuck out over the path, making Ker stumble. Leafy branches whipped at his face. He fell more than once, scraping knees and palms raw and bloody. As he began to lag farther and farther behind Liana, he tried to quicken his pace, but the path grew more treacherous than ever, full of sharp turns and jagged twists.

At last the trail disappeared entirely. A wall of trees stood in front of him, blocking his way.

He stopped, listening. He heard no sound but his own heartbeat. The insects had stopped their chitter; the birds no longer sang.

Around him, branches rustled, leaves moving to block the dim, filtered starlight. The forest grew pitch black.

He couldn't hear Liana or her horse anymore.

He was lost.

12

The Boar in the Grove

"May your life be full of magic."

—Zelloquan curse

Ker didn't do anything for a long time.

She can't have gone far, he thought. *She was just ahead of me.*

He moved to the left of his horse, looking for the trail, hand outstretched, feeling the bark of the trees. Figuring he'd missed the path, somehow, he kept walking. At last he stopped, forced to admit he'd walked in a complete circle. The oaks ringed him completely; his horse barely had room to turn.

Something rustled behind him. He whirled, crouched as if to fight.

The trees had receded, leaving a wide, straight path. It stretched a hundred yards long, and at its end he saw a glimmer of starlight. A clearing of some sort lay there.

Swallowing, he tugged his horse's reins and started forward. Branches wove a dense canopy of leaves overhead, and the darkness around him seemed almost tangible. Anything could be waiting to ambush him, he thought—waiting in the shadows or in the clearing.

Something chittered madly. Ker jumped, startled, as his horse neighed and jerked its head back, trying to get free. Its eyes rolled wildly. He gave the stallion some room, then moved close, making soft, reassuring noises as he stroked its neck. The horse calmed.

What was that? He searched the darkness ahead, then glanced over his shoulder, half expecting demons from Rhimalga to have followed him from the city.

There was nothing behind him but more oaks. They had closed in when he wasn't looking, and now the passage back to the paved highway was totally blocked. He had no way to go except forward. For an instant he had the impression he was being herded, like a stag in some hunt, toward an archer's blind.

Why?

The chittering came again, louder than before; then a small, dark, heavily furred creature of some kind dropped to the ground in front of him. Catlike eyes peered at him for an instant, then it scurried to the left and vanished among the trees.

Ker sighed in relief. Only an animal! But that still didn't explain the moving trees. What had happened to Liana? And where was Gar Galimu?

Still wary, he continued down the path, but nothing more happened. Reaching the end of the tree tunnel, he paused and looked around for an instant, studying the clearing and the trees ringing it.

His apprehensions slowly faded. The place was beautiful, like something out of fable. Stars glittered brightly overhead, and the short-cropped grass glistened like burnished silver with the morning dew. He could see as though it were day. Tall trees ringed the glade, noble oaks and gray-sided birches. Doves sang softly. A low breeze whispered like a woman's voice.

He moved forward as though in a dream, tugging the horse's reins. He could feel the magic all around him, running through the ground, coursing through the grass and trees, charging the air with a vibrant *aliveness* unlike anything he'd ever felt before. Euphoria filled him; he wanted to sing and dance in celebration of life. Throwing back his head, he laughed until tears rolled down his cheeks and he could barely breathe.

At last he stopped and wiped his eyes dry. He felt more relaxed than before, like all the tension of the night had slipped from his body, leaving him at ease for the first time in weeks.

He noticed a low mound rising from the glade's far corner, and on top of the mound sat a waist-high block of white marble. He led his horse over to it.

On the block of marble lay a short sword of the finest steel. Intricate gold-and-silver inlay decorated the razor-sharp blade, and small sapphires and chips of rubies had been set in the pommel. But despite the sword's beauty, it had a plain, worn leather grip. Ker picked it up, feeling the perfect weight, testing the balance. It fit his hand as though he'd used it all his life.

A spear leaned up against the other side of the stone. It had a six-foot shaft and a silver head that ended in a needle-sharp point. Setting down the sword, he hefted the spear. It had a good feel—light enough to be thrown a fair distance, but still heavy enough to be used for thrusting in hand-to-hand fighting as well. He set it down, too, figuring the weapons belonged to Gar Galimu.

"Is anyone here?" he called.

Climbing to the top of the stone, he slowly turned, scanning the clearing for any sign of Galimu. The trees stood like silent watchers. The place was deserted.

He heard a grunting sound behind him. Whirling, he found a large boar standing at the far edge of the glade.

Where did it come from? he wondered.

His horse scented the boar and reared suddenly, jerking the reins from his hand. He dove after them, which only frightened the stallion more. It skittered back, then turned and fled in the opposite direction. Cursing silently, he watched it disappear into the trees.

He turned to face the boar. It was larger than any he'd ever seen before, standing almost as high as his shoulder. The fur around its neck bristled with steely spikes. It must have weighed four hundred pounds at least, he figured—mostly muscle and bone. With foot-long upturned tusks, sharp incisors, and rock-hard hoofs, it could easily kill him.

The boar pawed the ground, sending great clumps of dirt and grass flying. Its eyes were shiny and black as it watched him.

Scrambling back to the stone, Ker snatched up the sword in his right hand and the spear in his left. He'd hunted all his life, listened to the guards' tales of slaying monsters the like of which no man had ever seen before. Of course, those had been just stories—but now he wished he'd listened to how they'd slain the creatures!

Where did it come from?

The boar charged.

Ker dropped the spear and leaped onto the stone and backed to its center, gripping the sword with both hands, ready to bring it down on the boar's skull as hard as he could. He didn't know if he'd be able to kill it or not, but he planned on hurting it as much as he could if it came any closer.

It circled the low mound at a run. Ker turned as well, always facing it, holding his sword ready to strike.

At last the beast slowed. Raising its snout, it snuffed the air. It seemed uncertain whether to come closer or not.

Where did it come from? Ker wondered again. He risked a quick glance around the glade. All the trails had vanished—including the one he'd followed into the clearing. The forest seemed to swallow everything—paths, horses, people. Why would it do that? Someone had to be responsible.

It was as though everything had been prepared for their coming: the trees leading him into the glade, the sword and spear waiting on the block of marble, the boar showing up. It seemed as if his adventure in the forest had been planned just so he'd end up fighting! And only one person would be able to do all that: Gar Galimu!

What had Liana said? He often wandered the forests—disguised as a giant boar? Like this one? It had to be!

He searched for a blue halo of magic around the boar—and found it an instant later. The animal shimmered with a deep, clear azure glow that matched the sky for brilliance, and as he strained to look beyond the outer shell of its skin, he saw a flickering golden light, as bright as the sun, that seemed radiate from its heart.

He swallowed, then lowered the sword, letting his sight slip back to normal. It *had* to be Galimu.

Once again, only a giant boar stood before him. It had stopped pawing the ground. It remained there like a statue, and Ker had the impression it was studying him for weaknesses.

"I know that you're Gar Galimu," he called, "and I won't fight you."

The boar grunted an answer, taking a step closer. Its muscles tensed as if to spring. But it didn't.

Ker swallowed. "I know you're Gar Galimu!" He seized the spear, in one motion turning and throwing it off into the trees. It hit wood with a solid *thunk.* Bending, he dropped the sword at his feet. Its steel blade clattered loudly against the marble. Still the boar didn't move.

Ker hesitated for an instant, wondering if he could have made a mistake. *No,* he thought, remembering the blue glow with the golden light shining inside, *this has to be Galimu. No animal could look like that.* Gathering his courage, he jumped to the ground and stood boldly in front of the boar, staring it straight in the face.

It trembled for a second—then charged straight at him. He gaped in shock and fear. It was on top of him before he could move.

At the last instant it veered to the left, the edge of its shoulder just grazing his side. The force of the blow sent him sprawling across the grass, the air *whoosh*ing from his lungs. The dew's wetness began seeping through his clothes. Gasping for breath, he tried to think.

The boar wheeled at the far end of the clearing and began to trot back toward him, slowly gaining speed.

He saw the sword on the block of marble, barely ten feet away. He had to get back to it—that was his only chance! He tried to push himself up to his feet, but a sharp pain shot through his left arm. It suddenly slipped out from under him with a ripping sound, and he felt something grate in his shoulder. His whole side pulsed with waves of agony.

Pricking up its ears, the boar lowered its head, tusks inches from the ground, and charged straight at him a second time.

Ker struggled to get his legs out from under him, but kept slipping. His left arm seemed to be on fire. His whole body shook.

With a low growl of rage, the boar was on top of him. Ker threw his right hand up to protect his face, twisting his head away and squeezing his eyes shut.

He felt a rush of air and smelled something musty, then a shadow passed over his face. Prying his eyes open, he saw the boar bounding across the glade. It had leaped over him.

Why? he wondered, through a haze of pain. He could barely feel his arm now and seemed to be drifting away from the world. His head pounded. The clearing wobbled unsteadily.

The boar seemed to be facing him. Abruptly it leaned back and stood on its hind legs. Its hide shimmered and rippled like a banner in the wind. Its front legs grew longer, thicker, straighter, the hooves splitting apart and re-forming into long, tapering fingers. Its face twisted. The long white tusks shrank and vanished. The snout pulled back to become a human nose. The spikes around its neck wavered and suddenly became a shoulder-length mane of silky black hair.

And then the change was complete: a tall, massive man dressed in black animal skins stood before him.

Ker could barely see. He seemed to be drifting in a pool of warm water.

"I am Galimu," the man said. His voice was low and powerful, more like an animal's roar than a human's speech. "I am Galimu, and you are mine."

He stalked forward.

The air seemed to roar in Ker's ears. Then darkness swooped down and he knew no more.

13

The House in the Wood

> It is the nature of magic to be unnatural—for magic is the unbinding and rebinding of the fabric of the world. Perhaps we trust magic-users too much. Do they truly know the forces with which they tamper? Are their dabblings and experiments truly safe?
>
> —Tellerion
> *Speculations*

The next few hours were a blur to Ker: at times he seemed to be hanging upside down while the world spun around him. At other times he gazed up at the leaves of trees while he seemed to rock slowly from side to side, like a baby in a cradle.

At one point his mind grew clear and he found himself in Gar Galimu's arms. The man bore him silently through the forest. Trees whipped past on either side. Through gaps in their leaves he saw the sky overhead: pale blue with the new dawn, unmarred by the slightest wisp of cloud.

He closed his eyes, remembering his fight with the boar, remembering Gar Galimu's transformation. He recalled the pain in his arm, but that seemed long gone: he felt nothing now. His whole body had become a leaden weight, dragging him down into darkness.

The world slipped further and further away.

The next time he opened his eyes, he lay on something soft and warm. His clothes had vanished. Smells of damp humus and decaying leaves rose around him. From the feel of his bed, he realized he lay on moss. He struggled to sit up, but winced in sudden agony when he moved his left arm. Both shoulder and elbow throbbed painfully. He sank back.

Turning his head, he looked out into a dimly lit room. The walls were textured like tree bark and filled with nooks and cupboards.

Stone and clay bottles had been stacked everywhere. A rich green carpet of moss covered the floor, and across the room a small fire burned cheerfully on a wide stone hearth. Gar Galimu crouched beside it, the flames making his face appear longer and sadder. He glanced up, met Ker's gaze, then smiled and looked down.

Ker noticed that a small stone pot sat by the fire. Something faintly luminous boiled within. Galimu stirred it occasionally with a long wooden spoon, often adding pinches of dried herbs from bottles to his left and right. At last he picked up a clay cup, dipped it into the liquid, then climbed to his feet and crossed to Ker's bed.

Ker sat up, self-conscious, forcing himself to ignore the pain in his arm. Again he tried and found he couldn't move his left hand. That whole side of his body felt thick and heavy. His shoulder ached.

"Be at ease, child," Galimu said. He put one hand behind Ker's head and placed the steaming cup at his mouth with the other. "Drink this. It will still the pain." He began to pour the liquid.

Ker had no choice but to drink. Even before the scalding stuff reached his stomach, he felt the difference. Rather than growing dull, his senses expanded. He grew aware of every corner of the room, every mote of dust in the air, every line and feature of Gar Galimu's face. Then his sight seemed to drift up and away from his body. He looked down into himself as if from a great height, recognizing, then, what was wrong with him: he had a dislocated shoulder and torn ligaments in his elbow.

Breathing deeply, he found himself relaxing, lying back on the bed of moss. Galimu no longer seemed so threatening; he was more like a kindly uncle than the giant boar that had attacked him. His face was as heavily lined and creased as tree bark, and his long, thin fingers resembled roots. What had Liana said? He was older than mankind?

Leaning forward, Gar Galimu gently probed Ker's shoulder, finding the displaced bone and the joint where it belonged. Ker felt no pain.

"Close your eyes," he said.

Ker did so.

In the distance he heard something scrape like fingernails on slate, and then he heard a popping sound and his left arm felt different—no longer heavy, but normal. There was still some throbbing, but it came from his elbow rather than his shoulder.

He opened his eyes. Gar Galimu smiled down from his wrinkled face. "Move your fingers," he said.

Ker turned and gazed down at his hand. It seemed miles away. He willed the hand to close, and one by one his fingers obeyed. He made a fist, then let it unfurl. Slowly, he sat up. He stared at Galimu.

"The injury will no longer pain you," the man said. His voice was low and heavy with age. "Does it feel correct?"

Ker flexed the hand again. He felt a quick twinge in his elbow, but that was all. "Yes—thank you," he said. "The pain is gone, except for the elbow. I heard something rip in it when I fell."

"Hmmm." Taking his arm again, Gar examined it carefully, then nodded. "Yes, I see it now." Softly he hummed, stroking Ker's elbow, and beneath his fingers the skin took on a faint blue glow.

Ker felt a deep warmth spread up his arm. It was a pleasant, tingling sensation that made him want to sleep. He built a picture in his mind—the tissue pulling together, the ligaments rejoining, the bone growing heavier, stronger.

Gar Galimu leaned back. "It is done," he announced.

Ker stared at his arm, slowly bending it, feeling its strength—it seemed as good as before. The draft Galimu had forced him to drink began to wear off and the world grew close again. Swinging his legs off the bed, he stood. The soft, mossy floor gave under his weight, tickling his feet.

He was suddenly cold, and shivered. "Where are my clothes?" he asked.

Galimu pointed to a trunk against the wall. "There. Take them."

Ker crossed and threw back the trunk's lid, finding his silver tunic neatly folded within. It had been washed and dried. His sandals lay beneath, also clean. He slipped them on, then turned and gazed at the small looking glass that stood in one corner.

His hair had been combed and cut, his face washed until it glowed with health. Stretching, he found all the aches and pains of travel had vanished. He looked fine. He'd never felt better. It was as though he'd slept for a week. Drawing a deep breath, he turned to his host.

"Thank you for everything—" he began.

"It was my duty. That I injured you was not intended—I meant to pass by without touching you, but I have grown old, and clumsy in my age. I beg your forgiveness, young sir."

"Why—yes, of course," Ker said quickly. "But I must beg a favor of you as well. First—how long have I been here?"

"Scarcely half a day. Tell me what favor you ask. If it lies within my power, I will grant it."

"Do you know what happened to Liana?" he asked.

"Who is Liana?"

"She rode into the forest with me."

"The Wind. Yes, I recall it."

"Where is she now?"

"Wandering." He shrugged. "The Syrnae lead her in circles."

Ker guessed the Syrnae had to be the forest's trees, the ones that moved. "We came to seek your help. My master was injured last night—he was hit by a poisoned spear. He sent us to find you."

"Who is your master?"

"His name is Biur. He serves Derethigon. I'm Ker, his apprentice."

"Very well, Ker. I am Gar Galimu, Seneschal of Shonora Anasith—whom you would call Shon Atasha. I will summon the Syrnae. They will find your master and bring him here to me."

"How can trees bring him here?" Ker asked.

"Trees?" Galimu roared with laughter. "Trees? No, the Syrnae are the tenders of this forest. It is they who guard it from harm, just as I guard them and all their kind. Magic is dying in the world, and their race had all but vanished beyond this place. Such is the great cycle." He sighed, then rose. "Wait. I will summon them."

He went to a round stone door, pushed it open, then passed outside and disappeared from view. Suddenly a horn wailed, a long, low, mournful cry like that of some wild beast in pain. Ker leaped to his feet. Galimu returned in a second, leaving his door wide.

"They will soon come," he said.

"What about Liana?"

"She will be brought here as well."

"And my horse?"

"It already sleeps in my stables. The Syrnae tend it well, Ker—it had been ridden hard and needs time to recover its strength. All will be mended in time. My promise binds me to your service."

"You're very kind," Ker said, feeling the truth of his words. "Were I not apprenticed to Biur, I would gladly serve you as my master."

"Make no promises you will not keep," Gar said, laughing lightly. "Come, tell me of your journey. I have heard little of the world beyond this forest, save what little the Syrnae hear and pass on to me. Few men travel this corner of the Earth: I bid you, speak of what brings you here."

Haltingly at first, then with greater speed as his imagination supplied the details and caught him up in the story, Ker told him of the theft of Shon Atasha's bones, of the wizard and his great engine, of how Biur, Liana, Zeren, and he pursued him down the ancient highway. He told of Loq and the demons in Rhimalga, how they'd been tricked into the house and how he'd discovered the deception. And he told of their flight and Biur's wound. Lastly, he told of Biur's destruction of the city. "And then Biur sent us here to find you—to cure him of the poison," he finished.

Gar Galimu shook his head. "Evil times are upon us. I had no knowledge of such happenings—and I wish you had no cause to bring such sad news." He cocked his head to the side, listening. "The Syrnae wait. Will you see them with me?"

Ker grinned. "Please!"

They went through the stone doorway. Outside, hundred-foot-tall trees loomed over them, spreading heavy branches wide. Dim green light filtered down to the forest floor. As soon as Galimu stepped out, a chittering sound rose from all directions.

Ker stared at the shadows around them. Catlike eyes stared back.

"Come," Galimu said, beckoning.

Small, round creatures seemed to tumble from the darkness in all directions. They climbed down from the trees, crept out from the shadows, slipped up from the earth itself. Hundreds of them clustered around, eyes bright and intense, and their chittering became a deafening roar.

Ker recognized them as the same sort of creature that had startled him and his horse on the forest trail. He got a good look at one for the first time. It had the slitted gray-green eyes of a cat, and a coat the color of well-tanned leather—to all appearances soft and sleek. A roughly triangular head, with a small black nose, bristling whiskers, and needlelike teeth, sat upon a rounded body with short limbs ending in miniature hands much like his own, each with four slender fingers and a thumb.

"These are the Syrnae?" he asked in amazement.

"They are kin to all the woodfolk. Do not be fooled by their form: they are shape shifters and affect this guise for reasons I do not comprehend. It is enough that they wish it."

"How will they be able to bring Biur here?"

Galimu smiled faintly. "They will manage." Turning, he sat cross-legged on the forest loam. Some of the Syrnae climbed up his arms, sitting on his shoulders and in his lap. Others just lay in the soft piles of leaves, or leaned against one another. Galimu laughed. They chittered happily.

Then he began to speak to them in a tongue Ker didn't understand. It was beautiful, full of trilled sounds and rolling vowels, almost a song. The words had a liquid quality, flowing and sinking and rising. Ker felt a power in them and knew that they were magic.

At last the Syrnae all rose and disappeared among the trees. Gar waited until the last one had vanished before standing.

"Come," he said. "Let us wait for their return. The Wind will soon join us, and then Biur."

For the first time, Ker noticed that the house was formed of living trees. Seven of them grew in a giant ring, their ten-foot-wide trunks forming the walls. Branches grew in toward the circle's center, twining together to form a sort of roof. Between huge roots, an immense granite door had been set. Ker guessed it must weigh hundreds of pounds. He knew he could never have opened it.

Galimu crossed and closed it with one hand, then sat on a high stone bench to its right, beckoning for Ker to join him.

After Ker had seated himself, Galimu said, "I have watched you with care, healing your injuries. I can feel the magic that lies coiled within you, yet I sense other things, too—strange things that I do not understand. Your face is not the same as the rest of you."

"What do you mean?" Ker asked too quickly. He had a terrible feeling in his stomach, suddenly, that something else had gone wrong.

"It is different, I perceive, from the rest of your body—as though you wear the face of another. It does not seem a part of you. *Here.*" Extending one finger, he traced a line along Ker's jaw, up around his forehead and down the other side of his face.

Ker jerked back. Sharp pain jolted through his face, as though his cheeks had been jabbed by a hundred different needles. A fierce ache spread outward through his body from the places Galimu had touched. His whole face blazed with pain. His hands flew to his face, rubbing it frantically.

It felt very cold, as if made of ice.

He seemed to be falling down an endless black pit.

He heard screaming. After a moment he realized it was his own.

14

The Geas of the Syrnae

> Any traveler entering lands of which he has no knowledge or experience should be wary of all creatures, especially small, furry, seemingly friendly animals. Often such beasts feign docility so they can get close enough to attack unwary humans.
>
> —Pere Denberel
> *Atlas of the World*, Revised

Ker heard silence burring in his ears, felt himself scream and scream until his throat went raw and silent. *He couldn't move.*

Something smooth and cool traced the line of his jaw. In his mind he saw the hand of Derethigon reaching toward him, growing longer, stretching to infinity. His eyes were gone. His mouth was gone. He couldn't breathe. His lungs burned. An ache grew inside him—he thought his chest would burst—

He imagined his face peeling back, floating free of his body, falling—forever falling . . .

From miles away, he heard a voice. Gar Galimu seemed to be singing softly, calmly. Ker felt himself floating in the dark, in a warm, cleansing pool of water. The pain in his chest eased.

He imagined himself raising his hands (as light as feathers), running them across his face (as cool and smooth as glass), feeling the contours of marbled lips and nose, brushing softly against closed eyelids.

He could almost see.

The water around him grew warmer, then hot. Jagged bits of light broke the darkness, like bits of some thin shell being torn away. He could sense the blue glow surrounding his body. There was a calmness in him such as he'd never known before.

Gar Galimu's song became louder, stronger.

Colors washed around him, reds and blues, yellows and greens, swirling up into place like all the pieces of a puzzle come together.

He moved high above the Earth. Emerald sprays of water and brown splashes of land rolled beneath him. Clouds flowed like banks of white fog.

Laughing, he spread his arms and drifted.

He passed great forests, rivers, cities . . . passed grasslands, deserts, mountains . . . passed valleys, hills, oceans . . .

He saw the beauty and terror wrought by Shon Atasha in his fit of creation, saw all the beasts that roam the rim of the world:

. . . herds of two-headed goats with scaled limbs and spiked tails

. . . vast serpents whose coils spanned the lengths and breadths of rivers

. . . groves of flowers with bodies like beautiful women.

He saw unicorns running wild through the forests, their golden coats aflame beneath the sun; saw dragons circling great, towering mountains of fire and smoke; saw creatures with bodies like pillars of light.

The sun rolled across the sky like a giant ball, unguided by any hand. The seas flayed the rocky shores of a thousand different lands. Rivers raged; storms blew; winds howled through the mountains.

Ker threw back his head and laughed. He knew the power of the world and reveled in its splendor.

He came to an immense city that spread beneath him like an ocean of stone. Through labyrinthine streets wandered men and women dressed in black and gray. All wore white alabaster masks over their faces. Ker watched their movements, drifting lower, lower.

His attention focused on an ancient stone fortress atop a low hill. It formed the heart of the city: streets radiated from it like the spokes of a wheel; merchants hawked their wares around its base.

On the highest battlement stood a figure wrapped in black, watching the people below. Wind whipped at his cloak, tugging back his hood for an instant. Ker saw a gold mask half-hidden beneath it.

Memories returned: *Biur. Liana. The bones.*

The gold-masked wizard they sought.

The man seemed to grow aware of his presence. Turning, he looked up toward Ker.

Again Ker sensed a strange familiarity, as though he knew the wizard, but couldn't quite name him. He'd felt the same haunting half-memory when Zeren had first spun his wheel in Loq's barn.

But that seemed ages earlier, in times far removed. How could he possibly know the wizard? And yet he felt that they *had* met, that he needed to remember *where* and *when*. It seemed more important than ever before.

The wizard pulled back his hood, fully revealing his gold mask, then raised gloved hands to lift it away. But before the mask could be removed, the fortress on the hill faded. Ker's sight grew dark.

He cried out in shock and longing—heard his own voice (so strange in the distance).

He grew aware of silence around him. Gar Galimu's song had stopped, and with it, the stretch of his vision. Something dragged at his thoughts, pulling him up into brightness—

He opened his eyes and found himself inside the house, on Gar Galimu's moss bed. His face tingled. Raising both hands, he felt the stretch of every muscle, the pull of every tendon, the lines of nose and lips and chin.

He could see again.

He stared up at Gar Galimu, wondering what had happened. He remembered the other touching his jaw—then it felt as though his face had been torn off. But surely that couldn't have happened! Galimu was no god!

"I fear I injured you again," Gar Galimu said. "I had no intention of undoing whatever sorcery had been worked upon you."

"I don't remember—what happened?"

"Perhaps it is best if I do not say?"

"Tell me!"

"As you will. Your face was not joined to your head. I accidentally severed the ties holding it in place. I beg your forgiveness—I had no thought of harm!"

"I know that," Ker said quickly. "Your kindness and help are already more than I can ever repay. If it weren't for you, my master would die. That alone is worth more than my life!"

"Does your face feel as it should?" Galimu asked.

Again Ker ran his fingers over it. It felt the same as it always had. Standing, he crossed to the looking glass and studied his reflection, turning his head first to the right, then to the left. It looked the same as ever—as though Derethigon had never taken it. He nodded.

"Please tell me," Gar said, "why this was done to you. I have never seen such magic before."

Ker looked at the floor, ashamed at how he'd lost his face. "When I was younger and more foolish," he said at last, "I challenged Derethigon to an archery contest. When he won and I accused him of cheating, he took my face as his prize. That's how I became apprenticed to Biur—he offered to get my face back if I served him. In time, when Derethigon had grown tired of wearing my face, Biur brought it back to me. It seemed to become part of me when I set it in place—" He stopped, swallowing. "What did you do?"

"Your face was not truly a part of you. Rather than meshing with your body, it had been added on, as a tapestry might be fixed to a stone wall, but never truly a part of it. I have woven its substance back into your flesh; it is truly a part of you and may not be separated again, save by magic like that which took it the first time."

"Then I thank you for that," Ker said. *What would I have done,* he wondered, *if it came off without warning?* He recalled the smothering sensation and shuddered, knowing he would have died.

And then he wondered about the vision he'd had. Hallucination? Some fear-inspired dream? Or had it been a true look across the world at the wizard who'd stolen the bones of Shon Atasha?

Why was he wearing a gold mask?

How could I know him?

"Your friend Liana will soon join us here," Galimu said. "Let us wait for her outside. The afternoon is pleasant; we may still talk of much."

"Will you tell me about the Syrnae?" Ker asked.

"If you wish."

Together, they went outside and sat on the bench again. The day had grown warmer; faint breezes stirred the trees around them. Syrnae stole from the shadows and clustered around them, watching their faces with solemn attention.

Ker managed to put his concerns away for a time. He'd done everything he could for Biur and Liana—it was up to Gar Galimu now.

"What do you wish to know of my friends?" Galimu asked.

"You said they were shape shifters—what do they really look like?"

"They are as they are. What is reality but what you see?"

Ker sighed to himself. Now Gar was talking in circles, like Biur. He glanced down at one of the Syrnae, which was slowly fingering the leather straps of his sandals. Then movement caught the corner of his eye. The trees to his left had begun to stir, twisting their roots and wading through the ground as a man wades through water. He realized they were drawing back to form a large trail.

"Is Liana coming that way?" he asked.

"Yes. She will be here in moments. I feel her approaching."

Ker closed his eyes and tried to sense what his host felt. His attention expanded, all his senses reaching beyond his body. He smelled the rich, damp smells of growing things, broke down the scents into plants and animals, most of which he couldn't identify. He heard the whisper of his own breathing; then Galimu's; then even that of the Syrnae around him. He heard the barest rustle of wind in the trees, the ruffle of the Syrnae's fur, the creak of Galimu's bones as he shifted in his seat. Then, in the distance, he heard the soft tread of hooves on dirt—the rub of leather tack—a half-sigh that might have come from Liana.

"I hear it, too!" he said. He sat up straighter, watching the path.

Liana rode into view. She seemed tired, ragged. Dirt smudged her cheeks and forehead and she had dark circles under her eyes. Her long golden hair had become matted and tangled, losing much of its sheen. Even her green robes had frayed from catching on branches.

Ker stood and waved, calling a welcome.

Smiling a bit, Liana urged her horse on. It plodded forward dumbly.

She dismounted, stretched, and smiled at the Syrnae that suddenly clustered around her. Several took the reins from her hand and led the stallion off behind the house—to the stables, Ker guessed.

Liana curtsied to Gar Galimu.

"Please," he said to her, "you are tired. I know why you and Ker have come. I already sent for Biur and he will soon be brought here. Until then, rest; my home is yours."

"Thank you, Gar Galimu," she said. "Do you remember when last we met?"

"I have met many Winds, but never one in human guise."

"It was many years ago. You were like an uncle to me. My sisters and I played with you in the trees—you called me Tessele."

Galimu's dark face broke in a smile. The skin around his eyes crinkled. "Yes, I remember Tessele!" He laughed. "How the gods have changed you, my little Wind!"

"All things change in time," she said. "Even you look older."

"I am," he said sadly. "I have grown tired and clumsy, as Ker will tell you. When I tried to play with him, as I once played with other bold young men from the Summer Kingdoms, I nearly killed him. Alas! It is too true."

"All the world has come to bad times," Liana said. "He told you of our quest for the bones?"

Gravely, Galimu nodded. "Yes, a terrible story, indeed. Ah, Tessele, what problems have come to our world! Tell me again what happened. I must consider everything carefully."

Liana told him then of all that had happened to them over the last few days, faltering only when she came to the part about her horses. Ker too felt the shock and horror of their deaths again. But Liana finished the tale quickly, then looked up at Galimu's face as if searching for reassurance.

Gar slowly rocked back and forth, deep in thought. His brow furrowed. At last he sighed.

"Yes," he said. "I share all your pain. Indeed, this theft may be the worst thing to happen to our world in many centuries."

Ker studied the ground in silence. He felt a quick stab of fear and uneasy apprehension. This was the adventure he'd always longed for—but now he wondered if he really wanted a part in it. How could he ever help Biur defeat a wizard and his demons? He had enough trouble learning even the simplest magic.

Liana rose. "I must rest," she said, "or I'll be of no use to anyone."

Galimu nodded to the door. "A soft bed waits for you within. I will call you when Biur arrives."

"Thank you," she said, and left them.

Gar turned to Ker and spoke softly, gently: "Something troubles you. Will you tell me what it is?"

He looked up at Galimu's face. "I'm not sure what to say. I feel so useless to Biur!"

"There is no such thing as a useless man. From what you told me, I see that you helped him in many ways."

"But I know so little." He had trouble keeping the bitterness from his voice. "I can't use magic, can't help Biur or Zeren fight demons—can't do anything. I don't even know what a Wind is!"

Gar Galimu only smiled. "A Wind is just that—a being made out of air, such as Liana. A god has given her a mortal's body; there is no great secret."

"And magic? Is there no great secret to that?"

"Of course not. Has your master told you nothing?"

"Hints, just hints, and never anything more. I can see magic around me, trace its patterns, but . . ." He shrugged helplessly. "I'm just supposed to watch."

"Perhaps he has not had enough time?"

Ker thought of the rush of their journey and reluctantly agreed. "Biur always seems in such a hurry, he never has time to stop and explain even the simplest things, like how magic works, or how to open a Gateway—anything."

"I will tell you of magic," Gar Galimu said, "for it is the essence of the world. Listen well: this is a lesson which all men should know.

"Everything around you—the trees, the animals, the sky, and the earth—all this is bound together by the lingering power of Shonora Anasith's will, which created them. To most beings this force is invisible. Others, such as myself, such as my beloved Syrnae, such as your master Biur, and now you, can see it. Our wills are strong. We are the gifted ones of our world. We can reach out with our minds and turn the Earth-bound strength of Shonora Anasith to our own uses. I see that the embers of your mind already flare with such a power; you too could manipulate the forces of the world, if you truly wished. When you do, you will know what it is to wield magic."

"But what can I do until I learn?"

"Learn? What is there to learn, except form and custom? If you saw a pebble and wanted to move it, would you study engineering for ten years to work out the problem?"

Ker laughed. "No, of course not!"

"What would you do?"

"Pick it up and move it."

"Magic is the same. There are forms and customs to which your talent must be bound. These are a matter of learning; the ability to use magic is not, for it is already within you. Biur, as your master, must force discipline on you, force you to use your power wisely and sparingly. As you know, magic takes its price from those who use it."

"Like Biur getting old."

"Exactly. I have heard of men using up their whole life's energy in a second by trying impossibly huge feats of magic, like lifting mountain ranges into the sky, or ripping islands from the bottom of the sea. They were fools. But learn from them, for even fools can be teachers."

"You're saying I can make my own magic?"

"Magic is not created; it is always there. Magic is the power to manipulate the world around you to your own designs."

"But I could use it . . . *now*, if I wanted to?"

"Of course."

Ker felt his heart beating fast and hard. "I want to try it, then. *Now.* Will you help me?"

Gar Galimu smiled. "If that is what you wish."

"It is!"

"What would you like me to do?"

"A—a Gateway, like Biur opened. I want to open one, too."

"Ah? And where to?"

Ker looked around and finally pointed to the other side of the clearing. "There."

"You should have no trouble. Go ahead."

"Just like that? Shouldn't I . . . do *something* first?"

"If you wish. What did you want to do?"

"I need you to tell me!"

"No, you do not."

Ker sighed. It seemed Galimu wasn't going to be much help. Turning, he looked across the clearing. It seemed far away now, impossibly far. How could he possibly open a Gateway?

"Well?" Gar Galimu said. "Proceed. Stretch out your hand, that you may better feel the magic."

Ker blushed and did what Galimu told him. He let his sight slip into the blue and, sure enough, the air in front of him took on an oily quality, as though he looked through hazy water.

Tiny sparks and streamers of deep azure swam before him. Focusing his gaze, Ker imagined their joining together, moving, forming into a huge dark rectangle.

As he concentrated, he saw them slowly begin to drift together, gathering up into a huge misshapen disk in the middle of the air.

Distantly he heard Galimu say, "See? You can do it. Now: shape it into the form you want."

Ker's arms felt like deadweight. He forced his right hand up, felt the power gathering within him. Mentally reaching forward, he tried to bring the blue into an even shape, form sides, straighten them out. A stream of blue electricity shot from his fingertips, forcing the Gateway into a skewed, almost square shape.

Then he imagined the Gateway opening, and darkness rose before him. He thought of the far side of the clearing, picturing it perfectly in his mind, and the darkness seemed to open up—and he was there.

He relaxed and pulled back. Blinking, he found himself back in his own body again, standing before his crooked Gateway. He felt a deep sense of satisfaction, of accomplishment, and grinned to himself. This was what he'd always longed to be able to do.

As the Gateway's matte black surface rippled like taut canvas in the wind, he felt an icy cold radiating from its heart. The Gateway collapsed a second later.

"I did it!" Ker said. He sat heavily, feeling drained, as though he'd just sprinted a mile. His breath came in gasps. Now he knew how Biur felt after opening a Gateway: exhausted, ready for ten long hours of sleep. "I did it!" he said again, more softly.

Gar Galimu smiled. "It will become easier after you've done it several times, and after you make yourself a wand."

"A wand?"

"It will focus the energy you use to open the gateway, much as a channel will guide the course of a river. It is much more precise, much more efficient, than using just your hands . . . and I have heard several wizards say it makes them look more accomplished and skillful."

"It worked. It's almost too much to believe," Ker said. The truth of it all had only just begun to reach him. He felt as happy as he'd ever been in his life. "Now I'll finally be able to help Biur and Zeren!"

"Haven't you been?"

"They could have done just as well without me."

"Had you not warned them, they would all be dead in Rhimalga now."

"But that was just an accident—"

Galimu laughed. "*No.* You are noble-born; they are not. Your experiences as a noble told you of the wrongness of the place. They didn't feel the things you did. It was your unique knowledge that saved them, as they may someday save you. Have you not wondered that Biur, Liana, Zeren, and you are so different, and yet so much alike? Your talents complement one another. Even I can see that you have all been selected by the gods."

"What?" Ker cried. "How can that be? Biur said the gods wouldn't interfere—that's why Derethigon sent Biur rather than go himself!"

"Yes. Derethigon *selected* Biur for the mission—just as he selected you, Liana, and Zeren, whether they know it or not."

Ker sat in silence. It all made sense now—why the Oracle had sent him to seek Derethigon's ruby, why the god had taken his face, then told Biur to give it back . . . it had all been arranged!

"And is the end of our quest already decided?" he wondered aloud, suddenly bitter. "Is everything we've done so far just some game to amuse the gods? How can we do anything that matters?"

Gar touched his arm. "Do not think such things. Only my master Shonora Anasith knows the future. The gods have no knowledge beyond the present . . . they may well fear the theft of the bones and the destruction that may follow. For a thousand years have they slipped apart from humanity. For a thousand years have they drifted through time like feathers on a lake. That they even bothered to wake from their torpor to arrange your mission is enough to cause me grave concern."

"Then nothing is certain?" Ker asked.

"Nothing, save the gods are now afraid."

Ker shivered. The gods afraid? He thought of Derethigon and the other god he'd stumbled across in Theshemna. They had such power! *And the thing that could make them afraid* . . .

Gar Galimu gave him no more time to think about it. "Here is your master," he said.

Ker looked up and noticed that the wide path to the house had grown full of Syrnae. They carried Biur on a stretcher of tree boughs and moss. Behind them, riding one black stallion and leading another, followed Zeren. The Rashendi looked exhausted, sagging in his saddle.

Ker stood, watching his master's pale, haggard face as they bore him into the house. Galimu followed them, then stopped and turned to Ker.

"You must wait out here," he said. Then he entered his house and pulled the granite door shut with a grating sound.

Most of the Syrnae drifted off into the woods, disappearing into the shadows. The remaining few helped Zeren dismount, then led the horses off in the same direction they'd taken Liana's mount.

The Rashendi noticed Ker and hurried to join him. "What's going on here?" he demanded. "Where is this Gar Galimu?"

"He took Biur into the house."

"Those little animals came out of nowhere," he said. "They swarmed over Biur and I thought they were trying to kill him! When I drew my knife, they jumped on me and took it away. Then, without a word, they lifted Biur onto that stretcher and carried him off. They would've left me there if I hadn't ridden after them!"

"I'm afraid it's my fault," Ker said. "I forgot to tell Gar Galimu that you were there, too."

"Thanks," Zeren grumbled. He glanced around at the trees, then the house. The forest had grown quiet. "At least I'll be able to get a peaceful night's sleep." Going to the bench by the door, he lay down. Within seconds he was snoring softly.

* * *

Hours passed and the dim green light grew faint. Night fell. Soft patters and rustles came from the forest around them, but Zeren still slept, his cape drawn tightly around his shoulders.

Ker found himself pacing. He jumped at every strange noise. He had too much nervous energy to sleep, and he felt completely rested anyway—whatever magic Galimu had used to heal him had left him completely refreshed, though he had no idea how long the feeling would last.

At last he went to the nearest tree and sat with his back to its trunk, staring at Galimu's house. Blue fires flickered around the door and through small gaps in the roof, casting a pale glow through the air.

He heard a low voice whisper: *"Man."*

Slowly Ker turned his head. Slitted cat-eyes peered from the shadows where Syrnae crouched.

"You can speak!"

"When we choose to." The shadows seemed to riffle and change; an indistinct shape emerged, roughly man-sized. A light-skinned, human hand stretched out to touch his wrist. "I am named Kalan."

"I'm Ker."

"We will talk with you now."

"Who—the Syrnae? All of you?"

"Yes. Come with me?"

Ker rose. "Let me tell Zeren."

"He sleeps. You will return before he wakes."

He hesitated. "Very well."

"Come." The Syrnae took his hand and led him toward a winding trail that had appeared behind them.

They walked in silence. The forest had grown quiet; even the night birds no longer sang. At last the trees fell away to either side and Ker stood in a small clearing. Thick, ankle-high grass glistened with dew. Bright stars studded the velvet sky, providing enough light for him to see clearly.

Hundreds of Syrnae gathered there, a sea of dark bodies and gleaming eyes. They moved back, making a path for him. Kalan pulled him forward into the center of the group.

The two of them stood there, taller than all the Syrnae. An immense circle formed around them. Ker shifted uneasily as a thousand eyes studied his every movement.

"Why did you bring me?" he asked.

"Man," said Kalan, "we have studied your gods. We too are

children of Shon Atasha. In the night, when our dreams rise above the land, ofttimes we watch the future. It is a mist through which events break like sun through clouds. This night we have seen our deaths."

"No!"

"It is true; we have seen it."

"Perhaps you were wrong." Ker began.

Kalan shook his head. His body shimmered and began to change back into that of an animal. Abruptly he became a man again, as though his thoughts had come to a focus. "The sides were drawn before your birth. Many generations have looked to the coming battle. There is nothing that can be done."

"Kalan—"

"You are our doom and salvation. We know you, Ker Orrum, and we lay this geas on you: you will return here before you die, and when you come, you will bring those who will follow after us."

Ker didn't know what to say or do. A coming battle? The death of the Syrnae? Those who would follow after them?

"You must promise," Kalan said. "Swear you will do this one thing for all our kind. Swear it for our master, Gar Galimu. When we are gone, others must serve his needs."

"I promise," Ker whispered. "If it's in my power—and if what you have said comes to pass—then I will return here and do whatever needs to be done."

"We thank you," Kalan said. Then his face and body seemed to melt and flow like hot wax, shrinking, re-forming into that of a Syrnae. Slitted cat-eyes searched Ker's face for a long second before turning away.

The creatures slipped into the forest, leaving Ker alone. He blinked and they had gone. Wind whistled through the trees.

Following the path back to Gar Galimu's house, he thought of all the Syrnae had said. *A coming battle . . . generations . . . death . . .*

They could see into the future, but—like Shon Atasha—they revealed only what served their purposes. *A geas . . .*

He shook his head, bewildered. How could he be that important to them? Surely they'd mistaken him for someone else! Perhaps they'd wanted Biur or Zeren—

Finding himself at the trail's end, he noticed at once that Gar Galimu's house no longer flickered with the blue fires of magic. The air had taken on an odd stillness, a crystalline calm like that of a lake before a storm. Something had happened, he knew at once.

He watched. Nothing moved for a long time. Zeren still lay on his bench, oblivious to the world. The Syrnae had vanished.

Then the granite door began to open.

15

The Gates of Zelloque

Who has not heard of Zelloque, the greatest city in all the world? The poets describe it better than I; I will say no more than that it is the center of civilization, where anything can be had for a price, where everyone who is anyone lives, where all the marvels of the universe can be seen or heard or felt.

—Pere Denberel
Atlas of the Known Lands, Revised

Gar Galimu led Biur to the doorway. They stood there for a second, silhouetted against the lights inside the house, one figure tall and strong, the other old and bent.

Ker ran forward. When he got close enough to see Biur, he stopped and stared in shock.

A web of fine wrinkles covered his master's tired face; Biur seemed to have aged many, many years since the day before. His hair, now brushed back over his head, had thinned and silvered; his cheekbones now protruded sharply in his gaunt face, and dark circles surrounded his deep-sunken eyes. But Biur still moved with the same quick grace, still smiled with the same cheerfulness that had made him seem so vital only a day before. And as he stretched, he no longer seemed quite so feeble. His movements were still strong, certain.

Biur laughed. "Ker, if you could see your face . . ."

Ker shut his mouth with a snap and quickly bowed his head. "I'm g-glad you're all r-right!" he managed to stammer. He felt strange inside, shocked and disoriented. His stomach twisted itself into knots.

Biur had been young and strong a day before; now he'd become an old man, drained of life. *Will this happen to me?* Ker's hands were cold. He couldn't meet Biur's steady gaze and felt ashamed because of it. He blushed.

"Have I changed so much?"

Not knowing what to say, he only nodded.

"Such is life. I have but one thing to tell you—one lesson, if you wish to call it that."

Ker looked up.

"Do not judge by my appearance. When you first met me, you thought I was an old man. Now again I seem so. *Or do I?*" He straightened, suddenly, and covered his face with one hand. Softly he whispered. When he drew his hand away, he had become young again, his face smooth, his skin unlined.

Ker gasped. "You're—"

Then in the blink of an eye the magic faded and Biur was old again. Biur smiled faintly. "I am as I am. To change my face is not to change my nature. I could alter my looks if I wished; I do not choose that vanity. You will understand when you are older." He shook his head. "Too much time has already been lost for such talk." Turning to Galimu, he said, "I thank you for your help, sir. The gods will surely reward you."

"I serve only Shonora Anasith, as you know. That is the only blessing I need; to help you is to help my true master."

Liana joined them. "We will leave, then?"

"With your permission," Biur said to Galimu.

"Of course. I will summon your horses." Taking a small wooden horn from a peg near the door, he raised it to his lips and blew a long, loud note.

As the horn's sound slowly faded, another, more distant horn sounded in reply. The noise awakened Zeren. Seeing them by the door, the Rashendi hurried to join them, running fingers through his hair and brushing imaginary dust from his clothes. He too stared at Biur, Ker noticed. But he only nodded to himself, as if he'd expected the change.

In seconds four Syrnae led their mounts around the side of the house. The horses had been groomed until they almost shone, with plaited manes and tails, clipped and polished hooves, and neatly brushed coats. New packs had been tied in place behind the saddles: trail provisions and fresh bedding, Ker guessed. The horses seemed well rested; they moved quickly, prancing, eager to start.

"All has been set for your journey," Galimu said. He motioned with his hand and the Syrnae scurried back into the forest. "May Shonora Anasith speed your mission."

Ker found the horse he'd ridden the night before. As he stroked the stallion's neck, he forgave his steed for bolting the day before, when Galimu first appeared in the clearing. The others mounted, and he did the same.

Without further farewells, Biur clicked to his stallion and started into the forest at a trot. The trees pulled back in front of him, leaving a wide path. Liana and Zeren followed.

Ker hesitated a moment. "Good-bye," he called to Galimu. "Thanks again for everything."

"You will return here soon enough," Galimu said. "This is not meant to be our final meeting." Humming to himself, he went back into his house and pulled the door shut.

Puzzled, Ker stared after him for a second, then wheeled his horse around and galloped after the others. He caught up and rode behind Zeren. The Syrnae and Galimu both had told him he'd return. How could they know?

The spirit of Shon Atasha burns in them, like in the Oracles. Like in Zeren.

He brooded on their words, trying to find some hidden meaning. Nothing made sense! Either the gods *had* been directing them, in which case everything they'd done had no meaning; or they'd been on their own, which meant they could be trying to save the world from an evil wizard and his demon army. Who was right? Gar Galimu or Biur? *Could* the gods have arranged everything that had happened, like some mad game? *Would* Derethigon have let Biur die? Would Derethigon have let *him* die?

The idea made him uneasy. He didn't want to think about it. He *wouldn't* think about it, he vowed. At least, not until he knew more.

The path through the trees led straight to the black highway. Biur didn't pause for a second's breath. Hooves clattering on the paving stones, his horse headed back toward Rhimalga at a gallop.

The night wore on. Biur kept them at a rigid pace: five minutes running, ten minutes walking, then another five minutes running. The horses sweated; foam ran down their sides. Ker ground his teeth and forced his mount on, even when it stumbled from weariness. He refused to be left behind. His muscles ached, but he clung to the reins and silently cursed the wizard they sought: for Liana's horses, for Biur's transformation, for the destruction of Loq's farm. He would have his revenge! And, like a powerful drug, his anger and hatred pushed him onward.

The forest fell away around them. Hills rose. Sheep clustered on some, gray shapes in the darkness; on others stood the tumbled-down ruins of shepherds' huts. Still the road ran straight before them. Still they rode on. Overhead, stars began to pale; a faint glow appeared to the east, marking the coming sun.

A sea of shadowy whites and grays suddenly appeared before them, washing across the road. They had reached the desert that had once been Rhimalga. Wind had drifted the sand into huge dunes and gullies, completely covering the black stone highway. Not a brick remained to mark the city's passing.

Biur raised his hand, signaling a halt. "We will rest here," he called.

Dismounting, he hobbled his horse, then wandered on alone. Sand crunched under his feet. At last he stopped and slowly turned in a circle, studying the destruction he'd wrought. He sighed and knelt, scooping up a handful of sand, letting the tiny grains trickle through his fingers. His hands balled into fists, hit the dunes, pressed flat against the ground in anger and frustration. He wept quietly for a time, alone.

At last Ker moved to join him. "Is something wrong?" he asked. "What can I do?"

His master said nothing for a long moment, looking out across the desert. Ker saw pain etched deep in his face. "Think of the people who died here because we were too slow to arrive. Because *I* was too blind to see the demons. All that remains is desolation. Who will remember the people now? Who will know of my failure here? *Nobody!*" He spat the words. "*Nobody!* We are callous creatures, we humans."

"Biur . . ."

Biur looked up, as if noticing Ker for the first time. "We've lost too much time to stay here long. First a day at Loq's farm, then another in Rhimalga and Galimu's forest. I fear we have given this wizard time to create more problems for us. He must surely be far ahead by now, perhaps far enough so we won't catch up until he reaches Zelloque."

Zelloque, the greatest city in the world.

Suddenly Ker remembered his dream in Galimu's house, remembered seeing the gold-masked wizard standing atop a fortress battlement. Could that place have been Zelloque? He felt the excitement and apprehension growing within him.

Quickly he told Biur what he'd dreamed, describing the immense city with its white domes, golden spires and large, straight streets that radiated from the fortress at its center. He told of the long, dark piers stretching into the harbor, told of the ships moored there, told of the gray clouds and the threatening storm and everything else he'd noticed.

Biur frowned. "That *does* sound like Zelloque," he said. "But why would *you* dream of the wizard?"

"Gar made me drink something before he healed my arm—"

"What do you mean, healed your arm?"

"Didn't he tell you?"

"No. What happened?"

Ker told him of all that occurred after he and Liana entered the forest.

"No wonder they say he is mad . . . but that still leaves my question. Healing draft or no, why did *you* dream of the wizard? Why not Zeren, instead?"

Ker shrugged. "Does it matter?" he asked. "How can we know whether the wizard is there *now?* How much farther is Zelloque?"

"If he did not stop," Biur said, "he would be in Zelloque now. We must ask Zeren; he will know whether you looked upon the present or the future. All Rashendi deal with dream and reality." He turned back toward the others. "Come."

Liana had led the horses off the road and begun rubbing them down with soft cloths from the saddlebags, as if trying to lose her thoughts in labor. The desert, Ker guessed, reminded her of Rhimalga, of how her horses had been butchered by the demons. As she worked, the four stallions browsed on thick green grass. Zeren had stretched out just beyond them, beneath a low tree. Eyes closed, he appeared asleep.

Biur walked over and sat beside the Rashendi, shaking him awake. Zeren blinked and stared blearily up at him.

"What is it?" he asked. "Time to leave?"

"Ker, tell him what you told me."

Again Ker related his dream of the city.

"Well?" Biur asked, as Zeren sat quietly, lost in thought. "Did he see the present or the future?"

"A possible future, I think," he said. "It's difficult to tell. There was a storm . . . and you can see no clouds in the sky now. Zelloque is not so far away. And all the people wore masks, going about their normal business as they did in Rhimalga. Stealing a hundred thousand faces would surely take more than a day, even for an army!"

"Then we must hurry," Biur said. "If Zelloque *is* the wizard's destination, I will open a Gateway to bring us there."

"But won't the wizard know?" Ker asked. "You said—"

"I know what I said. Too much time has been lost for such caution; I thought, at first, that we would catch the wizard on the road. Now that seems impossible. I will open a Gateway beyond Zelloque, near the end of the Insel Sea, and we will ride back to the city. If all goes well, and this time it *must*, the wizard will not notice magic that far away, or will ignore it."

"A good plan," Zeren said, "*if* it works. Nothing has yet."

"Accidents and chance," Biur said. "Things could have gone better; so too could they have gone worse. We all might have died in Rhimalga."

"Or lightning could've struck us, or the ground could've opened up and swallowed us," the Rashendi said harshly. "*If* such were Shon Atasha's will. Your plans have been poor, with little thought ahead."

Biur said nothing. At last he nodded curtly. "I know little of such things, it is true. But we must look to the future, not the past."

"What if the demons took over more towns?" Ker asked. "Shouldn't we find them first, before going to Zelloque?"

"Once we find the wizard no more towns will be ravaged," Biur said. "I believe, however, that the wizard was merely testing his power at Loq's farm. And the demons in Rhimalga were meant to stop anyone from following his trail. He will not waste his time and strength needlessly. Whatever plans he has for the bones will doubtless require much of his power."

"But there's no way to be sure," Zeren said. "For all we know he may be destroying every town through which he passes. Few men outside the Rashendi see the future clearly . . . or even the present. *You* can't know what this thief has done, *can* you?"

Biur made no reply. Standing, he walked over and joined Liana by the horses. Ker sat and watched him go.

Zeren snorted. "Wizards!"

After resting for a short time, Ker, Liana, and Zeren mounted their horses. Biur stood in front of them, his wand held straight out. Ker watched him carefully, trying to learn every movement, every gesture. Tracing a quick pattern in the air, Biur began to sing in a low voice.

The world grew dark around him. Electricity ghosted over his body. The hills around them flickered with light; the road's jet black stones took on an oily sheen; the air grew misted and thick. Biur raised his wand and a crackling stream of blue fire leaped from his arm in a low arc, then rose up in a roaring wall of flames. Slowly they faded, revealing a matte black Gateway fifteen feet high and five feet wide.

Its surface rippled slightly as Ker watched. Again he felt the cold that seemed to ooze from the Gateway's depths, felt a disjointed sense of falling when he looked straight into it.

Liana rode through first, followed a second later by Zeren. Glancing back over his shoulder, Ker saw his master swing up onto his horse. Then Ker turned to face the Gateway and spurred his own steed forward.

The stallion ran straight for the Gateway, gathered itself, and leaped. Darkness washed over Ker, then the familiar brilliant white light blinded him. As cold ripped through his nose and into his lungs, he gasped for breath. Then suddenly, it was as though he'd completely stepped into the netherworld, and for the first time he had no trouble seeing, no trouble breathing. The place had odd, disturbing dimensions; the air seemed unnaturally thick and heavy, as though he looked out through thick glass or deep, clear water. A white, tunnellike passage stretched far ahead of him.

Liana already rode far ahead, with Zeren some twenty feet behind. Kicking his horse when it faltered and tried to turn back, Ker followed. Icy walls slipped past to either side; the air grew colder. Plumes of misted breath streamed from his horse's nose and mouth.

At the end of the passage stood a large blue-black Gateway. They plunged through, into burning air.

Ker shivered and blinked rapidly, rubbing his eyes. His horse had stopped. They were on a rocky beach, he saw; the sea lapped almost at their feet. Liana and Zeren had already dismounted; only Biur had yet to arrive.

Twisting around in the saddle, Ker looked back at the Gateway. Its surface shimmered ever so faintly. Biur appeared through it, then it folded into itself with a soft, whispering sound.

Ker turned his attention back to the waves. He'd never seen the sea before, never seen any body of water larger than a small lake. The tales he'd heard as a boy in Vichir hadn't prepared him for the sight of mile after mile of water, stretching almost as far as he could see.

Dawn broke over the long, dark chain of mountains lying across the sea, sending wavelets running with pink and gold and silver. Far out over the water, he noticed the triangular white and blue sails of ships. The air held the sharp tang of salt and seaweed.

He turned. The beach sloped upward and he couldn't see what lay beyond. Spurring his horse, he rode toward the top of the incline, pushing through high tangles of yellow-green marsh grass and brown, thorny weeds. When he reached the crest, he stood there for a moment, just looking at the lands below. A vast plain—larger than any he'd seen before, larger than he'd imagined existed in the world—stretched away from him, running mile after mile after mile until it finally ended with verdant green foothills and smoke-colored mountains far in the distance. To his right, even farther away, he saw the sparkling curve of the blue-green sea as it continued; and to his left lay a hazy smudge on the horizon. The smudge could only be Zelloque.

Most of the plain had been cleared of trees and brush, leaving stretches of open ground that had been divided into a patchwork of small, square plots of land. A single black road cut through the fields, heading right and left.

Scattered stone houses and barns, with their red-tiled roofs and whitewashed walls, broke the monotony of landscape; here and there a small village stood. Men, women, and teams of horses and oxen moved through the fields, all signs of life and normality that reassured him. The wizard and his demons clearly hadn't been here.

"*Ker!*" he heard Biur shout.

He turned his horse and plunged back through the tangle of grass, down to the shore where the others waited.

They headed down the beach toward Zelloque for many hours, the horses moving at their own comfortable pace. The sun rose higher; the day rapidly became uncomfortably hot and sticky. Ker sweated, his tunic sticking to his back, his legs rubbing raw against his horse's sides. Grimacing, he shifted and tried to find a more comfortable position.

Soon they came to a small cove where several fishermen had pulled small, single-masted boats up onto the beach. The stench of seaweed and rotting fish was overpowering, and it made Ker faintly nauseous.

Dozens of large nets had been spread out over the sand. Barefoot old men and boys, dressed in loose cotton shirts and pants, stepped cautiously across the strands, bending now and then to mend breaks or untangle bits of shell and seaweed. Behind them, on a small dirt road, more men stood around a horse-drawn cart. They seemed to be haggling with a merchant over a set of scales as fish were being weighed.

Biur held up his hand. Ker pulled up his stallion beside the others. Dismounting at the wizard's command, they led the horses forward, stopping ten feet from the edge of the nets. An old man limped over. He smiled at them, showing chipped yellow teeth.

"Would ye be wanting fish?" he asked, his accent thick and strange. "If so, talk to the men at the wagon. They'll give ye a good price, not like the mongers in the city."

"We have no need of fish," Biur said. "I serve the god Derethigon. In his name I bid you, tell me the news of Zelloque."

"How would an old man know the city's gossip?"

Biur leaned forward and winked. "Men do not live to be old without making many friends." He glanced over at the fishermen by the cart. "I imagine you know more of Zelloque than any of the others here."

"What news is there?" the old man said, but he grinned more broadly than before. "What news can there be? The gods stay in their palace in the sky; the Great Lord stays in his fortress in the city. No new taxes are being collected. The people still eat fish. All is the same as yesterday; all will be the same tomorrow." He shook his head, as if thinking the answer were obvious, then looked at them slyly. "Why would a servant of a god ask these things?"

"It matters little," Biur said. "I have come on a minor errand with some friends. We thought we might rest a while in the city before returning home, if the place is hospitable to strangers."

"Aye, Zelloque is always known for kindness to travelers. Go, then, and good fortune to ye. Mind the nets, though!"

"We will!"

They rode around the drying nets, the horses skittering back a bit whenever the waves rolled in and splashed across their legs. Ker kept looking out to sea, admiring the trim-sailed ships to which he could put no name. Galleons? Triremes? The stories he'd heard in Vichir mentioned them but briefly.

The horses moved back to dry sand and continued down the beach. As they followed the winding coast, they found more and more small coves and inlets filled with fishermen drying their nets; most of the men and boys cheerfully called a welcome and waved. Ker waved back.

The day grew yet hotter. After stopping once to water the horses and eat a quick meal at a brackish stream, they rode on. The coast never really opened up to show Zelloque ahead, and Ker grew tired, his excitement fading. His eyes hurt from watching the sun shining on the sea.

Then they rounded a turn and Zelloque lay before them.

The walled city lay on the other side of a huge harbor. Dozens of long, dark piers stretched out over the water, and tied up at the pilings were more ships than Ker had thought existed in the world. The piers stretched back to a large open area where thousands of crates and cloth bundles had been piled. Beyond the open area stood rows of enormous brown-brick buildings: warehouses, taverns, offices for city officials. A seemingly endless flood of men and animals loaded and unloaded cargoes, argued, shouted, cursed, or just wandered the streets, adding to the confusion. Even across the water Ker could hear the dull roar of noise.

"Where are they all from?" he asked.

Zeren rode next to him. "All over the world. See? Those ships with the blue and green banners are from Coran, and those two galleons are from Lothaq or Selambique. And those farthest from the shore—yes, the ones with three masts and banks of oars—*those* are mercenaries from Viandas. The Great Lord of Zelloque uses them as his navy. The rest are traders or private ships. And some belong to pirates."

"Pirates?" Ker asked.

"There are always too many of those. They find it easy to sell stolen goods here, where nobody cares where they came from—only that the price is low enough to make a profit. And the Great Lord of Zelloque has made bargains with many of them. They leave his ships alone, and in exchange he lets them into his port without trouble." He sighed. "The world is old and decadent; I can remember the time when the Great Lord's mercenaries pursued pirates across all the civilized lands, driving them like sheep to the slaughter. They say the Great Lord is old and tired and no longer cares. So it is with the world."

After a minute, they continued along the shoreline toward the city. Thousands of small one-man fishing boats had been beached here; miles of gray nets lay spread out upon the sand. The path became impassable without treading on the fisherfolk or their belongings.

Biur wheeled his horse to the right and led the way up over the dune, to the great plain Ker had seen earlier. A broad dirt road ran parallel to the beach. Hundreds of people and strange, exotic beasts traveled it, walking or riding in horse-pulled carts. The people's clothing fascinated Ker, and though he tried not to stare, he couldn't help himself. Most men wore silk shirts and pantaloons like Zeren's, only theirs were brilliantly colored, full of bright reds and electric blues, dazzling sun-yellows and shimmering greens, glowing pinks and vibrant purples. The air rippled with color.

And the animals! Weird beasts of burden with shaggy blue-black fur, huge broad backs, and long, pointed faces, their jaws opening from time to time as they passed, showing long rows of needle-sharp teeth. And there were small, hissing lizards in cages on carts, and there were piglike animals with large cow eyes, and chickens and goats and sheep and all the other animals familiar to him.

As his horse wove in and out of the crowd, following the others, Ker found his heart pounding faster and faster. *Zelloque.* He'd longed all his life to travel to the Eastern lands, to visit the great cities and see all the places of legend, and now he was finally here.

The city's immense outer wall grew nearer. Beyond it he could see the tops of buildings, several standing at least a hundred feet high. Domes of gold and silver capped the tallest of the buildings, and where the sun gleamed off them, the whole city seemed alight with hot white flames.

They passed tall, eight-legged, spiderlike beasts with black chitinous skins and multifaceted eyes; they passed a group of wagons pulled by giant tawny-furred creatures that reminded Ker of cats, with their slitted amber eyes, except for their triple-jointed legs. They passed long caravans of traders from distant lands, fishmongers from along the coast, merchants and seamen, nobles and peasants.

Then they reached the great wall. Ker leaned back and looked up at the battlements, where soldiers dressed richly in red and black silk and leather patrolled. The wall itself had been built of ten-foot-thick blocks of granite, forming an almost impenetrable barrier.

A gate appeared ahead. Its twenty-foot doors had been pulled open, allowing people to enter. Twenty soldiers, splendid in polished black leather armor, flowing red capes, and red-plumed helms, stood in lines to either side of the huge oak doors, watching everyone who passed.

Then the soldiers looked in their direction and tensed. Several reached toward their swords.

Ker kicked his horse and caught up with Biur. "Turn back!" he whispered urgently. "They're going to stop us!"

"They will let us by."

A lieutenant with his gold-inlaid helmet and intricate silver breastplate to mark his rank, motioned to a couple of his men.

Stepping forward, one seized the bridle of Biur's horse as the wizard passed, halting him. Another stopped Zeren.

Ker glanced over at Liana. She continued on through the gate as if nothing had happened. What was going on? Why would the city guard stop them? He bit his lip, then reined in his horse and stayed next to Biur.

His master smiled reassuringly. "This is but a formality."

"You will come with us," the lieutenant said in a loud voice. Turning, he strode through the gate, red cape fluttering out behind him. The soldiers pulled Zeren and Biur's horses along, taking no notice of Ker.

Four more soldiers, swords drawn, fell in step behind them.

16

The Great Lord's Festival

> The laws of Zelloque have long been known for their fairness. The Great Lord will execute just about anyone.
>
> —Uli Dorbant, before his execution

A wild festival was in progress. Thousands of men and women filled the streets with an endless parade of colorful costumes, some wrapped in ankle-length robes of shell-encrusted silk, some wearing ivory masks over their faces, some dressed in bizarre animal pelts, with great claws of carved white bone strapped to their hands. Others just wore their brightest and their best. Merchants hawked wares on corners; booths containing games of chance and skill had been set up in the middle of the street; people played and laughed and danced to the music of wandering minstrels. Children ran and barking dogs followed. Crowds pressed around them.

"Make way!" the lieutenant shouted. "Make way!"

Reluctantly, it seemed, the people shifted, leaving them a narrow corridor next to the great wall.

The guards brought them forward to a door set deep in the wall. No windows looked out; Ker couldn't tell if the entrance led to a single room or a whole hidden building. Zeren and Biur dismounted, so he did the same.

Still puzzled, but no longer quite so apprehensive, he studied everything and everyone around him. The guards looked almost as bored as Zeren. Biur had said this was just a formality—but why would they separate the people able to use magic from the rest of the men and women entering the city? And why hadn't they stopped Liana?

"This way," the lieutenant said. Taking an enormous iron key from the chain at his belt, he unlocked the door and pushed it open, its huge iron hinges squealing in protest.

They followed him into a small, dark room. Water had seeped up through the stones in the floor, forming small puddles, and the air reeked of mildew and rotting wood. Ker guessed few people used this room.

The guards lit a tiny oil lamp and set it in a niche high in one corner. It burned smokily, filling the room with a hazy glow. A wooden table loaded with books, papers, and various small objects Ker couldn't identify sat against the far wall, along with several straight-backed chairs.

The lieutenant flung his cape out behind him, then sat behind the desk and opened the huge leather-bound book that lay there. Taking up a quill pen, he dipped its point into a jar of ink and looked up expectantly. "Names?"

"I am Zeren Kentas," Zeren said, "of the Rashendi."

Nodding, the man wrote it down.

"And I am Biur."

"What about the other?" the lieutenant asked, looking at Ker.

"He is my apprentice," Biur said. "He knows little of magic yet."

"I see that. The gods have blessed me with one small talent myself—that of recognizing men who use magic."

He doesn't look like a wizard, Ker thought, letting his vision slip into the blue that showed him magic. The chamber leaped to brilliant life—fine azure lines ghosting over Biur and Zeren and even him, sparks flickering across the paving stones at their feet, traces of cyan lingering on several scrolls on the desk . . . but as for the lieutenant, nothing!

"A useful talent, in this city," Zeren said a bit sourly, "but surely such things are no longer necessary. I know of no other place that inconveniences travelers so."

"Yes." The man nodded as he wrote. "But as they say, when all things are seen, it is best to be honest. The Great Lord values honesty in all people. And still, it's best to know who's in the city. History has shown that—"

"Do your duties now include lecturing travelers?" Zeren demanded.

The lieutenant frowned, growing silent.

Biur said quickly, "There is a festival outside—what does it mark? The fishermen we spoke to said nothing of it."

"The Great Lord declared a holiday this morning in honor of

Suthyran, his new counselor. It's the first public festival in nearly a month. Tonight the Great Lord has promised to slaughter a hundred of his best oxen, so there will be free meat for anyone who comes to the palace gates. Later, troupes of performers will play in all the squares. This will be a night to remember!"

"Indeed," Zeren said. "*If* ever we get out of this room. It stinks in here!"

"But before you join the revelers, I must ask what business you have in the city."

"We have come to visit a friend of mine," Biur said.

"Good, good." He wrote that down, too. "You won't be doing any trading?"

"No."

"Very well. You may go; there are no further questions. Enjoy the festival, Biur . . . and may the gods favor you and your friend."

Zeren pushed past the guards.

As they led their horses past the booths selling food, the crowds grew thicker, closing in around them once more. Ker smelled roasting meat and newly baked breads, saw people nibbling sugary candies and sweet, ripe fruits of all description. People clustered thickly around the booths. He caught up with Biur.

"The lieutenant," he began.

"Yes, I saw. He lied to us; the gods have not blessed him with anything, other than a sharp wit and a quick tongue."

"I don't understand. Why would he lie?"

"In Zelloque, the people fear all magic and are suspicious of all wizards. Which city guard would be most noticed? Which would be made an officer? The one who can see magic, but cannot use it himself. He should never have told us. He must have grown old and lazy in his job . . . perhaps he even believes in his talent now. It is no matter and no concern of ours." He paused, glancing at the crowds. "Mount up. We will make faster progress if we ride."

Ker did. They continued in silence for a time.

The music around them grew louder. Men and women dressed in green and red silks fluttered past, hands linked in some intricate dance. Biur and Zeren had begun to get ahead of him, so Ker touched his heels to his horse's sides and tried to catch up. His master glanced back at one point and called something, but Ker didn't catch the words.

A lady wrapped in coil after coil of yellow snakeskin pranced under his horse's nose, and his stallion shied back, plunging to the left, through a sudden gap between dancing people.

Ker pulled firmly on the horse's reins, but the animal refused to obey, throwing its head forward and trying to jerk free from his hands. It darted between two booths selling vegetables and circled around, emerging on the other side of the street—and trotted in the opposite direction of Biur and Zeren. Laughing children scattered before them.

Reaching the end of the street, the horse stopped abruptly. It glanced first to the left, then the right, hesitated for an instant, then plunged down a dark, garbage-filled alley, leaving the noise and bustle of the festival behind. Then they turned a corner and faced a brick wall thirty feet ahead.

The stallion halted. Ker swung from the saddle and seized the halter, swinging his horse's head down. He looked at its eyes. They were dark and seemed to shine in the dim light, as though made of black glass.

"What's the matter with you?" he demanded. "Have you gone mad?"

He felt a sharp, tingling sensation, then the horse's coat rippled and flowed like water beneath his hand, twisting in upon itself. In the shadows of the alley, darkness writhed.

Ker dropped the reins and backed away, crying out in shock and fear. No one heard him. He turned to run, but stopped at the corner, looking back, sensing something familiar in the transformation. Rather than repel him, the sight drew him closer. He felt a thickening of the air, smelled ozone—

The stallion's body grew smaller, its shape more certain in the dimness. Distinct lines appeared—and suddenly a small, dark-haired man stood before him, dressed all in dark, leathery clothes that rustled like windblown leaves when he moved. His face was rounded, resembling a cat's. The saddle and packs now lay on the refuse at his feet.

"*Kalan?*" he asked slowly.

"Yes, man." The Syrnae walked toward the mouth of the alley, paused for a second, sniffed the air. His nose wrinkled at the decaying fruits and vegetables piled high around them. "Let us leave this place."

"What happened to my horse?" Ker demanded.

"It still rests with Gar Galimu."

"But—he would've told me if you were coming!"

"I did not tell him. I chose this task for myself."

"But what am *I* supposed to do now? I haven't got the money to buy another horse!"

"Money?" Kalan asked. "Your words are strange to me."

Exasperated and angry, Ker didn't know what to do. He stared at Kalan in frustration. "You should've stayed in the forest," he said bitterly, "or told me you were coming. Now I've lost the others, haven't got a horse to carry all this"—he kicked at the saddle and pack—"and *you're* here."

"Forgive me," Kalan said. "I meant no harm—only to help you."

Ker picked up the saddlebags and the pack containing his blanket. He thrust them into the Syrnae's arms. "Carry these," he said. Then he picked up the saddle and slung it over his shoulder, shifting the weight until he found a comfortable position.

Then he stopped and dropped the saddle heavily. "Why don't you think first, Ker?" he muttered to himself. "Kalan?"

"Yes, Ker?"

"I'm sorry, but . . . well, why didn't you *tell* me you wanted to come?"

"I will help you find the bones."

"Yes, but—" He sighed. "Well, can you turn yourself back into a horse? It would make things much easier."

"As you wish," Kalan said. He set everything down. Then his body seemed to swell, his features becoming indistinct, his arms and legs lengthening, his clothes becoming a black pelt that stretched across his body—

And then the change was done and again Ker looked at his stallion. It seemed no different from before, but he approached it hesitantly, nonetheless. His hands shook a bit as he heaved the saddle onto Kalan's back and tightened the cinch. He found himself sweating, knees and elbows suddenly weak. Then he swung up into the saddle, giving Kalan free rein, and bent forward to whisper into his ear.

"Back to the festival. We need to find Biur and the others."

Snorting, Kalan turned and trotted.

Before they reached the festival, the mouth of the alley filled with men. They all stood there silently for a second, watching Ker, silhouetted against the brightness of the street, and Ker felt a sudden pulse of fear. Several of the men slid knives from their belts. One of them stepped forward.

"That's a nice horse you've got there, boy." His voice was low and thick with an accent Ker didn't recognize. "How about letting me ride it?"

Kalan wheeled and ran down the alley, back the way they'd come. Rounding the corner, again they faced a fifty-foot-high brick wall—the side of a building. The buildings to the left and right were even taller. Small windows for dumping garbage opened onto the alley, but no doors—they were trapped.

"Climb the walls!" Ker said.

Kalan looked back at him and snorted derisively.

"Then—grow wings and fly! Do *some*thing!"

Kalan reared back, his fur all ashimmer. Ker found himself rising higher and higher into the air—ten feet above the ground, fifteen. He grew dizzy and squeezed his eyes shut, then forced them open. The Syrnae's legs were pulling in closer to his body, which was grown thicker, faintly serpentine. Scales gleamed like polished ebony in the dim light. Instead of hands Kalan had giant black claws.

A distant voice shouted, "You can't get out of there! Make it easy on yourself—we don't want to hurt you!"

Ker blinked and the picture came together for him. Gasping in shock, he realized he sat astride a giant black dragon. Kalan breathed heavily, his whole body trembling from the change—as if this shape had almost been too much for him to assume—as if he couldn't hold on to it much longer.

"Just a minute more," Ker urged. "They'll be here in a second!"

Kalan threw back his head, drawing in a sudden *whoosh* of breath. The dragon's jaws snapped once, shredding the halter and bit, freeing its mouth. Ker clung frantically to the bucking saddle. As the dragon's chest expanded, the leather of the cinch creaked and seemed about to break. Kalan give a little shrug. The saddle jerked violently to the left, then the right, inching higher up his body, circling the dragon's thinner neck.

Lowering his head near the alley's paving stones, Kalan moved forward.

The first man rounded the corner at a run, a knife clenched in one hand. Kalan lashed out with his tail. Bones crunched and the man reeled back. He struck the wall and collapsed with a gurgling cry.

The four other men stopped and stared from ten feet down the alley. Their mouths hung open in shock; their eyes gleamed wide and white with fear.

Muscles rippled like liquid steel in Kalan's scaled shoulders. He lurched forward into full view. Throwing his head back, he roared. The sound was deafening in the narrow confines of the alley.

The men dropped their knives and fled with screams of terror. In a moment, they were gone.

Kalan drew back into the darker part of the alley. Slowly his transformation began again—the shimmering of his hide, the drawing in of his body, the re-forming—

And once again Ker sat on an ebon black stallion. Kalan pranced impatiently for a moment, then turned toward the street. As they passed the man whom Kalan had struck, Ker saw that he was dead—his chest crushed to a bloody pulp. He shuddered and couldn't look away for a minute, triumph and horror fighting for control of his thoughts.

Then the body vanished into the shadows behind them. They reached the street and rode out into the sunshine. Bright music and lithe dancers swirled.

Before they'd gone fifty paces, Ker heard a heavy tread behind him. Then rough hands seized him from behind and tore him from the saddle. The festival swung around him, dizzy colors all mixing together in the shock. He caught a glimpse of a deep red cape, black boots, a helmed face—*a city guard.*

Strong hands wrenched his arms behind his back and bound them together with rope; someone stuffed a bitter-tasting gag into his mouth.

"That's him! That's the one killed Jerro in the alley!"

The taste in Ker's mouth was overwhelming. It bore up through his mind with a scream of sound and color . . . and then darkness.

He felt himself falling.

17

The Halls of Narmon Ri

> Is it any surprise that Zelloque is decadent? Consider well the wealth that flows into our city from the lands the Great Lord's armies have conquered, from the traders who use our city's thousand-odd warehouses, from the pirates who make our city their home. There is an air of spoilt opulence here that makes me sick at heart.
>
> —Olam Werren, before his execution

Ker woke slowly, each muscle in his body a distinct pain: his arms felt swollen and heavy, like someone had wrapped them in molten lead. His head pounded. His mouth was dry and full of something thick and foul-tasting.

He opened his eyes, and found himself lying on his side, on a bed of moldy straw. His arms had been tied behind his back and his mouth stuffed full of dirty rags.

They fear magic, wizards. Of course they'd bound him.

Dim light filtered down through a pair of narrow slits set high in the wall over his head. A crow perched in one and watched him, its body almost too large to fit. Opening its beak, it cawed once as if in chastisement. One glance around the cell revealed everything to him—the bedrock floor, the thick stone walls, the sturdy-looking oak door that provided the only entrance and exit. He felt a growing sense of horror.

The palace dungeon.

Swinging his legs over the side of the bed, he managed to sit up. For a moment he couldn't remember what had happened to him, but then it all flooded back: the guards leaping at him, someone shoving a foul-smelling cloth into his face, the last voice that accused him of murder—

He shuddered. How would Biur find him *here?* How—

A small window set in the middle of the door slid open. A wrinkled old face, framed with long, dirty gray hair, pressed to the opening. Bloodshot eyes regarded him coolly for a second, then the window slammed shut just as quickly as it had opened.

"He's awake now," Ker heard a gravelly voice say through the door.

"Good," said another, richer voice that somehow seemed familiar. It wasn't Biur's voice, nor Zeren's—but it held a kind note, which Ker welcomed more gratefully than anything else. "Open up."

"Careful! Don't want no sorcery worked down here. The master'd have my hide!"

"Open the door, I said!"

"Aye, sir. Here, it's done, 's you can see."

With a click and a squeal of rusted hinges, the door swung out two feet, then stopped.

"Hurry up!"

"That's as far as she goes, sir. This one's been stuck, long 's I remember. The master says—"

"Leave us. *Now.*" The tone left no room for dispute.

Ker heard shuffling footsteps, which grew fainter and fainter and finally trailed away. He sat up straight, straining to see and hear—

And caught a low murmuring song. The oak door glowed faint blue for a second, then it soundlessly swung back—to reveal a tall man dressed in long, flowing velvet robes the pale color of starlight, and holding a wand.

Threnodrel!

But the wizard made no move to free him. Ker thought, suddenly, that his old teacher didn't recognize him, that he'd leave and abandon him there. But Threnodrel stepped forward with a sigh, shaking his head, and tucked his wand away with a quick wave of his hand.

"Well, Ker," he said, "I see you didn't take my advice in Vichir. I've never seen anyone who looked as miserable as you do now! I had a suspicion it was you they'd arrested, when I heard the guards describing the demon they'd captured in the market-place. Of course the charges are ludicrous—you're supposed to have turned yourself into a fire-breathing dragon and eaten fifteen peasants. You didn't, did you? No, of course not, I can see you're not a shape shifter. But how did this story get started, hmm? And what are you doing in Zelloque—you didn't follow me here, I hope?"

He stepped forward as if to untie Ker, but the crow in the window gave a little coughing sound. Threnodrel stopped and looked up at it for a second. The bird cawed and cocked its head to the side.

"So *you're* at fault! Well, it won't do to have you caught here, will it? Go find his companions and tell them where he is—and that I'll help him as best I can. I am Threnodrel, court magician to the Great Lord of Zelloque, Narmon Ri himself. *Go.*"

With a flutter of wings, the crow vanished. Ker saw a lingering trace of blue where it had been standing and realized with a jolt that the crow had been Kalan.

Threnodrel sighed and removed Ker's gag, then set to work untying the ropes. Ker spat the rags from his mouth with relief. His lips were cracked and dry, his throat raw and bloody when he tried to swallow, but couldn't. Then his arms and legs were free and the wizard knelt and began to massage his leg muscles vigorously. Ker winced as sharp pains shot through his calves, but the cramps soon passed as circulation returned.

Threnodrel stood. "This way," he said, helping Ker rise. "You must prepare for your meeting with Lord Ri. I will vouch for you—but that may not be enough to win your freedom. Wizards are not in favor in this city, as I'm sure you noticed."

"Water—" Ker mumbled. Bits of lint from his gag still stuck to his tongue. He tried to wipe them away with his tunic's filthy sleeve, but only made things worse.

"Outside. Come." Then Threnodrel took Ker's arm and, half carrying, half dragging, led him forward.

Ker's legs ached and his knees kept trying to buckle. The world swayed dizzily as they moved through the door and turned left, into a long, dimly lit passage. Torches set in deep recesses along the walls flickered, throwing weird shadows around them. Water ran down the stone walls and pooled on the floor. The air held the sickly sweet smells of decay. Age-blackened oak doors, most of them solidly barred, lined the passage. Ker heard small scuttling noises from several cells. He shivered at the thought of the poor creatures locked within.

The dungeon guard, a small, gnarled old man with long gray hair, waited at the end of the hall. Instead of a uniform, he wore a tattered gray tunic and scuffed boots. His eyes were small and red, like an animal's, and he kept nodding his head and grinning madly.

"Yes, yes," he said, voice oddly hollow, "you'll take him, won't you, high one? Yes?" And then he laughed—a bizarre choking sound that made Ker shudder.

Threnodrel said nothing. He turned to Ker and pointed toward a niche in the wall. Ker looked and saw a bucket sitting there. A thin layer of green scum floated on top of the water inside, but he grabbed the dipper and drank eagerly.

The passage through the halls of the palace became a blur to Ker. He dimly remembered guards who challenged Threnodrel, then stood aside for the wizard when he voiced his claim on Ker. He had fleeting impressions of beautiful women dressed in dazzling gowns of silk and lace, women who moved away with squeals of fear when Threnodrel approached.

When his mind cleared, he found himself sitting on a narrow bench in a small, dimly lit room. Small globes of pale blue and red light slowly drifted through the air near the ceiling, as though moved by small drafts of wind or their own strange whims. Ker found himself clean and dressed in pantaloons cut much like Zeren's, only made of some soft, white material like fine wool. He wore a pale blue shirt with white laces up the front and new leather sandals.

Beneath the shifting light, Threnodrel sat at a high table in the middle of the sparsely furnished room. The wizard's eyes were closed and he seemed asleep. But when Ker stirred, he opened his eyes, smiling faintly.

"You feel better now, don't you? I gave you a healing draft of my own mixing—made of the leaves of various plants that only grow on the Plains of Pendilop. Now you must tell me what brings you and your friends to Zelloque; the shape shifter was rather vague. We have an audience with the Great Lord in a short time and I must know everything if you're to keep your head."

Ker told him then of all that had happened—how he met Derethigon and lost his face, how Biur had given it back . . . how Derethigon had sent them off to find the wizard who stole the bones of Shon Atasha. He told of the demons in Rhimalga, of Gar Galimu and the Syrnae. Then he told of how Kalan had snuck away with him and how they'd been cornered in the alley by a band of men trying to steal a horse.

When he finished, Threnodrel nodded slowly. "Such thieves are not uncommon in this city. I think the Great Lord will believe your story—he *is* a sensible man, wise and just in his own way." He looked up at the colored lights for a moment. "The time has come for our audience. Follow me, and remember to say nothing. I will speak for you."

* * *

The audience hall of the Great Lord of Zelloque bustled with noble-born men and women, minor lords and their ladies, the wealthiest merchants of the city. They crowded the floor and clustered on the thick gold and red carpets nearest to Narmon Ri's throne. Jugglers and acrobats moved among the rich, plying their trade; servants carried trays of exotic delicacies; minor magicians floated multicolored spheres of light into the air, then burst them one by one like so many soap bubbles.

People drew back when Threnodrel appeared, Ker saw at once. They didn't deign to notice the wizard; one by one the small groups of talkers just somehow managed to drift either left or right, away from the wizard. A path to Lord Ri's throne cleared before them. Ker looked up at Threnodrel's face; it was set in determination . . . as if the wizard was at once accustomed to and angered by the way they shunned him.

At last they neared Narmon Ri. The Great Lord of Zelloque sat on a high golden throne against the far wall. Flowing black curtains of the finest velvet and ermine covered the wall behind him, setting off the brilliant splendor of his bejeweled green silk robes. An area of perhaps twenty feet around the dais remained clear at all times.

Two heavily muscled city guards, hands resting on the hilts of their swords, stood to either side of Lord Ri. Their dark eyes moved constantly, Ker saw, missing nothing in the hall.

To one side of the throne, surrounded by ten city guardsmen holding drawn swords, stood a ragged line of prisoners. Heavy iron chains bound their arms and legs. To the other side of the throne stood a longer line of richly dressed men and women—those seeking an audience with the Great Lord, Ker guessed.

"Ker!" someone cried.

Ker started, then saw Biur in the line of supplicants. His master motioned them over. Ker started forward, but Threnodrel put a hand on his shoulder and stopped him.

"No," the wizard said. "You will have time for that later. First we must see the Great Lord. Join the line of prisoners. I will speak to Biur."

"But—"

"Do as I say. *Now.*"

Ker nodded reluctantly. He knew better than to argue when his life might well be at stake. "As you wish." Turning, he walked slowly toward the line of prisoners. The guards moved aside and let him pass as if they'd expected him. He entered the circle of prisoners and stood next to a twisted old man with only one eye. Nobody spoke. A general feeling of despair radiated from those around him, and Ker shivered uneasily.

He watched as Threnodrel embraced Biur like an old friend, then spoke to him in a quiet voice for a minute. At last both of them nodded and parted, Biur returning to the line of supplicants, Threnodrel heading toward Ker. The wizard passed the city guards and stood next to him.

"What did he say?" Ker whispered.

"Little. Kalan had already told him what happened. I promised that you would be treated fairly. They haven't found the engine yet—the others are still searching for it, and the bones. He believes they will be found soon, and I know he's right. Such things cannot long remain hidden." There was certainty in his voice.

It struck Ker how much alike the two wizards were. "You know Biur well, don't you?"

Threnodrel nodded. "I served him as a boy. He taught me much. Be silent now, the judging will begin."

The Great Lord of Zelloque raised one hand. The audience hall grew quiet. All the people of the court moved forward to hear the cases Narmon Ri would judge. There was a strange eagerness about them—a bloodlust, Ker realized suddenly. They wanted nothing more than to see the prisoners executed . . . him among them.

One of the guards turned and motioned for Ker and Threnodrel to approach the throne. The wizard nodded and Ker moved forward, knees weak, stomach queasy. He felt apprehensive, with all the people watching him, but decided to try and look brave. He was, after all, a noble himself. He held his head up higher and arched his back. Ten feet before Lord Ri's throne he stopped and bowed, as he'd been taught. Beside him, Threnodrel did the same.

"Speak, my wizard," Lord Ri commanded. He sounded bored and amused. "Of what crime is this boy charged—and why do you speak for him?"

"My Lord, the boy is charged with transforming himself into a dragon and devouring various peasants in the marketplace."

A gasp went up among the watchers, but Narmon Ri merely regarded Ker shrewdly. "Go on."

"My Lord, his name is Ker Orrum, and he is the second son of Baron Orrum of Vichir, a minor barony far to the west. He was charged with this crime by various criminals after defending himself against their leader, who tried to steal his horse. Look at the boy, my Lord! No witnesses saw him turn himself into a dragon. And his accusers would not dare to venture into your court, lest they be hanged for their crimes."

"Why do you speak for him, then?"

"My Lord, I was once his tutor in history. I like the boy, although he is a bit stupid and brash"—Ker stiffened a bit, but forced himself to say nothing—"and I have no desire to see him hurt for a crime he didn't commit."

The Great Lord of Zelloque nodded slowly. "Are those who accuse Ker Orrum here?" he asked, looking slowly around the room. Nobody moved. "Very well," he continued. "I—"

Lord Ri broke off as the curtains behind him parted and a small, thin man dressed in gray robes stepped out, a long black cloak flowing shadowlike behind him. A drawn hood covered most of his face, but Ker could see pale lips, a short gray beard, and eyes that shone unnaturally bright. Something about the man made him faintly uneasy.

"What is it, Suthyran?" Lord Ri asked impatiently.

The dark-robed man bent forward and whispered in the Great Lord's ear. Narmon Ri froze. He frowned, then paled, then began to tremble with rage.

Suthyran stood, turning to look out across the hall. At last his eyes settled on Ker—and stayed there. Ker had the impression the man recognized him . . . and hated him more than anything else in the world. He trembled under the man's dark scrutiny.

Suthyran, he thought. Hadn't the festival been in his honor . . . as the Great Lord's new counselor?

Narmon Ri stood. The two bodyguards stepped closer to their lord, hands slowly caressing the hilts of their swords. The Great Lord turned and looked directly at Biur.

"Seize that wizard!" he shouted, pointing.

Ker jumped, startled. He tried to run to his master, but Threnodrel locked his arms around Ker and held him back despite his struggles.

Guards materialized from the crowds of nobles around Biur. Four of them grabbed the wizard's arms while another two pried his jaws apart and forced a gag into his mouth. The others bent his arms behind his back and chained them together while still more city guards shackled his legs. They knocked him to the ground and stood over him, swords drawn, as the Great Lord descended from his throne. The lines of audience-seekers drew back in fear and shock.

"Let me go!" Ker said, struggling to get free from Threnodrel's iron grip.

"Shut up, boy," the wizard hissed in his ear. "Something's gone wrong—you can see that! Wait. Watch—there's no help for Biur here, now. Can you help him if the Great Lord cuts off your head?"

Ker stood still, biting his lip, knowing his old teacher was right. Biur would've said the same thing, if he'd been able to speak. Finally Threnodrel released him. Ker tried to look away, but couldn't. His eyes were locked on Narmon Ri as the Great Lord stood over Biur, sneering.

"So, Wizard, your plot's been uncovered by my counselor. You would have murdered me, eh? Well, my torturers will have their sport with you. Tomorrow at sunset you will be taken to the marketplace to suffer the Death of a Thousand Brands." He gestured to the guards. They grabbed Biur's chains and dragged him off through the crowd.

Narmon Ri ascended his throne and sat heavily. He was breathing hard; Ker guessed the Great Lord hadn't moved that quickly in many years.

But Narmon Ri hadn't finished. He gazed down on Ker for a long minute without speaking. His eyes were dark, unreadable. Ker had a sinking feeling in his stomach. Then Lord Ri said:

"Boy, I have been told of your part in this plot. You will die at sunrise tomorrow. So be it."

"That's a lie!" Ker screamed. "I never—"

Threnodrel struck him hard across the mouth, knocking him to the floor. Ker lay there, stunned, staring up at the wizard's impassive face in shock and anger. Threnodrel too had betrayed him. A ringing filled his ears. He could scarcely believe it. He could still feel the wizard's handprint on his cheek.

"I'll kill you for that," he said in a low voice.

Guards moved forward and took his arms, heaving him up to his feet. They twisted his arms behind his back and pulled him toward the door. He didn't struggle . . . yet.

Too many of them here—

"Wait, my Lord," Suthyran said. His voice was low and smooth—not the voice Ker expected.

The Great Lord of Zelloque held up one hand. The guards halted. Ker twisted around to look behind him.

There was a strange eagerness in the counselor's voice. "The boy is not evil—merely misguided. He would make a good servant, I am sure. Will you give him to me?"

Lord Ri nodded. "If you want him."

"Thank you, my Lord." He bowed, then turned to the guards. A faint smile passed across his face for an instant; then it was gone. "Take him to my chambers."

The guards pulled Ker away. The ringing in his ears grew louder; the room misted over. Far away, as if in another world, he could still hear the Great Lord speaking to Threnodrel:

"Suthyran assures me you knew nothing of their plot, but I can't allow you to remain in the city now, after what happened. I ask you, therefore, to leave of your own free will before the week is over."

Threnodrel's answer was the final, crushing blow: "Yes, my Lord. That would be best."

The guards left him in a cool, dark place. An odd, sweet smell filled the air, but he scarcely noticed.

Ker lay on the floor, on some musty-smelling carpet, for a long time. He felt a great yawning emptiness inside, a sense of utter desolation more terrible than any he'd ever felt before. Worse than losing his face to Derethigon, worse than discovering the demons in Rhimalga, this fear and despair built and built inside him until he could think of nothing other than the fate Lord Ri had decreed for Biur. The Death of a Thousand Brands—it sounded horrible.

And Threnodrel had betrayed them both.

He knew it; and the thought filled him with pain. He silently cursed the wizard for all he'd done.

At last his anger pushed him to action. Determined to escape and free Biur, Ker climbed to his feet and stood uncertainly for a second. Hands in front of him, he slowly moved forward, feeling for the wall. He bumped into a table, skirted it, continued. A second later he touched heavy cloth—a tapestry or curtain of some kind. He grabbed it and pulled as hard as he could.

The curtain came loose with a tearing sound and brilliant sunlight flooded in through the window, making him blink and shield his eyes. Ker leaned forward and gazed out between the bars. Below lay the palace's central courtyard, where dozens of city guards marched in formation. Even if he managed to get outside and scale the walls, Ker knew he'd never get past the men below.

Reluctantly, he turned from the window—and stared in horror across the room. Eight cages hung from hooks set into the far wall, and inside each cage sprawled the naked, decaying corpse of a man. Their bodies bore the marks of whips and brands; an expert torturer had worked on them for hours. And as Ker moved closer, repelled yet fascinated, he saw that their faces had been cut away with what must have been dull knives.

The cage farthest to the right swayed slightly. Blood slowly dripped from the corpse within, spattering on the cold stone floor. The man couldn't have been dead for long.

Is this how Suthyran amuses himself? Ker wondered. He felt sick. *Is this what he plans for me?*

18

The Great Lord's Counselor

Is it any surprise that Zelloque is magnificent? Consider well the wealth that flows into our city from the evil lands the Great Lord's armies have rescued from tyrants, from the generous traders who use our city's public warehouses, from the seamen who make our city their home. There is an air of friendship here which makes me glad at heart.

—Olam Werren
Collected Works (posthumous publication)

Ker turned away from the nightmarish sight and faced the window again. The sky was fading toward purple; it would soon be dark. If he didn't escape now, he feared he never would. How long did he have until Suthyran came?

He glanced around the room again. Odd pieces of furniture—mostly carved wooden cabinets—had been pushed up against the walls, and several heavy oak tables sat in the middle of the floor. The table nearest the cages held instruments of torture—branding irons, braziers full of coal, thumb screws, whips, and all manner of other devices whose purposes Ker could only begin to guess. On one table by the window, however, sat old scrolls, books, and a small oil lamp. Ker crossed over to them and idly began turning pages and opening scrolls. Most of the writing he couldn't decipher, but there were passages that he could understand:

. . . that human flesh is a great delicacy to demons and can be used to lure them into this plane. To keep them trapped, two spells . . .

Ker let the scroll roll up. Magic. Why would Suthyran want old magic books . . . unless he was a wizard?

He rummaged through the rest of the pages frantically, looking for a clue, anything to tell him more about the counselor. As he seized a crumbling old scroll, something long and white fell out and clattered to the floor.

He picked it up. It was a slender wand made of carved ivory, just like the one Threnodrel used. Then Ker knew the Great Lord's counselor *had* to be a wizard. It all made sense: Biur's capture, Threnodrel's exile, old scrolls dealing with demons, the mutilated, faceless bodies in the cages . . . had the people of Rhimalga been similarly butchered? He thought so. Suthyran, he realized, was in league with the wizard who had stolen the bones from Ni Treshel—perhaps he'd even summoned the demons himself.

Quickly Ker tucked the wand into his shirt. If he couldn't escape by any other means, he'd try to open a Gateway.

He continued around the room. In one corner sat a small bed. Ker guessed Suthyran slept there after amusing himself by torturing people, by cutting off their faces. What kind of man could do such things? Again he wondered, *What if I'm next?*

He had to escape. He had to rescue Biur, then find the bones of Shon Atasha. Suthyran had to be stopped.

Maybe Zeren and Liana can find them, he thought suddenly. Suthyran couldn't possibly know about the other members of their party, could he?

He wasn't going to help Biur or himself by asking questions he couldn't answer, he decided. With the windows barred, he certainly wasn't going to get out that way. Perhaps there would be a secret passage, like the ones in his father's castle?

Ker began a slow circuit of the room, pushing likely-looking stones in the walls, feeling for hidden buttons or levers. At last he approached the back wall where the corpses were. The smell nauseated him, but he forced himself to continue. Several of the cages swayed a bit, and as he moved forward, he noticed with revulsion that several large white rats stood in the cages . . .

Eating the bodies.

When the rats saw Ker, they stopped, lifted small pink noses to the air, then turned and darted between the cage bars. They dropped to the floor and scurried along the wall to disappear through a small stone grate set in the floor.

Ker hurried after them, then bent and studied the grate. Its bars were covered with slime and rat droppings. Suthyran probably let the blood run down into the sewers. In any case, the bars were set too close together for him to squeeze through, and the passage beyond them looked much smaller than his shoulders. He wouldn't have been able to squeeze into it, even if he'd been able to lift the grating. And, far down in the drain, he thought he saw the glint of tiny rat-eyes studying him.

He stood with a sigh. In a way, he was grateful he couldn't fit into the sewers.

Bolts rattled behind him. Ker whirled in time to see the door swinging soundlessly open. Suthyran stood outside, still dressed in a gray shirt and pants with a black cape. His hood had been thrown back, revealing his full face for the first time. He had a light gray beard, small blue eyes, a small nose. He smiled mockingly, entered, and closed the door behind him.

"What do you want of me?" Ker demanded.

Suthyran said nothing. He walked forward, toward Ker, absently picking up a whip from one of tables. He let it uncoil across the floor, smiling as if at some private joke, then cast it aside.

"Pretty one," he said. His voice was low and smooth, soothing. "You are my special toy. Your blood will be my life."

Ker felt cold all over. He gestured at the men in the cages. "Is that what you're going to do to me?"

"No, pretty one." Suthyran laughed softly. "I have better things in mind for you." He moved forward again, slowly, surely, like a spider stalking its next victim.

As Ker backed away, he bumped into a bench—which had a large branding iron lying upon it. Seizing the iron like a club, he rushed Suthyran.

The counselor made a quick gesture, and twisted lines of blue lashed out from his fingers. The lines wrapped around Ker's body, binding his arms, tightening until he couldn't move, couldn't breathe.

Suthyran crept closer and kicked Ker's legs out from under him. Ker fell with a jar and gasped in pain. Still the lines tightened about him.

"You must wait a while longer, pretty one," Suthyran said. "I will return for you later, when time allows such pleasure." Chuckling, he crossed to the cabinet and unlocked it with a small key from his pocket. Inside, on hooks, Ker saw white ovals. In the dim light he couldn't be quite sure what they were. He didn't think he wanted to know.

Suthyran took one out and, as he turned toward the window, Ker saw that the counselor held what looked like a mask. The eyes were holes through which darkness showed.

With one hand Suthyran stripped off the face he wore and hung it on a hook. Ker stared. The front of Suthyran's head was smooth and pale as ivory, without place for eyes, nose, or mouth. Slowly the counselor fitted the mask into position, closed the cabinet door, and turned back to Ker. He was smiling faintly now—the mask had come alive. Suthyran's new face looked younger, stronger . . . the face of some city guardsman, perhaps, or of some young merchant.

"I will deal with you tonight," he said. He made a curt gesture and the bonds around Ker loosened a bit—enough for Ker to breathe, no more. Nodding to himself, Suthyran turned and left.

Ker wept. His whole body ached and he didn't want to think about Suthyran, or the bones, or what fate might await him. *The wizard had no face.* His nightmares came back to him. Again he ran through endless corridors pursued by faceless demons. Again they mocked him, calling, *"We have your face . . . your face . . . your face."*

He knew why Suthyran had taken him. The counselor wanted his face.

Eventually it grew dark out and the stars shone through the open window. They were bright, sharp, remote. Ker stared at them. He felt empty inside, as though all the anger had been drained from him. Whatever magical bonds held him seemed to suck his strength away; he felt a heavy numbness all through his body, in his arms and legs, deep in his chest. Still he struggled to free himself.

At last, exhausted, he had to admit failure. The ropes were stronger than he was. He looked out the window once more, but the sky had grown cloudy and he couldn't see the stars now. He could scarcely see anything around him, he realized.

He let his vision slip into the blue of magic and looked at his bonds. They glowed azure, deep azure like the noontime sky. As he studied them, he could almost *feel* their smooth, slick texture: and then he *was* feeling them—tracing their loops and turns in his mind, following their twining pattern around and around in endless spirals. *Here* the wizard had joined two lines together; *there* he had woven them around and around; *here* he had twisted them all together into a knot.

It was like the time with Gar Galimu. Ker remembered all that he'd done there, how he'd opened a Gateway, how he'd used magic then by himself.

Ker could *feel* his bonds, *feel* the power within them straining for release. He let his thoughts flow from his body and into them. Slowly he forced the patterns to change, to loosen, to dissolve, and around him the blue glow of magic flared brighter and brighter—and Suthyran's ropes started to break up, to dissolve.

Ker felt a rush of excitement, of strength unlike anything he'd felt before. His fingers tingled. His whole body seemed vibrantly alive as the magic poured into him and filled him with its energy. Distantly, he himself cry out in pain, in pleasure—

And in a quick, hot burst, Suthyran's ropes vanished. Gasping, Ker lay on the floor, exhausted. Already his arms and legs ached with the pinpricks of returning circulation.

His success in freeing himself elated him, and he understood at last what Gar Galimu had meant about magic being the ability to manipulate the forces of the world around him. He'd done it!

Slowly, painfully, he levered himself to his feet. He had to escape before Suthyran returned.

After checking the door and finding it still locked, he faced the wall. Galimu had said a wand would help him. He took out Suthyran's and held it firmly in his hand. Drawing a deep breath, he looked for the blue of magic, found it, tensed.

Then he raised the wand before him, just as he'd seen Biur do so many times, just as he'd done in the forest what seemed aeons ago, and he concentrated on shaping a Gateway. The sparks in the air drew together. The wand moved in his hand like a painter's brush, directing, steering, shaping.

Now! And the Gateway took form.

He concentrated not on where he was, but on where he wanted to be: the alley where Kalan had turned himself into a dragon. As he pictured the place in his mind, his thought seemed to flow from his body. Distantly, he heard himself singing, but the words were strange, only half-understood. He saw lines of force twisting away before him, roaring up in cold blue flames. Then the flames covered him, and he slipped through them into brightness and shadow. He had the impression of ever-shifting patterns, of crisscrossing lines, of circles and diamonds rushing past at impossible speeds. Finally the blue flames opened up before him and he gazed out into the alley.

Shivering a bit, he opened his eyes. He stood before a slightly lopsided Gateway perhaps eight feet high and four feet wide. It was matte black and shimmered faintly, as though some unseen wind ruffled its surface. From its depths came a cold, cold wind.

Better than last time, he thought.

Without hesitation, Ker stepped through it.

19

Idol Bones

> Once, long ago, the gods wandered the world in mortal guise. They saw people at their tasks, plowing the fields, and they said, "It is not good that men work so hard," and they created a giant hairy beast, the Nuk, from the clay of the Earth and set him laboring in the fields in man's place. After the gods left, the Nuk kept to the fields, plowing deep furrows, harvesting the grain, threshing it. However, the Nuk did not like to work so hard for man's benefit. He let himself melt in the next rainstorm and went back to his home in the ground. And man had to work for himself once more.
>
> —Traditional

Ker stepped out into darkness and for an instant didn't know where he was. Then the smell told him—the reek of spoiled fruit, of open sewage, of mold and decay. He'd made it into the alley, just as he'd pictured in his mind.

The Gateway behind him shimmered. He let it collapse.

Slowly his eyes grew accustomed to the dark. He could pick out the walls of buildings around him; he could see the piles of garbage. Only then did he let himself relax a bit, the tension draining slowly from his muscles. He was safe. He'd escaped from Suthyran. Drawing a deep breath, he realized how tired he'd become—all he wanted to do was lie down and sleep. He shook his head, trying to clear his thoughts. No: he certainly couldn't do that, not with Biur captured and set to be killed.

The humid air felt charged with electricity, as though a storm were about to break. He studied the thin slice of sky showing between buildings and saw no stars . . . just a thick slate of darkness, like a shadow hanging over the city.

Then he remembered what Biur had told him about magic spreading like ripples in a pond, how wizards could sense magic around them, and felt a sudden panic again. He ran toward the mouth of the alley, weaving among piles of decaying garbage. Rats bolted for cover as he passed. Rotten fruit squished under his feet. If Suthyran *had* sensed his opening a Gateway, he didn't want the wizard tracking him down again.

He turned the corner and saw the street ahead. The festival had ended; not a single person passed the mouth of the alley. He moved forward cautiously, listening, watching, but heard little. Somewhere distant, a dog barked; farther still, a wagon slowly creaked its way through cobbled streets. A faint hint of music hung in the air, delicate strings and pipes that played almost too softly to be heard.

When he stepped into the open and looked up and down the street, he saw only a scattering of people. Several were drunk and staggered a bit as they walked, each helping the other home. A few more tucked their heads down and hurried on unimaginable errands.

All the shops were closed. Doors had been locked, windows shuttered. From upper stories came the faint gleam of lantern light.

Ker turned right, heading in the direction he'd last seen Zeren and Liana heading. Perhaps there would be inns ahead. He glanced down at the gray clothes he wore, at his baggy pants and shirt, and for a moment thanked Threnodrel for giving him a disguise good enough to pass by any guards he might meet. He'd be a servant, he decided, on a late-night errand for his master, if anyone asked. That would get him by.

As he passed cross streets, he glanced up and down their lengths. Some held small metalworking shops or tanneries; others, small homes set close together. All the buildings seemed dark, brooding as they leaned far out over the cobblestones. He pressed on, saying nothing to the few people he passed. Once a small group of guardsmen marched by, swords swinging by their sides, deep red capes fluttering out behind them, and Ker caught his breath and said nothing—and they ignored him in return. When they were gone, he breathed out in relief and found his hands were shaking. Still he continued on.

At last he came to streets with rows of small inns. Light streamed from open doorways, flooding the street with bright illumination. From some common rooms came sounds of minstrels and story-tellers; others echoed with loud, bawdy drinking songs. Signs hung over the doorways of the fanciest places, proclaiming names like The Dreaming Crow and Inn of the Bright Pleasures.

Lightning flickered somewhere overhead, and a slow rumble of thunder followed. Ker glanced up and, when lightning struck again, saw dark, swollen clouds moving lower. Still, it hadn't begun to rain yet, and his hopes of locating Zeren and Liana and Kalan had risen considerably with finding the street of inns. When he stopped and glanced through each door he came to, he found scatterings of fat, richly dressed old men—probably visiting merchants—or plainly dressed pilgrims to the Oracle outside Zelloque. These inns were expensive, the best places to stay in the city, and he knew Biur would never have taken rooms at such. Still, Zeren probably would have, and with that thought, his search went on.

As he progressed down the street, the inns became smaller and more run-down. Few had signs. Here Ker began stepping in and asking the few servants on duty whether they'd seen any of his companions.

In the first inn, the richly robed boy on duty sneered at him. "We wouldn't serve wizards here!" he said. "Try the slums. We don't want their kind about, scaring off good customers."

In the second and third, maids had shrugged.

In the fourth, he found Zeren and Threnodrel sitting at a table in the common room, eating a late meal of cold meat and sweet-breads. The place was empty, except for them and a young serving boy asleep on the wine counter.

Ker hurried in and they looked up at him in surprise.

"Ker—they let you go!" Threnodrel said.

Ker glared at him, but couldn't find the strength to do more than that. Instead, he sank down in an empty chair next to Zeren and looked at the food. The Rashendi pushed a plate of what looked like sliced duck toward him, but he found he wasn't hungry.

"I managed to escape, no thanks to you," he said. "If I weren't so tired I'd—"

"No," Zeren said sharply. "Threnodrel and I were just now discussing how to break into the Great Lord's fortress to find you and Biur."

Surprised, Ker looked at Threnodrel, who nodded briefly. The wizard said, "You must realize, Ker, how dangerous the Great Lord of Zelloque truly is. If I had dared to oppose him, do you think I'd still be free? Subtlety is always best, as Biur must have told you many times by now."

Ashamed, he nodded. "Yes. But I—" He didn't know what to say.

"Come now," Zeren said, rising and taking his arm. "This is far from the best place to talk—and we must tell Liana that you're safe. She was quite worried about you."

"Really?"

"Of course. We will need your help to take the bones."

"You've found them?"

"Not here." He glanced at the door, then the sleeping boy, and started for the staircase at the back of the room.

Liana was sleeping in a large room with two featherbeds. She sat up quickly when they came in, and when she saw Ker, she smiled. It was a radiant look of joy mixed with relief. He smiled back at her.

"I'm glad you're safe," she said softly.

"Did you find the bones?" he asked.

"Yes," Zeren said. "They're in an idolmaker's shop near the city gates. The idolmaker and his apprentices have been ordered to work the bones into statues of the eleven gods. The idols, they believe, are to be sent to an Oracle as a gift from the Great Lord." He shook his head. "No matter what we said, they wouldn't see reason—wouldn't realize they were carving the bones of Shon Atasha. They finally threatened to call the city guard if we didn't leave."

"And now what?"

"We must steal the bones this night. To do that we will need Biur. He is perhaps the most powerful wizard in Zelloque; far more powerful than Threnodrel. Now, tell us—quickly!—what happened to you."

Ker told them of all that had happened—of how Suthyran butchered men and took their faces, and how he didn't have a face himself, only pale, blank skin, without place for nose, mouth, or eyes.

"Then he is like you were," Liana said, "when Derethigon took your face? How strange. Biur never spoke of his god doing that to another, let alone to a wizard. And yet that is what must have happened. No mortal could give up his face and live, without a god's magic to keep him alive."

When he thought again of Suthyran, Ker remembered the strange familiarity he'd felt, almost as though he'd known the wizard. And the more he thought about it, the more it seemed the wizard had known him, too. Why?

He thought back to losing his face. His stomach felt queasy as he remembered Derethigon's burning hand reaching out to him, touching his cheek, tracing the line of his jaw, lifting away his face.

And he remembered trying to re-create his own face with the

magic wand he'd shaped from a fallen branch; remembered the face he'd created and how the image had come to life and seized control of his body. He'd thought it but a dream at the time, but now . . . He swallowed. The picture he'd created in his mind leaped out at him: *it was Suthyran.*

He knew it more surely than he'd ever known anything before. He knew that he had created the wizard—given him shape, given him substance. *He* was responsible for all that the wizard had done.

It was a sudden, harsh blow. He felt a sharp pain in his stomach and sank down on the bed, face gray, not daring to look at those around him. He felt the terror of all he'd done, felt the utter hopelessness of it all. *He* was responsible for everything that had happened.

"Ker, what is it?" Liana said.

He looked up at her, eyes blurring with tears. Haltingly, he told her—told them all—what he'd done on the road so long ago. And they looked at him with shock, as though he'd somehow betrayed them in the last few seconds: Liana as though he'd personally butchered her horses, Zeren as though he'd personally stolen the bones of Shon Atasha the Creator, Threnodrel as if he'd betrayed Biur to the Great Lord of Zelloque. And he couldn't meet their gazes.

Threnodrel recovered first. He looked down, studying the floor, as he said, "What's over is over and cannot be changed. You were used, Ker, by Suthyran. But know this: he is no wizard. He is a demon shaped of the netherworlds, born of cold and shadow. A lust for power must drive him as it drives few others of his kind. If he truly wanted to come to our world—as his actions show he did—then he would have found another way, had you not let him in. These things the old scrolls tell us. You are not to blame."

"Yes," Zeren said, "I too have read such reports. Fortunately, when he took control of your body, you managed to force him out—and he took on your appearance. Now that he is locked into your form, he must be partially crippled, since he has no face of his own. Perhaps we can use this to defeat him."

"I certainly hope so," said Threnodrel.

Ker shook his head. "But what will happen now?"

"At least twice before have such demons walked the lands of men. Always they wreaked havoc before they were destroyed. Thousands died in battle. Cities were pillaged, gutted, burned. This must never happen again. Suthyran must be stopped—at once!"

"That's what Biur told me," Ker said. Then he stopped,

remembering the Great Lord's death sentence for his master. He turned to Zeren. "You said you were going to rescue him!"

The Rashendi nodded. "Yes. The hour grows late; we must go now, if we're to succeed."

Threnodrel stood. "The demon Suthyran must be stopped," he said. "There are enough of you to free Biur; I will go to Theshemna."

"What good will that do?" Ker demanded.

The wizard looked at him. "I must tell the gods," he said. "They must act now or Suthyran may start whatever plans he has for the bones."

"Go, then," Zeren said, "and hurry!"

Threnodrel pushed back his chair and stood. His face was set in grim lines. Without another word he turned and hurried out the door.

Thunder rumbled outside, louder than before, closer. The heart of the storm would soon be there.

Liana slowly stood and went to the window, opening the shutters and throwing them back. It had grown even darker outside, and the air seemed very still. A gray fog rising from the dew on the cobblestones shrouded the streets.

"This storm," she said softly, "is not natural."

"What do you mean?" Zeren demanded.

"Look at it. There are forces at work here beyond those of nature."

Ker looked beyond the normal world and saw, then, what she meant: sparks of turquoise traced the clouds, sparks which twisted across the sky faster than storm winds could possibly move. He gaped in wonder. It was a spectacular sight, unlike anything he'd ever seen before.

"Faramigon's Eye," Zeren muttered.

"What?" Kel said.

"Faramigon's Eye—the storm that comes before great sorcery. I have heard of it, but never did I expect to see it."

"What does it mean?" Liana said.

"Some great feat of magic will be done tonight, something that will tear apart the natural fabric of the world. Already the Earth senses its coming. Shon Atasha the Creator bound his bones into the fabric of our world . . . who can say it does not share some of his power?"

"Biur said Suthyran would try to summon the demons who serve him!" Ker cried. "Could that be it—could that be what's causing the storm?"

Zeren looked at him sadly, strangely resigned. "It must be."

"Is there nothing we can do?"

"Nothing. We don't even know where Suthyran is right now. And we still have to find Biur."

Liana took herself apart from them. She knelt on the floor, staring up at the wooden rafters, but not seeing anything before her. Her eyes seemed to focus on something far, far away, as though she peered beyond the pall of the world and into the heavens, to the gods and beyond, to the spirit of Shon Atasha the Creator. Ker saw her lips move slightly in a half-voiced prayer.

He moved slowly toward the window to close the shutters. He couldn't help but glimpse the thick gray fog still creeping through the streets. Pausing for a second, he watched as strange, muffled shapes darted past: flashes of black clothing, a glimpse of star-pale skin, a pale, pale face turned up to look at the sky for a moment.

He closed his eyes. In his mind he built a picture of the wizard-demon they'd chased across half the world, saw his slender boy's body, saw his familiar stance and movements. It was like gazing into a looking glass and seeing the reflection move by itself. How many times had he looked and never seen the similarities between Suthyran and himself?

Suddenly he ached for the old, simple days of study. He cursed himself and all his weaknesses, cursed himself for trying to hide from all the terror he had wrought. He was a man now; no one could follow after him to set the world aright. Not his father, not Nowandin or Lerrens, not Biur or Threnodrel. He was adrift, his actions ripples in the pool of time, and all the waves couldn't be stopped.

"Derethigon," he whispered, "why have you abandoned us?"

He stood there, his breath ragged, tears hot on his cheeks, until he no longer thought of anything but the hurt inside him. Even the gods had abandoned him. An emptiness spread through him, a terrible, desolate feeling of helplessness. And then that too passed, and he stood alone with nothing inside him. Carefully, he closed and latched the shutters, wondering a bit what difference that would make. At last he wiped his face on his sleeves and turned back to rejoin the others.

Faramigon's Eye. The rape of the city had begun.

He realized he didn't want to die here, no matter what he'd done.

That rekindled the anger inside him, and again he longed to kill Suthyran himself. He thought of Liana's proud horses, butchered for their meat, their blood pooling around them, their insides ripped out, and knew he could kill the demon.

Ker looked at them each in turn. "We can't just wait here! You said you had a plan to rescue Biur. What are we waiting for?"

They said nothing for a long while. *"Well?"*

At last Liana spoke: "Zeren, you must set me free before the demons come to this place. That will be your only chance."

"Liana—"

"Do it!" Her voice was too loud, too shrill.

Ker studied her, puzzled. Muscles corded in her neck and arms. She was begging for release just as she'd done in Rhimalga. Then she'd wanted Biur to drive a dagger through her heart. Was it really death she sought—a final voyage to meet the Mad God? Or did she have something else in mind, some last trick?

"The magic may not work," Zeren said softly. "You might die."

"At your hands, or at the hands of demons—does it matter now? Will you surrender your one last chance to escape? Set me free and I will go to the rim of the world and bring my sisters back. Together we will wreak such vengeance as no mortal land has ever seen!"

An image flashed before Ker's eyes—but whether it was a true glimpse of the future or part of his own fragmenting imagination, he could not tell. Yet it caught his breath in wonder.

He saw Liana like a pearl of silver against the noon-black sky. Her body flowed and rippled in a river of light, expanding in ring after ring of power, running across the sky as a flood of white energy—

"Liana!" he heard himself whisper, feeling the torrent of events rushing past, feeling the tug of powers beyond his comprehension. His thoughts seemed to be rushing outward, ever outward, beyond the tavern, beyond the city, beyond the rim of the world.

He looked and saw her staring at him, a puzzled expression on her face. "Liana," he whispered. "It will work. I see it—your freedom—"

She said to Zeren, "The wheel turns: this you yourself have said. Do now what you must."

Zeren swallowed. "So be it." He drew his dagger as Liana knelt before him. She ripped her dress from neck to stomach. Slowly he placed the blade of the knife against the white of her flesh. A trickle of red appeared, running between her breasts, staining the silk of her gown. He hesitated.

"Do it now! All flesh is but illusion. I am not human."

"No!" He stood, throwing the blade aside, and cursed helplessly. He couldn't look at her beautiful face. "No, I cannot, Liana. I'm too weak. I love you too much to hurt you!"

She turned to Ker. "Then you must do it."

"Me?"

"You must. Trust me. Would you want all that we've done to have been for nothing? Do you want the demon and his deeds to haunt you for the rest of your life?" She retrieved the dagger and placed it in his hand, then slowly wrapped his fingers around the handle and guided it to her breast. "It will be easy. Just close your eyes and push."

Ker swallowed. He thought of his vision, of her flowing through the sky, brilliant and powerful—majestic. Deep inside he sensed the truth of it all; this was more than imagination or hope. Perhaps it was a vision sent from Shon Atasha himself. *Yes,* he thought, *what I saw is real. And this must be done.*

He closed his eyes and pushed the blade into her heart. It entered her chest easily, as easily as it would enter a sheath. He heard the blade grate against bone and winced. He released its handle and dared, finally, to look.

Slowly, like a dry leaf falling from a tree, Liana slipped to the side and lay still. He saw no magic, saw nothing at all. There was a gentle expression on her face; slowly, blood trickled from her wound. For a second Ker panicked, a sudden chill sweeping through him.

Then he smelled ozone in the air, along with something else—something strange and urgent. He tensed, eager—and afraid.

A thin white mist came from Liana's lips, swirling up, hovering just below the timbers in the ceiling. This was nothing like what he'd expected, and every inch of his body shrilled warnings.

Zeren slowly skirted Liana's body until he stood next to Ker. Laying a light hand on Ker's shoulder, he pulled him back to the wall.

"Don't watch," he said, covering his own eyes.

But Ker found he couldn't look away. The scene fascinated him. As the mist thickened, the atmosphere in the room grew charged with energy. Blue sparks crackled over Liana's body; the air felt heavy—as though a storm were about to break. The air pushed against Ker from all sides at once. His ears ached. His head pounded. He knew then that he looked upon the sorcery of a god—this was no light magic such as Threnodrel or Biur might do.

Liana's body was shriveling away, skin stretching taut over her frame. Her bones themselves seemed to turn to dust, leaving her skin a dry, empty husk—and then it too was gone. Only her pale blue gown lay upon the floor.

The mist, thicker and heavier than before, whipped around the room like a whirlwind. Ker's hair ruffled. Around them, dust stirred, lifting into the air, making Ker's eyes tear. A table overturned with a solid thump. Pitchers and mugs smashed into the walls, ceramic shards ringing like hailstones on a tile roof. Ker's tunic snapped in the gale. He laughed in the wildness of the wind; stood, spreading his arms, embracing Liana in all her savage fury.

For an instant he stood in the eye of the storm, wrapped by deadly calm. Head reeling, drunk on power, he threw back his head and laughed.

Let the Dark One come for them now; let the demons smash in the door! He felt the tingle of power deep inside, knew it waited for the right moment to rise and burn through his body. He was apprentice no more, but a wizard himself, with all the power within him at his command!

Every facet of his life slipped into place: the delicate machinations of the gods, all that Gar Galimu had said, all that Zeren and Threnodrel had hinted at. He felt the flame inside him grow, kindled by his confidence. Closing his eyes for an instant, he saw the intricate patterns of blue magic spreading through his body, felt the fire in his veins, in his mind. He could trace all the patterns in the universe. Suddenly he saw all the intricate relationships between objects, the lines of force that held them together, the lines of force that could be torn apart and molded together. He saw himself as a bright flame burning in a sea of blue.

This was a wizard's power!

The mist moved toward the window and he followed. Before he could get the shutters open, they blew apart, splinters of wood raining across the street.

He laughed out into the night, drunk on the power around him. Liana howled, a savage sound full of emptiness and pain. And then she was gone.

Ker turned back to the room, looking at Zeren's stunned face. The Rashendi stared at the window, his face white. His hands twisted; his shoulders shook. The knife—still dark and wet with Liana's blood—now lay on the floor at his feet.

Ker swallowed. *He loved her,* he knew suddenly. And then all the terror and apprehension crashed over him like a wave in the darkness. He knew all that Zeren had suffered in those last minutes—tasted the fear that he'd kill her when he thrust the dagger through her heart.

The white of her breasts. The smell of her hair as he touched the blade to her skin. The red of her blood as it trickled from the wound. Her last, forgiving look as she felt the blade entering her body, but didn't dare cry out lest the slightest noise make him think he'd hurt her. The last sight of her body before it faded, vanished into mist.

He felt the power receding, leaving him aching with the emptiness of its passing. His vision of the power within him faded as well. He thought, *Not yet. The time has not yet come.* He tried to swallow and couldn't.

Struggling to his feet, Zeren crossed to the window and pulled the remains of the shutters closed. Only the frames remained whole, and they offered little concealment from the street and probing eyes.

"We must get Biur now," Ker said. "Zeren? Zeren?"

"Yes," Zeren said distantly.

20

The Tunnels Below

All things are forgotten with age: memory fades or people die or places just fall into disuse. As the oldest city in the world, Zelloque is full of the odd corners and forgotten passages which make habitations for cutthroats and thieves.

—Ciol Bartiv
A Tour of Zelloque

They left the inn not long afterward. Fog rolled between buildings like banks of clouds, making it hard to see more than a few feet ahead, and the air had taken on a chill that made Ker shiver. Lightning flickered overhead almost constantly now, and an icy rain fell. In seconds Ker's clothes were soaking wet; his shirt stuck uncomfortably to his back and arms as he moved.

Zeren turned left and set off at a fast pace. Ker jogged to keep up. *At last,* he thought, *we're finally* doing *something, instead of sitting around and talking about it.*

Doors had been bolted and windows shuttered against the storm. Not a trace of light showed from any of the buildings ahead. Not even a stray dog could be seen wandering the street. The silence was unnatural, oppressive; the fog seemed to swallow sound. Even their footsteps sounded muted, distant.

"It's so cold!" Ker said, after they'd been walking for several minutes. The buildings here, from what little he could see during flashes of lightning, were tall and imposing, with high stone arches and intricate woodwork.

"It's Faramigon's Eye," Zeren said. "Normally it's very warm at this time of the year. This cold will, undoubtedly, destroy much of the city's food crops. It's that wizard-demon's doing! The forces that hold the world together are unbalanced. When the storm breaks, you will know its full weirdness. All in Zelloque will feel it."

"Where are we going?"

"Kalan found a secret passage into the dungeons. Threnodrel and

I were to meet him by the main gate. We planned to go together to rescue Biur."

Zeren grew silent, and somehow Ker didn't feel like asking more questions. They continued at a good pace, threading their way through the foggy streets. The whole trip took on a strange, dream-like quality, and Ker imagined their leaving their world and walking in another. Wisps of fog were people all around them. If he strained into the silence, he could almost hear the roar of a thousand conversations.

Then came a blinding flash as lightning struck somewhere close, and the crash of thunder that followed was almost deafening. Ker shook his head and forced his fantasy world away. There were more important things to think of—first of all, rescuing Biur. And then the bones . . .

He became aware of a presence beside him. A light hand touched his shoulder and he jumped, startled. Turning, he found Kalan walking beside him—again in human form, again dressed all in black.

"Don't sneak up on me like that!"

"I ask forgiveness, Ker; I meant no harm."

Zeren had heard them. He turned and motioned for them to hurry up, and when they were all together, he turned and pressed on. Ker could hear him gasping for breath and knew the Rashendi wasn't used to such exertion.

He said to Kalan, "I'm sorry, I didn't mean to yell at you. It's just this storm! I . . ." He didn't quite know how to put his uneasiness into words. Instead, he changed the subject. "Zeren said you were going to meet us at the main gate."

"Yes. That is why I came. Strange creatures move through the streets. I have watched them, and though they dress as guards, they are not. I came to warn you."

Zeren stopped, turned. "What do you mean, they're not?"

Kalan shrugged a bit. "Just that they do not move correctly. Their walk is strange, hunched over, and they do not march in formation like other guards I have seen."

Ker swallowed. "They sound like demons."

"Yes," Zeren said. He stopped. "Fortunately, we're almost there. You lead the way, Kalan—you know where this passage is better than I."

"As you wish." The Syrnae started forward.

"Where is it?" Ker asked. "In case we get separated, I should know."

"The guards have their barracks and offices inside the wall that circles the city," Kalan said. "There is a secret passage from one of the offices into the dungeon. Perhaps it would be used if ever prisoners seized weapons and tried to escape; perhaps it serves another purpose. Still, it's there, and that's all we need to know to rescue Biur."

"How did you discover it?" Ker said, a bit suspicious.

Kalan shrugged a bit. "Such things are easily found, if you know where to look, and as what."

As what? Ker wondered. *He must've shape-shifted into—a cat?* He looked at Kalan uncertainly, wondering again what the Syrnae truly looked like.

They left the tall, imposing mansions and passed through a run-down part of the city. A tall, fat man dressed in muddy greens and yellows staggered out of the fog and almost walked into Kalan. The Syrnae danced back nimbly. When the fellow pushed at Kalan and missed, he almost fell. His clothes reeked of stale wine, Ker noticed, wrinkling his nose in disgust.

"Why don't you watch where you're going?" the man whined. Then he wandered off down the street.

"Drunk," Zeren said, shaking his head. "This city is old and decadent. The Great Lord wouldn't have allowed such things twenty years ago."

"We are almost there," Kalan said. He moved forward cautiously.

Ker noticed a few more drunks slouched in doorways and tried not to stare at them. Most of his father's soldiers drank, but never so much that they didn't know what they were doing. He'd never seen such a depressing sight before, and for an instant felt glad of the shroud of fog.

Ker could barely see Kalan's back, fifteen feet ahead. Then the fog parted for an instant and he saw the city wall straight ahead, perhaps two hundred yards away. Its wet stones shone like glass. Swiftly the fog closed and only his brief, tantalizing glimpse of the wall told him that they'd almost reached their destination.

Sounds of fighting reached them from somewhere ahead—swords ringing on swords, brief curses, shouts, a scream of pain that cut off abruptly. Ker couldn't tell from how far away or from what direction the noise came. He drew up beside Kalan and stared into the grayness, straining to hear.

Zeren pulled them both back into the shelter of a doorway. "Quiet now!" he whispered. "We don't want to walk into them."

"Kalan can find them," Ker said.

He shook his head. "Too risky. What if he got caught?"

"I will not be," Kalan said. He stepped out into the street before Zeren could protest. Spreading his arms apart, he seemed to wither a bit, to bend over and pull his legs to his chest. His skin rippled and pulled into itself, his arms shortening, his body shrinking. Black feathers sprouted from his clothing and pulled back against his skin. In a second, the change was done and Kalan stood before them as a large black raven.

He hopped forward a few feet, cocked his head to the side, then spread his wings and, with a couple of sharp flaps, launched himself into the air. Circling up between buildings, he gained height rapidly. Then the swirling fog closed around him.

Ker looked at Zeren, but there was little hope in his voice as he said, "They must be the first scouts Suthyran sent out—some of the demons Kalan saw earlier."

"If so," the Rashendi said, "we have few hours left."

Kalan returned in a moment, gliding silently on widespread wings. He landed and seemed to stand up from the bird, skin rippling and re-forming into his human shape, black feathers smoothing out into clothing once more. He looked slightly puzzled.

"Well?" Zeren demanded.

"Demons," Kalan said in confirmation. "They killed a group of ten guards and continued up the street. The way ahead lies clear."

"Good," Zeren said, and they pressed on up the street.

Soon they came to the high, thick stone wall surrounding the city. Kalan hesitated a moment, getting his bearings, then pointed to the left. "That way." Again they moved forward, still cautious, listening for sounds of more demons.

At last they came to a large door set deep into the wall, well back from the road. "There," he said softly, "is the place the guards sleep."

"How did you get past them?" Ker asked.

"I walked among them. They did not wake. If you move quietly, you will not disturb them."

"Very well," Zeren said. "Lead the way!"

Kalan walked up to the door and pushed it open. It moved easily on well-oiled hinges. Ker followed the Syrnae into a small hallway lit only by a small lantern. The walls had been whitewashed recently and the smell of lime was overpowering.

Kalan turned right without a second's hesitation. They passed a half-dozen doors that opened into rooms full of rows of cots. On the cots sprawled men in various stages of undress. Armor and uniforms hung from pegs in the walls. It would be easy, Ker thought, for the demons to slaughter the guards as they slept. He knew, somehow, that Suthyran counted on that.

Still the passage continued, stretching ahead as far as Ker could see. They passed empty offices, interrogation rooms, holding cells. All were empty. Few of the cells looked as though they'd been used recently; many had broken bars, locks rusted shut, or piles of old uniforms and weapons stored in them.

At last Kalan turned and entered a large meeting hall. Ker and Zeren followed close behind. A large table with well-padded chairs to either side took up most of the space, and the smell of must and slow decay hung in the air. They skirted the furniture carefully. The only light came from the hall.

In the near dark, Ker tried to watch Kalan's every move. The Syrnae seemed to shimmer and ripple as he neared the stone wall at the back of the room. At last he seemed to flow rather than walk across the floor. Reaching the wall, he crept up it, clinging like a spider to the stones, pressing and probing here and there with large, clawed hands. At last Ker heard a loud *click*, and Kalan dropped to the floor.

The Syrnae gave the wall a push with one hand and a small section of it swung back, revealing—darkness. A chill, damp wind came from it.

"This is the way," he said.

Ker hesitated. "How far did you explore?"

"I traveled the entire length, starting from the dungeon. The way is very straight, carved through the bedrock upon which Zelloque rests; we will not get lost."

"Hurry, then," Zeren said, stepping forward. "There can't be much time left." He seemed determined to take the lead, as though he were ashamed of his weakness at the inn and now wanted to make up for it.

"A number of old torches lie beside the door," Kalan said, as he followed Zeren through the door.

Ker brought up the rear. He had an uneasy feeling about the passage, but decided it was probably his imagination. The thought of walking hundreds of feet underground in absolute darkness made him more than a little nervous. Anything could be waiting to ambush them—demons, guards, or whatever sort of creatures lived beneath the city. Still, if it would free Biur . . .

Zeren had found the torches and taken three of them. Now he thrust one into Ker's hands.

"What do you want me to do with it?" Ker asked.

"Light it, of course." He made it sound self-evident.

"But—" Ker began. Then he realized the Rashendi didn't have a tinderbox, and probably expected him to use magic to start a fire. He'd never seen Biur or Threnodrel create one with their powers, but guessed it couldn't be too hard. Hadn't his master said fire was a prime facet of magic? "I'll try," he said hesitantly.

He let his vision slip into the blue of magic. He saw the torch, traced ever-so-faintly with blue. Reaching out with his mind, he felt the pattern of the wood, felt the patterns traced in the pitch and straw tied around its end. Next he thought of an open fire, picturing in his mind open flames dancing, how they would flicker, how they would burn. The patterns were there . . .

In his imagination, the flames he saw held traces of blue; the blue was twined like string, but also writhed like a fish on dry land.

"Yes," he whispered, knowing that was the pattern he sought, and he reached out with his thoughts, forcing the energy around him together, onto the torch. There he shaped it into cold blue flames. For a second he wondered what more he needed to do, but then the pattern came back to him and he kept the twined strands of blue central in his thoughts. Closing his eyes, he released the torch.

A hot white light flared before him, bright enough to penetrate his eyelids. He drew away, shielding his eyes. Slowly the white light faded to a more normal yellow.

Quickly he lit the other torches. For the first time he looked at what lay ahead.

They stood at the mouth of a tunnel that curved down and to the left. The walls here had been built of large stone blocks, but thirty feet farther he could see chisel marks where a passage had been cut through the bedrock.

"I meant for you to go back to one of the oil lamps," Zeren said. His voice sounded oddly strained.

Ker turned to look at him. "Sorry. I didn't think of that." He handed the Rashendi and Kalan each a torch, then started forward at an even pace. Behind him, he heard the others hurrying to keep up.

They'd gone perhaps a hundred yards down the tunnel when Ker heard a grating noise. He stopped and held up his hand for quiet, but heard nothing more—just his rough breathing, and Zeren's. Kalan stood as quietly as a ghost.

"What was that?" he whispered.

"Perhaps the door behind us swung shut?" Zeren said, not sounding very confident of it himself.

"Perhaps," Ker said. Swallowing, he decided to press on.

When he took a step, the stone floor beneath him tilted forward at a sharp angle. He fell on his back with a sharp cry of surprise and pain, then slid down.

Zeren and Kalan also fell, the Rashendi shouting in surprise, Kalan scrambling to try and climb back up to the tunnel. Ker had found the bottom by then and the others landed on top of him. He pushed them away and struggled to his feet a bit unsteadily.

A fifteen-foot section of floor had suddenly dropped them down into a pit, he saw at once. His torch had gone out, so he picked up Zeren's instead and swung it in a wide arc. It flared briefly, sending a flicker of light up to the tunnel ceiling twenty feet overhead.

"No," he heard Zeren mumbling, "no, no, no. Why do these things always happen to us?"

Ker turned. Zeren sat on the floor, rubbing his back. Slowly, awkwardly, the Rashendi climbed to his feet. He groaned a bit.

Ker turned his attention to escape. *With a bit of effort,* he thought, *we'd be able to climb back up the slide to the tunnel.* But that wouldn't get them past the pit. He cursed their luck, guessing one of them had accidentally set off the trap—probably the grating noise.

Then he heard the muffled sounds of human voices. He sighed and closed his eyes. *All we need is to be discovered here. Then we'll all be able to join Biur for his execution tomorrow.*

The voices grew louder, and in a minute five men appeared at the sheer end of the pit. They all carried torches and wore the uniforms of city guards. Several were yawning and all looked more than a little sleepy. And each one held a drawn sword.

Their leader stepped to the edge of the pit and looked down. He grinned. "Well, it seems we've caught three little rats in our trap, haven't we?" He motioned toward the wall at his feet and Ker noticed handholds had been carved there. He guessed they weren't the first people to fall into this trap. "Climb out of there. We'll take you to see Captain Mirane. He'll know what to do with night prowlers like you!"

"Yes, do that!" Ker called up to him. "Take us to your Captain. I'm sure he's a reasonable man."

"Sure he is." The guard's grin turned into a harsh laugh. "He'll make certain you get a nice trial, before your execution."

"I am of the Rashendi," Zeren said stiffly. "You would do well to remember your manners!"

The guard spat. "I may get to kill you myself."

"I'll see you banished for that!" Zeren said. "I serve Shon Atasha the Creator, and his power—"

"Shut up! You there in the black—you climb out first. Slowly! I wouldn't want to have to give the captain a corpse to question, would I?"

Kalan climbed out. Two of the guards seized his arms and bound them behind his back. Then Ker went up, and they did the same to him. Zeren came last, protesting all the while. After they tied his hands, they gagged him. Then he just glared.

"That way," the guard said, shoving Ker down the tunnel.

An hour later they were dragged into a small room to face a tall, muscular, dark-haired man in an immaculate red-and-black uniform. He had a short black beard and carried himself with an air of authority. Ker didn't have to ask to know that this was Mirane, the captain of the guard.

At first he just walked around them, studying them, looking them over. He smiled a bit at Zeren's gag, but made no effort to remove it. Then, after nodding for a moment and chewing on his lip, he went back to his seat and flopped down. He glared at the two guards who'd escorted them in.

"You woke me up for *this?*" he demanded.

The first guard paled. "Sir, I thought it important."

Ker stepped forward. "Captain Mirane," he said, "it *is* important. A matter more urgent than you realize brought us here."

"Oh, I'm sure of that!" he said sarcastically. "It's always important when people break into sealed passages in the middle of the night. Trying to rescue a friend of yours from the prison? Of course, of course. It's always that, isn't it?"

"No," Ker said.

Mirane leaned forward, elbows on the table, chin cradled in his hands. "This should be an entertaining lie."

"I'd speak better if I were untied. And I'm sure my friend would very much appreciate it if you ungagged him."

"Very well; there's little chance that you'll escape." He smiled. "I must admit you're the most improbable band of people ever to try to rescue someone from the Great Lord's dungeon—the guards say you weren't even armed with a knife!" He chuckled at that. Leaning back, he motioned to the guards, who drew daggers and cut them free.

Ker rubbed his wrists. "Thank you."

"It's nothing. Now, tell me your story. It had better be entertaining—I don't enjoy getting up in the middle of the night."

Ker drew a deep breath and launched into their tale. Zeren cut in at times, adding details, corroborating wherever necessary. When they spoke of the demons in Rhimalga, Mirane leaned forward, his interest obvious. And when Ker spoke of Suthyran and named him as the one who'd stolen the bones, Mirane only smiled.

"Now," Ker said, "the demons are loose in Zelloque. There will be a battle here—and you'd better alert your men now, while you still can."

"And you must help us reclaim the bones of Shon Atasha," Zeren said. "Suthyran must not be allowed to defile them!"

Mirane frowned, scratching his beard. He looked at Zeren, then at Kalan, then at Ker. Then he sighed. "What you say makes a certain amount of sense, in some ways," he said. "I find it easy to believe Suthyran plans ill for Zelloque; never did I trust him and his soft ways. Now he leads the Great Lord around by the nose like a noble leads a prize horse. No decisions are made that Suthyran does not approve. Still—everything you say is so fantastic, so unbelievable!"

"It *is* that," Ker agreed. "But it's also the truth. It would be easy enough for you to check every detail—just look outside at the storm, or go to the idolmaker's shop and see the bones for yourself."

Zeren added dryly, "Or wait just a few hours more."

"What do you mean?" Mirane demanded. "Wait for what?"

"This storm—Faramigon's Eye—only comes before great sorcery, when the forces that hold the world together are unbalanced for a time. Tonight the storm will hit; therefore, Suthyran must be about to strike. And, as Ker told you, the Winds are coming. When they arrive, the streets will not be safe for man or demon."

As he said that, a loud roar came from outside—like a thousand voices screaming in terror. The walls shook; dust sifted down from the rafters. Mirane leaped to his feet, startled, his red cape flowing around his shoulders.

"What was that?" he shouted over the noise.

Ker smiled. "The Winds are here. The battle has begun."

21

The Winds in Their Wildness

There is a reason wizards are suspect in Zelloque: in this of all cities wizards seem to go insane with frightening regularity.

—Tellerion
Speculations

"No!" Mirane said, shocked. Still the walls trembled. Still the Winds roared. "That can't be!"

"You *must* act now," Ker said, "before it's too late."

The captain of the guard just looked at him. "I thought you were lying to save yourselves."

"Everything we told you is true." Zeren shook his head. "We must stop Suthyran at any cost—that's more important than any one of us. I would gladly die to destroy him and recover the bones he stole. Do you have the same loyalty to the Great Lord and Zelloque?"

Mirane bristled. "I swore to serve them both until my death!"

"If you want to save Zelloque, set my master free," Ker said. "He'll know how to stop Suthyran—and the Winds. His name is Biur, and he serves Derethigon. He's being held in the Great Lord's dungeon."

"I know of him. He's scheduled to be executed."

"Then get him out!"

"Yes." Mirane looked more confident. Now that he had a purpose again, he seemed to regain a measure of control. His expression became—not grim, but perhaps anxious, as though he looked forward to the coming fight. He strode to the door and pulled it open, shouting, "Guards!"

A half-dozen came running, swords drawn. Their faces were very, very pale and they kept glancing up toward the ceiling, as if half expecting the Winds to rip through the roof at any moment. Their knuckles were white and their hands shook.

"Call out the rest of the city guard," Mirane ordered them, over the noise. "There are demons in the streets outside. Zelloque has been invaded! Defend the Great Lord and his people! *Hurry!*"

They just stared at him for a moment, shocked. Then they turned and ran. Ker could hear them shouting orders, rousing the men, calling on all their reserve forces. He smiled a bit in relief. Now, with luck, the city would have a chance against the demons.

Mirane turned to Zeren and gave a short bow. "My apologies for the delay. I see now that I should have listened to you immediately—then, perhaps much of the battle would already be over and we could concentrate on fighting the Winds—if that's possible."

"You shouldn't have to fight them," Zeren said. "They were to kill demons only—"

"But when they find the demons are dressed as guards, how will they tell the difference?" Mirane said. "No, we will be attacked from two sides at once. I pray the gods will let this wizard of yours end the fight quickly."

"If such is Shon Atasha's will," the Rashendi intoned.

Mirane glared at him. "It had better be! Now, follow me—we'll set Biur loose, then see what can be done against Suthyran."

He led them down a short flight of stairs to another tunnel, this one well lighted by torches. Guards stood at attention and saluted as they passed, and Ker was glad to have someone in authority on their side for once. Now they were getting things done.

"Where are we going?" Zeren asked, panting for breath.

Over his shoulder, Mirane said, "This passage leads directly to the palace. It's the fastest way there—especially now, with the storm, the demons, and the Winds above."

"Wait!" Kalan said loudly, stopping. They halted and looked at him. Cocking his head to the side, he seemed to listen. Then: "Men are fighting ahead."

"I don't hear anything," Mirane said doubtfully.

"I am not human," Kalan said. "My hearing is far keener than yours can ever be. I hear men fighting."

Still the captain of the guard hesitated. Ker said, "Is there any other way to the palace from here?"

"Perhaps through the catacombs beneath the city. But it wouldn't be as fast, and I'm not certain of the way—I haven't been through them in many, many years."

"It would be better to take a few more minutes and arrive safely than to force our way through a battle," Zeren said. "Surely you agree?"

"Of course." He started forward again, though softly now, and loosened his sword in its scabbard. "The tunnel branches ahead. We can enter the catacombs there."

In a minute Ker heard the sounds of fighting from ahead, the ringing of sword on sword and sword on stone, battle cries, screams of pain and fear. Then, as they came to the split in the tunnel, he saw the fighters: a dozen-odd guards slowly forcing a small band of dark-robed demons back. Both sides fought savagely, but the city guards outnumbered their opponents and were slowly winning out. As Ker watched, two demons died, skewered on the long, slightly curved swords of the guardsmen.

Captain Mirane paused for a moment, watching his men. His hand dropped to the hilt of his sword and caressed it for a moment. Ker thought he wanted to join the battle, to kill demons himself, but at last he cursed and looked away. Taking a torch from its holder in the wall, he started down the left tunnel, toward the catacombs.

The tunnel wound deeper into the earth; the ceiling lowered and the walls closed in. Now they had to travel single file, in places stooping to pass. Ker quickly lost all sense of direction. *It's like we're in Theshemna again,* he thought, remembering how Biur had taken him through the twisting corridors in the Palace of the Gods.

Twice more they heard sounds of fighting. Both times Mirane paused, listened, swore softly to himself. But he pressed on.

They came to another split in the tunnel. As Mirane moved to the right, someone down the left tunnel shouted his name.

He paused, holding his torch higher, looking into the darkness. "Who's there?"

"Caroltan, sir!" came a distant cry. "Wait!"

In a moment, a man staggered into the torchlight. Blood soaked his whole left side from a deep gash, and he pressed both hands to the wound. Panting, he collapsed before them.

Mirane ran forward and bent to tend the wound, but the man shook his head. "Demons," he whispered, "everywhere—dozens of them, coming from the dark—"

"Where?" Mirane demanded.

"In the palace . . . only a few of us escaped—"

"What do you mean, escaped?"

"We . . . ran." He couldn't meet his captain's gaze.

"And the Great Lord?"

"I don't know."

"How are your wounds?" he asked, pulling the man's hands apart, looking at the sword cut.

"I'll live, sir."

"I was afraid of that," Mirane said. He covered the man's eyes with his hand, then drew his knife. "Don't be afraid," he said, as the man tensed. "You won't feel a thing."

He drove the blade up under the man's jaw and into his brain. The guard flopped back and lay still.

Ker stared at the body in shock. "Why did you kill him?" he demanded.

Mirane stood. "Desertion," he said briefly. Ker could hear the strain in his voice, and knew, then, that it was something the commander of the guard had to do. It was not a duty he envied.

Captain Mirane bent, pried the sword from the dead man's fingers, and offered it to Zeren. "Here."

"I would be next to useless with that," the Rashendi said, his distaste obvious. "Give it to Ker, or to Kalan."

Kalan shook his head. "No. I have no need of such."

"I'll take it, then," Ker said.

Mirane tossed it to him. Blood still dripped from the blade; the grip was still warm from the dead man's hand. Ker felt uneasy as he hefted it.

The captain of the guard didn't give him a chance to think about it. Ker barely had a chance to take a practice swing before Mirane was off at a run again and he had to follow or be left behind.

They traveled in a gloomy silence now. Mirane walked ahead, alone, and now and then Ker could hear him whispering curses. Most seemed directed at Suthyran and his demons. Still they went on. At times Ker thought their journey would never end.

At last they came to a narrow, winding stone staircase that curved up and around, out of sight, and here Mirane stopped. Somewhere close, water dripped. They were so far underground Ker couldn't hear the Winds anymore.

"This is it," the captain of the guard said. "It leads up into the dungeon." He climbed the steps two at a time and the others followed.

Twice he came to trapdoors in the ceiling; twice he drew keys from his belt, fitted them into locks, pushed the trapdoors open. The sounds of the Winds grew steadily louder, rising from a hum like that of bees to a deep, throaty growl.

At last they climbed out into a small, dark room without windows. A desk in one corner held stacks of papers, sets of keys, a half-empty bottle of wine. This had to be the dungeon master's office, Ker knew.

Mirane went to the small door and pushed it open, leading the way into a narrow hallway lined with doors. Light flickered from small lamps set deep in walls that ran with water. Mold covered everything. A strong, cold breeze blew through the corridor, making Ker shiver. Terrified whimpers came from many of the cells.

"Your wizard should be here somewhere," Mirane said. "These prisoners are all scheduled to die."

"Biur!" Ker called. "Where are you?"

Someone banged on a door to the left. Ker ran quickly, eagerly toward the sound. At last he came to the right cell. Standing on tiptoe, he could just see through the small viewing slot. Biur lay inside, bound in chains and gagged. He'd been banging on the door with his feet.

"This is it," Ker said, standing back.

Mirane produced another key and fitted it into the lock. When the door opened, Ker rushed in and took the gag from his master's mouth while Mirane unlocked Biur's chains.

Dirt streaked the wizard's face, and his hair was matted and filthy. Bruises on his face showed where he'd been beaten. Nevertheless he smiled as Ker helped him to his feet; he stretched stiffly, wincing at various pains. His legs shook so much he could hardly stand.

"Can you walk?" Ker asked hesitantly.

Biur looked at him and his eyes were alight with power. "Magic," he whispered, "can work miracles." He closed his eyes for a moment and mumbled something. Slowly his hands moved, tracing patterns in the air. A blue glow appeared at his fingertips, spread across his body.

When Captain Mirane noticed, he leaped back with a curse and drew his sword. Ker grabbed his arm and forced it down.

"No—let him alone for a moment! He's healing himself."

Mirane lowered his sword. "He's not angry because I helped to lock him up?"

"Of course not. He knows that was Suthyran's doing."

The glow had completely covered Biur. His voice became stronger as he sang, and the power of his words swept through Ker. The bruises and cuts on Biur's face healed in an instant; the lines of stress faded. His hair grew thick and white. Even his ripped, filthy robe became whole again. When he stopped singing, the blue glow faded, the magic done.

"Now I am ready," he said.

Mirane swallowed nervously. "This way," he said. He gave Biur plenty of room as he pushed past, heading for the stairs to the upper floors of the palace.

Ker touched the wand he'd stolen from Suthyran, making sure it was safe, then followed.

The Winds howled outside, not far away. The whole palace was in a panic. Servants ran from room to room, some screaming, some crying, some clutching small bits of gold or silver they'd managed to snatch from one of the court's nobles. Corpses lay everywhere: guards, mostly, but a scattering of noblemen and ladies and their attendants as well. Pools of blood slowly congealed on the intricately mosaicked floors.

It had taken half an hour of winding through hallways and dozens of rooms to reach the huge audience hall, and they hadn't seen any signs of the Great Lord or his personal guards.

Biur looked around, shaking his head. "You must find the Great Lord," he told Captain Mirane. "If he still lives, order may yet be restored. He must show himself—gather his servants about him in an army!"

"Where would he be?" Zeren said.

"I thought he'd be here organizing the fight," Mirane said, "but I see no sign of him. None of the servants would be here if he'd left. Perhaps he's in his private chambers, planning his attack."

"Which way?" Biur asked.

"There." He pointed toward a small marble staircase in the corner. It led up to a wide balcony.

Biur went up the steps at a run, Ker following almost on his heels. At the top, they found two large, gold-inlaid oak doors. Ker pushed at them, but they'd been sealed from within.

Mirane pounded on them with the hilt of his sword. "Open up! It's Captain Mirane!" He paused, listening, but heard nothing. "Guards! Open up!"

"Well?" Biur said, looking across the balcony. There were no other doors. "Can we get in another way?"

"None that I know of. And these doors are almost a foot thick. We'll never be able to break through!"

"I will open it," Biur said.

Mirane moved back a few feet, watching the wizard with mingled awe and fear. Slowly Biur placed his hands together. When he drew them apart, his silver wand was there. He began to sing in a low voice, tracing patterns in the air before him.

Azure sparks ghosted over the door. The wood and metal seemed to writhe like a thing alive, pulling back, twisting away. It opened up before them until a hole large enough for a man to step through had appeared.

Biur lowered his wand and sagged to the side. Ker caught him and held him up, draping his master's arm around his shoulder. Even such a little magic seemed a great drain, and he wondered if his master would be a match for Suthyran when the two met. He forced the idea from his mind. Of course Biur would win: anything else was unthinkable!

Mirane stepped through the opening first, and the others followed. Ker came last, after his master.

They had entered a small, private audience hall. The silver-tiled ceiling arched ten feet overhead, to where a single crystal chandelier holding dozens of wax candles dangled, its light reflected a thousand times in the silver. Tapestries sewn with gold and silver thread hung the walls and carpeted the floor, and recesses to the right and left of the door held gold statues of the gods. Everywhere he looked Ker saw dazzling gleams and reflections.

It took him a minute to spot Narmon Ri. The Great Lord of Zelloque sat motionless on a low throne, robes of blue and gold flowing around him. Despite the splendor of his clothes, he seemed lost in the room, his costume dull and unimpressive by comparison to all the wealth and beauty around him.

Mirane ran forward and bowed. Slowly, the Great Lord of Zelloque stood. He moved forward even more slowly, down the three small steps from his throne until he stood before his captain of the guard.

"Rise," he said.

"My Lord," Mirane said, standing, "I have brought friends to help you. Suthyran has betrayed you and let an army of demons into the city. Zelloque is being destroyed! You must appear before the people—marshal your forces—lead them into battle as you did in your youth!"

"Fool!" the Great Lord shouted, slapping Mirane. "You have been tricked. That wizard"—his finger stabbed at Biur—"tried to kill me! Arrest them, or you will share their fate!"

"But—"

"Arrest them all!" Narmon Ri shouted. "They've destroyed my city! It's *they* who led the demons in! Suthyran warned me. I should have listened to him! And now they're trying to kill me—they're all trying to kill me!"

"My Lord," Mirane said, stepping forward. "It isn't true! Listen to me—*Suthyran* is your enemy, not they!"

"No!"

"Yes!" Mirane said. He knelt before the Great Lord of Zelloque, grabbed the hem of his gold-and-blue robes, kissed it. "My Lord, I have served you well all my life. You know this. I would never do anything to betray you. I—"

"Lies!" Narmon Ri shouted. He drew a knife from the sleeve of his robe and plunged it down into Mirane's back. Then he drew back, screaming, "Lies! Foul lies! You've betrayed me as well! *Traitor!*"

Ker gasped in shock at the Great Lord's sudden attack and instinctively moved forward to help. Biur grabbed his arm.

"No," he said. "Let Mirane speak. His wound is far from fatal. If the Great Lord will not listen to him, he certainly would not listen to us. And he must be made to listen. That is the most important thing right now!"

"Yes, master," Ker said, though it hurt inside to stand by helplessly while Mirane bled. If only he could do something—anything—to help.

He breathed a little easier as, slowly, the captain of the guard climbed to his feet. He staggered back, half turning until Ker could see his face, twisted with pain. Fortunately, his armor had turned the knife's blade from his heart; now the point protruded from his left shoulder. Blood flowed freely from the wound, spattering on the carpets at his feet.

"My Lord," he said softly, the strain making his voice break.

"Traitor!" Narmon Ri cried, laughing. "At least I shall watch you die, as the poison drains your life."

"Poison?" Mirane said slowly.

The Great Lord climbed the steps, sank back on his throne, a smile twisting his face. "Can't you feel it? It starts as an itch in your hands, Suthyran told me." He seemed to take great pleasure from his words, like a child showing off a new toy. "Then it spreads to your face, your chest, your stomach. Slowly, elegantly, it eats away your insides."

Ker whispered, "Can you help him?"

"No," Biur said. "I know little of poisons—if what the Great Lord says is true."

"If?"

He shrugged. "He must be insane, or drugged. That is how Suthyran must have won such influence over him. And what can be done? Who knows the working of a madman's mind? Telling Mirane he will die may be just a subtle torture. Only time will prove it true or false."

Mirane trembled. He stepped back from the Great Lord, bowing low, although he gasped in pain from the effort as the knife turned in his shoulder. Then he drew his sword.

"My Lord," he said, "forgive me. What I do now, I do for the good of Zelloque. Once you would have approved."

"No!" Narmon Ri screamed. "Don't kill yourself—not yet! I want to watch!"

"You may watch what I do," said Mirane, "if you wish." He stepped forward and, with a quick, clean thrust, drove his sword up into the Great Lord's chest. Blood spurted from the wound in a long stream. The Great Lord screamed, a wild, bestial sound like an animal in pain.

Ker gaped in shock. Blood poured from Narmon Ri's mouth, dribbling down his chin. He beat feebly at the sword as his blood continued to spurt in smaller and smaller jets. He writhed and twisted, making a little choking, crying sound.

Mirane leaned on the sword, driving it farther into the Great Lord's body. It made a sound like fingernails on slate as it slid through bone.

Then Narmon Ri, the Great Lord of Zelloque, gave a final gurgle and died. Mirane reeled back, leaving his master stuck there like an insect on a pin. The Great Lord's blood covered him. He looked down at his hands, up at what he'd done, and wept.

Slowly he sat and stared at the floor. Ker broke free of Biur and ran forward to help him. He knelt, longing to do something to ease the pain, not knowing what. Mirane looked up at him, eyes dark.

"No, boy," he whispered. "Stand back. Nothing can be done for me now." He suddenly clutched his stomach and doubled over, moaning, his whole body tense. In a moment, when the pain eased a bit, he whispered, "I feel the poison. It . . . *aanhh!*" And then he slipped to the side and lay still, his eyes fixed on something far away. The Mad God, the God of Death, had taken him.

Ker stood, sick at his stomach. His head hurt and his eyes burned, but he couldn't look away.

Biur touched his shoulder. "Come," his master said gently, pulling him toward the door. "Nothing more can be done here. We must get the bones *now*, before it's too late. I hear Liana and her sisters outside. They will deal with Suthyran's army. When the bones are safe, we can return to kill Suthyran."

"Yes, Biur," Ker said. He looked at his master. Biur appeared very old, very tired, suddenly.

Outside, the Winds roared.

The palace had grown very quiet; all the servants had either found hiding places or fled. They went through the empty rooms quickly, meeting no resistance. In the main entry hall, Biur stopped them.

"Which way is fastest to the idolmaker's shop?" he asked. "I gather from the lack of guards here that the battle has moved out into the streets. It would probably be dangerous to try to reach the bones that way. How did you get here?"

"Mirane brought us through the catacombs under the city," Ker said. "We heard fighting there as well."

"That is to be expected," Biur said.

"There is a secret tunnel," Kalan said.

Zeren snorted. "Filled with demons and guards, the last time we looked."

"No, I meant the other—the one in which we were captured. Its entrance and exit are both hidden; there are a few other entryways, and they are hidden as well. Surely the demons have not found them."

Biur nodded. "Yes. That way will do. Lead us to the entrance."

Kalan turned. Again they went through the corridors, winding down past abandoned guard posts, back to the dungeon. In the entrance, Kalan paused and examined the stones to his right. Finally he reached out and pushed one as hard as he could.

It moved back. With a grating sound, a section of the wall slid aside, revealing a narrow passage. Zeren and Biur each took torches from notches in the wall. Kalan led the way.

Behind them, the door slid shut. Ker glanced over his shoulder, but saw nothing. He guessed it had closed by itself. At least the demons wouldn't be able to follow them.

The tunnel curved down and opened up before them, into a wide, high passage that stretched ahead as far as the light showed. Ker listened for the Winds, but heard nothing. They were too far under the city. Zeren set a quick pace while Kalan scouted ahead for traps. Nobody said anything: demons might be nearby.

Ten minutes later, they came to the trap they'd fallen into earlier. It hadn't been reset.

Ker went first. Zeren dropped his torch to him, then climbed down, followed by Biur. Now, Ker saw, the incline didn't look quite as steep as it once had. Kalan ran up it easily. Ker followed and grinned at the Syrnae, who grinned back. Then came Biur, who walked up it with ease, and Zeren, who tried but kept slipping back to the bottom again. Finally Ker and Kalan slid back down and helped pull him up.

"Is it much farther?" Biur asked, when they all stood at the top.

"No, master," Ker said. "We'll be there in a moment."

"Good," he whispered.

They made it to the meeting room five minutes later. The first thing Ker noticed was the sound—a dull, incessant whine from far away. The Winds, he thought.

Then he and Kalan slipped out into the hallway. The lamps still burned, which he thought was a good sign, and he saw no trace of bodies—there hadn't been any fighting here. For an instant he had a terrible thought: what if the demons had butchered the guard while they slept? Well, if so, nothing could be done about it now. He listened, but heard nothing; the passage seemed safe enough. He motioned to the others, and they quickly joined him.

They crept down the hall softly, passing the offices, the holding cells, the interrogation rooms. At last they came to the rooms where he'd seen the sleeping men.

Ker peered into the first. It was deserted—and all the armor had been taken from the pegs in the walls. Sighing in relief, he knew then that their warning to Mirane had done some good: the city guard had been prepared before the demons attacked. Perhaps they were fighting even now in the streets.

"Wait," his master said, as he started forward again.

"Yes, Biur?" he said.

"We know where the bones are, but we also need something to put them in—a wagon or cart of some kind. We will not be able to carry them ourselves, you know."

"There is a large warehouse not far from here," Kalan said. "I saw it earlier. Something there will be able to carry them."

"Then you will show me where it is," Biur said. He looked at Ker. "You must go with Zeren and help him as best you can."

"Wait!" Ker said. "Shouldn't Zeren and I get the cart?"

The wizard shook his head. "No. If we run into demons, you would not be able to drive them off; Kalan and I can."

"Yes, sir." Though he longed to go with his master, Ker realized he'd be of more use with Zeren. "As you wish."

"Good," Biur said. "Then we're agreed. Lead the way."

Ker headed for the door. When he turned the corner, he found it had been torn off its hinges. Through the opening he saw Faramigon's Eye.

Rain pounded down. Lightning flickered constantly overhead, lighting up the whole sky as brightly as dawn, and thunder was an incessant roar. Only the howl of the Winds was louder, a wild, gyrating scream of power that set his teeth on edge. He shivered suddenly, uncontrollably.

"The bones are to the left," Kalan said, "and the warehouse lies to the right."

"Then we will part company here," Biur said. He nodded to Ker and Zeren, smiling with assurance. "I will join you soon." Then he turned and ran into the storm, followed by the Syrnae.

Ker swallowed. "Good luck," he whispered.

"Are you ready?" Zeren asked.

"Yes!"

"Then let's go." He stepped out into the rain and Ker followed.

They'd gone perhaps fifty feet, keeping close to the wall, when Ker heard a loud shout behind him. He turned. Through the curtain of rain he could just make out a large band of men who'd come from a side street.

He squinted. No, not men, but demons: they walked bent over, and most wore black cloaks and hoods. Their faces were pale, human—torn from guards or innocent citizens they'd murdered, he thought.

"Run!" he shouted, leaping forward. "They've seen us!"

The Rashendi glanced back with a low curse. "The shop is just ahead," he called, "the tall building on your left!"

Ker tucked down his head and ran for his life. *Fifty yards, forty.* His breath came in sharp pants; his lungs burned and his gut felt like he'd swallowed a handful of marbles. *Fifteen yards.* Risking a glance over his shoulder, he saw the demons were gaining on them. *Almost there . . .*

He reached the idolmaker's shop, skidding on the slick cobblestones in front of the entrance. The door stood open, the outside lock smashed. Ker ran in anyway and held the door for Zeren.

The demons had almost caught the Rashendi. They screamed at him, their words harsh, grating, and they threw knives that went far wide of target. Zeren pounded into the shop with them almost on his heels.

"Close the door!" he screamed.

22

The Demon's Engine

"You can run from a wizard, but if he wants to find you, he will."

—Coranian Proverb

Ker slammed the door shut behind the Rashendi. Fortunately, the inner locks hadn't been destroyed; he rammed their bolts home. Over the roar of the storm he heard a nerve-grating cry of rage and frustration. The door shuddered as the demons pounded on it with their wooden clubs and swords, trying to break in.

Zeren stood beside him, bent over, panting loudly. His face was gray and he trembled all over. Ker would never have guessed the Rashendi could run so fast.

For the first time he looked around the idolmaker's shop. The windows had all been shuttered tightly against the storm and thieves, and deep shadows pooled across the floor. Zeren lit a small oil lamp and set it in a niche in the wall. A warm yellow glow filled the room.

It was a medium-sized shop—about the size of the banquet hall in Baron Orrum's castle—with a high beamed ceiling and thick stone walls. Benches and tables covered with tools stood everywhere. Works in progress took up most of the floor. A dozen huge blocks of white stone—the bones?—sat on low, wheeled carts. Each piece was in a different stage of carving. Some stood in rough poses, arms outstretched or held high overhead as if in invocation; others were just hulking shapes whose forms seemed almost-but-not-quite human; others still were just eight-foot-high white cubes with charcoal markings on their sides. Chips of stone and dust littered the floor.

Against the far wall stood more of the immense stone blocks, these covered with large pieces of sail canvas.

Zeren hurried forward to the nearest block, touched it gently, almost reverently. Then he cursed. "It's marble!"

"Check the other ones," Ker said. He ran to the back wall, to the canvas, and pulled it away. More blocks stood behind it. Work had already begun on two of them.

But there was something strange about them, something he couldn't quite identify, a *presence* that seemed to hang over them. He felt an odd tingling in his hand as he touched first one, then another. The sensation was pleasant, soothing, like stroking the back of a favorite dog. Small blue veins marbled the bones. He could feel something alive in them, something powerful, and he let his vision slip into the blue of magic. The bones glowed brightly, rivaling the sun. Ker drew back.

"I've found them," he said in a low voice.

But Zeren was already at his side, running his hands across them, caressing them as a man caresses a woman he loves. He sighed in relief. "They are safe!"

The wind moaned outside, louder than before. The stone walls seemed to tremble. Overhead, dust sifted down from the rafters, and the thick wooden beams creaked loudly, as though they might cave in at any moment.

Ker caught his breath, suddenly afraid. The wind slacked a bit; outside the demons began battering the door with something heavy. The bolts showed no sign of giving, though.

"Will they break through?" Zeren asked.

He shook his head. "Not yet. The door's thick." *I wish Biur would hurry.* How long before the demons found a way around the door—or before the Winds brought the roof down on top of them?

Against the far wall of the shop, something stirred. Ker turned, sensing something odd. Darkness gathered: the air took on a thick, oily sheen, as though he were looking through a thick glass; a blue spark appeared and hung suspended five feet from the floor.

"Zeren—" he began.

The spark grew brighter, larger; spun into a disk as big as his hand, rapidly enlarging: a foot in diameter . . . two feet . . .

It exploded with light. Wave after wave of searing blue washed across the room. The brilliance blinded Ker for a second, and he threw up his hands to shield his eyes, squinting, trying to see.

The light subsided, revealing a matte black Gateway. Its surface rippled a bit, then grew still.

And Kalan stepped out of it, into the idolmaker's shop. He'd taken on human guise again. A long, black cloak was wrapped tightly about his shoulders.

"Where have you been?" Ker cried. "What's keeping Biur?"

"We have found a great engine, one large enough to carry the bones from here. Soon Biur will come. He wishes you to clear a place for the engine; it is large."

Ker nodded. "Of course."

Quickly they set to work. The three of them together could barely shift the largest blocks of stone, even though they sat on carts. Groaning and straining, they managed to push them out of the way. They shoved the first one up against the door, then used others to block the windows. Ker hoped they'd help keep the demons from breaking in.

Finally a large space had been cleared in front of the Gateway. Ker studied it a moment before nodding in satisfaction.

"This *is* enough room?" he asked.

Kalan shrugged a bit. "I will tell Biur." Then he turned and ran toward the Gateway, leaped into it—and disappeared.

In seconds Ker sensed a change in the air; a prickling started at the base of his neck and crept down his spine. The world seemed to be slowing around him. The whistle of the Winds outside became muted and dull, and the demons' incessant pounding vanished to a dull roar somewhere in the back of his head. He turned to the Gateway and let his sight slip into the blue of magic.

Azure lines laced the black surface of the Gateway, radiating from the center like the arrow-straight spokes of a wheel. They began to bend and twist, to spiral out and pull back, forming a new checkered pattern of diamond shapes. Blue flames danced. The Gateway began to expand again, growing taller, wider. Ker felt a sharp, cold wind on his face.

Then the magic was done. The Gateway stood thirty feet high, almost touching the ceiling of the shop. The storm outside howled with renewed force, shaking the walls, and the noise of the demons' attack grew still more frantic. They seemed to be hacking at the door with swords. Ker could hear the ring of metal on wood, the deep *chuck* as blades caught and for a second wouldn't pull free.

Then, from somewhere inside the Gateway, Ker heard a strange creaking, grinding sound that set his teeth on edge. He took a step back, uncertain. What sort of engine had Biur found?

A long wooden pole pierced the Gateway fifteen feet over Ker's head . . . and it kept getting longer and longer. Finally it grew into the prow of a ship, and a great wooden wheel broke the Gateway's surface five feet from him.

It was the engine Suthyran had used to steal the bones, he realized suddenly, amazed. Biur stood on deck, his arms spread wide in an embrace to the world, and in his right hand he held his wand. He sang those strange, rhythmic words Ker could almost-but-not-quite understand, and his wand shone as bright as the sun, radiating wave after wave of light, each pulse matching the rhythm of his words.

Again Ker marveled at the machine. Close up, he saw that it had indeed once been a true ship such as the ones he'd seen in Zelloque's harbor. Four immense wooden wheels had been added, each twenty feet tall—as high as the deck—and various doors and hatches had been cut into the hull just as he remembered.

It's not going to fit, he thought then, remembering the tall masts with their ruined rigging. *It's going to catch on the top of the Gateway—*

A dry cracking startled him, until the remains of the first mast appeared. It had been sheared off cleanly, seven feet above the deck. Then the second mast broke, and the whole engine squeezed through and glided to a halt. It filled the idolmaker's shop, the tip of the prow almost touching the front wall, the stern a scant five feet from the back one, the remains of its masts almost grazing the ceiling. Slowly the Gateway collapsed in on itself.

Biur turned and disappeared from sight, but Ker heard him walking inside the hold. He soon appeared at the largest portal in the machine's side, and from there he called down, "Ker!"

"Yes, master," Ker said, running.

"Take the end of this board and pull it out," Biur said. He moved back until Ker saw what he meant: part of a ramp. It had been pushed up into the engine's hold. Kalan moved up beside him and helped him pull out the board. It fell into place and seemed to lock on some hidden catch. Biur trotted down to the floor.

He turned once, surveying the room, and when he saw the bones against the wall he nodded. Pausing, he listened. "Quiet!"

Then Ker heard it, too—a rising moan of wind, with an undercurrent of other noises. At first he thought it was thunder, but the other sound went on too long for that, and it was gradually growing louder. In a few moments, a series of loud booms shook the shop's walls, syncopated by sounds of breaking glass and brief, distant shrieks of pain or fear.

Suddenly a half-dozen roof tiles snapped off and blew into the sky. Through the holes Ker could see a swollen gray sky, clouds swirling and boiling like water. Tornadoes leaped thousands of feet into the air. Far off, he heard another crash and guessed a building had collapsed. More tiles flew from the idol shop's roof, and the wind whistled as it sought the new openings.

"The Winds . . . ?" he whispered.

"Hurry!" Biur said. "They're destroying the city. Get into the engine!"

Zeren bolted up the ramp with Kalan close behind. The roar of the Winds grew deafening.

"How are we going to get the bones inside?" Ker shouted.

"I will do it. Go on—join the others!"

Ker backed away, then ran up the ramp and paused just inside the engine. The gale whipped at his hair, his clothes. He watched as Biur spread his arms wide.

A wand blazed in the wizard's left hand and his whole body had taken on a glow that seemed to pulse like a human heart. His face was bright as the sun at noon: radiant, powerful. Again he sang. Ker could see the power moving in him, channeling through his body. Biur pointed his wand and blue fire leaped away from him. It struck the first bone and wrapped around it, crackling with blue electricity like a thing alive . . . the bone slowly rose into the air and moved toward the engine.

Ker backed away from the hatch. The bone, shimmering blue, drifted past him and slowly settled onto a bed of straw. Then another bone followed, and another, and another, in a silent, graceful dance.

Ker turned and ran to the front end of the engine, where a rough ladder had been cut into the hull. Seizing the first handhold, then the next, then the next, he pulled himself up onto the deck.

The air had taken on a strange crystal clarity. Nothing seemed real. Light flickered all around him; sheets of electricity rippled across the deck at his feet. Most of the tiles were gone from the shop's roof, but he could no longer feel the Winds and the force of their passing. An unearthly calm had settled in. The ceiling's huge wooden beams stood out, stark and skeletal against the sky.

He looked to the left. Two tornadoes moved far away, sweeping across the city, sucking up whole buildings as easily as a man picking up a leaf. Banks of dust and smoke rolled like banks of fog. Fires turned the whole eastern sky a deep orange-red.

He turned to the right and gasped: a third tornado was bearing down on them from a hundred yards away.

23

Ni Treshel

> The Rashendi are a strange people, obsessed with Shon Atasha and His power. They search the world for splinters of His bones—and take them back to their homeland, where they store such relics away from other men. What do they do with these bones? Nobody knows for sure. Perhaps, one day, they plan to put them all together and create Shon Atasha anew.
>
> —Tellerion
> *Speculations*

"*Biur!*" he screamed, but his master didn't hear.

Then the tornado was on them. Ker felt rough hands of air tearing at his clothes, trying to lift him, but he grabbed the deck's railing and refused to let go. Ripping, tearing like paper, most of the roof flew into the sky and quickly vanished from sight. He saw a half-dozen demons stream straight up and vanish into the funnel one by one. Then he was looking into the black heart of the Wind, into the eye of the tornado.

For a second, there was calm. He hooked his leg under the railing, took a firmer hold, and squeezed his eyes shut.

Then the Wind jerked at him again. A deafening roar filled his ears and he felt something hard and heavy strike the back of his head. For a second he saw nothing but blackness, felt nothing but pain. He heard himself screaming something, but couldn't understand the words. His throat was raw, bloody.

Finally the tornado passed and he just lay there, gasping. He felt a dull, distant itch at the back of his head, touched it, found his hand covered with blood. Dizzy, he closed his eyes for a second, feeling sick. With a low groan, he forced himself to sit up.

The roof was completely gone, and most of the huge oak beams with it. Others had fallen in among the half-worked statues. Most of three stone walls still stood, but the fourth was half gone. Dust drifted everywhere, obscuring his sight.

Far off now, the Winds roared, mocking.

"Biur?" he called, coughing. "Kalan? Zeren?"

He heard movement inside the engine. Kalan's dark head appeared through the forward hatch, followed by his body. The Syrnae saw him and hurried to his side, knelt, and, looking concerned, said, "You are not well?"

"No—I'll be all right. What about Zeren?"

"He is seeing to Biur."

He had a bad feeling in the pit of his stomach. "Why? What happened?"

"One of the falling beams struck him."

Ker leaped to his feet and ran to the hatch, ignoring his own hurts. His head pounded with a needle-sharp pain that made him gasp. As he lowered himself down the ladder, his blood-slick hand slipped from a rung and he fell. He landed on his back in a pile of straw, the breath knocked out of his lungs for a second. He forced himself up. Forcing his way between the bones, he staggered down the ramp to the floor of the shop.

Debris littered it. Fallen stones, wood, pottery, and bits of statue lay everywhere. Zeren was just ahead, bent over something. Ker ran to him, pulled him aside—and saw his master lying there pinned under one of the ceiling beams.

"Biur," he whispered.

Blood stained the front of the wizard's shirt and trickled through his silvered hair. His face bled freely from a dozen cuts. The pain must have been terrible, but his eyes were open and when he saw Ker he smiled a bit.

Nothing could hide the strain in his voice as he said, "The play is done. Take the bones and go while you yet can."

Outside, the Winds whispered. Ker heard them and trembled. He felt a growing ache in the middle of his chest. "No! We can still get you out. There's time—"

Slowly the wizard shook his head. The effort seemed to cost him needed strength. He could barely whisper: "I would only die sooner if you tried to free me. I am the Dark God's now. Serve Derethigon well, Ker, for he is a demanding master." And then he shut his eyes and spoke no more.

"Biur . . ." Ker said. His eyes burned and his vision darkened until he could scarcely see. A ringing filled his ears. He stood, fists clenching and unclenching, rage and pain filling him, not knowing how to stop the hurt.

Zeren took his arm and led him back to the engine. "Sit and gather your thoughts," he said softly. He went into the machine and Ker could hear him talking in hushed tones to Kalan.

Ker sat there, thinking of all Biur had done for him, of all he owed his master. Getting his face back, allowing him to come along when they went to find the bones, showing him the way to unlock the power within him—Biur had done all these things, and never once spoken a harsh word or shown anything but kindness toward him.

And now he was dead. *Dead.* The whole scene was a surreal nightmare, playing and replaying itself in Ker's mind, turned a thousand times worse by his imagination. How could his master be dead? How could Derethigon let it happen?

He remembered what Gar Galimu had said—that it was all a game to the gods, that people were the pieces and the world the board. Did Biur's death really mean that little to Derethigon?

"Derethigon, please hear me," he heard himself whisper. "Bring him back to life. Your power can do that. *Please* bring him back!" And then he was sobbing and pounding the deck with his fists, and the tears came, and all the rage and frustration poured out like an endless flood.

As the roar of the Winds became louder, Ker grew despairing. He was helpless to do anything, to stop the Winds or bring Biur back to life. And it was all his fault. *He'd* let that demon Suthyran into the world. *He'd* caused the destruction of Zelloque, the greatest city in the world. If he'd listened to Biur when he had the chance, if he'd never challenged Derethigon . . .

Zeren came and sat beside him, putting his arm around Ker's shoulders. They drew comfort from each other. Ker knew, suddenly, that Zeren missed Biur almost as much as he did, that they both felt the same yawning emptiness inside.

"Come," Zeren said at last. "We must not stay longer. You have to open a Gateway to Ni Treshel for us."

"What does it matter now?" Ker said. "The demons are gone. Suthyran must be dead. How could he survive the Winds?"

"I don't know. But we're still alive—mightn't he be as well? And the bones have to be returned to their shrine. Biur wished it so. I believe he managed to get all the bones inside the engine. Would you throw away everything he worked for—everything he died for?"

Numbly, Ker shook his head. He felt tired and old and just wanted to be alone in his misery. But Zeren took his arm and pulled him to his feet.

Ker walked into the engine's hold, passed Kalan without a word, and climbed the ladder. He reached the deck and stood in silence for a moment. *I'll try not to let you down, Biur,* he thought. Drawing the wand from his pouch, he held it before him as he'd done before, as he'd seen Biur do so many times. And when his vision slipped away into blue, he saw the deep, deep azure sparks hanging in the air before him.

He willed them to move, to draw together. He felt rather than heard himself begin to sing, and the patterns in his voice matched the patterns in the air, the rising and falling tones, the hissing sibilants, the rhythm of the words. A new strength filled him. Fire coursed through his body. He felt power in himself like none he'd ever felt before.

Blue flames leaped from the tip of his wand, touched the ground, and shot upward. Behind the flames he saw the fabric of the world folding back, opening into the netherworlds. When the blue flames subsided, a thirty-foot-high black rectangle stood there.

He closed his eyes and let his mind flow through the Gateway and into the cold, white land of the netherworlds. He concentrated on the city of Ni Treshel, the gleaming white temples, the buildings with their gold domes and high crystalline spires.

And then again the fabric of the universe seemed to open before him like a giant gate folding back. It seemed as though he gazed through an immense window onto one of the rolling green meadows just beyond Ni Treshel. For an instant he could see the city's buildings not more than two hundred yards away.

Slowly, keeping both ends of the Gateway open, he retreated back to the engine. His mind flowed back into his body and he stood on deck once more, staring at the matte black rectangle before him.

Now what? some part of his mind asked. *How do I make the engine move?*

He willed it to start forward. He imagined the wheels turning one by one, then all together. He let his mind flow out and tried to feel the engine around him—and failed. A bitterness filled his mouth. He tried again and again—a dozen different ways. Nothing worked.

How had Biur made it move? How had Suthyran? He stopped and tried to think. He knew he was doing something wrong. What would Biur do? What *had* Biur done? He didn't know, and it was too late to ask.

He risked a glance around. The Gateway seemed to be holding steady with only a small part of his will focused on keeping it open. He looked over the shop, hoping for some clue to help him. Nothing seemed of any aid. And outside . . .

Far to his right he saw two of the tornadoes beginning to move toward him—it would be some time before they reached the idolmaker's shop.

"Zeren!" he shouted.

The Rashendi stuck his head through the open hatch. "What?"

"I don't know how to move the engine. What should I do?"

Zeren stared at him, then cursed and ducked down out of sight. "I'll look for something to start it down here," he called.

The wind whipping around him was growing steadily stronger as the tornadoes approached, Ker noticed. He began to pace frantically. Then he noticed two thick ropes lying half-coiled on either side of the deck. They were fastened to huge iron rings—perhaps for anchors?—and the first tornado hadn't been able to tear them away. Perhaps they could pull the engine through the Gateway . . . or get Kalan to.

Wind whipped his hair. He looked up at the tornadoes. They were moving faster than he'd thought. They'd be over the shop soon.

"*Zeren!*" he shouted again. In seconds the Oracle reappeared. "I'm going to throw the anchor ropes over the front of the engine and into the Gateway," Ker said. "Kalan can pull it. Tell him to go around to the bow. He'll know what to do. Hurry!"

"What? How can *he* pull it?"

"Trust me. There's no time. Do it now!"

Zeren's head disappeared. Ker heard him giving Kalan instructions.

He had to get the ropes over the side. Turning a bit, he raised his wand. Hopefully he'd be able to shift the ropes in the same way his master had moved the bones into the engine.

Slowly he let his thoughts expand. Again he heard himself singing, and patterns took shape in the air around him. He gave them focus and forced them around the end of the first rope, using them to pull it across the deck. Then the rope snaked over the side and jerked taut against the ring in the deck.

Gasping, Ker let up. His head ached fiercely, but he gave a shout of triumph. He'd done it! But his hands were shaking, and now something burned in his stomach. His whole body seemed drained, weak, as if he'd used up every last reserve of strength within himself. For a second his attention wavered and the Gateway began to collapse. He forced himself to stand straighter and reshaped the outline of the Gateway.

The tornadoes were approaching. He could see the debris caught up in their swirling funnels now, whole buildings being ground to dust, human bodies, dead horses, huge logs, blocks of stone. He saw uprooted trees and shattered carts, smoldering galleys from the harbor, hundreds of demons with broken bodies and twisted faces. He gaped in shock and fear.

Then his attention turned back to the final rope. Slowly, carefully, he extended his wand again. He felt the power flowing down his arm as he began to sing, saw the shimmering blue lines of magic appear and wrap themselves around the end of the rope. It began to move slowly but surely, inching its way across the deck. At last it dropped over the side and jerked tight against the ring in the deck.

Ker ran forward to the prow and looked down at Kalan. The Syrnae grabbed the end of each rope and leaped through the Gateway.

When a minute passed and nothing happened, Ker began to wonder what was going on. He glanced to the right. The tornadoes were scarcely a hundred yards away, and the grinding, rushing sound they made was awful to hear. Then the ropes jerked once, pulled taut, and the engine started forward with a jolt. Ker barely managed to keep to his feet.

The ship's prow nosed into the Gateway and vanished from sight, and the Gateway seemed to move toward him. Darkness swept over Ker. The last he saw of Zelloque was a glimpse of one tornado about to touch the idolmaker's shop. This time he had little doubt the whole building would be destroyed.

He blinked and it was as though he'd stepped through a curtain. The sudden quiet roared in his ears. The engine's wheels squeaked and groaned a bit, and the deck creaked—those were the only sounds. He stood, shivering, in a vast cavern of snow and crystal. Everything around him gleamed brilliant white on white. Ice frosted the deck beneath his feet. His breath misted in the air.

Looking ahead, he saw Kalan. The Syrnae had transformed himself into a dragon, as he'd done in the alley in Zelloque what seemed years ago. He'd folded his huge wings along his back, and thick sheaves of muscle strained beneath scaled skin that might have been made of burnished brass. Kalan held the rope ends in his broad, toothy mouth. Steam rose from every part of his body.

The end of the Gateway appeared before them. Kalan moved faster, in a strange waddling gait, and Ker had no way to gauge their speed. It might have been as fast as a horse's gallop.

Then Kalan passed through the Gateway and the engine thundered after him. Ker gasped, suddenly breathing hot summer air. The bright sun blinded him.

The engine slowed and stopped. Only then did he see the hundred-odd soldiers in red-and-black uniforms surrounding them with drawn swords. The men stood motionless in a semicircle before the engine, looking up at Ker. The breeze snapped and billowed their long red capes.

Ker shivered and let the Gateway collapse.

They'd stopped in the middle of a wide green meadow. Several hundred yards away rose the first of the temple buildings. Beyond stood Ni Treshel, with its tall, thin towers, gold-domed roofs with tapering silver spires, and immense marble shrines to Shon Atasha. The whole place seemed alive with excitement. Beyond the soldiers a large crowd of brightly dressed men and women had gathered.

Kalan's dragon body rippled like a tarp in the wind, then seemed to pull into itself, blurring, changing—shrinking to the shape of a human once more. Kalan blinked, slowly looked around him, then shrugged a bit and folded his legs and sat.

One of the soldiers—an officer, from the gold trim on his helm—stepped forward. "What do you want here?" he demanded.

Ker closed his eyes for a second, then opened them. "I serve Derethigon," he said. His voice was strong, hard. "By my master's orders we have brought back the bones that were stolen. They lie in the engine's hold. Your men may remove them, if you wish."

Zeren had climbed out of the hold and strutted up beside the ship, looking proud of himself. The soldiers bowed a bit to him in deference.

"No," he said. "The Rashendi will remove them. No others may touch the bones of Shon Atasha the Creator. I have returned with them, as instructed!"

The officer waved to his men and they began to disperse, heading back toward their various posts. The crowd of townspeople surged forward, surrounding Zeren, lifting him high on their shoulders. They bore him back toward the center of town with many cheers.

Ker looked down at the deck, realizing how tired he was. His whole body ached. Everything they'd done that day just now began to catch up with him, and a numb shock settled in. He slowly walked to the hatch, climbed down into the hold, and wove his way between the bones to the side portal. He paused there for a second, looking out at the beauty of the Rashendi's valley—how vibrant and alive compared to Zelloque!—then jumped to the ground. Kalan wandered around toward him. Of the vast crowd that had encircled the engine, now only a handful of soldiers remained.

"I'm Captain Wextet, sir," the officer said with a slight bow, "from Sonkitu, here by the request of the Padah of Ni Treshel."

Ker looked at him dully. "I'm Ker Orrum," he said. "Why did they ask you and your men to come here?"

"To prevent the theft of any more bones. Now I want to thank you for helping to return these. I know the way of wizards—you'll leave before the Rashendi can thank you properly. But I want you to know how much they appreciate it, even if they don't show it right now."

Ker shrugged. "It's the bones that matter, not those who serve them. I have done my master's will. That is all."

"As you say," Wextet said. He turned to his men and ordered them into position around the engine. Then he turned and started toward the town without a backward glance.

Ker heard a strange half-whistling, half-singing in his head. It vanished in a second when he rubbed his temples.

"What now?" Kalan asked. "What will we do? Where will you go?"

"I don't know," Ker said. He thought about Zeren and the Rashendi, and knew he didn't want to stay here. These people could never be his.

"Perhaps Theshemna?" Kalan said. "Perhaps you will take me with you? I have heard great tales of its many wonders."

Ker heard the same whistling again, and started. He listened, concentrating, and suddenly heard a deep, rich voice, full and terrible with its power. A god's voice: Derethigon's voice.

"Come to me, Wizard."

"Yes," Ker said. "We will go to Theshemna."

He took out his wand and held it before him. The power seemed to come easily this time, flowing up through his body like water in a spring. He opened the Gateway, and together they stepped through.

24

To Serve the Blind Archer

To serve the gods is madness, and to refuse, insanity. There is a fine distinction.

—Tellerion
Speculations

Ker stood alone in the throne room of the gods, on the carpet whose patterns shifted constantly. He'd left Kalan at the castle's outer wall. He knew he had to face Derethigon by himself.

Men in blue-and-gold breeches, with silver-inlaid steel breastplates and deep blue capes—the gods' honor guard—stood stiffly at attention to his right and left, their hands resting on the hilts of their long, slightly curved swords. Above, pale globes of light floated in an intricate dance, a glowing kaleidoscope of color. Eight of the guards fell in step around him as he moved forward, toward the eleven high stone thrones at the far end of the room.

Derethigon sat there. The god was huge and splendid in long red robes made of some shimmering material, more imposing and powerful than Ker had ever seen him. The air around him almost seethed with energy.

Ker bowed low before his god.

Derethigon spoke, his voice low and rich, full of the roar of the sea and the songs of the birds, the rush of the wind and the patter of rain. "Biur is dead."

"Yes, Derethigon," Ker said.

"Know this: once it was my power to make life from death, but that power is gone from me, taken by my brother Kharthtugon, who rules below. I could not bring Biur back even if I wished to."

Ker started. "You heard my prayer in Zelloque—"

"Yes. Now the time has come for you to serve me in Biur's

place. Know that I am satisfied with you, for the bones of Shon Atasha have been returned to Ni Treshel and the one who stole them is gone from this world, his body crushed beneath the rubble, his spirit vanished to the shadowlands whence it came. Go, then, Ker Orrum. Take Biur's rooms as your own. You will hear my call when I have need of you."

"Thank you, Derethigon," he said, and bowed, and turned to go.

The honor guard escorted him outside.

The palace remained the same as before. The ceiling still vanished among high, white clouds; the walls were still made of gigantic stone blocks without seams or mortar—and they were still so far away he could scarcely see them. Fields stretched to his right and left, and, misty in the distance, stood a huge forest unlike any on Earth. Far away to his left, on the horizon, rose foothills lush with high, green grass where horses browsed.

Kalan waited for him at the edge of the long, black road that led into the hills, toward the rest of the palace of the gods. The Syrnae had kept his human form and showed no interest in changing back to a small, furry animal. Ker smiled and greeted him warmly.

"Ker," Kalan said. "What will you do now?"

"I am to replace Biur as Derethigon's servant." Then he grimaced. "I forgot to ask about my duties!" *Dumb, as usual. Can't I do anything right?*

"He will summon you when he needs you," Kalan said.

Then Ker heard a distant voice calling his name. He looked up, bewildered, surprised.

Two people were riding toward him, one on a black stallion, one on a bay. Their horses moved quickly, faster and faster, hooves striking sparks from the black stones. Ker could scarcely believe his eyes. A woman in flowing green gown rode the bay stallion, and her long, golden hair flew wildly behind her head.

"Liana!" he shouted. *"Liana!"* And beside her—wasn't that Threnodrel?

He felt a sudden, swift rush of joy and ran forward, shouted their names. Liana still lived! Then both she and Threnodrel reached him, dismounted, and they all embraced one another. Ker had never been happier in his life.

"Threnodrel—I'm so glad you're still here!"

"I'm glad you got back safely, Ker," the wizard said with a half-smile. "The gods refused to help us when I asked them, and by the time my audience ended, Zelloque had already been destroyed. I had no knowledge of whether you had succeeded or failed. I'm just glad you're still alive."

"And Liana!" Ker said. He hugged her again. "I thought you were dead! Or, not dead . . . but at least gone. I didn't think I'd ever see you again!" And he whispered, so that none of the others could hear, "Thank you, Gods, for giving her mortal form once more."

She pulled away, laughing lightly, and hushed him before he could speak. "Ker—look at yourself. You've changed!"

"Changed? How?"

"You're older," Threnodrel said. "Magic does that, you know. You look . . . perhaps twenty-five."

"That old?" he said, amazed.

They all laughed at his expression. "Come," Liana said. "We know what happened. Word has spread through all of Theshemna that Biur is dead, but that the bones have been recovered . . . by you."

"Not by me—by all of us. Nobody could have done it alone." Ker grinned. "But you're in human form again. What happened?"

"I brought my sisters back to Zelloque, as you saw. But they were wild, and savage in their wildness. They would not stop at destroying the Great Lord's palace, so they moved through the streets, leveling the city, turning it to dust. I fled before them, for I feared that I too might learn to revel in the destruction, and never return to my friends here. So I came back to Theshemna to beg the gods to restore my human form, but before I did, one of them changed me. Now I am as I was, and as I hope I always will be. I thank whichever god took pity on this poor Wind!"

"The other servants of the gods have prepared a banquet in our honor, Ker," Threnodrel said. "They wait for us now."

Ker smiled. "Lead the way."

Later, after the banquet, Ker came to Threnodrel's room in the palace of the gods. He knocked lightly on the door.

Soon it swung open. Threnodrel nodded to him, then moved back that he might enter.

"Something troubles you," Threnodrel said. "What is it?"

Ker hesitated. "I don't feel . . . *right,* being Derethigon's servant. Why did he ask me? What if I can't do what he wants? Biur didn't have time to teach me his magic!"

The older man sighed and put his arm around Ker's shoulders.

"He taught you better than you think. You can sense magic around you, use it, shape it to your will. That's more than most people can do after a lifetime of study. To learn more than that will require time, and more study, and more practice."

"Will you teach me?"

"No. Your time for teachers has passed. The rest remains for you to do yourself."

"That's what Biur said."

"Then trust him—and trust yourself. If you do, you won't disappoint those around you."

Ker smiled. "Thank you for the advice. It's a big help."

Then he heard a whistling sound in his head, and Derethigon's rich voice filled his mind: *"Come to me, my wizard. I need you now."*

"Derethigon calls me," he said. "I've got to go." Turning, he strode through the door, tall and proud and satisfied deep inside.

He had confidence in his abilities, and he planned to make himself the finest wizard possible—no matter how long it took, no matter how hard he had to work. He only wished Biur could have seen him now. He knew his old master would have been happy.

Epilogue

A stranger came to Vichir one night. He wore deep blue robes and rode a proud black stallion. A hood hid his face in shadow. When he came to the drawbridge of Castle Orrum, he stopped and called to the sentries on duty.

"Dero, Rammur—go tell the baron that he has a visitor."

"Who are you?" Rammur demanded. "How do you know us?"

"Just give your master my message." He spurred his horse and entered the castle's main courtyard. There he dismounted.

A stableboy came running to take his horse's reins, but the stranger shook his head and held them himself. "I won't be staying long," he said.

The baron soon entered the courtyard through one of the side doorways, followed by Lerrens and Rammur. Frowning, he held his head high.

Then the stranger drew back his hood.

"Minnan, my son!" the baron said, starting forward. "What brings you—" Then he grew silent, and an uncertain look crossed his face. "You're not Minnan, are you?"

The stranger shook his head. "No, Father. I'm your other son."

"He's dead!"

"No, Father. I'm alive."

"What sorcery is this? You're too old to be Ker. I'll have you run out of Vichir—"

Ker raised one hand. "Peace, Father, peace. I serve Derethigon, the Blind Archer, and magic has . . . aged me beyond my years. I *am* Ker."

There was recognition in his father's eyes. "Ker—it *is* you, isn't it?" For the first time Ker saw his father smile.

The baron stepped forward and hugged him awkwardly. Ker

hugged his father back. It made him feel good inside, fulfilled, somehow, now that he'd come home. "Yes, Father."

"Thank the gods you're still alive! I'd given up any hope—we'd all given up hope—when you never returned! But now you're back for good?"

"No, Father. I'm a man now, and I have work. The Oracle's prophecies were right—both of them. Or at least they can be. I've just got to work to make them come true."

"But magic . . . I have not spoken of this before, Ker, but now it is time you knew. At your birth a healer from Zelloque came to Vichir, a healer who was also a witch. I called her to help your mother. The witch used her powers to save you, but killed my beloved Maelera in the process. Maelera was hideously deformed." He shuddered. "Magic! How can you be sure that nothing will go wrong?"

"Who can ever be certain of anything? What I know is this: I have responsibilities in Theshemna, and a god trusts me to carry out his will. If Derethigon has faith in my abilities, that is enough to satisfy me."

"Very well. As you say, you *are* a man now, Ker, and you must make your own decisions. Tell me—how long can you stay?"

"Not long. I just wanted you to know that I'm well, and if you'll have me, I'd like to come home and visit you whenever I can. But now I must go."

"Of course," his father said. "Please—come as often as you can. We—*I*—missed you, Ker."

Lerrens pressed his hand to Ker's shoulder. "You've turned out well, Ker, better than I'd hoped. May the gods go with you."

The baron echoed his words. "Can you—will you—come back again in ten days? Minnan will be here then. We'll all have a lot to talk about, I'm sure."

Ker smiled. "Yes, Father. I'll come."

And then he mounted the stallion, turned, and rode out into the night, bound for Theshemna.

JOHN GREGORY BETANCOURT was born in Missouri but grew up in New Jersey, where he still lives. His father is an archaeologist, and the author spent his childhood summers in Greece, Italy, Spain, and Turkey, among other countries. At age fifteen, he decided to become a writer; he sold his first story (a fantasy) at age sixteen. While a freshman in college, he became an assistant editor at *Amazing* magazine, where he worked while completing his B.A. in communications at Temple University. THE BLIND ARCHER is his second published novel, and he plans to write more tales of Theshemna.

Mr. Betancourt comments, "Currently I write full time, work for a literary agency, and am involved in an attempt to revive the pulp magazine *Weird Tales.* I've been fortunate in that all the jobs I've ever held have been in the science fiction field, and I hope to be able to say that for the rest of my life."